OTHER SYSTEMS

a Novel by Elizabeth Guizzetti

a 48fourteen Publishing Trade Paperback

Other Systems. Copyright © 2013 by Elizabeth Guizzetti. Cover Illustration by Elizabeth Guizzetti. Novel Edited by David Kostiuk. Printed in the United States.

http://www.48fourteen.com

ISBN-13: 978-1-937546-14-4
ISBN-10: 1-937546-14-4

This book is dedicated to my husband, Dennis.

*One night, many years ago, we sat on our bed
and you explained space-time using the blanket for the
universe…*

We are such geeks.

PROLOGUE

"NAX TO *ANTRIA*—YOUR CREW manifest shows that you are not in compliance with current Kipos Reproduction Law," were the most terrifying words Captain Cole Alekos believed he had ever heard until the night he awoke with someone pounding on his hatchway, the emergency lights flashing, and his youngest screaming through the adjoining door. He fought his way from the blankets. Tapping out his security code upon the embedded com screen next to his rack, he saw the unauthorized use of the shuttle bay airlock.

The inner airlock would automatically shut when the outer one was opened, so the *Antria* still had a viable atmosphere and functioning life support, but it was an emergency situation. Ignoring his six-year-old's screams, he locked the hatchway to Mark's quarters and slipped on a pair of coveralls. Cole's mind raced towards his adult offspring. Helen would always go to her station in an emergency. He trusted her. Harden would...

The thought of his daughter-in-law, Lucy, committing suicide foisted itself onto his brain. He considered that his eldest, Harden, might also be dead. The cool recycled air felt heavy in his lungs. He wished he had time to figure this out before he left his quarters, but his crew needed him.

Whether or not Harden was dead, Cole was the captain.

He opened the hatchway and climbed out of his billet. Like a well-run hive, the ship's officers were at work. The XO and navigator were still at the helm and running ship diagnostics. Cole went in to the join them. "Airlock malfunction," the XO said.

The cook was in the galley, starting pots of coffee and tea. The ship's doctor was helping him by putting chocolate biscuits on a tray. After all, most of the crew would not fall sleep again on this night. Glancing over, he saw Harden, alive at his emergency station!

However, as his son looked over the assembled crowd, Cole grew more worried. The engineering team was in disarray and Harden himself was only half-dressed. His curls were bent in random cowlicks and his face was cold, vehement. He looked like he might hit someone or possibly decompress the whole ship. One of the mechanics tried to speak to him, but Harden said something softly and took a step away.

Someone asked if there was a note. No, there wasn't a note, but the crew didn't need one to know why she had done it. No one was even surprised that it finally happened. Lucy had been getting up early since the forced abortion and following hysterectomy. She often felt ill lying down in the darkness. She had been whispering things Harden didn't like to hear. Harden had once tried to tell her he didn't care if they were sterilized. It was she that he loved. She screeched back loud enough for the entire ship to hear: "You never loved our son!"

No one ever knew what to say to her after that.

Cole would never forget the day the customs agents said in an icy tone: "Come into compliance with Kipos reproduction law or leave Kiposi space." He didn't care about himself. The fact they sterilized his kids and murdered his unborn grandchild disturbed and infuriated him, but there was little he could do. The fetus had been checked for defects and, according to Kipos Reproduction law, terminated. However, Lucy had been regularly seeing the ship's doctor. His tests concluded the only *defect* was it would have been born a Khlôrosan.

"We all loved her and we will all mourn her," Cole said in his captain's tone, more to the crew than to Harden.

Harden hissed at him, "Shut the fuck up."

"Son," Cole tried to reach out and pull Harden into a hug, but Harden pushed back.

"Don't. Touch. Me." He panted out. "I can't breathe!"

"We will have a memorial service at 09:00," Cole said.

"There are too many people here! Not one of you cared enough to stop her!" Harden punched at the nearest wall until the ship's inner hull groaned. He screamed at the crew until they backed away. "I have an IQ of 168, and they still murdered my son! You let them murder my son for a fucking contract!"

Cole did not justify himself. While there was not much truth in the statement, there was enough to make it sting.

Helen slipped in front of her brother. She drew him into a hug and rested her forehead against his. "No one could ever love Lucy like you did, but I lost my sister-in-law tonight and Mark did too... and we did love her," Helen whispered.

Harden asked, "Mark knows?"

"With all the noise you're making, everyone knows," Helen whispered. "No one blames you. It was her choice."

"Will you make the same choice?" Harden whispered back, but he was visibly calmer.

"Fuck no, and neither will you."

"Someday you might wake up to the alarm sounding and discover you are wrong."

"No, I won't."

Cole realized they were alone as anyone could be on a starship. He could hear the constant murmur of the engines, the cook still in the galley banging around, and muffled speaking and weeping in the galley or the lounge. Above it all was a higher voice wailing: Mark was still locked in his billet.

Tears left red blotchy trails down Helen's cheeks, but Harden's eyes were still dry. He looked exhausted. It was cruel to leave them, but knowing that Helen could deal with her elder brother better than he could, Cole hurried back down to his quarters and unlocked Mark's hatchway.

A bundle of terrified six-year old threw himself at Cole.

He scooped up Mark, along with his ratty quilt and an even rattier stuffed kitten, and carried him back to his berth. Not able to figure out a better way to break the news to him, Cole said, "Lucy is dead."

Mark wiped away tears and choked out a bit of snot, then asked, "Really dead? Worse than Mommy? Not even a radio transmission?"

Was six old enough to understand that death was permanent? Cole couldn't remember what he knew at six and he wasn't around when his adult children were Mark's age.

"Really dead."

"I want Mommy."

Fuck the black and all her stars, Cole hated talking to his wife. It wasn't that they argued. Since the separation they were incredibly civil to each other. However, though he was only thirty-five, every day he spent in the black seemed as if Rosemary had aged another year. He hated seeing her dry hands, the lines on her face that grew deeper. However, what he said was, "Sure, buddy. I'm sure Harden needs to talk to Mommy, too."

He carried Mark into his billet and hit the com. He told his XO to place a call to the *Endeavor* and then opened the hatchway. "Hel," he said. "Bring your brother to my billet. I'm calling your mom."

He could split the call, but figured Mark would want to be with his elder siblings. Depending on the boy's immediate need, either Harden or Helen was his favorite person.

Helen guided Harden inside and to sit on Cole's berth. His elder son looked as broken and old as anyone could possibly be at twenty-two. Cole lit two cigarettes. He handed one to Harden then took a deep drag on his own. Out of habit, Harden nodded in thanks.

Mark, who had always hated the smell of tobacco, made a face, but stood on the berth between them. He wrapped his left arm about his big brother's shoulders. With his right hand he stroked the top of Harden's head as if he were the ship's cat. "It's okay. It's okay. We'll call Mommy for you."

The Antria; Canis system
April 10, 2967 K.E.

FIFTY YEARS ON KIPOS MIGHT equal a decade on the flotilla, but it was less than a year for Cole and his offspring flying at near light speeds. Giving up the profitable transport routes and focusing on new tech and exploration was the single best decision he had made since becoming Fleet Captain. Any semblance of the boy Harden had been had died with Lucy, except when a new planet came into view.

Of course, there were other reasons to sell off the transports, the biggest of which being the encrypted message loading from the Feed at that moment. Cole slid his finger over the touchscreen and entered his password. With the inevitable delay between the series of alphanumeric symbols and the key, he didn't bother studying the transmission until it finished. The contracts from the Kipos government had come in. Ten long-range transports were ordered to Earth. Missions for the greater good of Kipos never came as requests.

Relieved, he smiled at the back of his daughter's head three short meters away. Cole had the urge to kiss the top of Helen's short dark curls, but made it a rule to never embarrass any of his offspring with public affection. It had been Helen who had discovered the speculated mission plans and he wanted to assure her—or perhaps himself—that he had finished the transactions in time. The population of Kipos was currently just under a million and, for the past planetside decade, one in every two women was pregnant with a *defective* child who was often terminated.

Though Cole didn't care to see the Home World, there were plenty who did. Cole had quietly sold the long-range transports to their captains and plans for the high-speed space elevator to the government. He transferred personnel to protect his two elder kids and any friends who were worried about spending all that time in the black.

There could be no denying what the computer models said: within eleven generations Kipos would hit the event horizon of failure. Time was short. It would take over two centuries to get to Earth and back at ninety-six percent of light speed.

Kipos was colonized in 2384 C.E. and breeding for the nonnative species had always been somewhat problematic. The progression from Homo sapiens into Homo kipos might have been slower if they hadn't developed a gene modification therapy to help them thrive. Then colonists of Kipos had created Cole's species, Homo khlôrosans, by slicing together human DNA with the Khloro ray.

While the Homo kipos struggled for survival, Homo khlôrosans flourished. Within three generations, they were hailed as the miracle that would stop the downward birthrate. The Kiposi were given great tax deductions to interbreed with them. Cole's people could take greater g-forces and radiation than the average Kiposi, and with no histamine reaction to the grav-couch's nanomite technology. Indeed, it seemed Khlôrosans were made for space travel and the dueling suns of Kipos.

From the humans, the Khlôrosans had inherited hair on the heat centers of the body—the top of the head, armpits and genitals—but apparently this was not enough. The Kiposi had a love/hate relationship with their genetic experiments. They needed them to survive and yet variations in the species were scorned as inhuman.

It was true that the Khlôrosans tired more easily. With only an average of a million sweat glands and a sluggish circulatory system, they were also more susceptible to heat exhaustion. The most visible difference between the species was that most of a Khlôrosan body was not covered with hair follicles, but rather embedded with the opalescent microscales of their batoid ancestors. It didn't matter that these microscales seemed to protect them from cancerous lesions. It didn't matter to the pundits or politicians that the Khlôrosans were basically the same as everyone else, especially after twenty generations of interbreeding. It didn't even matter that the New World Dictionary defined human as: "any sentient primate species classified in the genus of Homo."

Khlôrosan, clone, or other genetic experiments of the Kiposi who wished to live planetside or accept government contracts had to be sterilized. Many fled. Khlôrosan fleet captains including Elias Brody, Andrea Tolis, even Cole's own mother made a killing on packing their transports with grav-couches stacked deck to deck, carrying refugees off planet and organizing a flotilla of ships orbiting Outpost 3. Kipos law simply did not apply that far in the black.

Cole did not have that option. It was his side of the fleet that provided these people with needed supplies. Besides, he and his offspring—at least the elder two—were explorers. They would never be happy in the dying flotilla. Harden and Helen were already looking to design their own ships. They wanted to break the light barrier. They wanted their names to live on forever. Maybe everyone does in their twenties.

Helen had already given her brother most of her savings for his insane experiments as the unwitting mateodeas, damselflies, and bees danced while playing with the fabric of space-time. Her only demand: "I want to fly our ship first. You can be captain if you want."

Harden argued just to be contrary, but in truth he was more than willing to give his sister that honor. Even at sublight speeds, Helen shined far beyond her peers and she was certainly a better pilot than her elder brother. There was nothing she could not fly.

Harden already discovered a way to move messages faster than light by stabilizing tachyon particles. Now he searched for a way to make it practical. He was sure there was a way to move a whole ship without killing the crew and destroying the equipment. Each relative morning, he played with the laws of physics. Each relative afternoon, the *Antria* sent messages via the Feed to Argent's Spacedocks and to the kids' mother on the *Endeavor*. Harden once told Cole that he did not worry that death chased them. When someone on the team died moonside, the work could continue uninterrupted because he was alive in the stars. Only once did Cole hear his son mutter to Helen: "Mom ages in front of my eyes, but Lucy will always be twenty-six. I must hurry."

Cole was almost positive Harden didn't care if traveling faster than light would send them spiraling back in time or hurtling forward. His son's work was simply a way to ignore the fact that Lucy was gone. Suicide was her right, but his son just shut himself off into his physics puzzles.

As for Mark, who the fuck knew what that kid was thinking most of the time? He was the most insolent, brooding seven-year-old Cole had ever seen. He was too young to have much of an opinion about being sterilized—thank the black he didn't even remember it—but he was a useless parasite aboard a starship. Though he was growing out of the age where he appreciated his sister's pseudo-mothering, the only time he smiled was when Helen got off work. She never failed to ask what game he was playing, whether he wanted to talk to her or not. Helen always made sure that, when they contacted the *Endeavor* about the FtL project, Mark got a few minutes to talk to their mother about his own interests, even if his chatter bored everyone out of their minds.

Her own grades suffered because of it. Helen passed her sublight exam early, but she had another two years of engineering school, three if she didn't focus. Cole wanted to send Mark to his grandmother, but he promised his ex-wife to keep the kids together. That had been a mistake.

It was all a mistake. To marry Rosemary—another captain—and bring her aboard his ship with a full crew and believe she would be happy doing nothing. They were both so young when they met. He was retrofitting the *Antria* with new engines on Kipos's largest moon. She was the captain of a short-range transport. They had their fun and she got pregnant. Cole's mother gave him leave so he could be there when Harden was born. Worked out fine, except Rosemary got pregnant again. Still, the *Antria* was ready and Cole had a contract to build the first of five outposts.

Rosemary raised Harden and Helen until they were fourteen and twelve respectively. She made them call Cole each year on his birthday, Landing Day, and New Year's. She sent him yearly photographs, which seemed to be every few months to him. Cole was twenty-eight and Rosemary was thirty-seven when he got back to Kipos. They still tried living together. They even became officially married. What a nightmare. It was beyond him why they believed a third child could lessen the perpetual fighting. Once pregnant, Rosemary either did nothing or screamed at him.

Mark had just finished potty-training when Rosemary announced she was going back to her own ship. Cole threatened to keep the kids. She said, "Clever kids need more than just a transport. Perhaps Harden really can break the light barrier with the Alekos family's resources."

Cole called her an unnatural mother.

She had been perfectly calm and he could remember her words from the tone. She was serious, but there was no malice. "If you ever lay a hand on them or separate them by time," she said, "I will find you and blow you out of the sky."

He laughed. Neat trick, considering her transport had no weapons and was made for short-range travel between Kipos and her three moons.

"A mother's love can defy the laws of physics," she said.

They both had known their kids' best hope for a future was a stretched life at near light speed, or even faster if Harden's work with dark energy and tachyons panned out. As long as Cole kept flying, they could live out centuries planetside. It was possible that the reproduction laws would change or he might even find a planet that could be colonized by the flotilla.

If he found such a planet, a doctor would reverse the vasectomies on his sons and the tubal ligation on his daughter. The Alekos fleet wouldn't die with them. Cole knew grandchildren were a far-fetched dream, but it kept him flying.

PART 1
SEATTLE, EARTH

CHAPTER 1

May 31, 3062 C.E.

ABBY LIKED THE NIGHT. HER mother often warned her of the dangers, but colors seemed to brighten against the darkness and she had found friends in the stars. When she was little, Grandma had taught her to see the constellations. Since then she loved drawing pictures in the sky. She adored every story about the stars whether it was historical, scientific, or mythological. There was some light pollution in her neighborhood, but this late many of the buildings went dark. As she looked into the sky, she could make out parts of the Dragon, Lynx, Big Bear and Little Bear. To the southwest, she could see the Dancing Virgin and to the east: Pegasus. Even if she could not see them, she knew there were other constellations, other systems with other planets.

Besides, Tara was with her. Her sixty pounds of energy and brindled fur was the real reason Abby was out on the street gazing at the stars. Behind her, she could hear the buzz of the solar streetlights and the muffled voices of her family, her neighbors and animals that lived in the commune. Ignoring the mosquitoes, she glanced at her handheld. The time shone 10:15 p.m., but she was in no hurry.

She waited for Tara to finish her business, scooped it up, and threw it into the methane generator as she flashed her keycard at the door, which in turn, opened on her approach. She glanced over her shoulder, careful that no one would follow her inside.

Abby ducked under a cobweb as she put the metal scoop in the tool closet. She couldn't locate the lucky spider that lived in the corner. Perhaps it was out hunting, keeping the silverfish at bay. She was too big to be a spider's prey, but Abby still ran her fingers through her black hair hoping that it had not caught a ride. The thought gave her the shivers.

She passed her family's apartment and went to the communal wash-room. As she cracked opened the heavy metal door, she heard excited panting in the stall. *Disgusting.*

Not the sex. Abby was a woman of seventeen, only two months and six days from being eighteen. She prayed nightly that someone would speak to her parents. She knew she would enjoy the touch of a husband. She even had one in mind.

It was the washroom that was repulsive—and annoying since there was only one per floor. She considered going upstairs, but the second story had two known huffers and an elderly man who wandered up and down the hall looking for his wife, or his cat. He was often only half dressed with spittle hanging from the corners of his mouth. The poor man could not always remember things. He had outlived his son; the commune took care of the man as well as it could.

Though irritated, Abby understood the washroom might be the only privacy that anyone could have. These two did not want to be caught. She hoped it was not who she thought it might be. She prayed it was not.

"Lei Abigail!" She heard Grandma call down the hall in Mandarin. "Lei Raymond, go find that wild sister of yours."

Abby rolled her eyes.

Grandma only spoke English in the factory, where it was required. She hated that her daughter had married a white boy. She hated that Cameron Boyd insulted the family by giving his two eldest children hard to pronounce American names. Worse, on the birth certificates, the given names were listed prior to the surnames: "Abigail Boyd Lei" and "Raymond Boyd Lei." Still, Boyd Lei's offspring stayed out of the cold quarrel and answered to both versions. Even though, Grandma had trouble with "Raymond" and "Abigail," she never had problems with any of their neighbor's names whether they were of English, Egyptian, or African origin. The Thinking Machines left Earth prior to Grandma's birth, but she was sure that each generation without them became more stupid and careless and less honorable.

"I'm here," Abby called back in English.

Ray walked down the hall. "What's taking so long?" he asked, though he obviously knew the answer.

He moved passed Abby to look through the crack in the door. Though he was a year and a half younger, he was gaining on her in height. It was still shocking to her that a few months before her little brother had become a man of sixteen.

"Curious?" Ray asked. He obviously was.

They never spoke of such things openly, but Abby knew that he was sensible. Like her, he did their parents' bidding and adhered to the commune's edict: he would take no lover that was not his wife in order to protect himself from diseases that could not be cured. Yet, he could not deny his interest.

"Just waiting," she said.

Abby held her breath as Rory Dale Bao exited the washroom. The woman was Mary Rogersdottir, a widow from the fifth floor. Her pale cheeks were flushed with embarrassment as she hurried up the stairs. Abby blushed too. Rory looked smug.

Abby pushed past them into the washroom where the smell of just-sprayed vinegar assaulted her. Ray followed. "Wait!" he said. The word might have multiple meanings, but in this case he only wanted to check if anyone else was still lingering. Abby and Tara went in the stall while he washed up in the sink. She knew he would not tease. He never did when she was upset.

Once she had finished, he went into the stall and Abby washed herself in the sink. She looked in the mirror and wondered why Rory didn't like her.

Her black hair was a few decimeters lower than her shoulders; her eyes were wide set with gold flecks in liquid obsidian. No mark lined her countenance because she rarely saw the sun. Maybe it was because she was mixed. She briefly wondered if Rory liked white girls best, but no, she had seen him with Li Bao Mei and Shaniqua Travis. She had seen him with lots of girls.

Maybe it was because she wore the same two dresses over and over, both demurely cut to cover her knees and elbows. One was blue cotton while the other was gray. She wore no lace or satin as Mary did. They simply did not have money to spend on frippery.

Abby wondered aloud, "What would happen if Mary got pregnant?"

Ray answered, "I wish I had known she was so lonely. Maybe I could marry her."

"How can you say that?"

As he came out of the stall, he asked, "Why not? She owns her apartment. She doesn't work, but with my work in the garden, we'd have enough to get by… and I'd be close, able to keep an eye on things at home."

Abby put her hands on her hips. "She's nine years older than you and has a son."

"So?"

"You're sure you'll be able to raise her son before having a child of your own?"

That was the crux of the issue. As the first-born son and daughter, both Ray and Abby were to be married to someone to pass on the family names. Ma and Da simply did not believe in second attachments once children were involved. It confused the inheritance laws. The rivalry between full siblings was hard enough.

The mixing of religions was another reason. Mary was pretty and generous, but she had strange ideas. She did not even believe in praying to one's Honored Dead.

Abby doubted aloud, "I can't see you enjoying going to the chapel to pray in a flagrant public display more than in the silence of one's own home."

Ray said, "You won. Would you shut up now?"

His eyes were not cold or angry even though it wasn't the first time Abby had bashed one of his ideas.

She nodded, slightly guilty. "Sorry. I got carried away."

He just shrugged. Once the door to the washroom was opened, she felt his calloused hand touch her shoulder. Though Abby was glad for the affection, she hated that it was coming from her younger brother. It should be she who comforted him. It wasn't so long ago that she had kissed his skinned knees, but now it was her heart that was flayed.

AS ABBY LAY IN THE darkness, she listened to the heavy snores and soft breathing of her family. Her parents had a cot and her grandmother had another. Tara slept close to the door each night since the huffer had broken in. The offspring all slept together on a straw mat covering the concrete floor next to the methane stove that was off for the summer. Even if Abby's heart throbbed too much to sleep, she was glad her brothers and sister were lying beside her. Their physical closeness somewhat mollified her hurt.

Born in the year of the Serpent, Abby was the eldest, then Ray, a Ram. Jin, the Monkey, was fifteen. Joseph would have been thirteen, but was no longer there. He and Grandda had died from the winter chill. There was a little shrine of a baby photo and a jade rooster that sat untouched, high on a shelf. The youngest was Orchid. Perfect Orchid: kind hearted, honest, trusting, pretty, born in the Year of the Pig. She had three older siblings to protect her and guide her into an agreeable marriage once their parents fell due to old age. Most of the time, Abby did not feel jealous, just wistful that her sister had an easier time of things. After Orchid, their parents were careful not to have any more children. Their bread coupons and commune rations could only go so far.

Abby wished she could turn on the Cloud just to focus on something else, but it would wake Da, who always slept lightly, or Orchid, who slept beside her.

Instead she focused on the history of her city. She knew all the great legends. According to one story, a doctor paid a mighty chief for his name. The chief had felt that naming the city after him would cause his soul to live on in unrest, but the money, which was used for the good of his people, changed his mind.

In another, a man became king by building the first sawmill. Eventually, much of his history was lost, yet his legacy lived on. The city started to grow larger as it terraformed the landscape by engulfing trees, filling in mudflats, and lowering the grades of the nearby hills. With a voracious hunger, it fed off the small villages and absorbed their people. Yet Seattle needed more in order to become the economic center of the Americas.

Nestled between a deep harbor and mountain ranges that kept her safe, she rose higher. In between the steel, fresh fruit grew on trees. People raised and ate the flesh of animals alongside those who made fresh bread.

In this golden era, people lived for a century or more. Babies did not die from the cold winter, as a flip of a switch could magically circulate heat or cool air within any building. However, this world was no utopia.

People became so healthy that bodies rejected food and girls flowered too young. The uneducated ones procreated too early and often, but America and other first world countries did not care. Some extended their life with robotics and gene therapy. Even during the age of the Thinking Machines, rich humans did not notice until it was too late and the resources of the Earth had become scarce.

Crowded countries sent their people into space. They first built colonies on Luna and Mars. In the early days of colonization, nothing was wasted. They even used old technology and rubbish. From there, they settled on Ganymede and Triton for a time, but since humans are curious creatures, they looked beyond Sol's system.

Ships carried three hundred thousand souls looking for new homes. History said at least five ships—a quarter of their number—exploded once they were out of the solar system.

Yet Earthlings did not see the price of wasting the planet's resources until the day it became too expensive to send excess people into space. Ganymede collapsed as people flooded back to Earth. Colonies simply died out on Triton and Mars. Then, once Luna was cut off from humans, other stars became impossible dreams. Earth lost contact with the colonist ships completely when the last of the Thinking Machines left. They had no time for such a mentally limited species as humans and planned to reconnect with their missing brothers.

When the water level threatened the cities and the levies broke, what was originally Seattle's downtown was gradually reduced to ruins. At the first sign of weakness, ancient skyscrapers were deconstructed for their wealth of steel, glass, and asbestos. The United States dissolved into territories and then further into citywide fiefs.

Every winter, when the rains came, more lowlands disappeared as the hills became steeper, giving rise to a number of squalid, peripheral, island suburbs. The original city was now a steep hilly peninsula with five-story tenements made out of concrete and covered in aluminum. However, even though it was crumbling, trucks funneled into Seattle and ships carried the city's goods to the rich markets of New Delhi and Johannesburg via the deep harbor and plentiful fresh waterways from the winter's unending rains.

Abby knew she had no reason for self-pity, living in her family's safe apartment while many were homeless. Besides, she loved her job. As a librarian, she cut through the algorithmic gatekeepers and filtered the unending information of the Cloud in order to find knowledge. She could be working in a factory—or worse—if she ignored logic and lost the trust of her parents.

She knew what Rory was. She would not throw away her only treasure on a man who chased anything in a skirt. Yet she ached for his sparkling blue eyes. She loved and hated the electricity that ran down her spine and into her toes each time Rory looked at her.

At that moment she wished to run down to the docks and climb on one of the metal ships that brought apples or grain across the Pacific, but it was a fleeting aspiration. The only women down there were tainted unfortunates. Mostly robot covered in human flesh, they were too stupid to be called AI and too broken to work at the most menial of tasks. Not even the sailors touched them anymore. She chastised herself and prayed for a sensible wish: a gentle man who would love his wife like her father loved her mother.

CHAPTER 2

June 1, 3062 C.E.

ORCHID NUDGED UNDER ABBY'S ARM and snuggled closer for warmth. It was their morning habit to wait to leave the comfort of the blankets until the last possible moment. Abby traced her sister's ear and pushed away the long black strands until Tara whimpered. She wanted to be let outside.

Abby glanced up at the blue numbers on the white wall: 07:59. Ray would be in the garden. Jin, Grandma, Ma, and Da would already be on their way to the factory. Though she might see a few adults seeking the truth, her days during the summer were mainly spent watching children too young to work or too poor to have a stay-at-home parent. The library paid only minimum wage, but her wages were in cash. The library provided Abby with free Cloud access and allowed her to keep her little sister with her during the day. Orchid, who was cleverer than required for factory work, tended to get bored and into mischief. Except at harvest, she was mostly in the way around the commune and its gardens.

Abby and Orchid waved goodbye to Ray and Rory, both of whom tended the commune's enclosed hectare of land. Even this early in the morning, the men's faces were ruddy from the wind that funneled between the ancient buildings.

Ray waved and shouted, "Be careful!"

Abby and Orchid walked down the concrete path, past the coffee house filled with unemployed men, past another tenement, and across a rundown park to the library that had been standing since the twenty-first century. It used to be brick, but the mortar had long since wasted away. Steel and acrylic enclosed it, but there was a viewing window on the front so people could look in and see the old construction.

On the west side of the building, an ancient totem pole stood sentry. Whenever Abby looked at the monument, she felt sad. As the library had been, the pole was encased by acrylic in order to protect it from environmental decay and human vandals. Now the acrylic was covered in scratches, bird droppings, and layers of graffiti. The structure was a ghost of its former self. Abby couldn't even remember what the First People's symbols had been. There was nothing to tell her except the unending information on the Cloud, but half of that was dog shit anyway.

She glanced over her shoulder to make sure no one got too close before she swiped her key through the reader. Once inside, Orchid kicked off her outdoor shoes and ran ahead of her sister to crank on the power. Abby locked the door behind them. Everyone liked to turn the crank a few times; filling the cells with charge was fun in its way. Abby heard the wheel buzz as Orchid pushed the handle flat and the turbine began to move, filling the library with light and electricity. There was no need to turn on the heat in June. Abby took a cloth and spray solution to disinfect the handles of the door and the adult section's touchscreens, then they both went to wash their hands.

With stocking covered feet, they skidded across the old polished concrete floor into the children's area. "Pick out today's stories. I'm going to check the Cloud," Abby said.

The day's news seemed pretty standard:

[MURDER/SUICIDE ON FIRST HILL: Traffic was backed up for nearly an hour after Jon Duk Go, age 39, jumped off of the Madison Street Overpass. He survived the fall, but did not survive getting hit by a milk truck. Fortunately, the driver of the milk truck was not charged with vehicular homicide, nor did he lose his job. While traffic was backed up on Old Highway 5, no other injuries resulted in the accident. However when the police went to inform Duk Go's family, they discovered that his estranged wife and children had been stabbed in their sleep...]

The South Branch was close enough to Madison, that it was likely a few patrons might be interested in this tragedy and she needed her facts straight. Abby opened up another window and typed in the headline. Seven different news sites all gave similar stories though a few were sensationalist; one blamed the wife for "corrupting her marriage bed." Abby scanned a few more articles and comments until she found the reason for the estrangement. Their commune had kicked him out after it was discovered he had beaten his wife and his children repeatedly. He sued with charges of adultery upon her, but the wife and their children were allowed to stay in the commune. Proof that she had been found innocent.

Abby went to the next article.

[SALMON COUNT IS UP: Bad news for the greedy owners of fish factories, but good news to struggling families! This year's salmon prices are expected to level out at $700 per kilo. This is after six years of wild fluctuation in the salmon market...]

Abby sighed. She did not believe the owners of fish factories were any greedier than anyone else, but the idea that any "struggling" family could afford even a kilo of salmon was a joke. This story was only good news for the wealthy. She did not bother looking up any other sites. She focused upon the next story.

[COMMUNE FIRE ON FIRST HILL: The 1425 Building on Seneca and Boren burnt down this morning due to faulty wiring...]

She glanced at the other news websites. Abby was relieved to see it had been in a building where she did not know anyone, then rebuked herself for her coldness.

As she scanned down the newsfeed, Abby saw a story near the bottom that interested her:

[VOICES FROM THE STARS: A transmission from an unknown source is bouncing off the satellites orbiting the Kepler Belt. Telescopes were pointed towards the transmission. Lights were seen, but they were moving too fast.]

Abby skimmed the rest of the article until the last line read:

[Could it be a sign from God? Are these the days foretold?]

She looked at the line again. She hated the "Sign from God" threads that ended news stories lately. She started scanning other news sites, hoping for more information, but they were just reposts of the original thread.

For twelve centuries, America had been a melting pot of geographic differences and religious thought. None of the ancient religions had survived intact, though some people leaned more towards one belief or another. Abby believed in a mixture of the ancestor worship that Ma had taught her, Grandma's animal zodiac, and the God to whom Da prayed.

She knew that Da's God wasn't the same Suffering God to who the head librarian Mr. Johnson and Mary Rogersdottir worshiped. A heavenly, long-suffering man just seemed implausible. Moreover, He might learn to hate the ones He had died for. She liked the idea of the Honored Ghosts of her ancestors watching over her family. Offering them protection and guidance, they had to care about what happened to their decedents. Grandma's words rang in her head: "A serpent's too clever for her own good!"

Abby hated that she embodied all the negative traits from the Year of the Serpent. Every time Grandma read the stars, she told Abby in one way or another that she was destined to be a scheming, selfish, and obsessive woman. After all, she worked in the warm, clean library for minimum wage while most of her family worked in a factory that paid twice as much, and Ray worked honorably in the commune garden, which provided them with extra rations.

However, there was hope. Grandma said if Abby wanted to better herself, she should patiently wait for a man born in the sign of the rabbit, who would pacify her questioning nature. If she was a good wife, she would temper his self-indulgence. Abby considered this point often since Rory was born under the sign of the Rabbit. If he would only talk to her parents, she knew they would say yes.

Her thoughts were interrupted by a knock on the window: a man dropping off his daughter and son. She let them in and once the children kissed their father goodbye, they took off their outdoor shoes and washed their hands. They ran shrieking to Orchid, who picked them up and spun them around in turn.

Abby set up the main entrance lock so it would accept library account numbers, but not allow in the homeless. Knowing this time of year, it was unlikely any adult would come in seeking information, Abby kept her browser pointed at the article "Voices in the Stars" but turned off the screen so no one would see what she was investigating or change the topic. She hoped by afternoon there would be more information.

As he did each day, Mr. Johnson came in at exactly 9:30. He settled himself behind the information desk, far away from the children's department. It wasn't that he was aloof. Indeed, Abby's employer tended to be kindhearted, even to the homeless who slithered up to the library's solar lamps for warmth. Over fifty, he was just beginning to show his age. He couldn't hear the chirping voices of children as well as he once had, nor could he see them without his thick glasses. Even in June, he wore a sweater to hide the slight shiver of his limbs. Abby brought the old man his morning cup of tea and inclined her head at him in respect before she went back to work.

She set up the projector and began the children's stories. Though she read the highlighted words underneath the animated characters to the children, her mind was on the "Voices in the Stars." A man came in and requested information about salmon prices, which Mr. Johnson looked up, but otherwise it was a quiet day until noon.

At that time, a well-dressed young man paced at the door. He glanced behind him before he flashed his card. His behavior seemed strangely hesitant; he unwittingly encouraged the attention of all the children. Abby started another story, *Ruby Red and Snow White*. She closed the clear polymer doors behind her and set the lock. The children could see her, but they could not disturb the patron if they got bored.

Abby approached him and asked, "May I help you, sir?" She placed her palms together and bowed in respect.

He glanced back toward the door prior to bowing in response. "Can I speak to a librarian, Miss?"

"I am the assistant librarian."

He pulled out his handheld. "I saw a story called 'Voices in the Stars' this morning. I seek the truth."

She gestured at the contact point. "Yes, I saw the story this morning too. Let me see what the current information says. May I bring you a cup of tea?"

He declined and sat in a nearby chair. She sat down at her station and slid a finger across her touchpad to restart it. "Voices in the Stars" was already there.

She matched the story with Seattle's two major news stations. The search engine brought up the government satellites station, ten magazines, and two Cloud pages about a movie and a symphony with the same words in their title. Twelve daily news sites repeated the same story, with hundreds of comments about "God punishing the unfaithful," how "the honored ancestors abandoned the Earth," or how "God's will is to destroy the world."

She quickly typed in her secondary password to Seattle.gov. She scanned the police reports until she saw orders for the landing of an alien culture and riot control. She glanced up at the patron, who began fidgeting. She looked for something newer. Unfortunately, every station and newsfeed seemed just to be a repeat of the original story. She bit her lip. The orders from the city-state said to deny all possibility of invasion. Abby stood up and bowed. "I have come to a conclusion, sir."

"So it's an invasion like everyone says?"

Abby said, "Doubtful, sir. I believe it is most likely our lost brothers coming home. Isn't that exciting?"

The man looked pale. He bowed and walked out without answering her.

AT THE CHILDREN'S NAPTIME, THE University called the voices a hoax, a bad signal, or a comet. Religious conservatives preached that the ancients used comets and the stars to convey God's will. Abby could not deny her disappointment.

Orchid read over her shoulder. "What a load of crap. I'm really sick of people saying 'God's will' just because they don't know the answer."

Abby tried to look stern, but she could hardly stop herself from laughing. "Don't say 'crap.' I'll get in trouble," was the best she could manage. She glanced over at Mr. Johnson, who was with another white knuckled library patron. Both men's pallors were gray. Mr. Johnson poured a bit of whiskey into his teacup. He handed the patron the flask and he took a long swig.

"I would say it is our lost brothers coming home," Mr. Johnson said.

Abby perked up immediately. "Mr. Johnson, are you alright?"

He turned around. His eyes dripped tears. "Come, girls. Look what our friend brought up."

Government satellites from New Delhi captured images of the ten large ships heading directly towards Earth. Moreover, they were sending out signals on an unending loop. Some of it was static, but some of it sounded like words. Radio telescopes around the world worked together in order to capture and translate them. It was the same message repeated in many languages—English, Hindi, Mandarin, Cantonese, Japanese, Spanish, Italian, Afrikaans, Greek, Shona, Tonga, and others: "Brothers and Sisters, we come in peace and in need. We have found our way home."

The armada slowed at Triton and sent a message to the moon. No reply came. The colony had been abandoned centuries ago.

Mr. Johnson looked up. "Take my word for it. They will slow again on

Ganymede, then Mars, and then continue on to Earth. It is our brothers."

Earth sent out responses on the known frequencies, but the original message did not change. Abby wondered if there was more to the message than the governments of the world wanted them to know, but no amount of Cloud searching could find it before naptime ended.

Most of the parents returned at 5:30, but as the clock crawled towards 6:00, there were still children hanging around, getting hungry. Abby glanced once more at the "Voices in the Stars."

Mr. Johnson tapped his foot impatiently. "Miss Boyd Lei, soon we will know one way or the other, because at current deceleration rates, they'll be here in two days. God be with us. Find out where the little ones' parents are."

Abby scanned the old traffic monitors. Videos of rioting men filled their screen. "Mr. Johnson, look. It's my dad's factory," Abby said, turning the touchscreen toward him.

Orchid typed something into her handheld. She began pacing. She typed something else before she started chewing her nails.

Ten minutes later, Rory and Ray were at the library to escort them home. The men washed their hands as they came in and bowed in respect to Mr. Johnson. Abby could not deny that she was relieved to see her brother and friend, but there were still children in the library.

WHEN THEY FINALLY ARRIVED HOME, Grandma was in a tizzy. "The people..." she muttered and rocked herself. "Everyone has gone insane!"

Ma brought Grandma a cup of hot tea then sat down beside her. Grandma lifted the cup to her lips. Her hand trembled so badly, a few drops spilled on her dress front. Wrapping her arm around Grandma's shoulder, Ma whispered, "The girls made it home safe. We are all safe."

Da said softly, "People just walked off the job, but demanded their bread script. I tried to reason with them, but Davis—that hot head—riled people up! Soon, almost like a disease, fury spread throughout the workers. It got worse when the boss called the police..."

Jin broke in, "The mob was all over the district. They moved ahead of the police, screaming that we were being invaded."

Da said, "People threw stones and pieces of tile from the roofs and windows of nearby apartments in order to hinder the police. Several men were slain by lasers, but what was worse were the bodies of trampled women and children that littered the ground. The police were indiscriminate. All were guilty."

Jin interrupted again, "You should've seen Da. Shit, he was brave."

Da lightly smacked the top of Jin's head. "We're no longer in the factory."

Jin looked sufficiently chastised so Da said, "The boss gathered up the few women still there, had me protect them as he went around securing the factory. Most that was left were elderly women, boys and girls cowering under tables, some injured with laser burns. We waited the riot out."

According to the Cloud, the mob moved toward the breadlines. The clerks were wolf packed; some of them were even defiled. The police used nano grenades that gave the crowd large blisters all over their skin and made the bread inedible. Anyone unfortunate enough to eat the contaminated bread would quickly find themselves with blistered and swollen throats as they gasped for air.

Da told them there would be no supper except for the vegetables from the garden, but as they always had in their commune, Abby's family and neighbors pulled together. It was decided that able-bodied men and women would stand a two-hour watch. Abby stood with her father and Jin. Nothing happened that night, but the stars were beautiful.

According to the Cloud, the hysteria changed to a different form. Complaints of nausea and muscle spasms became common. Mayor Xiao promised amnesty if people went back to work. All of Seattle held its breath.

CHAPTER 3

June 2, 3062 C.E.

THE SUN WAS SHINING. THE factories were running. Restaurants and museums were open. The breadlines were calm. It seemed to be a day like any other, except Da walked Abby and Orchid to the library. He ordered them to wait for Ray in the evening. Abby thought her parents were being overprotective, but did not argue. After all, nothing happened at the library.

She refused to feel vulnerable, until a homeless man pushed past a woman dropping off her children. He ran down the steps and hid on a shelf that contained poetry drives. Abby called the police. It took them nearly thirty minutes to respond, but the man was happy to go. "Yes, take me. Jail's safer than the library."

The telephone started ringing. Sometimes Abby wanted to damn the Cloud. After fielding a few calls from the kids' parents, her father finally got through. She told him, "Don't worry. Tell Ma we're fine. He was just a frightened old man. The police took him."

Da asked, "The Cloud said Mr. Johnson has not come in?"

"No, but I have everything in hand," she replied.

"Damn. I'm sending over Jin."

Abby asked, "What about his job?"

"I'd rather have him lose the job than lose my daughters." Her father paused before he ordered, "Keep those doors locked. Until Mr. Johnson gets there, don't let anyone else in. If anything feels uncertain, head home. Bring the kids if you have to. Leave a note in the Cloud for their parents."

Abby promised to obey though it meant she was breaking library regulations. During business hours, she was supposed to let anyone in with an account number. She called the Central Branch. No one answered; eventually it went to the recorded message. She checked the Cloud; it was closed. Though the Cloud said the North, East, and West branches were open, no one answered there either.

She found the story about her branch. It was a total lie. There was no angry mob, and she had not done anything heroic. She glanced back at the kids playing with Orchid.

"I better sulfur the poetry area or we'll have lice. You okay?"

"Yeppers," Orchid said.

A chorus of "Yeppers" filled the children's area.

Abby went into the kitchen and unlocked the cabinet above the counter. She took out a jar of pesticide and went down to the lower level. She sprinkled some around the shelves and floorboards. She checked the old books. The man had completely ignored the polymer-coated volumes. He probably did not know their worth. Though she did not have time to look through them today, she ran a loving finger over their spines.

Orchid screamed. Some of the little girls began to cry. Abby ran up the stairs as someone smacked against the front window. The kids stared outside at a group of homeless men fighting in the lawn. Some threw punches. One was pawing at the door, whimpering. Another attacked a woman. Her bruised, sagging breasts were in clear view. Abby shut the curtains so the children could not see anymore and called the police again.

Abby jumped at the noise behind them. Jin knocked on the back. She let him in. "I'm so glad you're here. I was going to start another round of songs, but if you want to …" She looked around, not sure what Jin might want to do.

Jin said, "I'm just going to check the Cloud for a bit, but I'll be right there. Shout if you need anything. Hey, do you have anything in the kitchen? I'm starving."

THAT NIGHT, DA WAS SHORT tempered. He escorted Abby when she took Tara out and snapped at Abby to hurry her dog.

Abby did not argue openly, but thought *I doubt such a thing is possible*. There was another round of guard duty, but no one seemed to be on the streets that night.

The next morning, no children came to the library. Neither did Mr. Johnson. The Cloud reported that people refused to work. The general consensus was: What's the point? It was likely that an invading army was circling Earth. It was God's will whether Earth would live or die.

The Cloud stated that the mayor's office did not know the ship's landing site, but due to her librarian training, Abby knew almost immediately that the Cloud story was fabricated. She typed in her password to Seattle. gov. She did not have high security clearance, but she considered that the police and EMT's would be called to the landing site. She scanned their daily commands.

She showed her father. "Da, this has to be it!"

As the day went on, Grandma became more hysterical. Abby and Orchid were smart enough not to voice their opinions, but both of them silently rolled their eyes while they genuflected beside their family.

CHAPTER 4

July 5, 3062 C.E.

PEOPLE FILLED THE STREETS, NOT rioting in anger, but wanting to be the first to see the visitors. The hospital was full of people too, complaining of a smell that would not disappear.

The air was sweet with jasmine, honeysuckle, and other flowers of summer. Entrepreneurial spirits sold seasonal fruit, popcorn, and cotton candy. Others held handmade signs. Most said: "Welcome Friends from the Stars!" However, there were a few that said, "God made us this paradise. Go home!" Or worse: "God made humans in His image, what do you look like?"

Abby saw Rory in the throng and waved. Her heart started beating faster as he called out and pushed his way towards them. He inclined his head towards Da, Abby, and Orchid before he playfully slugged Jin and Ray's shoulders in turn. Tara growled under her breath and whined. Abby clutched her dog tighter. They walked beyond the horde enjoying the carnival like atmosphere over to a nearly empty field where plain clothes police had set up metal fencing and a plastic barricade with signs saying: "Don't crush the lettuce."

On the far side there were several men, including Mayor Xiao.

The translucent blue metal ship hummed above them. Even from the ground, Abby could see it wasn't a large ship, probably not more than sixteen meters in length and six meters wide. The roar of its engines brought the rest of the crowd, gawking toward the landing site.

Orchid pulled on Abby's sleeve. "This is not the ship that Mr. Johnson showed us."

Abby said, "Might be a short range ship. The larger ship is probably still above."

As soon as she said it, Abby knew it was true.

It hovered over the large green field of lettuce before it began to lower and fold its wings inward. Three lads jumped the barricade. Da and a few other clear-headed adults shouted at them. They did not back away and the crowd heard the screams of agony and terror before the great blue flames disintegrated them. Da checked Jin. Tara pulled backward on her leash, pawed on the ground and gently nipped at Abby's skirt. Orchid hid her face in Ray's shoulder. A few other boys tried to touch the ship, the heat radiated towards them and they screamed in pain. Half of the human throng still pressed forward, the other stepped back.

The hatch opened and six people exited: tall with dark hair, smooth tan skin that was unmarred by blemish, and wearing gray coveralls. They were ageless, with a strange sameness about them. They might have been twenty or forty years of age; there was no way to tell.

Abby asked, "Da, do you think it could be a family?"

"Perhaps. On such a long trip, families would want to stay together," he said as he raised his hand to tell her not to speak. He was trying to listen.

Mayor Xiao stepped forward. "Welcome home?" He pressed his palms together and inclined his head as did the City Secretary and Police Officers.

No expression came to the newcomer's faces, but they put their hands out. Abby remembered that long ago, when there were less people, shaking hands and embracing was customary. The mayor put his hand out the same way. The man clasped it. Abby guessed that was a good sign.

With a strange lilting accent, the newcomer said, "I'm Captain Saunders of the *Vos*. We tried to contact you, but it seems you no longer have over-air communications."

"My understanding is that we sent out messages." Mayor Xiao was a politician, not a scientist; he really did not know what the man was talking about. He wound up falling into the habit of nodding in order not to seem too stupid.

Captain Saunders began making an obviously prewritten speech, yet he told the crowd nothing. The other newcomers scanned the multitude, looking for something. Abby thought one looked directly at her, but she knew that was probably just foolishness. Remembering that there was more than one ship, she realized that an armada had encircled the planet. It seemed likely that they would be in orbit over the largest cities. The shuttles would spread out from there.

"What do you think they want?" Abby whispered.

"Obviously, they have come home," Rory said with authority. "The entire world is changing. Old rules will no longer apply."

He put his hand on her shoulder. An unwanted shiver of excitement ran down her back, but was dulled by her father's presence and her resolve not to be Rory's next conquest. She tugged on Jin's sleeve and changed places with him, using Orchid's fear as her excuse. Da raised an eyebrow at the younger man; his beliefs on the importance of virtue were well known.

Rory eventually moved away. Abby told herself that she didn't care, but she watched him go out of the corner of her eye. When she glanced back, she saw her father's green eyes studying her. She kissed the top of Orchid's head in order not to have to answer him. He said nothing, but put an arm around her. Da was always good at letting his children know his feelings without words. At that moment, Abby knew he was proud that he did not have to worry that his eldest would do something dumb, no matter how much she liked a certain young man.

Once the newcomers, the mayor, and a few other men that Abby did not recognize went into the ship to discuss communication methods, it was obvious there was little else to see. Though the boys wanted to stay, Orchid wanted to go home.

Da decided, "Let's go home."

WHEN THEY ARRIVED, MA WAS nearly in tears, wringing her hands and pacing. Grandma admonished the whole family for staying out so long then she kissed both Ray and Jin for being smart enough to not jump the barricade. Da wrapped his arms around Ma who sobbed in thanks that the boys who were burned at the landing site were not either of her sons. And she sobbed for feeling such disgraceful emotions.

Abby and Orchid glanced at each other and looked up at the wall screen. It was obvious Ma and Grandma had been watching the news covering the riots. Unending tides of people throwing bottles and garbage towards the shuttles in Rome and New Delhi. The newcomers simply turned around and flew away. They only landed where they were greeted with respect and friendship. Seattle, London, Johannesburg, and Tokyo were the only first landing sites that didn't riot. Paris and Moscow were second choices, but they greeted the newcomers with open arms. The family watched clip after clip of the shuttles landing until an hour later when the Cloud announced a town meeting at Seattle City Hall. The world rang with the news as the emergency broadcast signal went off upon their handhelds.

EVEN THOUGH THE BOYD LEI family went two hours early, it seemed that nearly all million residents of Seattle swarmed inside or around city hall, watching monitors in the foyer and outside the windows. The family was able to squeeze into the back and stand.

The smell of honeysuckle was overpowering. It became so hot with the crush of bodies Grandma took Orchid home. Two others quickly slipped into the spot they had relinquished.

The same six newcomers with impossibly clear brown skin and one-piece uniforms of pale gray marked with his or her insignias sat in plastic chairs facing the crowd.

After the mayor had introduced them, Captain Saunders said, "We have found numerous planets with more or less breathable atmospheres. We have colonized our best hope for the future. We once called this planet c of 75289, but now we refer to it as Kipos—the Greek word for garden. As you may remember from history, Japan, China, India, France, Italy, and Greece supported colonization.

"Kipos orbits the HD 75289 binary star system. We now refer to the A star as Ilios and the B star as Kokadelfi."

A photo of the solar system was projected upon a large screen. The slides changed a few more times, each photo showing different views and details of the system and planet as the man spoke: "Ilios is located 94.4 light-years from Sol and lies at the northwest edge of Constellation Vela with four other planets, surrounded by an asteroid belt."

A female science officer began speaking, "Kipos is, on average, a few degrees cooler than Earth. It has three large continents, though its total landmass is larger. When we changed the calendar to the Kipos Standard, we kept the same twelve months that you are used to with the Gregorian calendar. However, we have a twenty-seven hour day, three hundred forty-nine days in a year. Our months have twenty-nine days, except for December, which has thirty. December 30th is our New Year…" She went on about holidays for a time and then changed slides.

Another crewmember began: "Now in order to conserve resources during the journey to Kipos, a person must undergo what we call hypersleep in a gravity/stasis pod…"

Abby noticed as the science officer spoke that many of her neighbors drifted off into the glazed look of lazy listening. She wondered if they understood how long it would take to get there. Once a person was in a pod, he or she would not wake up until they arrived on Kipos nearly a century later. Everyone they once knew would be dead. This was a one-way trip.

A tall man stood up. "Since you will be traveling at near the speed of light, how do your vocal or ship to ship communications occur?"

The science officer had a look of contempt. "The short answer is tachyons, which are not bound by space time."

The audience seemed ready to move on, but Abby did not like the irritated way the science officer answered or their condescending gazes. The tall man asked, "Will you help us learn this technology?"

"Our ship orbiting with the East Coast plans to share technologies."

Ma whispered to Da, "Why are they so evasive?"

"They're no longer from Earth, Blossom. They've their own way of doing things. Honestly, the more science-speak, the less people listen," he answered.

The Kiposi moved on smoothly, now noticeably ignoring the man. They wanted people to understand their principle points.

Here it comes, Abby thought.

"We cannot take your old and frail or very young. Nor do we wish to split up parents from their small children. We can only take healthy young men and women over the age of twelve and under the age of thirty. Still, at the end of this journey, will be paradise."

A chance to see a new planet! Excitement rushed into her chest as Abby tried to think of a way to convince her parents. While she did not technically need their permission, she would be unhappy without their blessing. To sneak off and leave the planet without letting them know was childish and cruel—especially when there was no way back.

Da raised his hand. "If you take our young, who will work our fields and..?"

Abby carefully hid her disappointment. She knew her father would not allow his children to go. Maybe Jin, but not Ray. And certainly not his daughters.

The science officer said, "We are not taking anyone without their consent. For those that wish to come, you must be tested. You have ten days to decide. We leave in twenty."

CHAPTER 5

June 8, 3062 C.E.

ABBY WAS STILL HALF ASLEEP when she heard her father's handheld buzz. He answered it and spoke in a low, urgent voice that Abby could not quite make out. Then he and her mother whispered to each other in their cot.

Da gently nudged his sons with his socked feet. "Get up. Get dressed. This might be a better life for you. Come on, girls."

Abby pushed off the coverlet and yanked Orchid to her feet. Ma carried in a few buckets of water and started heating it over the stove. When the water was at a rolling boil, she poached seven eggs for breakfast. Grandma was stirring rice porridge clockwise for luck.

Da showed her his handheld. The night foreman texted him:

```
Night shift empty. You must see KOMI.
```

Abby typed the IP address into the wall screen. Images flashed of the Kiposi machinery drilling downwards and putting together ten pressurized, glass-enclosed cars to transport the new colonists from Earth to the mother ships. Behind the fences there were swarms of people, holding signs or gawking.

Their spokesman said cheerfully to the camera, "As you may know, one of the largest costs in space travel involves simply escaping Earth's gravity. Once built, the elevators cost very little to run since they are powered by Earth's own orbital rotation and magnetic field."

He went on, "We will be leaving these for your use to restart your space program."

Da said wryly, "And they've more room for colonists. I suppose we should see if any of you qualify."

The Boyd Lei offspring looked at each other; they could not believe it was possible.

"Why the change of heart, father?" Ray asked.

"They closed the factory. The fields are empty. I'm going to go in, just in case someone does show for work. Your mother will take you."

MEDICAL STATIONS WERE SET UP around Seattle. The school was four blocks away, while Saint Mary's Church was a kilometer. Grandma refused to leave the apartment. Though Ma required them all to wear their best outfits, Abby knew that she felt hesitant to be on the street for long. They headed for the school. Crowds of people shuffled in long lines to see the Kiposi doctors and find out whether they could make the journey or not. For some, it was in the hope that technology had cured their ailments. For others, it was simple curiosity.

As the line moved down the hall, it was split by gender. Before she lost sight of her sons, Ma reminded them, "Ray, watch your brother! Jin, you behave!"

Abby and Orchid followed their mother into Dr. Li Rao's makeshift office. She wore a one-piece gray flight suit and a smile on her heart-shaped face. On her shoulder there was a caduceus patch and an insignia with two bars. Her lilting accent was melodious, but Dr. Rao spoke in near perfect English. "What language do you speak at home?"

Ma replied, "English. Sometimes my mother will only speak Mandarin."

Dr. Rao switched to Mandarin. Ma answered in the same, "My mother would be so pleased. She worries that the old ways are dying."

It was those words that made Abby realize that Dr. Rao was not there by chance. She had been assigned to this neighborhood.

Abby listened carefully. If her family was able to go then she must learn to speak as the Kiposi spoke. "Excuse me, doctor, but do you speak any other languages?"

Dr. Rao turned to her. "Yes, I also speak Hindi and a little Greek. Not fluent, mind you, but I can get by. There are so many Greek words which have worked their way into the common vernacular of English, it's easy to learn."

Abby thought that was an interesting answer. Dr. Rao began interrogating Ma about her daughters' medical history. Abby heard nothing out of the ordinary, but Orchid was embarrassed by the questions as well as her mother's answers as they discussed the tests and inoculations that would be required.

Ma must have said nearly a dozen times: "They are good girls. No drugs, no boys. Abigail works as an assistant librarian. Orchid is in school. Very high marks."

Abby and Orchid sat through the various pokes and prods. Blood pressure, temperature, and urine were taken; tiny scratches were made across their backs with needles dipped in common substances found on Kipos.

Their mother's insistence that they were both virgins was not enough. Abby lay back first. "Hymen intact, a little stretched," Dr. Rao said. Abby saw the dictation recorded on a nearby glass tablet. "First day of last period, May 14th – normal. Six days. Minor cramps. No signs of cancer or disfigurement. To be expected at her age—in a good girl." Abby realized that Rao added the last part for the benefit of her mother.

Abby pulled on her underwear as the doctor checked Orchid. "Hymen intact. No signs of cancer or disfigurement. Menarche has not begun. Mother began at thirteen, aunt and elder sister at twelve."

Their backs were bared once more.

Dr. Rao scanned and made notes on her tablet.

"Good. No allergies!" Dr. Rao said. "Both girls are healthy. You've done well with them, Madam. Your sons have completed their medical exams. All are eligible for further testing, which will take place on 712 Jefferson Street on Saturday the eleventh. May I ask how old you are?"

"Thirty-three," Ma answered.

"Though you're a bit older than we are looking for, since you've bore four healthy children, I could examine you if you fear your children leaving you behind. What form of birth control do you and your husband use?"

"The Natural Calendar."

Dr. Rao squinted as she processed the words. She obviously had no idea what it meant. With a slight tone of condescension, she asked, "Moon Cycles?"

"Yes, but my husband is forty and my mother still lives."

"We would have to leave them both behind, I am afraid."

"Then I could not go," she said.

Arrogance danced in Dr. Rao's eyes. "Of course, we understand. I do hope that you will consider allowing the children to have greater opportunities than Earth could possibly give them?"

"Their father and I will speak on it," was the only answer Ma gave.

CHAPTER 6

June 11, 3062 C.E.

UNSURE OF WHAT TO EXPECT, Abby and her siblings sat down on long divided tables as instructed. Men in gray coveralls set plastic and glass touch screen pads in front of them. They were given the most basic of instructions and told they had an hour.

Nerves fluttered in her stomach. A recorded man asked Abby what certain symbols meant to her. She did not understand; she didn't know any of them.

"What do they make you think about?" The recorded man asked. "Look at this image. Just the first words that come to mind, Abigail Boyd Lei."

The black mark spread out and looked like it had wings so Abby said it was a butterfly. Another looked like a bird, monkey, rosebush, Sol.

She was asked to write a list of goals for her life. Taking up the stylus, she wrote directly onto the glass screen:

> *I originally hoped to be a librarian or a teacher. I helped raise my younger siblings and taught each of them reading as my mother had taught me.*
>
> *Now, we are asked to travel somewhere new. It is hard to have specific goals when the world has changed so much in a week. I would like to be married and have children someday. I do not know what types of jobs will be available to us, but I will work hard to the best of my abilities to be a useful member of the society on Kipos.*

She was given seven letters and asked what words she could make in three minutes. She was able to come up with sixteen words. The recorded man said there were over twenty-five possible answers; Abby assumed she had failed that part of the test. Next was a matching game that moved on to analogy patterns.

The recorded man asked her what other languages she knew. She informed him she was fluent in Mandarin and knew a little French.

"You have been granted fifteen minutes extra for each language." It began two more tests that covered the basics in reading, writing and listening skills. Mandarin was easy, French slightly harder. Yet, some of the questions were strange. The recorded man asked in both languages who she would like to marry.

In Mandarin, she answered, "I want to marry a man who loves me."

In French, she answered, "I'd like to marry a kindhearted man."

Then the recorded man asked her at what age she felt would be appropriate for her to bear children.

In Mandarin, she answered, "I am seventeen and ready to bear children once I find a husband."

In French, she answered, "At seventeen, I am old enough."

Again, she was given seven letters and asked to play the word game in Mandarin and French.

Finally, there was mathematics. The first few questions were sums and multiplication, which she flew through. The test moved on to ratios that were a little harder and equations of which she had never seen the like.

At ninety minutes, the recorded man said, "Thank you, Abigail Boyd Lei. Your test results will be sent to your home."

She left the room assuming she had failed. By the look on her siblings' faces, so had they. Ray shoved his hands in his pockets and suggested they all go get a bubble tea if the café was open.

Orchid agreed with enthusiasm. Abby and Jin agreed so they did not have to face the fact they were all idiots.

"Did you let Ma know?"

Ray shook his head and Abby pulled out her handheld and texted home.

She heard a beep with the reply:

```
Be careful!!!
```

Seconds later, the younger siblings got the same messages with the added words:

```
Listen to Abby and Ray!!!
```

Ray smirked. "We got to get Ma to lay off the bangs."

The four walked down six blocks to their favorite teahouse. It was packed with depressed adolescents and one happy business owner. Some were in corners typing on their handhelds. Others scowled into their tea. Most were not given the chance to take the test.

Ray whispered, "Don't talk about what we did today."

All agreed. Not seeing anyone they knew, Abby and Jin found a table near the back while Ray and Orchid ordered and watched the man behind the counter put the mix with the milk and tea. Orchid's favorite part was when he put it through the frothier and sealed on the cellophane lid to the thin plastic cups.

DA'S HANDHELD WENT OFF. HE told his offspring that they would be in charge of breakfast while he and their mother went out to the garden. They returned inside when a Kiposi buzzed the commune's secured gate.

Not knowing what else to do, Abby offered their guest a cup of tea and a seat. When he reached out for the cup, she saw that he had the soft hands of a man not used to doing manual labor.

Visibly uncomfortable in the room, he spoke directly to Ma and Da. "My name is Bob Tygh. I'm here to inform you that four of your children—Abigail aged seventeen, Raymond aged sixteen, Jin aged fifteen, and Orchid aged eleven—have passed testing. We'd like to offer them all passage."

Grandma held on to Ma, who wept with joy and sadness. Their father nodded with a worried look on his face.

Tygh looked directly at Abby. "I am sure a healthy girl like you will have no problem finding a kind hearted husband just as you said you wanted."

Abby blushed uncomfortably.

Then he continued, "It is best that the children take as little as possible. They will want for nothing." He began describing hypersleep in a gravity pod again. After he finished his tea, he took their thumbprints and printed out four boarding passes.

He answered a few more questions and said he hoped he would see them all at the elevator. "You are required to report on Tuesday, June 14th at the airfield. If you do not, your space will be given to those on the waiting list."

"Three days?" Da asked.

"We know this is a difficult decision, but we did not anticipate so many would want to come. This is the best way to proceed."

Tygh left a copy of a small booklet with photographs and information of the transport ships and Kipos. There was a link for the Cloud with even more information. Happy faces similar to their own smiled out at them. There were rivers, mountains, and trees so much like Earth's.

THAT NIGHT, WORD OF WHO else was traveling to Kipos spread quickly through the commune: Rory and another boy in Orchid's class were offered passage as well.

It was past midnight when the Boyd Leis were awoken by Mary Rogersdottir's scream. Seconds later, her broken body, blood and cracked head were on the pavement outside their window. Da ordered his daughters and Jin to stay inside, but the men went out to help Rory. Ma called the police, but they did not come.

THE NEXT DAY WAS LONG. No one spoke about much except Da, who refused to allow anyone out alone. Orchid wasn't allowed out at all. Jin escorted Abby to the library. No children came and when Mr. Johnson did not arrive, she called his house.

She gave her resignation.

He wasn't surprised. "Miss Boyd Lei, I suspect they'll take little Orchid and your brothers as well?"

"How did you know?"

"I've seen lots of kids in my time. May God be with you."

Sad to leave this part of her life behind, Abby roamed between the shelves of drives and polymer coated books. She picked up *Lieutenant Hornblower* by C.S. Forrester. She scanned the first chapter, though she knew the book by heart. It was Mr. Johnson's favorite and she had read the entire series to him over the course of the past year. She set it back with the wish there was more for her to do.

She locked up the library and went to the post office in order to mail her keycard to Mr. Johnson's home. She used the self-service machine since the town seemed to be deserted. Everyone was home watching the Cloud's surveillance of the last of the elevator being built. With shocking alacrity, robotic arms pulled carbon Nano-tube cabling as magnetic tiling was bolted into place on the elevator's crystalline structure.

That night, Abby and Ray took Tara out together. Long after the dog had done what she needed to do, they sat on the stoop.

Ray looked up at the stars and sighed. "I'm not going."

Abby turned to her brother. "What?"

"Someone needs to stay here and take care of the place. Take care of Mother, Father and Grandmother ...and Tara. She'll miss you like crazy," Ray said.

"Don't you want to see another solar system? Another planet?" Abby asked him and leaned forward to squeeze her dog. Ray was right, Tara was going to miss her.

"I don't really care about that."

"You're afraid."

"Yes, but that doesn't make my reason any less valid. You need to go.

Take care of Jin and Orchid. They won't be turned from this," Ray said. "My guess is that there will be many older folks without sons and daughters to care for them in their old age. Rory killed so he might go!"

Rory came through the door, obviously having heard them. "She jumped, Ray."

"She jumped," Abby and Ray repeated.

Rory took the steps down so he could look at the two of them. His blue eyes looked black. Abby thought, *If Ray was correct, Rory killed so he might go. If he killed once, he might kill again. But that makes no sense. Why would he need to kill Mary?*

"You know the Kiposi don't care if you've kept your virginity. The world is different now." Rory reached out and patted her thigh. Some of his old charm came back into his face.

Tara growled.

"I'll let my husband decide if he cares or not," Abby replied and stood up. At least on the stairs, she was taller than he. Seeing the fear and anger in his face, she knew Mary had been pregnant. The Kiposi had said they would not split up young families.

"You stupid girl, don't you see you won't have a husband! They have different rules than we do. Share my bunk. Let's leave all this nonsense behind."

Abby felt Ray shift, beside her. Tara's ears flattened and began a steady low growl. In order to diffuse the situation, she snapped, "You're wrong! Mr. Tygh discussed it with us. Men and women do marry on Kipos. So even if the rules are different, I will wait."

With her free hand on Ray's arm, she spun around and hurried up the stairs, into the commune, and back into the lighted hallway. Abby feared shaming herself and getting pregnant, but she was more afraid of what her brother would say if he knew that Rory's touch had made her tingle.

Perhaps, Rory was right and on Kipos the old rules wouldn't matter. Perhaps, she could choose to take a lover. If that were the case, she would ask Rory. Or, perhaps not. From what she had seen so far, Kiposi men were handsome; maybe she would find someone better. *If I can't have a husband, then I'll take whoever it is they have there. Jin is too young to say anything and Ray won't be there to care!*

CHAPTER 7

June 14, 3062 C.E.

THE FAMILY SAID GOOD-BYE OVER a lunch of chicken, carrots, and plenty of tears. Grandma said prayers and burnt incense. Ma kissed her children again and again. Da squeezed them hard. So did Ray.

Tara whimpered and paced, almost as if she sensed Abby and her younger siblings were not coming back. Tara was family, but she was seven years old, and Abby knew that she could not give up her entire future for a dog.

As they walked outside the commune, Orchid began to sniffle.

Da embraced his children once more and said softly, "Take care of them, Abby.

"Jin, I'm counting on you. You'll be the man of the family on the new world.

"Orchid, you listen to your brother and sister now. You better get going. You have a ways to walk."

The three took their first steps away from the commune. Abby glanced back. Her parents held each other. Grandma clutched Tara around her giant, furry neck. Ray watched them. She knew there was part of him who wanted to come, but fear and duty held him to Earth.

She waved once more at her dearest sibling. Her eyes were moist. She could not deny part of her wanted to return home. The sun was warm on their backs, but the blue skies saddened her. She would never have another day on Earth. She was glad when they made it down the hill and the commune was out of sight. Orchid was bawling and tears dripped down Jin's nose.

Abby reached around her sister's narrow shoulders and squeezed her tight, then pulled out a few tissues and passed them around. In a false cheerful tone, she said, "This will be a grand adventure, won't it?"

Jin followed suit: "I know we'll miss Ma, Da, Ray, Grandma, and Tara, but we'll have each other, alright?"

Orchid took the tissue and wiped a bit of clear snot and tears off her nose and nodded.

Abby went on: "I'm going to Kipos, but I'll take you home right now. Once we are around this bend, there's no turning back. Do you still want to go?"

"Yeah." The younger girl lifted her chin to look at her sister. "Remember when Mr. Tygh said that on Kipos I could go to school to become anything I wanted, maybe even a doctor. I like that idea. Ma and Da can't send me to the university."

Abby felt a lump in her throat. Orchid's reasoning was much more mature than her own.

"If I can go to school, I always thought it would be neat to invent something instead of just building something that someone else designed," Jin said. With a guilty look, he glanced up at Abby. "But I understand if I have to work."

Abby nodded. "My hope is that both of you can attend school."

Behind them, they heard: "Hey, guys! Wait!"

Rory ran to catch up with them. His forehead held a glaze of sweat. Abby waited for him to start making lewd remarks but he just fell in step. His blue eyes were filled with fear.

"There's nothing to be scared of, Orchid." Rory's voice held a slight tremble, as though the words were meant to make him more confident, not her. "We really are going somewhere new. Someplace better. I saw Ray before I left. He's a good man. You should be proud to have a brother like that."

"We are," Jin replied.

Jin and Rory walked behind them and, though it was uncomfortably sweaty, Abby held Orchid's hand as they hiked the two miles to the old airfield south of the city. They watched the elevator car disappear into the blue sky as the new colonists were sent up to the mother ship. With each step, it was hard not to get excited.

Rory stopped for a moment. His voice was pleading. "I did not kill Mary."

"No one said you did," Abby said. She wasn't sure if she believed him or just wanted to.

Rory spoke quickly. "She committed suicide when I broke it off with her. She didn't have any money for paternity tests and she didn't have time to put it together before the ship left. I offered to abort the fetus, but the Suffering God does not like abortion. Please, I need you to believe me. I did not kill her."

Jin nodded.

Embracing him with a quick and what she hoped felt like a sisterly side hug,

Abby said, "We believe you. Come on. We are almost there."

Ahead of them were layers of gated security and mobs of people. Pimps and drug dealers encircled the gate selling their wares. Thieves sold stolen or forged passes. Abby was glad that their boarding passes were hidden deep within her blouse. Rory shoved his hands in his pockets so no one could steal his. A man asked Abby what her price was, but Jin glared and took a step towards him.

She grabbed her brother's arm. "Let's keep moving. Soon it won't matter."

Jin reluctantly agreed.

They worked their way through the crowd of people holding hate-filled signs and the reporters with their cameramen. They circumvented families who were saying their goodbyes. When they reached the first manned gate, the guard instructed, "Put your right thumbprint here."

Abby told Orchid to go first. She whined that she did not want to be left alone even for a second, so Jin went first, then Orchid, followed by Abby.

Inside the gate, Abby gave their boarding passes to the second official scanning the documents. Once the lighted red star beeped, he allowed them inside the second gate. They walked through a meter of icy antiseptic spray. Once across the threshold, they waited for Rory as it dried.

They moved to stand in the next line when they heard shouting and saw three young men with guns storm the gate. There was a single shot and a scream. Jin picked up Orchid and grabbed Abby's wrist. He pulled the girls to the nearest barricade. Rory was right behind him and Abby felt his arms wrap around her head to protect her.

By the time they turned around the three men had been engulfed in flames. Abby covered her sister's eyes. Crowds of people screamed, but no one did anything. They just waited for the elevator doors to open.

Abby saw another young man and woman try to socially engineer their way through the gate. "We lost our passes, but we are on the list," the woman said, pointing towards the fence.

"Your irresponsibility is not our concern," the Kiposi said.

"What she means is my brother has them and he is already in there." After a few more minutes of arguing, the woman eventually gave up and walked away. The man grew angry that he was refused. The gateman hit a button and the man's body erupted in a blue flame. His howl of agony lasted a few long seconds before he was dead. Abby forced herself to find fault in his actions, not blame the Kiposi. "He wouldn't have just left. They didn't want to kill him," she whispered as she filed through the airlock and into the space elevator.

A Kiposi woman handed each of them a small roll of soft candy and a napkin. They were told to chew the candy or blow their noses to equalize their ears during the air pressure change. Most of the seats on the ground floor were full, but Abby glanced around hoping to find four together. Jin, however, rushed up the stairs, pulling Orchid behind him.

"Jin!" Abby called.

He glanced back with a smile and kept going. She trailed after them. Her brother pushed his way to an empty row of facing seats to make sure he and Orchid could sit next to a window. Once on the top floor, Abby glimpsed towards the sky, but she could not see anything but glittering cables against magnetic tiles and disappearing blue. Rory's hand was gentle on her back as he continued to guide her towards the others. Abby apologized to anyone grumbling about the pair of wild children who had just pushed past them. By the time they reached them, Jin was helping Orchid buckle herself in. Abby briefly considered reminding her brother to be considerate, but he had kept their little sister safe and found four seats together. She sat down next to Orchid without a word. Rory sat beside Jin.

Abby counted the twenty-five rows of ten seats. There were three floors: seven hundred and fifty souls per trip. According to her calculations, there must be at least ten trips in a day. Seventy-five hundred people from Seattle and there were nine other cities, making a total of 750,000 souls, plus the crew of sixty per ship, in addition to seed and livestock.

Her stomach lurched as the elevator started to lift. Before she knew it, the city was spread out north of her. Now there was really no turning back. She wondered what Ray was doing. Did he miss them? Did he regret his decision? She wished he were there to share in this adventure. As they rose, she could see the Puget Sound and the Olympic Peninsula. It looked like a child's model. Soon the distinct topography disappeared and she could only make out splotches of brown, white, green, and the blue of the Pacific Ocean. She mused that it was strange that the first time that she ever saw the Pacific were her last moments tethered to Earth.

She took one piece of candy and gave the rest to Orchid, who wolfed hers down. Abby blew her nose to equalize her ears, then wrapped her arm around her sister as the blue opened up to the black. Above them was a gray-bluish, conical shaped ship set against a field of stars. On what Abby assumed was the bow, the cone rounded to a bulbous sphere. Below this sphere were antennae and a large dish all of which looked like they might be retractable. Towards the aft was a large rotating wheel. Each spoke ended in a large thick box. Abby had no idea what any of it was for, but the constellations had never been so visible as they were at that moment. It had to be a good omen.

A clear acrylic hollow arm stretched out towards the elevator. It locked in place and the Kiposi technicians opened the airlock. An announcement told them to unbuckle their belts and file out in an orderly fashion. Abby found walking easy enough, but she felt slightly lighter than she had before the journey.

"Do you feel that? I bet there is lower gravity aboard the ship then on Earth. The technology on Kipos must really be amazing!" she whispered to the others.

Rory just nodded. His tanned skin looked very pale.

"You're such a weirdo," Jin said, trying to look indifferent but failing miserably since he seemed unable to stop grinning.

Not wanting to argue, but wanting to get in the last word, Abby said, "Imagine being part of a team that designs ships like this."

"Maybe I am," Jin said, still grinning.

"Come on!" Orchid said as she pulled on Abby's hand as they shuffled with the crowd towards the airlock.

Walking through the heavens, the view of Earth below was too amazing to fear falling. She wished she could slow down to take it all in, but the crowd and her siblings pulled her along.

Even for the ship's sterile cleanliness, there was a smell of oil and dry air. Abby was struck again by the similarities of the crew, but what was truly disconcerting were the insipid smiles on their too similar faces. Jin was confident, but Rory seemed as nervous as she was. Like everyone else, they tossed their tissues and candy wrappers down the marked chute.

They followed the crowd, who followed the rows of light embedded into the ceiling. As they entered the back of the hold, a hallway split and they were to be segregated by gender.

Rory looked ill.

Jin kissed both of his sisters on the cheeks. "I'll see you when we land. You be good, Orcs. Listen to Abby."

While her brother followed the other males, Abby considered how, in those few moments, his voice had become deeper. He was no longer the second son or Ray's younger brother. She mused, if Rory were allowed to stay with them, Jin would make sure that he would be regulated to the little brother position. If Rory tried to bed her, Jin would make sure he would also wed her.

Abby and Orchid followed a woman past large crates stacked upon one another and clamped to the walls. She could see by the writing that some were filled with supplies, others with seeds. Beyond, doorways led to long narrow passageways of smaller quarters. Abby and Orchid were told to relieve themselves, which they did on a cold metal public toilet that did not flush until its sensors determined that it was full.

Then they were led with two additional girls inside a tiny room with four narrow bunks that reminded Abby of a packing crate. The walls were solid, but the floor and ceiling was grating. Through the open spaces between the metal, she could see tiny spirals of piping.

The woman handed them each a tiny waxed paper cup of water and two capsules: one white oblong and the other a pink circular disk.

She said, "Alright, ladies. Just a sedative and an antihistamine." She watched to make sure everyone swallowed the pills.

The other girls kissed each other for luck and climbed into the two uppermost bunks. Orchid began to cry.

To distract her, Abby asked the technician, "My understanding is the hypersleep liquid acts like some sort of filter."

With a condescending smile, the woman answered, "That's right. There is a circulating current of highly oxygenated liquid and nanomites. You will sleep through the entire trip."

"Body functions cease?"

"They slow. Nanomites clean up any waste."

"Isn't that interesting, Orcs?" Abby put her arm around her little sister. She swore to herself she would find a job on the new world and send her siblings to school. Jin would design ships and Orchid would become a doctor. She would find a good husband and when they were ready, she would help her siblings to do the same. They would even help Rory. Even though she would never see her parents again, she would honor them and her ancestors by her actions.

Abby helped Orchid into one of the lower bunks. The air smelled honeysuckle sweet. She realized she smelled this aroma before. The day the Kiposi landed and again in city hall. She refused to allow fear to overwhelm her. Her eyelids felt heavy as she tucked her sister under the thin blanket. "We ask that our ancestors watch over us and Jin and Rory. Even on Kipos, please watch over us, Amen."

"Amen," Orchid echoed.

Abby tried to stand, but Orchid started to cry again. "No, don't go."

"Relax in there," the woman said. "Breathe deeply. You two are slender enough that you can stay in the rack with your sister if you wish, Abigail. It won't hurt anything."

Abby sensed that the Kiposi's cheerfulness was being forced now, but she wasn't really irritated with them as much as it had been a long day. Abby guessed that since so many siblings slept together that the Kiposi had gone through this many times before. Abby crawled under the covers. Orchid calmed down immediately. The Kiposi's relief was obvious.

"Our ancestors will watch over us," Abby brushed the hair off her sister's ear.

"Rory too," Orchid replied sleepily. "Remember the little book? It said there were cats. I'd like to have a kitten."

"I don't see why not, but I'll need to get a job first, okay?"

"Mmmhmm," Orchid replied sleepily.

Another girl was placed in the now-spare bunk and given pills. Once she lay down, the door closed. The air grew moist and the lights faded. The giggling above her silenced. Abby heard the girl crying. Orchid was asleep. She rolled towards the other girl.

"Homesick?" Abby whispered in the darkness.

A tired young voice whispered, "My mama told me that it would be a better life, but she was really sick. I shouldn't have left her. She your daughter?"

"My little sister."

The girl mumbled something else, but it was coated with sleep. Abby rolled back over. Orchid was dead to the world when the room filled with a thick goopy liquid. She felt her sister drifting away from her in the black. Abby sat up. Bumping her head on the bunk above her, she realized how long it took to put her hand to her brow. Even in the movement, Orchid did not stir. Suddenly, where there had been space a solid wall stood.

In seconds, the liquid seemed to expand. *Still a liquid, but heavier. Like gelatin? Am I wet?* Abby did not have the vocabulary to make her observations into complete thoughts.

She wanted to scream but no sound came from her. She was too frightened to close her eyes.

"Please don't be dead!" Abby tried to scream again. The black entered her mouth. It was filling her lungs. She was going to suffocate. She felt the ship move. *Should I feel acceleration in the gravity pod?*

There was flashing before her eyes, but she was deep in the ship. She could not see stars even if she pinched her eyes shut. No amount of struggling would move the black gelatin. Once more she tried to reach out to Orchid, but her sister was out of reach. *Calm down. This ship isn't moving. The ship doesn't leave for days. Days—I don't know how much time is passing. Is this a second or an hour? Let me out of this!!!*

Abby knew she was panicking. She had to calm down. *The Kiposi know what they are doing! Take a breath!* She became aware that she was able to breathe through the gelatin. Her eyes grew heavier. The current nestled her. Abby fell into velvet blackness, believing she heard music.

Intermission:
The Cerise on the run between
Argent and CD-39 4247
July 21, 3062 K.E.

COLE SIGHED AND GLANCED UP at his clock. He still had a half hour before Helen's ship placed the next set of tachyon generators for the FtL communications relay. He missed his daughter, but if he called her now, the time delay would be too noticeable to have a real conversation. He turned to the Feed.

[Disbelief today after the Silvio Beta tried to touch down in Rome. Black smoke filled the sky as Earthlings burned their own vehicles after the local government voted to trust the "Aliens." Angry mobs smashed shop windows, hurled firecrackers, eggs, and paint towards the ship. No one on the Silvio Beta was injured. They changed course and flew to Paris.

However, orbital scans showed the riots did not end after the Silvio Beta's departure. Dozens of people were arrested and firefighters were called to deal with six burned vehicles, including a police van, rubbish truck and four private cars.

A paramilitary officer was beaten to the ground by a mob. He emptied his gun into the crowd, injuring seventeen people and killing ten. The officer is currently in a Rome hospital suffering from shock and bruising.

President Carlos Giuliani was shot dead by another officer as he attacked Speaker Maxina Cato in her armored car with a paring knife.

Shoppers and school children were caught up in the violence that lasted more than four hours, with isolated skirmishes between protesters and police taking place across Rome. They hid in shops and emerged when the riots had ceased.

The city was left strewn with nano gas shells, poles, bottles, bolts and chairs. Violence slithered through Europe. In Milan, the Governor's mansion was briefly occupied. In Athens, the parliament was stormed. Read more: **feed/daily/news/article-1334655232/Earth/rome/riot**]

Cole rubbed his forehead in disbelief. Could it be possible that their progenitors had become savage? According to the reports, Earthlings were no longer explorers. The planet was crumbling and those living there had grown stupid, lazy, and weak. Kiposi teams were busy removing the wheat from the chaff of the youth of Earth, but even the best were nothing more than wanton savages. Once these rumors entered the general population, citizen groups demanded strict laws about personal responsibility. The Kiposi feared the barbarians would taint their grandchildren. There was no real plan yet. After all, the new colonists would not arrive for ninety-four years. The ideas that were floating around were no less than iniquitous.

Cole appreciated Kipos' fear and anger. However, he also realized this influx of DNA was attached to an entire generation of people. It was statistically improbable that all of them would be violent. Harden made it clear that his past injuries were making it harder for him to go planetside, especially without Helen heading up the team. Maybe some of the Earthlings could be taught.

Finally, Cole saw the automatic test message from the Hydra System. The tachyon stabilizer had been placed and was functioning. He told his console to dial the *Tycheros Asteri*.

Helen answered.

Cole smiled at her image through the monitor. "Your brother wants to go into medicine. Medicine!" he said.

Helen just laughed. "Are you concerned about the cost of the classes, Dad?"

"He fools around too much! He plays football in the corridors and when we dock—even for a day—he finds himself a date."

Her brow creased. "Well, he's seventeen. Honestly, I don't see what one thing really has to do with the other."

Cole could see she didn't. She still did a fair bit of fooling around herself, but it was never with the crew and always away from the ship.

"You're being more obtuse than Harden," he said.

Helen laughed again. Now he knew she understood even though she asked, "Does Harden think medicine is a bad idea?"

"Harden doesn't understand! He's focused only on expanding tachyon fields. He doesn't care what this means." Cole paused, "Honey, talk to Mark. Tell him what it's like to fly a shuttle and see a planet that no one has seen before. Did I tell you that he failed his flight test again? Your mother would be mortified."

He noticed the few seconds before she replied, "Mom would want Mark to be happy. He has to make his own choice."

Cole grumbled awhile and then admitted, "If he is to be a doctor, I'm going to send him with Harden to the spacedocks. Your *Revelation* will have a large science department and he has access to the *Cerise* for his residency."

Helen frowned. Cole knew she had hoped he would tell her to come get Mark or maybe even order her home. She had been flying a long time and the age gap had begun to widen. It wasn't optimal. Still, before her emotions got the better of her, she changed the subject. "Dad, did you read about the Earth missions?"

"I didn't know you did," he said, surprised the news reached her so fast.

"I heard there was some sort of riot in Rome?"

"Yes, I read that too," he said.

"I don't think it's true what they're saying. Earthlings cannot be savages anymore..."

"Neither do I." Though he longed to talk to her, he interrupted, "Did you want to talk to your brothers?"

"I suppose," she answered. She had obviously hoped to talk to him more as well.

It bothered him that he had hurried his most beloved offspring, but Cole hit the intercom touchpad. "Hey, guys, your sister is on the Feed."

He pushed back his chair and called out to the corridor, "Hey, Helly's on if you want to say hi."

Cole's closest friend and executive officer, Saul Evans, entered the office first, followed by Diane Richards, one of Helen's friends. Saul told Helen that the crew all loved her and missed her like crazy. He told her to be safe and not break too many hearts in the black.

Cole looked away and reminded himself Helen was a grown woman and, moreover, a captain. He could order her to drop tachyon stabilization relays all over the known universe, but her private life was her own. Still, the father part of him gritted his teeth. He knew that made him a hypocrite.

Helen was laughing by the time Saul said good-bye and left to allow the ladies to catch up. Diane always had amusing anecdotes and promised that she would send a package to Outpost 7 so Helen was never out of touch with what was happening fleetside.

Still, he did not call in the beautiful divorced engineer for Helen. He wanted Harden to see what he had been missing. Or even just smell her.

Diane's shampoo smelled like candied apples. Her overlaying natural scent could bring a man to his knees. Too bad she wasn't the type of woman to fall for a captain eighteen years her senior.

The women said goodbye as his sons arrived. Mark wore a wrinkled t-shirt; his dark curls had not been combed. At least he had the excuse of being a teenager. Harden could be as handsome as Helen if he tried. His elder son had been living on coffee and cigarettes. His coveralls and forearms were coated with grease and what looked like burns. He had dark circles under his eyes.

Harden mumbled a "hey" to Diane but didn't even look at her. His elder son generally liked women, but Cole decided that next time he would try a male. As a full heterosexual, Cole wasn't a great judge on male beauty, but he would do his best to distract Harden before he worked himself to death. At least at that moment, Harden was smiling. He stopped working long enough to give his sister an update on their ship's progress.

"So I hear you're thinking about medicine?" Helen said to Mark.

"Trying to talk me out of it?" Mark snapped.

"No," she replied. "Dad wanted me to, of course, but if you're sure that's what you want, then I think it's great. All I'll say is, I hope you'd want to be a ship's doctor, not planetside or in the Flotilla. Even Dad hopes that—though he'll never say it."

"The research is better planetside and the Flotilla needs doctors," Mark said.

Helen was moving farther out. Suddenly there was a twenty-second delay. Still, they could have a normal conversation for a little while longer. "Yeah, but I bet you'd have a much wider range of patient problems on an explorer. You might find new medicines. Who knows? You might even cure the deep space death."

Mark huffed, "I'll think about it."

Cole saw something change in his younger son's eyes. The idea of discovering new medicines attracted him in a way that Cole's "flying though the stars and discovering new planets" talk hadn't. Helen was always good at finding solutions that would benefit everyone. It was why she made such a great captain. The conversation moved from Mark's grades and CG instructors to Harden's exploration of the last planet and finally to the *Revelation's* tachyon generation engine.

If it worked, the ship would be Harden's masterpiece. Cole remembered the day his son had drawn the plans and sent word to his sister. It was insane and brilliant at the same time. If the damned thing worked, the *Revelation's* three-part engine system and tachyon stabilization unit would revolutionize space travel.

Yet, Harden was alone, lost. Cole knew Harden took a lover now and again, but it never lasted. No one enjoyed being dimmed by the shadow of the *Revelation*. However, Harden was an adult. Cole could not solve his problems for him. He just wanted his boy to get a good meal and possibly a good lay to clear his head.

The conversation was almost up when Helen told Harden that he looked thin and exhausted. Harden snapped back that he didn't need her to nag. Mark chimed in that Harden was averaging thirty-six cigarettes and four pots of coffee a day and he was getting a little worried too. A light slap on the head made Mark confess that he had started going through Harden's waste bin and counting.

The delay was over a minute now. Helen told them she loved them and would be sending reports on schedule. After her image flickered off, they just wandered back to whatever they were doing before. It was as if someone had just turned out a light in Cole's office.

No one felt it more deeply than Cole. He regretted not talking to her about the Earth problem. What was ten minutes of his time compared to the light years of space between them?

He rested his hand over the touch pad. He almost called her back, but didn't. A private note came through on the Feed.

```
Dad, if things aren't going right, maybe
I should come home after Hydra? Richards
can do this relay placement in Lepus; he's
ready to captain. I can hitch a ride back
with the Gnosi after O-9.
```

Cole thought carefully about what to say.

Helen, I need good captains more than I need
my daughter to nursemaid her idiot brothers. Richards would be decent, but he does
not have your passion. Sometimes Mark won't
listen to me, but we're fine here. Don't
worry.

He noticed another message going out on the family line. Fuck, Mark
or Harden had seen the conversation. He should have encrypted it. He
couldn't stop it, but he could figure out what was also being said.

We'll come get you even if I have to fly
this ship myself. So it might take a while.
What's the best way to knock Dad and Saul
out? Harden won't notice we changed course.

Cole shook his head. *Mark.*
A few minutes later, Helen wrote back:

Don't be silly. I just worry about you.
Please don't argue with Dad and Harden, ok?

Mark wrote:

Why not? There is nothing else to do on this
fucking ship.

Helen replied:

Mom once told me there is nothing lonelier
under the unending stars than when your
crew doesn't care about you—except going
planetside. That's how I feel sometimes. If
you go, I'm afraid you will be older than
me the next time I see you. Or dead from
old age. Just seeing Harden, I freaked. He
looks so old.

Cole knew that Helen was lonely. She had an older crew, but everyone
said Helen was one of the best captains they had ever had the fortune to
work under. What shocked Cole about this interaction were the kind words
from his self-possessed son.

Mark went on:

He's 31. That's pretty old. Of course, 27
is pretty damn old too. Now you're slow-
ing, maybe I should go planetside until I'm
30. It might be pretty fun to have a little
sister.

Helen's final message was:

We're coming up to the next drop soon and I
got to get back to the bridge. I love you,
Mark.

Mark kept typing so Helen could have a message when she got off duty.

> If Harden would quit smoking, take a shower
> once in a while, and get something to eat
> he'd be fine. I'll start nagging at him
> for you. However, I'm starting with "Helly
> says," so if you start getting pissed off
> messages it's your own damn fault for wor-
> rying so much. See aren't I a good big
> brother? This is gonna be awesome. I love
> you too, little sis. Bye.

Rubbing the palm of his hand over his smooth face, Cole thought about telling Helen to come home and get back on the timeline with the family, but the relay contracts were government work. He needed a captain he could trust.

He told himself things wouldn't change as much as Helen feared. It was only two more relative years at most which wouldn't seem like more than a year to her. She would be back to test fly the *Revelation* before heading back into deep space. The age gap was lengthening between her and Harden and narrowing between her and Mark, but she would not be younger than Mark unless he went planetside for school.

The ship's computer still held some of the general classes from when his two elder kids started their university level work, but Cole brought up a new window and asked for the Fleet Educational Feed. He scanned the pre-med university courses. There were more specialty courses than he expected. He doubted Mark could get through it. Still, for Helen's sake, he had to keep the family together.

For Rosemary's too. Every once in a while, he felt guilty that he had to break his promise to her when the Alekos Fleet was awarded this contract. Cole closed his eyes and he could see the curve of Rosemary's neck and her crooked smile. He remembered how, when they were not fighting, he could rest his head on her lap and she would run her finger behind his ear.

He missed the smell of her next to him when they slept and how some-times in the morning she would kiss his shoulders in hope that they would fuck. He told himself that he would not miss her if not for the kids, but he knew that it was a lie. There had been plenty of other women, but they just did not compare. Most of them were ultimately forgettable.

Cole hit the com and shouted, "Mark."

Mark snarled his way back into the office. "What now?"

"So I've been looking at some of the Feed courses. They're expensive, especially these anatomy simulations, but I suppose if that's really what you want—you're going to need to buckle down in biology."

Mark's face was cautious. "What about flight school?"

"This list of classes doesn't seem to think you need it. Talk to Spiro and see what he thinks. He's qualified to fly a half-light shuttle."

Cole wished his son didn't look so surprised, but was glad he was smiling. Mark hadn't smiled in a long time. He was left to his own devices too often, especially since Helen was away.

"Doc took flight as an extracurricular to get out of art or singing or bowling or whatever. Figured it would be good to learn." Mark paused, "I just get nervous at the stick—especially with you screaming at me."

Cole shrugged. "You're going to be in school for another six years. Just hang out in the simulator until you are ready. We'll do some more practice flights and you can take the test again. You have plenty of time."

Mark nodded. "Dad, don't forget to call Helen on her New Year like you did last year. It's in two weeks and three days. I put it on the ship's calendar so you and Harden will remember."

Cole chuckled, hiding the irritation in his voice: "You'll find nobody knows as much as they did when they were young. Go nag your brother. Tell him if he is really smoking that many cigarettes then he's taxing our life support system."

"Is he?" Mark's face showed his worry.

"No." Cole shook his head and sighed. For a boy raised on interstellar ships, Mark had very little faith in their systems.

PART 2
EARTH TO KIPOS

CHAPTER 8

Year Unknown

WHILE MOST OF ABBY'S JOURNEY was lost to the deep blackness, when her body fell into REM sleep, she dreamt of the changing stars. She saw the Dancing Virgin from the other side. The Dragon loomed so close. Abby felt like she could reach out and touch his stars.

Intermission:
The Revelation outside O-5
May 18, 3114

COLE WATCHED AS THE FTL checklists were completed twice. Helen had been using the sublight engines until they reached deep space beyond O-5, then they would open up the tachyon generation field. Part of him felt guilty for disembarking his own ship to watch the test flight, but Saul could handle anything that would come up on the *Cerise*.

There had been a decade of simulations, but in the back of his mind, Cole still wondered if Harden had truly let go of Lucy. Cole hoped that Harden did not hold to a hidden belief that the *Revelation* might bring him back to the moment when he lost her.

No, Cole assured himself. Harden would never drag Helen into that. Still, he could not deny that, unlike the *Cerise* or even his new flagship the *Discovery*, there was something feminine in the ship design. Every detail had been considered. While it was comfortable and even familiar, Cole could not shake the feeling that all of this had been intended for a woman. The bridge command station was filled with upholstered leathers to soften the hard polymers and lights. The walls were painted cool blues and greens.

Cole left the bridge and headed back down the corridor. He noticed the tiny windows and the locking handles within the doors mirrored the shape of the arches on the top of the hatchways. The lounging area and galley were connected in an open plan. The billets were designed specifically for expanding and contracting families with easily doubled berths. Two billets were connected via a head and then surrounded by a heavy carbon wall lined with steel ribs and hydraulic stabilizers.

Cole noticed the arch again underneath the handrail, punched out of the metal in a repeating pattern as he headed back down to the shuttle bay and science decks. During the flight test, Cole would be aboard the *Revelation Alpha* shuttle with Mark and the ship's doctor Phoebe Willows. If anything went wrong, the plan was to travel at sublight and catch up to the *Revelation* before everyone expired. Phoebe was solid. Harden trusted her completely.

Just as they had planned, Harden commanded the ship and Helen would fly it. Rosemary would be so proud of them, but Cole had to admit, the idea of his son and daughter at the helm made him want to puke. He trusted them and their crew, but he literally hurt with worry.

Diane was always Helen's first choice as an engineer, but the choice of the mechanic—and the fact that Helen married him after only six days—shocked the family. Brian Tolis—(a Tolis!)—was the best mechanic that money could have hired, yet Harden had gotten him for practically nothing. His degree was in engineering; his love was getting his hands dirty. He claimed to want just his share. So far he had not tried to send the technology to his family, but the Tolises owned three times as many ships as the Alekos family. They would want it. Helen had fallen in love with him; she might not see the danger. Harden simply would not notice. And Mark simply did not care.

As Cole entered the shuttle deck, Harden did not say anything except, "There is another discipline report. We had a camera witness this time."

He did not have to ask. He never should have left Mark with Harden, but he took the tablet. "Did you punish him?"

"Why would I?" Harden's tone indicated he had not thought to discipline his younger brother.

Cole didn't say that was exactly the problem. "Mark's a minor and you're the captain. You are ultimately responsible for his behavior."

"Well, now you're here."

"Only for a few days. If you don't want to keep him…"

"I don't want him."

Mark came down the stairs. He had obviously heard them. "Make a hole."

"What's wrong?"

"Nothing. Are we going?" He pushed his way into the shuttle without saying goodbye to his elder siblings. Maybe that was for the best.

Phoebe looked embarrassed, but said good luck and embraced everyone. Cole kissed his daughter and embraced Diane. He shook the men's hands and went into the shuttle.

Phoebe started the engines. She asked Mark if he wanted to watch, but he shook his head and closed his eyes as the shuttle disembarked the cargo hull.

Cole glanced behind him. Mark's head was in his hands. His cuticles had been bitten raw.

It was a major accomplishment of Harden's that even the *Revelation's* shuttles were faster than any shuttles before them. Though the acceleration and decelerations to near light speed would burn through a fuel cell and cause massive vibrations to the outer hull, the internal hydraulics and insulation stabilized the space inside the ship so the crew could function.

Mark opened his eyes once they were flying and steady.

Through the monitor, the three watched the bridge of the *Revelation*. Wearing a full helmet and pressurized environmental suits, Helen flicked on the tachyon engine. It began running smoothly. Seconds later, she reported a tachyon field surrounding the ship.

Harden gave the order.

Mark closed his eyes. Cole lit a cigarette and took a deep drag.

Through the monitor, Helen hit the throttle.

In less than a second, The *Revelation* was gone.

Cole relayed an FtL test message.

"We read you, *Alpha*," his daughter said through the com seconds later, "All systems in the green."

"What about backwards thrust?" Mark asked.

Cole never wanted to smack his younger son as much as he did at that moment.

Helen replied, "Probably works fine, but it won't be tested for a bit. Seriously, Mark, nothing's wrong."

"What about physical symptoms?" Mark asked.

Helen sounded perfectly content as she answered, "The stabilization units seem to work. Did you forget our brother's a genius?"

"Don't take your environmental suits off unless absolutely necessary, okay?"

Harden snapped. "Fuck, Mark, shut up already. You'll see us in three days."

Helen turned to Harden. "He's just worried."

"He can still shut the fuck up."

Mark went to a stasis pod and lay down. It wasn't on. Cole considered activating it as he wondered if maybe a few days sleep would put his son in a better mood. Not having to deal with him on the shuttle would definitely put Cole in a better mood.

Phoebe asked Harden to send out a copy of their physical readings as Cole turned to the discipline report.

HARDEN HAD LEFT THE VID file on the tablet. The shuttle *Beta's* recorder had switched on when Brian and Mark entered. Brian's hand was on Mark's shoulder and he shoved Mark into a seat. They were close to the same height, but Brian probably outweighed Mark by ten kilos.

The rover bot sat motionless as they shouted at each other. At first, Cole wasn't sure what they were screaming about until Brian said, "I don't give a fuck if she's your sister. She's my wife!"

All right, so they were arguing about Helen.

"If you ever touch her again, I'll throw you from an airlock."

What had Mark done?

"What the fuck does it matter? You'll all die out there anyway!" Mark's eyes were edging on hysteria. "Harden said FtL is the easy part.

Stopping will be hard. He doesn't even think he can do it. That's why he dragged Helen into this!"

Brian calmed down as Mark's anger continued to grow: the difference between a man and one who is only nearly one.

Brian said, "Helen is here because this is her dream."

Mark shouted something half unintelligible about her backward dreams. All Cole got from the rant was that Helen was stupid, possibly retarded, as was Brian. It was just as well they couldn't have children since they would pass on mental defects.

Brian's eyes showed that he understood everything, but he did not take the bait. "We are not leaving this shuttle until you calm the fuck down. I don't care if I have to shove you in an environmental suit and tie you to this seat until your father gets here. Your sister has a lot of shit to do. The one thing she doesn't need is you impairing the crew."

"I don't impair anyone," Mark snapped, but his voice was calmer.

"Shit, we're going to change space travel. Don't you think I have more important things to do than talk to you right now?"

Mark was silent. His face showed anger simmering under the surface, but it was abating.

Brian said softly, "Look, if it all goes to hell, I'll put Helen's life above all others. *Beta*, *Gamma* and *Chi* are launch ready. But if she lives and we die, she'll have survivor's guilt, so you'll need to take care of her."

"I don't want my brother to die either."

"Neither do I. He's crap for a captain, but all in all I like the guy."

Brian began typing a command to the roverbot:

```
If Revelation's destruction is confirmed
to be imminent, retrieve Helen Alekos and
bring her into a functional shuttle. If
Helen Alekos is wounded and cannot pilot
the shuttle, bring her to these coordinates
and replay emergency message on a loop. If
time allows, rescue Harden Alekos, Diane
Richards, and Brian Tolis in that order.
```

The roverbot's screen flashed:

```
Cannot comply. Contradicts previous order
by Captain Harden Alekos.
```

Brian asked, "What is the previous order?"

```
If Revelation's destruction is confirmed
imminent, retrieve Helen Alekos and bring
her into nearest functional shuttle. If
time allows, rescue Diane Richards, Brian
Tolis, and Harden Alekos in that order. If
all humans are wounded and cannot pilot the
shuttle, fly to these coordinates. Replay
emergency message on a continuous loop.
```

Brian looked at Mark. "I'm liking your brother more and more. Harden's the captain. I have to abide by his order, but if I can get him out, I will. However, what you have to understand is I'm a damn fine mechanic. My ships don't just break."

The roverbot stared blankly ahead as if Brian had never spoken. As the guys left the shuttle, the camera flicked off.

COLE PINCHED HIS BROW, YET, he couldn't help but smile. Helen had picked well. He should never have doubted her.

From the pod, Mark said, "I pushed her. I didn't mean to push her into a cabinet. I didn't mean to hurt her."

"You're restricted."

"Figured." He laughed. "What's it matter? We're in a shuttle."

Cole shook his head. *Why must Mark always challenge me?* Mark being restricted to their quarters was just as much a punishment for Cole. "And you'll be restricted on O-5, but we'll talk about it later."

"I thought Harden and Brian were going to kill me."

"If you were a year older, they might have," Phoebe said softly to Mark and then said to Cole, "Helen had a minor contusion and a scrape. No permanent damage."

Once the data came over the Feed, Phoebe ordered Cole to take the helm. Somewhat in shock, he did so. Phoebe had always seemed soft spoken, but she wasn't one to waste words either. Well, Harden's doctor would need to be pushy.

She went back to the pod and touched Mark's hand. "They're okay. The readings all look good. Want to see?"

Mark sat up and rubbed his nose. He went to the screen. He glanced at the crew's reading. "Dad, look. Harden's blood pressure is too high, but Helen's heart isn't even racing. Neither is Brian's or Di's. They are safe. He just smokes too much."

He eyed his father's cigarette.

Cole took another drag. "Dealing with you is enough to drive anyone to smoke."

Phoebe looked half worried, half embarrassed at witnessing yet another tiff. Changing the subject, she said, "Now that we know the engine works, let's hope for stability."

She reached out for Mark and squeezed his hand again. "Let's do an anatomy simulation. There's no reason for you to fall behind."

Amazingly, Mark complied.

THE *REVELATION* FLEW TWO LIGHT years in three relative days. The only hiccup was a broken LED on the control panel and that was just a circuit that loosened due to the ships vibration during a sling shot maneuver.

Cole ordered all his ships to be outfitted at once, including his new flagship still in Argent's spacedock, the *Discovery*. He would have to hope that the mods held on some of the older transports. Even if the engine could be upgraded, there was no guarantee the hulls of the older ships would stay together at FtL or if the stabilization units would work with the older tech, but that wasn't his biggest concern as he stared at his monitor getting ready to place the call to the Fleet Liaison on Argent.

Cole had explained to his kids that he would sell the engine schematics to the government for open distribution. They would receive royalties each time the engine schematics were used in the building or remodification of a ship, but the Fleet Liaisons would do much of the groundwork for infrastructure as well as selling the engines to ships outside the Alekos Fleet. Helen had agreed, but Harden hadn't cared one way or the other. Yet now, as Cole sat there with his hand on the com, he knew he needed to contact Brian's mother.

Their greeting was somewhat curt. Cole said quickly, "So the kids completed their test run. All systems were in the green. Since your son is now my son-in-law, I just wanted you to have the schematics."

Before he changed his mind, he typed in Andrea's ship address and a copy of the engine plans flew towards her ship at no cost.

Andrea Tolis was shocked. "I never considered you a romantic."

"I'm not. I'm already regretting this, but I suppose a wild test pilot needs a damn fine mechanic to keep her ships running."

Andrea laughed. "Perhaps. My understanding is your daughter will run your fleet?"

"That's still the plan."

Over the Feed, single share certificates from twenty-five long-range transports came with his name as beneficiary. Upon his death, the shares would revert to Helen and Brian assuming they stayed married. If the marriage dissolved, Brian would regain the shares. Andrea was a smart woman.

She said, "I wasn't ecstatic that my son ran off with an Alekos, but they seem happy. Helen's the type of woman who is good for him."

"He's crazy enough about her to put up with us," Cole replied, "He's been more than kind to Mark."

Andrea smiled. "Nineteen is always difficult. I remember knowing everything. Yet for some reason, my mother didn't trust me to command her flagship…"

"He wants to be a doctor," Cole admitted.

Andrea just laughed. "You think you have problems? My youngest ran off to be a mechanic, though he has all the skills and resources necessary to captain his own ship."

Their goodbyes were much warmer.

AS COLE KNEW THEY WOULD, the government moved fast. Though planetside it would take months, on their timeline within relative days, all outposts had orders to be fitted with tachyon generators to make them orbit outside planetary time. Helen and Harden made the Alekos family a fortune, but they didn't even care. After the nearly non-stop work of the project and Helen's work in deep space, they were looking forward to their vacation on O-5.

COLE WOKE UP. REALIZING HE was alone; he saw the wall com buzz. He hit the panel with the very strong fear that Mark had gotten in trouble again. Mark was supposed to be restricted, but Cole had met a woman whom he dearly wanted to share his bed with for a few hours. The woman who had come and gone had not been traditionally pretty, but had her own variety of the wild charm common in pilots that Cole found attractive. She responded to him as he had hoped and fulfilled his needs with vigor and passion. He remembered inviting her to stay the night; she declined. Cole had not felt rejected at the time or now, but now she was gone, he regretted how he had allowed his physical desire to take precedence over his duty as a father. Again.

It was just Harden and Phoebe. A "hold on" and a second later, the screen split: Helen and Brian in bed. His chest was bare, but she was wearing a cotton chemise. Brian's hand rested on the blanket where her thigh was. He was her husband, but it still annoyed Cole.

"Phoebe asked me to marry her. I need witnesses," Harden said.

Helen made a happy little scream.

Brian said, "That's great, brother."

Helen said, "Phoebe, what are you going to wear?"

"What does that matter?" Harden looked exasperated then terrified. "Helly, think small. If we do it before the *Cerise* or the *Tycheros Asteri* arrives, it doesn't have to be a big deal. Just us."

Helen replied, "I know that. I'll be right over with Diane." She disconnected.

Cole rang for Mark and heard the radio buzz through the door. *Damn his stupid irresponsible son.*

He opened up the drawer and took out his favorite photograph: eighteen-year-old Helen playing cards with Rosemary. Close to winning the hand, Helen was laughing. He had also unwittingly captured Harden and Lucy reading to Mark in the background. Of course, Mark had been an adorable three, not the monster he was now.

He set the photo down and went into the head. He turned on the shower and let the water pass over him. This time of night on the outpost, he had all the hot water he could ever want. However, what he wanted was his wife to come in, kiss his shoulders, wash his back, and tell him how to deal with their son, but Rosemary had been dead for nearly a decade on his timeline, a century planetside.

MARK WAS PLAYING SKEETBALL WITH a teenaged girl when Cole entered the arcade. His obvious irritation at his father's presence suggested he had left his radio on his berth on purpose.

"What's up?" As Mark threw another ball, it hit the edge of the 50-point hole, then rolled into the 40-point hole. "Fuck," he said.

The girl looked guilty. "Sorry, Captain Alekos."

They had been fooling around for the night, but she didn't want to get into trouble. Fleet parents communicated too easily. She probably wasn't allowed to swear. He let Mark get away with too much.

"Harden's getting married," Cole yelled over the noise of the bell.

"And?" Mark replied without looking at him.

"He really wants you there. So does Phoebe."

"Phoebe?" The surprise wiped the sullenness off his face. He glanced at Cole and back at the girl. She was already looking away. "When did all this happen?"

"I don't know. They just called us about thirty minutes ago. The wedding is going to be in a few hours. That's why I came to find you."

Mark looked back at the girl. "You want to finish the game? I guess I gotta go."

Once they were out of the arcade, Mark looked down the hall. "You think Harden's rushing into this?"

"Worried for your brother?"

"No, Phoebe. As for Harden, I'm not sure I'd even like the guy if he wasn't..."

In reflex, Cole slapped his son. Mark's right eye watered from the blow, but he looked surprised more than hurt.

"Your brother has taken care of you when I haven't been around. If he's cold... it is because a captain sometimes has to be," Cole said lamely as he felt the guilt drip into his chest. He had never hit any of his kids before. Even if Mark was being argumentative, he only acknowledged something they all felt. As brilliant as Harden was, he didn't take care of himself and certainly no one else.

Mark hissed, "That's shit. Harden didn't take care of me. Mom left; you left. The only person who has ever wanted me around is Helen, but you didn't want to burden your favorite with her idiot brothers."

"I love all my kids," Cole said. He thought, but did not add: *but right now I don't like you very much.* "You've been screaming at everyone, starting fights. Are you on drugs?"

Mark's laugh edged on hysteria again. "You don't even know me."

Helen approached them, wearing a dark green lace-covered dress and a concerned look.

She touched Mark's reddened cheek. "Have you been fighting?"

Mark narrowed his eyes. Cole knew what he was going to say before he opened his mouth. "I wasn't fighting. He hit me."

Her eyes flickered up at Cole, but her voice remained calm. "Why?"

"I told him the truth," Mark said.

"Which is?"

"They're rushing into marriage. Phoebe will be hurt," Mark said.

"It's her mistake to make. She loves him. She might be good for him. Help keep him in this world. They've even talked about adopting a child."

"When he hurts her, I'll be on her side, not his," Mark said. He did not sound worried for his mentor; his snotty tone was full of triumph.

Cole was beginning to wish he had hit Mark just a bit harder. He tried to remember how he disciplined the elder two, but neither had been this insolent. Due to Harden's natural shyness and his crush on Lucy, he never got in trouble. Like most good pilots, Helen had been a bit wild, but a firm word from a senior crewmember or the threatened loss of stick-time could send her to tears. Mark would consider the loss of stick-time a reward.

With her soft, calm voice that left no room for argument, Helen replied: "Go get dressed. We are going to a wedding and have a family breakfast. Right now, this isn't about you. We'll talk later."

Mark opened his mouth, and then shut it. He sulked off without a word.

Helen turned to Cole. "I'm staying on the *Revelation*. I've been away too long."

He focused on his daughter. "What?"

"I'm an explorer and there are other barriers to conquer besides FtL. Harden and I have spoken about folding space, proton entanglement…"

Giving Helen an ultimatum was always a bad idea, but Cole could not stop himself. "If you do this, you'll no longer be considered my de facto replacement."

Helen replied, "Richards enjoys infrastructure contracts and wants the chance to captain. He's ready for it. Give it to him."

"If I pass on without naming a replacement, your brothers will sell off their share of the fleet. Harden'll hide in his puzzles and Mark'll go to the Flotilla, if not planetside."

She said, "If you no longer think I am capable of sound judgment, we'll find someone else prior to your imminent death."

"Stop being so rational," Cole huffed, but he knew she was right. Father or not, boss or not, he could not argue with her. Her brothers certainly couldn't. "Obviously you will take my place, but how it will look to others…."

"I'm not worried about how it looks to others. I'm worried about Mark," she said still using her captain's tone.

Helen would neither confirm nor deny Cole's shortcomings as a parent or the challenges of raising Mark. She accused him of nothing; she would just take care of it. There were a million things Cole wanted to tell her. Instead he said, "Honey, I sent Andrea the engine schematics."

It took her three seconds to go from shock to smiles. "So you approve of Brian now?"

"I'm getting used to the idea."

Helen embraced Cole around the neck. "Thank you."

"You shouldn't thank me. Your brothers certainly won't. Do you have any idea how much money we would have made if we had sold Harden's invention to the Tolises?"

PART 3
KIPOS

CHAPTER 9

THOUGH ABBY HAD DREAMS OF the dark velvet wetness within the gravity couch, she was dry when she opened her eyes. Orchid was lying beside her, not quite awake, not quite asleep. Stretching. Darkness melted away and the room grew brighter.

The same Kiposi technician who had put them to sleep entered with a tray of pink strawberry milkshakes. Abby took one and sipped. The thick cold liquid felt good on her dry throat.

Orchid frowned and said in a flat voice, "This is not strawberry. It should be fruitier—this just tastes sweet."

The Kiposi seemed too happy to be deterred, "The important thing is that they are nutritious and easy to digest."

Abby gave her sister a pointed look. "Don't worry, ma'am. We'll drink them."

Orchid reluctantly agreed.

The two girls in the top bunks did not rise or take the shakes.

The technician hurried Abby, Orchid, and a young blond into the cargo bay as two more Kiposi entered the room.

Abby glanced back, but could not see what had become of the girls. The blond had begun crying again into her hands. She could not be older than thirteen.

"Come here." Abby put an arm around the crying girl and held her sister with the other.

Behind them, the technician whispered into a white glossy pad: "Container 0753: Dead loss two out of five."

A chill went down Abby's spine. In front of them, other sleepy half-drugged Earthlings drinking fake strawberry milkshakes filed towards the airlock to their new world. With nothing else to do, Abby led the girls the same way.

The little blond slobbered about her mama. Orchid looked terrified, but put on a brave front. Without any confidence, Abby gave the girls each a kiss on the top of their heads. This seemed to calm the blond.

As they exited the ship, Abby expected another space elevator, but they were in a giant hanger. From the hatchway, they were led through a scanner.

A Kiposi technician said, "Alright, Abigail Boyd Lei, Orchid Boyd Lei, and Sadie Cho Jeffers, follow me." She chatted with a false merriness in her voice. "I didn't realize the three of you were acquainted."

"Sadie was put in the bunk next to us," Abby said, "She's traveling alone."

The technician nodded and swiped her finger across her tablet. "Sadie Cho Jeffers, it appears that generations back, your ancestor had a sister who was a first generation colonist. So you have an aunt. She and her husband are excited to meet you. Would you like to see a picture? This is Danielle and Jacob Blackwell."

Sadie nodded primarily because she was too scared to do anything else. Abby and the girls looked at the tablet. It was a portrait made to look unposed. Danielle sat in the chair and Jacob leaned over behind her. His arm was on his wife's shoulders. They were smiling. Really smiling. There were some Caucasian features upon Danielle, but otherwise Sadie's "aunt" looked like every other Kiposi: tan skin, brown hair, brown eyes. Abby guessed they might be thirty, but it was hard to tell.

Since Sadie was too frightened to speak, Abby asked, "What do they do?"

"Do?" The technician obviously did not understand.

"For jobs?"

"Jacob is a firefighter and Danielle is a land surveyor, though she requested leave to raise and educate Sadie."

"I bet your relatives will be nice." Abby squeezed the girl.

"Do we have family here?" Orchid asked.

The technician tapped something into her tablet. She glanced back up at them, but did not meet Orchid or Abby in the eye. "No, but don't worry. Everything's in hand."

AS THEY WALKED DOWN THROUGH the corridor, Abby noticed that, though everyone spoke English, the accents seemed wrong. Words seemed slurred. And worse, all the Kiposi still had insipid smiles plastered upon their faces. She tried hard to listen, catching only snippets of conversation. The plan had changed the two centuries that the transports had been away. She discovered that, once the ships were filled with Earthlings, names and test scores were sent ahead and relatives of children paid no bonds, assuming that they would pay for their higher education and assimilate them into gentle society. Other children would be adopted, but the adoption bonds were expensive.

Abby didn't understand. The Kiposi said nothing of bonds or taxes when they were encouraging them to leave their lives behind and journey across the galaxy.

They crossed a sky bridge and down a flight of stairs to where there were seven buses, the tops of which were covered by what looked like might be solar panels. Abby looked for the two suns, but it was a cloudy day.

What was most disconcerting to her was that there were still no sign of the males. No Jin or Rory. Sadie looked afraid as they entered the bus, but Orchid said, "Of course, you will sit by me."

The three squished together on the bench seat meant for two. From what she had seen of it, Abby was most surprised at how much the New Alexandria Aerospace Port looked like Seatac International Airport. Long tarmacs surrounded by cement buildings and trees. A few radio towers. Most looked similar to those they had on Earth. There were even airplanes. Only the spaceships looked different.

The bus stopped in front of a building and a list of names was read. Sadie Cho Jeffers was one of them.

"Abigail and Orchid Boyd Lei," she whispered, "maybe my aunt will allow me to write to you once we are settled."

"Jacob and Danielle Blackwell. Sadie Cho Jeffers," Orchid said.

They hugged once more. Sadie got off the bus.

Abby looked out the tinted window and watched the Kiposi technician introduce the girl to her new relatives. Danielle embraced her. She looked truly happy. Jacob looked a little more pensive as he patted her shoulder, but that was to be expected. He had just become a first time father to a thirteen year-old girl. Sadie looked a little frightened; she waved once more as the bus pulled away. Orchid waved back. Abby doubted Sadie could see them through the tinted glass.

The bus stopped a few more times. Names were read; women and girls got off. Families were quickly introduced and the bus moved on.

The Kiposi seemed efficiently organized. Some found comfort in that. Abby did not. The bus stopped in front of a large concrete building. As they disembarked, Abby heard male voices and shouts. She hoped to see her brother and the other men, but they could see only more Kiposi. Their faces held contempt and lechery. Abby wished they were still smiling.

Though sensing something was wrong, Abby tried to reassure her sister, "It's okay. I guess it's like a commune for those who don't have Kiposi families."

There was nothing to do except follow the crowd. Inside the building was a maze of female technicians, a dentist, and a doctor. A laser shower burned off the topmost layer of their skin, a second beam burned off excess body hair. The hair on their heads was washed, oiled, and perfumed. By the time they hit the dryer, Orchid was in tears.

They were both given their clothing, hot unsweetened tea, and tiny sandwiches. Abby did not know what to do. She sat down on a nearby sofa with her arms around Orchid. Something about this was very wrong. She pushed terrible thoughts out of her head by focusing on one point: *No matter what happens to me, nothing will happen to my little sister.*

They sat huddled together for about an hour until Orchid fell asleep with her head in Abby's lap. Once she did, a Kiposi immediately brought over a blanket and another cup of tea.

While Orchid slept, Abby watched for some clue of exactly what was going on. Needs were met quickly. If someone cried, a woman comforted her. If they were hungry, they were fed.

Lost, Abby prayed to her ancestors for guidance and bravery.

She witnessed men enter individually or in small groups. They would be introduced to women and then they would each take one away. Abby also saw a man get on one knee to offer marriage to a twenty-five year old woman. He gave the woman a laundry list of reasons why she should accept; the woman did. The others clapped to show their approval.

Abby saw one woman tell a girl that she was her new daughter. The girl could refer to the woman as "Mother" or "Mom" as she preferred. The girl did not seem too excited, but called the woman "Mother." The woman wept happily and kissed her.

Abby had snuggled up to her sister when a woman led a group of five men into the room. Three were dressed identically in uniforms. The one dressed in a gray suit was quite a bit older. The other, a thirtyish year old man with a brown suit and dull eyes, looked over a list of test scores and abilities and spoke to one of the Kiposi technicians. He didn't look at the women at all.

The party crossed the room and stood in front of them. Abby sat up and shook Orchid awake. Looking down on her, the dull-eyed man said, "Miss Bodlay, come with me." It was an order given by a man who was used to getting his way.

Abby did not bother to correct him; instead, she glanced at Orchid. "And my sister?"

The man said, "I don't need two."

Abby did not stand up, but tightened the grip on her sister's arm. "I promised not to leave her!"

One of his men reached out and grabbed Abby by the shoulder and yanked her to her feet. She momentarily lost her grip on Orchid. She clutched at her sister again and cleaved her to her chest. Other women began to take notice. Some cried. Others told the men to leave the girls alone. The Kiposi tried to calm them.

"ABBY!" Orchid screamed.

Suddenly, her sister was still. Abby could not hold her dead weight and Orchid slipped away as two of the men ripped them apart.

Abby elbowed her captor in the face. He loosened his grip and she tried to get to her sister. Another man grabbed her by the hair.

She cried out. "Orchid! What have you done?"

No one answered. She tried pushing the man away, but her scalp felt as if it might rip. His other fingertips seemed to drill themselves into her neck. The dull-eyed man picked Orchid up and put her on the sofa. "Let the woman go."

The two men complied, but Abby felt no sense of relief. She was so angry and frightened she could barely focus.

"Abigail Bodlay, according to testing, you have a fine mind and the needed genetic structure. This can be pleasant or not. You're mine now, a member of my household," the dull-eyed man said.

"Please, my sister…"

The man's mouth turned into a smile, but his eyes did not. He leaned down to her and she felt his soft manicured finger against her cheek as he spoke in the slightest of whispers: "She has been sedated. Obey or I will kill her."

Abby obeyed.

CHAPTER 10

ABBY HUGGED HERSELF AS SHE walked down the hall behind the two men. She wanted to scream or fight, but she was too frightened even to cry.

The dull-eyed man said, "Colton, if you please."

The older man, Colton, took off his jacket and put it around her shoulders. "Your sister will be alright, Miss. It was just a little sedative. You're being quite foolish to carry on so."

"But what will happen to her?" Abby dared ask, but one of the guards dug into her neck in response to her question and pushed her along. "She's just a child!"

Colton said softly, "Miss Bodlay is to be treated with kindness."

The guard replied not to the elder but to the dull-eyed man. "Forgive me, Kyrios."

Abby still did not bother to correct his mispronunciation of "Boyd Lei." She was a century away from home. She knew he wouldn't care. Kipos did not care. The black sky did not care. She wished she could see the two suns, but it was night. The best she could do was look at the unfamiliar stars and moon. There should be three moons, but she could only see a single reddish sphere.

"It must be Semi," she whispered to herself. "Where is Selene and Argent?"

Colton told her that Selene would not rise for another hour, and Argent would not be visible that night but was often visible during the day. She glanced back at the concrete building one more time. She had to remember where it was. She had to find Orchid again. She had to find Jin.

The men led her to a vehicle with six wheels. In the soft moonlight, it glittered like silver, but as they moved closer it became a dull slate gray.

Colton opened the door and she slipped into the soft upholstery. He buckled her in with a five-point harness.

Colton asked, "Warm enough, Miss? Certainly you are not dressed for such a cool night." He flipped open a compartment and pulled out a blanket and tucked it around her.

Abby said, "It was summer when we left Earth."

Colton and the dull-eyed man sat in the front. One of the guards sat beside her and two others sat in back. They spoke softly to each other. She looked out the window and tried not to be disappointed in Kipos. It felt as if she was just in another ecosystem of Earth. It was temperate. There were large trees that cut into her field of vision. Beyond was only black sky.

As they pulled into the road, the pitch of the engine changed. Abby felt the car attach itself to the magnetic strip and accelerate. From a sign, she knew she was heading northbound on Speedway 17.

Colton said, "Exit 156."

The on-board computer created the route and took over steering. It seamlessly merged with traffic. The car remained a steady 150kph the entire way.

Colton swiped a long finger across the touchpad in the dash. "Dr. Taggert has been summoned, Kyrios."

Somehow from the tone that Colton spoke, Abby knew Kyrios was not the dull-eyed man's name but a title of some sort. Abby focused on what she knew, but the only facts she had was that the Kyrios was a man used to getting his way.

The guard beside her was silent. His breath was even, but not quite relaxed. His dark eyes were watching for danger, though he did not expect it from her. She could see that the crease of his pressed slacks hid a scabbard holding two narrow blades against his long leg. She guessed that the other leg held another set. Under his jacket, he wore a harness that held a silver pistol of some sort. He was shaven, but his dark coarse hair pricked through the skin. She could smell just a touch of sweat under the spicy scent of his deodorant.

Behind her, the other two guards were mumbling about a concert and television show—subjects that had nothing to do with her. Colton and the Kyrios spoke about someone they referred to as the Kyria. All she could make out was: "The Kyria has everything prepared" and "The Kyria does not wish to meet Miss Bodlay at this time. Send the car around back."

Once off the speedway, Colton took over driving again. Abby tried to keep her directional sense as they drove through a small shopping district and into a residential neighborhood. Golden lights lined houses and shops. There was a bump as the vehicle went off the smooth paved road and onto a long tree lined gravel drive. There were long yellow wild-looking grasses leading up a hill to a large brick house surrounded by a hedge and a manicured green lawn. As instructed, Colton went around back. The house was filled with servants, but no one looked at her. They all inclined their head at their Kyrios.

She was led past a door and down a white painted hall and brought into a white room where a man with graying hair wearing a gray suit was waiting. The walls were bare, but there was a bed covered in thick blankets and an empty desk with a chair. He inclined his head at the Kyrios and cracked his knuckles with an air of uneasiness. He said softly to Abby, "I am Dr. Taggert. We need a sample."

Abby looked at the men, not knowing what they were talking about.

Very slowly, Taggert said, "Urin-nate in thiiisss cuuup."

"I speak English." Trying to act braver than she felt, Abby did her best eye roll. She looked around. He opened the door to a private toilet. She snatched the cup from him and went inside.

There were no windows and the only door was the one she came through. Not knowing what else to do, she peed in the cup, washed her hands and handed over the sample. The doctor dipped a stick into the urine and waited. It stayed white. Everyone left, except Taggert. He looked over her charts. He took her temperature and blood pressure that was automatically filled into his tablet. "You seem healthy enough."

Then he left, too.

A woman wearing black slacks and a black blouse with white piping entered with a meal of hot soup and bread. She had a pinched smile on her face as she set the food down on the desk.

"Where am I?" Abby asked. "Do you know what they want from me?"

The woman did not answer her. She opened the closet and laid out a white nightgown on the foot of the bed, then turned down the covers. Abby looked at her soup; it looked like it had bits of potatoes, carrots and white meat chicken. She took a bite. She had guessed correctly about the potatoes and carrots, but the meat wasn't chicken. Its texture was more like rabbit. She couldn't describe it in her mind. "What's this?"

The woman only said "eat" in a heavily accented voice as she finished her chores.

Abby repeated, "What is it?"

The woman took on the air of an exhausted mother with a fussy toddler. The look of disgust was apparent as the woman pulled her out of her chair and dragged her into the bathroom. Her hair was brushed, braided, and then she was told to brush her teeth.

"Hurry up," the woman snarled as she began undressing her and pulled the nightgown over her head. She pushed her to the bed and left.

Abby checked the door. The knob turned freely. It was unlocked. She slowly opened it. The guard outside yanked the knob from her hand and pushed her back in. "It is your bedtime, Miss."

"Do you know what they want of me?"

The guard took a step towards her. "It is your bedtime," he repeated. Abby stood her ground. His voice held a hint of violence. "I'm not used to having to give an order twice, but you're a dumb little thing, aren't you?"

She tried not to run to the bed. Once she was under the covers, the man closed the door and she was alone.

FOR THREE DAYS, THIS WENT on. The maids woke her, brought her food, bathed and dressed her in simple white underwear, bra, socks, and a black knee-length skirt and matching blouse. Her clothes felt like good quality cotton, though Abby had no idea if it was cotton or a synthetic made to feel like cotton. The label wasn't in English, French, or Mandarin. She wondered if it was Greek, but her questions were not answered. If she pressed the maids, they called her stupid and lazy. They slapped her hands away from her food before she finished or twisted the braids tighter and slapped the top of her head with her hairbrush. They just laughed when she cried and taunted her in a language she could not understand.

Alone in her room, she paced. Her windows did not open nor did they seem to be made of glass. Abby wondered if it was made of a clear polymer, but even if it was silica based, it was unbreakable. Nothing in the room seemed to be able to be broken.

She tried praying to her ancestors, but she felt nothing. She had no candles or incense to burn. She wondered if she had traveled too far for anyone to hear her. She gave up on prayer and paced again.

The door was kept unlocked but guarded. The guards did not say much, but they shoved her back into the room. Once she tried to get by, she ended up over a man's shoulder and tossed on the bed. Her fists had no effect, neither did tears.

When dusk fell, the doctor came and took a urine sample. The first three days, the stick remained white and he left. On the fourth day, the stick changed to pink.

Abby did not know what they were checking for, but she was afraid when the dull-eyed man came into her room with a scowl and the obvious intention to stay. She tried to back away from him; he had her by the shoulders. "Lie down."

She began to cry.

The dull-eyed man glared at Taggert and then at Abby. "Stop that! You're supposed to be wanton." Back to Taggert. "What's wrong with her? She's supposed to be wanton!"

In reply, Taggert gestured at the pink stick and stepped towards his medical bag. Abby was still sobbing when Taggert came close with a syringe. A slight prick in the arm. Dizziness as her muscles relaxed. The doctor sat her down on the bed. "Lie down. Quiet now." She didn't want to, but she didn't have the will to fight.

The dull-eyed man didn't even bother to get completely undressed. He just pulled down his pants and began getting himself hard with his hand.

"Lie down," the doctor repeated and she felt him pull off her undergarments. There was a sharp pain deep within her. *He cut me open!* She wanted to scream or cry, but neither her vocal cords nor her tear ducts worked.

She heard the doctor leave the room and the movements and whispers of the dull-eyed man somewhere close by, talking to himself. A few moments later, the dull-eyed man climbed on top of her. He had used some sort of lubrication that felt cold and slick as he entered. The friction began to burn as he pulled on her flesh. She tried to look into his eyes, but his were clinched shut. She pushed up on him, but she was too tired to struggle.

It was over quickly. He left. She was alone again in the dark.

Abby told herself to go to sleep. If she did, she would wake up safe on the straw mat with Ray, Jin, and Orchid. Tara would be snoring at her feet. If she told them of this nightmare, her brothers and sister would tease her for believing in it. She would walk Tara and go to work. If she could only go home, she would never again fantasize about seeing any place beyond Seattle. She would marry the man of her parents choosing and give him children. He would be kind and gentle. They would send their children down to their grandparents' or their Uncle Ray's on Sundays so they might have a little time to their selves, just as her parents did before her.

LIGHT FROM THE FIRST SUN filtered into her closed eyes. The color told her she was not home. Looking at the sheets, she spilled tears over the blood and semen. Though she knew it was morning, she had no true concept of time. She didn't know what year it was. She prayed to her ancestors to find her. She begged that the same fate had not befallen Orchid. She wondered if Jin was able to stay with Rory. She prayed her brother was not alone. She hid under the covers when the maid arrived.

As she had done every day before, the maid pulled Abby out of bed, bathed her, told her to brush her teeth, braided her hair, and dressed her in the same outfit of good quality.

Abby tried to remember all the facts she learned about the Kiposi, trying to find some clue.

Fresh fruit and toast was brought in. Abby thanked the woman. There was no reply. She ate her breakfast in silence and watched the second sun rise.

The woman cleared her plate and left.

She wanted to lie down, but she did not want to touch the bed. The floor was smooth and cool. She glanced under the table, chairs, and bed. There was not a speck of dust. *When was it cleaned? When I was in the bathtub is the obvious answer,* she told herself. *I need to pay better attention. I'll figure out when they are not looking. I can escape. Three guards, at least one male servant, and three female servants.*

She went back into the bathroom. Besides the white polymer and steel of the fixtures, the only other things inside were hand towels and a bottle of foamy soap. She doubted the latter was poisonous.

Too soon, the blue sky changed to gold. She could not see the sunset from her window, but knew Ilios was setting. Taggert returned along with two maids. She tried to fight them as they removed her clothing. She ran away and tried to get the window to open. She desperately searched for a hidden latch.

Terror of being raped again filled her. She screamed, "No! Why are you doing this?"

Taggert backed her into a corner and gave her another injection. She could not fight. He placed her on the bed. This time the women stripped her completely naked, wiped down her body, and brushed her teeth.

She was so tired. It was as if sleep had come over her, but she was still awake. As if marching into battle, the dull-eyed man came, took her with his eyes closed, and left. Without a word. She did not expect that the second time would actually hurt worse than the first.

Abby was left aching and wanting to urinate, but she could not make herself move. Eventually, she felt the feelings come back into her muscles. She rolled off the bed and went to the floor, curled around the dull ache inside her, and let herself sleep.

In the morning, the maid kicked her in the thigh to get her off the floor and called her a savage poutana.

Abby assumed the maid was calling her a savage whore, as that is what she had become. She was too cowardly to end it or even to fight. They bathed and dressed her in simple black. They brought her food. The next three days and nights were the same. Afterwards, the dull-eyed man did not come again.

She watched for him out her window, but she saw only the thick leafed maple that shaded the east side of the house. Beyond, a gravel path and a hedge. Nothing more. She remembered that the colonists brought seeds and fruits with them to transplant. This tree wasn't as old as the colony, but probably a century at least.

Some days, she felt brave. She fought or threw her food at the maids. The women just slapped her and warned, "Should I call the doctor? He will sedate you, poutana."

Abby did not fear being slapped as much as she feared sedation, but she obeyed. However she could not stay silent, she begged them, "Please, do you know where my sister is? My brother? Where am I?"

No one spoke to her except to order her in or out of the tub, turn her around, or position her in a way to make finishing the job easier. If obedience wasn't immediate, a slap was administered to whatever body part was closest. She tried to mark the days by scratching her nail through the paint, but the next morning the wall was repainted and her nails were cut to the quick. Since there was nothing else to do, she kept track in her head.

CHAPTER 11

July 3, 3163 K.E.

TAGGERT AND THE DULL-EYED MAN came back when the sky was still blue. Abby backed into a corner. There were no threats made this time. Taggert just put his arms around her and said, "It's just a little blood."

Before she was able to react, the sample was taken from her neck. They did the test and a minute later, an inane grin splayed across the doctor's face. The dull-eyed man looked relieved.

Taggert said, "You're with child."

Abby did not know what to think about that. "Are you sure?"

"Yes."

She asked the dull-eyed man, "What happened to my sister and brother? Will I see them again?"

He replied, "I see no reason why you should concern yourself with them."

"They're my siblings!"

The dull-eyed man sighed. "We plucked you from a dying planet and have given you a safe home. What else do you need?"

"My sister was only eleven! And you made us into brood mares!"

"What else could you be?"

"I can read and I like languages. Perhaps I could learn to be …"

"You're a foolish girl," he said.

"Not so foolish. I know a babe that grows in a lonely belly will be sickly. You seem to want this child. You said I had a fine mind, but what good is it except to find a way to escape from a rapist."

The dull-eyed man's face twitched. He was too serene as he covered his rage. "Taggert, get out."

"Kyrios…" Taggert glanced at him and back at Abby, but his fear of his master won out. He left.

Butterflies did jumping jacks in Abby's stomach as the dull-eyed man backed her into her chair. Without raising his voice, he said, "If you try to escape, misbehave, or further disrespect the maids and guards, I will bind you to the bed until I can cut the child from you. Then I will take you in my private shuttle and throw you out of an airlock… or perhaps I will just go get your sister. Imagine her young flesh opening to me."

Abby started to cry into her hands.

"Consider all I said, before you make any more threats. Unlike you, I am capable of doing everything I say." He left.

Taggert returned. He looked relieved that she was completely undamaged, however his look also made it clear that she was at fault for disparaging the Kyrios. He said, "You cannot understand the pressure the Kyrios is under!"

AS DUSK DARKENED THE ROOM, there was a soft knock on the door. Abby expected it was the maids coming to taunt her, but instead a beautiful woman in her late twenties/early thirties entered wearing a gown of water blue silk. She carried a small tablet with a stylus. Her black hair shimmered in the darkness, as did her sad eyes. Her Asian features were much less pronounced than Abby's, but they were there.

The woman spoke quickly as if she was trying not to lose her composure. "I am the Kyria of this house – my name is Peony. Barnett and I had one child together, but it was born mutated and died. Three more were terminated. Many are now."

"Barnett?" Abby said. "The dull-eyed man never told me his name."

Peony looked at her, trying to discover the meaning of this. "He doesn't speak to you?"

"No, he barely looks at me, except to threaten."

"He would never harm you," Peony said.

"As long as I am pregnant, I do not fear him. I fear for the others he might hurt!"

Peony did not answer her so, Abby went on. "They talked about the jobs we would have, the opportunities. We came to a new world only to discover that we have become slaves!"

Peony said, "We don't believe in slavery. You are indentured to the government for seven years or three children. We purchased your bond."

"No one talked about being defiled. I'm sure if you had told us that, a lot less people would have come to your garden!"

Peony's mouth opened, but not a sound came out.

The acid in Abby's voice was accompanied by spittle. "Your Barnett did not ask me if I wished to carry his child. He tore Orchid from my arms. I'd have done anything to keep her safe. You stole my baby sister from me!"

Peony flinched at that. "Orchid was young?"

"Not even twelve. Too young to mother a child safely. She hadn't even flowered yet."

"I assume you mean menstruated?"

Shocked to hear the word used openly, Abby could not speak any more. Peony thrust the smooth acrylic pad into Abby's hands.

"This is for you to learn about the world that you have come to. We're not evil, just people in need. A child Orchid's age would be adopted as a daughter. She will be educated and married in a decade. You need not worry about her."

Abby sniffed, the corrosive anger burning up her throat. "And my brother? He had just reached manhood."

"Your twin?"

"No. Fifteen when we left Earth."

"He might have gone on to the mines on Argent, a farm, or he might have been adopted."

By the fear behind Peony's eyes, Abby decided that it was the former, yet they did not want her to worry about such things. Abby said nothing. The tablet was at least an escape from the monotony of the white room.

Working to keep her voice under control, Peony said, "One of our oldest and most trusted servants is Vivian. She will be overseeing your needs from now on. I will send a man to escort you through the gardens once a day as long as you behave."

Not waiting for a reply, Peony crossed the room, her black hair swinging. Once she shut the door behind her, Abby could hear her sobbing.

"Justify it all you want, Lady, but you enslaved us! Your paradise has become tainted," Abby shouted to the door. The anger dissipated and tears welled up in her eyes. Setting the tablet upon her desk, she sat down on the floor and began to sob.

The door reopened, she glanced up with the thought it might be Peony, but instead it was an elderly man in a guard's uniform with a face coated in sheer disgust. He took a few steps towards her. Abby scooted towards the wall.

He hauled her up by the arms. Her tiptoes just brushed the bare floor as she struggled to regain some sort of balance. "You will not raise your voice to the Kyria again." He let her go and turned around.

Abby's arms were red, but she was uninjured. She crossed the room for her new source of information. She sat on her bed and typed "Orchid Boyd Lei" into the search engine on her tablet.

A little cartoon cat popped up shaking a scolding finger at her. She received the message: "I'm sorry but that subject is forbidden for someone of your age. If you continue to search for this, I will be required to send a message to your parents."

She wondered if there was a way to turn off parental controls, but realized if she tried, it would send Peony—or worse Barnett—some sort of message. She bit her lip and typed in Orchid. Photos of the Earth flower came into view, but orchids were too hard to grow on this planet. None survived colonization.

Abby tried "Jin Boyd Lei." She received an error message. This cat looked quite a bit sterner since "Boyd Lei" had popped up again. Abby considered what she knew about parental controls from the library. There was a list of explicatives, body parts, and sex acts that came standard. Parents could add to the list in their own words and phrases too. She typed "Jin." Articles popped up, many about an actor/singer named Jin Rao.

There was also a somewhat famous surrealist painter who went only by the name Jin. She also found a commentary about the Djinn of legend and how they affected life on Kipos. She skipped those. As she scrolled further down, she found an article about a man named Jin Su who had saved a family of cats from his neighbor's house when it caught on fire. The neighbor's adoptive daughter was screaming about the kittens. Without thinking, he ran in to the house and rescued them. Getting the commendation from the Kyrios was nice, but seeing the look of admiration in the girl's eyes was the reward he most treasured.

Unsure why she felt so emotional about a fluff piece, she let the tears flow.

CHAPTER 12

July 4, 3163 K.E.

PEONY WAS GOOD TO HER word.

The next morning, an old woman entered Abby's room along with the regular maids. She was round about the middle and slightly hunched, but even for her advanced years, she was a force like no other. She fluttered about and ordered Abby to eat more of her breakfast and scolded the other two for rushing her. She asked them, "What else do you have to do today that's so important?"

One of the women said something in a language that Abby did not understand.

The old woman crossed her arms beneath her ample bust and replied, "We follow the Kyria's orders in this house or I will ask for your resignation."

The women remained surly, but did as they were told.

Abby decided to chance trying to talk to her. "Ma'am—is Ma'am how I should refer to you? It's a sign of respect to one's elders on Earth."

"It is here too, Abigail, though you may call me Vivian, if you wish. I am your servant and the little one's servant as well. I have looked forward to this day for many years."

"Thank you. And how should I refer to my escort?"

"Why all these questions? Has no one told you anything?"

"No, Vivian, ma'am. I'm sorry."

Vivian glowered at the other maids. "We'll be setting this right starting today. How far did you get in school?"

"Until I was thirteen. I entered a work-to-learn program as a librarian for two years."

"Interesting," Vivian said, though Abby was sure the old woman did not find it interesting at all. "Now you may be aware, the word library on

Kipos is a room in a private home devoted to study. What is a librarian on Earth?"

Abby had not been aware they did not have public libraries on Kipos, but she answered, "I helped people find truthful information on the Cloud. I taught people to read books and watched children who were too young to work, including my own youngest siblings. Orchid and Jin are here somewhere on Kipos."

Vivian ignored the last statement. "That sounds like a perfectly respectable job."

The maids remained silent until Vivian left. When Abby was in the bath, the younger maid whispered, "We went to school until we were nineteen for this crap job. Earthlings only go to school until they are thirteen? No wonder the only way to insert you into society is on your back."

There was nothing to say.

THE SUMMER SUNS WARMED HER shoulders through the black cotton. The second sun glowed red in the sky and changed the colors, ever so slightly, to olive and teals instead of green and blues. Her white socks took on a hue of pale pink. Used to Sol's light, Abby could not help but be surprised.

This is what she had longed to experience. With the warmth of the suns in the afternoon, it was easy to forget what had happened to her. Her escort, Robert, was a trim man with the manner of a kept wolfhound. Abby guessed he was nearing forty-five by the tiny crinkles that lined his brown eyes and a crease that never left his brow. As with all the Kyrios' personal guards, he wore the black and purple uniform and, even within the safety of the gardens, he was fully armed.

From her window, Abby had not realized the house was so monumental. Hectares of stone and brick were surrounded by a few kilometers of garden in every direction. Yet, even for its vastness, each grove had its own sense of enclosure. One basin lined with flowers dipped into a stand of citrus trees. Another dropped down to a pond. Abby could hardly believe all this belonged to one family.

Robert chose a path that took Abby past twenty marble sculptures interwoven through blossoming trees, which surrounded a cruciform canal ending in a large fountain. He walked slowly so she could take it all in.

"Have you ever been off planet?" she asked.

Robert spun around so fast at first she thought he might strike her, but he buried his fingers into the back of her neck and forced her to look up at him. His voice was soft, but held a perfect warning. "Abandon plans of escape, girl. I might not hurt you while you carry a child, but I have ways to make you uncomfortable."

She whispered, "All I wanted to say is that I have never seen the red sun 'til today. On Earth, there is only one and it is yellow."

Robert's face showed his surprise and he released his grip. "So I have heard, but I have only seen these suns."

"The light seems different on Kipos," she said.

"No doubt."

They walked further into the garden into a hedge maze with stone benches surrounded by different varieties of roses, generations of mutations of the Earth flowers. Few had thorns and, while they were scented, most smelled strange and unfamiliar. Some colors seemed to shimmer in the sunlight.

Though there were men shaping the shrubbery, it was nearly silent. There were no children playing or dogs barking. Soon there will be a child to play among these statues. *Can I even imagine my child growing up in such a place?*

"Do you have dogs here?" she asked.

"Extinct," Robert said.

"Oh, I had a dog on Earth."

"It is dead now," he said.

Abby stopped walking and turned to him. "I know of time dilation."

Robert's fingertips drilled into the flesh of her shoulder. "Watch that tone with me, girl. The Kyria asked that you are treated well, but you're the property of the Kyrios. You understand?" He punctuated his speech with a little shake.

As meekly as she could, Abby answered, "Yes sir."

They walked back to the house in silence. He saw her to her room, reminded her to behave and that he would see her tomorrow.

ALONE AGAIN, ABBY PACED. THERE was so much out there to explore. It was unfair that she was caged.

She looked up dogs. As Robert had said, they were extinct, except for some feral hybrids that skulked outside the cities. However, cats had lived in some of the ships and now on Kipos, as they were lightweight, easy to transport, and clean. She wondered if Orchid had gotten a kitten. *Does my sister and brother ever think about me? Does Orchid live in a room like this? Does Jin?*

Abby felt so lonely.

A new thought entered her mind: *Maybe if I behave and ask nicely, I could have a kitten.* She shook the notion from her head. It wasn't hers, she was sure of that, but there was so many things that she did not know. Abby had no idea what the morals of the planet were. Obviously they thought nothing of ripping a family apart and raping them. *No, not both of them— just her. Peony obviously believed pedophilia was wrong.*

Abby tried to calm down and think. Barnett had threatened to kill her, but never raised his hand. He hadn't wanted anyone to overhear the things he had said. The guards were ordered not to hurt her either. She hoped beating women was against the law. She hoped killing people was against the law.

She opened a search window on her tablet and typed: "Murder laws." Though there had been five cases of reckless manslaughter, there had never been a murder on Kipos. The article identified murder as a public wrong, which meant it hurt society as well as the victim.

She typed in "rape law" and received a warning for use of the word "rape." However, due to the word "law" in the request, it offered suitable suggestions, including a link to the governing statutes brought to the original colony.

Based loosely on Noah's law, common sense, and the Constitution, it stated:

[All humans have the right to life, liberty and the pursuit of happiness. While there is a need for just law, most problems can be resolved with prudence and care if we just do unto others as we would have them do to us].

[Article 1: Freedom of speech and religion. There can be no persecution due to one's religious beliefs as long as they don't contradict other laws.]

There was a link: <u>Give me an example</u>. Abby tapped it with her finger.

[Example: human sacrifice is murder.]

She tapped on it again.

[Example: Even if your God puts one gender above the other, beating one's spouse is assault.]

Abby felt a bit of relief.

[Article 2: Prohibition of theft. Work for what you need, do not steal from your fellow colonists. These charges are punishable by indenture.]

[Article 3: Prohibition of any sexual practices in which any participant cannot or do not give consent or which has been medically deemed harmful for offspring including pedophilia, bestiality, rape, and incest. These charges are punishable by chemical castration and payment for the victim's recovery.]

On a link to The Kyn point of view, Abby saw the Kyn took even a wider stance on sexual immorality, which included any acts that could not be used for the purpose of procreation. They considered the genetic experiments, such as the sterilized Khlôrosans and Garo, to be beasts that would taint their human blood. She saw a link to Reproduction Laws, but held off clicking on it. Instead, Abby opened up another window and looked up "the Kyn."

[The Kyn are the only surviving religious group on Kipos comprised of Homo Kiposi. They believe in one deity who is the God of All and the Designer of the Universe. They can be traced back to the Sons of Isaac and Ishmael, which in turn, can be traced back to a cease-fire between Jewish Peoples, Muslims and Christians in 2238 C.E. in an attempt to curb the Veneration of Science on Triton.

While some Kyn live integrated within Kipos society as well as the private fleet, many tend to live in small clustered patriarchal villages outside of the cities. In conservative factions, Kyn women tend to be in charge of running the household, while the men work in various gainful employment around their House of Worship. They wear black and gold robes to set themselves apart from the rest of society. Due to their strict dietary, morality, and cleanliness laws, Kyn have a longer life span (142 years) than the average Kiposi (123 years). Mutational defects are virtually unknown in their chromosomes; however, they do have a higher infant mortality rate due to no immunity to G.I.D.]

Abby went back to the article that she was reading.

[Article 4: Prohibition against killing another human being, including an unborn except in cases of incest or birth defect. Murder is a capital offense and punishable by lifelong indenture to the government subsidized aero-space short range fleet. Wages are to be garnished for the victim's family.

   a) The lesser offense of Manslaughter is punishable by a decade of wages paid to the victim's family or indenture to the victim's family if one can not pay.

   b) Assault is punishable by paying wages or indenture to the victim's family until both mental and physical wounds are healed.]

On the bottom of the article was a link to <u>Indenture Bonds</u>. Abby clicked on it, but did not read it, because on top of the new page was a link to <u>Indentured Earthlings</u>. She clicked on that.

[Indentured Earthlings are typically young, unskilled laborers arriving on Kipos under contract to work for the government for a fixed period of time, typically three to seven years, in exchange for the costs of their transportation. Though this was an unpopular decision, it is obvious from the <u>Original Fleet Reports</u> that Earthlings must be separated and assimilated into Kiposi homes in order to maintain societal paradise.

Children under the age of sixteen have no bonds and can be adopted for a fee of 5000 credits and proof of a stable home environment, which includes the opportunity for higher education.

As the age of majority on Earth is sixteen, anyone arriving between the ages of sixteen and twenty-one are to be bonded to work or to reproduce if they cannot be adopted into families with loving parents. They are not paid wages, but treated as part of the family so as to not disturb the natural order of Kipos. Males will be given exercise via manual labor, a healthy diet, and time to study in order that they may go on to lead productive lives.

Per their terms of indenture, males are required to produce four healthy children or to be indentured for seven years.

Females are required to produce three healthy children or to be indentured for seven years or until the age of twenty-

five, whichever period is shorter. They may
do minimal chores if the family is without
servants, but they should be well fed and
not pushed beyond their natural capacities,
especially during pregnancy. Women of Earth
seem sturdier than their Kiposi counterparts, but have a larger variation in hor-
monal responses.

If any child is born with birth defects or shows signs of savagery, the Earthling parent will be sterilized and forced
to work on public projects for seven years.
If an indentured servant runs away without
just cause, he or she will be publically
executed.

Men and women over the age of twenty-
two can be married with a fee of no more
than 500 credits and proof of a stable home
environment. These fertile people generally expect monogamous relationships, and the
legal requirements of marriage will still
apply...]

The article went on, but Abby feared reading to the end. She began
scanning for Indentured Rights. They were few. She discovered that she
could not be killed or starved. She also realized that being female did offer
her more protection.

Her health and well-being must be taken into consideration. Corporal
punishment was allowed on men with just cause, but not on a woman for
fear of causing damage to her reproductive organs. If an indentured man
harmed the woman that he was to impregnate in any measure, he would be
castrated and sent to work in the public fleet. It went on and on...

She feared for Jin. She prayed that he had been adopted and not sent
to the mines on Argent. She thought about Rory. He wouldn't mind being
sent to stud, but he would not like that it wasn't his choice in the matter.

Abby did not agree that she was a savage or that she and her counterparts would have destroyed Kipos' paradise, but she had read about such prejudices in the library. Throughout Earth's (and she guessed Kipos') history someone, whether by race or creed, was always getting shit on. Kipos' survival depended on people multiplying quickly. They would force themselves to believe what ever was necessary in order to do so.

At least she had a few rights, but not knowing what to do, she paced.

CHAPTER 13

ABBY FELT NAUSEOUS AS SHE looked down at her dinner. She had eaten the same soup every night since she arrived. She did not want to eat another bite. She pushed it around with her spoon, left it on the table, and lay down in her bed. The room rolled. She shut her eyes tightly and wrapped her blanket around her. She turned towards the wall. Lying down made her want to vomit more, so she got back up. She tried the door; it was unlocked.

The guard outside was watching a sports program on a tablet. He looked up at her.

"Please don't hit. I need…" she started to say.

"Yes, how can I help you, Miss Bodlay?"

"I need the doctor. My name is Boyd Lei."

The man swiped out a message on a piece of acrylic. "I'll let Doctor Taggert know, Miss Boydlee. He will be here in a few moments."

"What's that?" she asked.

"Just a radio," he said.

"A what?"

He smiled as if she was a little girl. "Ray-dee-o. I tap out the message or change signals and use my voice."

"But how does it work? I never saw one like that."

The man shrugged. "Radio-waves, I guess."

"We had handhelds that used radio waves back on Earth too; they just looked really different than that."

The man gave her an encouraging look of a kindergarten teacher. "Really?"

Taggert came down the hall carrying his black bag. He wasn't wearing his suit jacket and Abby noticed the yellowing stains on his shirt. *Does he live here?*

The doctor frowned at her nearly full bowl. "You must eat. This will calm your stomach."

The injection just made her sleepy. She took a few bites of soup, only not to get in trouble later. She climbed into bed.

She awoke to find her hair soaked in vomit. Vivian and Peony were above her. They pulled off her dress and helped her into the bath. Vivian and another angry maid stripped the bed as Peony washed Abby's hair.

"I don't like it. Don't make me anymore soup."

Once Abby was in a fresh nightgown, Peony tucked her back into bed. "Please, someone help me," she whispered. "I'm trying to be good. Why won't you help me?"

Peony did not answer her. No one did. They simply left.

THE NEXT NIGHT, IT WAS the same soup. Abby didn't eat it. She typed in "bubble teas." It was a popular drink among the youth of Kipos, but they did not have tapioca for the bottom. They used fruity chews. *Why did I not ask if they had tapioca before I got on the ship?*

Ignoring her soup growing cold, she looked up "recipes" on her tablet. There were plenty of Earth recipes with minor modifications for ingredients that were not available on Kipos. Spaghetti, meatloaf, and chops with golden squash were top recipes, but beef was unknown. The colonists used mutton or something called savra in place of beef or pork.

Chicken was available, but on Kipos, it was more expensive than mutton and savra, as it was all grown on Argent. While Argent and the Fleet consumed vast quantities of poultry, generally, the Kiposi felt that the small amount of meat wasn't worth the hassle of defeathering and the cost of transportation. Yet people on Kipos did eat eggs; they were easy to transport and prepare.

Abby typed in "savra." It was a ten-legged lizard with a slightly rounded body, a broad head, and a tail that was two-thirds its body length. Gene therapy, loss of habitat, and the process of domestication had turned this once feared predator into human prey for food and leather. Adults were opalescent black with a creamy white underside. Juveniles were born white with a striped pattern for camouflage. As they age, the stripes thicken until they merge. Adults were big—nearly five to seven meters in length. Their heavy skins lost the opalescent sheen during the tanning process, but still made excellent leathers. At least in regards to cooking, savra's cuts were called similar names to pork: chop, bacon, loin, ham.

Another delicacy was the Khloro Ray. When humans arrived on Kipos, the rays filled the skies, but after only two centuries the wild rays were hunted to extinction for their skins, meat, and DNA.

Fish and gastropods were abundant.

She thought, though Peony and Barnett seemed to be wealthy, perhaps the soup was all they could afford. Either that or they had eccentric tastes. She decided it must be the latter.

THE NEXT DAY, THE SUN was out. Robert knocked on her door and Abby realized he was the closest thing she had to a friend. As they walked, she decided that, even though he was quite a bit older than she was, he was still handsome. She found herself wishing she knew him better. She imagined, maybe, if he grew to love her, he would draw his weapon from its holster and protect her from his evil employers. They could run off together and raise the baby. Then a terrifying thought entered her brain: *Would he be able to raise my child as his own? Yes. He is a grown man. The real question is: can I raise this baby? No matter how this baby was conceived, I'm the child's mother...*

"I hope to be a good mother," Abby said softly and rubbed the slight bulge on her stomach.

Robert glanced over at her and smiled, but did not speak.

"What are you thinking?" Abby asked.

"Nothing really."

Abby wondered if there might be other complications. "Robert, are you married?"

"No."

"Why not?"

"Never found the right woman."

"I wasn't married either. I still lived with my parents on Earth."

He nodded, but did not say anything.

Thinking of something they might have in common, she blurted out, "Do you like bubble tea?"

"Isn't that for kids?"

"Oh, I guess. I like it though. There was a teahouse near my commune and we used to go there because it cost two credits for a really big cup. Orchid—that's my sister—used to always get fruity flavors- strawberry or melon. I liked Thai or honey milk…"

Abby realized Robert wasn't listening to her babble. She tried changing the subject. "What kind of music do you like?"

"The popular stuff. Bonefish, Star's Revenge, and the like…"

"I don't know them, but I'll look them up on my tablet."

"You do that."

The Bonefish was a loud band with a good beat. They made her want to dance. Star's Revenge seemed almost tribal. The lead singer did lots of vocal acrobatics in his songs. She clicked on links to other suggested bands. It was an enjoyable way to spend the day and as she lay in bed that night, she thought about things to tell Robert.

THE NEXT DAY, IT WAS drizzling. Water squished in her shoes as they walked down to the pond. She picked up a polished stone and skipped it across the water. "So I looked up those bands you told me about," she began, "And my tablet also suggested I look up Cold Spirals and Wildin's."

Robert sighed. "Yeah, those are good too. Damn, why did you want to go out in this weather?"

Abby fell silent beside him. Abby didn't understand her sudden urge to put her arms around his flat middle just to see what he would do. Maybe he would hold her. Maybe… but if he didn't … if he truly felt she was nothing but an irritant, her heart would break. She worded her answer carefully. "In Seattle, it often rained. Ray—that's my brother who stayed on Earth—worked in the fields, rain or shine."

"Is your brother older than you?" he asked.

"No. All my siblings were younger."

"Was he stupid or ill featured?"

"No. He felt someone needed to take care of our parents and grand-mother," Abby said.

Robert laughed. Something hollow in his voice made her cringe.

ABBY TYPED ORIGINAL FLEET REPORTS from Sol. Even as she scanned the list of articles, she understood. Two centuries ago the intentions had been only to get fresh infusions of DNA. However, when Sol's colonies had all been destroyed and the Kiposi were sending their communications back home, it was decided the Kiposi had evolved, while Earthlings were obviously lesser beings.

She saw something from Captain Saunders.

```
[Earth supports seventeen billion Homo sapi-
ens who practice primitive religions. They
have widespread beliefs in animalism and
ancestor worship, that is to say they wor-
ship the ghosts of their dead or the spirits
of animals. They have primitive engineering
methods and medical practices; thus, most
of them are infected with lice and disease.
     The very mention of invasion sends
these people into riots. We have witnessed
rape, hysteria, and destruction of life and
property even before we arrived.
     However, upon arrival, Seattle resi-
dents either greeted us openly or huddled
in their hovels with the wish to be ignored.
We were forced to kill three boys who jumped
the barricade and touched the ship as we
```

were landing. There are so many of them I do not know how to find their families in order to compensate them. None have stepped forward.

Many are trained to do mining, farming, and other agriculture endeavors. Less than 10% will be good breeding stock. We shall attempt to remove those specimens from general population...]

Abby scanned lower.

Another article claimed, now that the first generation of Earthlings had settled on Kipos, they had "scientific" proof of Homo sapien weakness. On the journey to Kipos, forty percent of all the Earthlings had histamine reactions to the nanomite and oxygenated water in the grav-couches. Nearly all of these reactions had been fatal. This was twice the amount of an average Kiposi population and among the Kiposi less then ten percent of these reactions led to deep space death. The Kyn refused to mate with Earthlings until it could be proven that they were not barbarian. If these issues were all true, it was just another form of bestiality.

The final article spoke of the changes in society since the development of the Alekos FtL engine. With faster than light technology and more efficient nanomites, Kipos sent another ten ships to Earth. They felt they could get another million souls from the next generation. They wanted humans and cows specifically. Earth revolted and won by sheer numbers alone. Five ships were limping back to Kipos at sublight speeds carrying 75,000 calves and 50,000 humans.

Abby set down her tablet. She could not believe she had been so naive. Ray would have been dead when they landed. Had he married and had children? Did she have nieces or nephews on those ships? Would there be anyway to ever find them or were they lost to her, just like Orchid and Jin?

Since she could do nothing else, she paced.

CHAPTER 14

August 3, 3163 K.E.

ABBY HAD EXPECTED SOME MORNING sickness, but she had not expected it to last all day. She woke up feeling fine, but shortly after breakfast, she felt woozy. The sun on her shoulders made her feel better, but after going back into her room for her lonely dinner she felt worse. She hated going to bed because bile would rise in her stomach and her mind would rove.

Taggert just chirped that it meant the baby was developing well and told her to drink water. Vivian instructed the younger maids to bring her crackers, but they acted as if they were bringing her gold and told her not to fill up on them.

Robert thought, if she wasn't feeling well, perhaps she should stay in bed. Abby had a tantrum—there was no better word for it—crying and screaming at him. She threw herself on the bed. She knew she was acting obnoxious, but he took the bait. She sobbed into his chest about how lonely she was.

She wailed until Vivian told Robert that exercise was important to the fetus. He would just have to put up with a nauseous walking companion and Abby had to put up with a surly one.

The summer suns melted the anger away from Robert's face and made Abby glow as they walked down into the kitros grove, where Abby informed Robert that the word was "citrus" in Earth English.

They encircled the pergola, covered in deep scented purple flowers. Robert did not know the names of it or any other flower, but he let her pick one and wear it in her hair as she wished.

The ground was slick. They strolled amongst the statues and she took his arm for balance. He wrapped his strong arm around her and told her to be careful. She felt safe, safer than she had since she arrived on Kipos.

She began to salivate from the thought that he might lean down and kiss her lips. He let her go, but did not push her away as she held his arm. The electricity flowed through her fingers as she felt his strong arms under his jacket.

Her heart whispered that if Abby could learn to love what Robert loved, she might be worthy of him. Then he would protect her from what's coming. She asked if he knew any of the stories behind the statues. He did not. He simply did not have time for things such as gardening or sculpture.

They spoke on music again and again. Abby tried asking about novels, but Robert didn't like to read. He spent his off hours watching action movies and football. She told him that they have football on Earth too. She learned that, in his opinion, the New Alexandria's team sucked this year, but he supported their city. The Kyria always bought season passes for her men on the New Year, so he was able to catch a lot of games. Abby began watching the games on the Feed so she could talk about the exciting plays.

She discovered that he was born in New Alexandria, one of the seven cities of Kipos. Yes, Robert had been to all seven. Other than regional differences in weather or exports, they were all basically the same. His mother had been a hairdresser, his father a tailor. There was plenty of work since the higher level AI left.

That struck Abby as interesting. "Did you know the AI left Earth too?"

"How would I know that?"

Abby shrugged, as she did not have an answer, then asked, "Is there any AI left on Kipos?"

"There is rumored to be human-level androids, but I certainly have never seen one. We have lots of bots programmed to do various menial tasks: surveillance, harvesting crops, factory lines, etc."

As interesting as the topic was for Abby, Robert simply did not have much more knowledge about the AI. "You'll have to look in your tablet," he said when she tried to question him further.

She asked if he ever had any pets. He told her that his family had a cat when he was younger. She asked what kind it was. Robert said it was just a white cat. It was named Angelica for his mother's favorite actress. However, the cat was no angel.

Though he had originally been a customs officer, Robert had no love for politics or law. An injured shoulder took him off the line of duty and he went into private security. He had been working for the Kyria for seven years.

As the baby grew and Abby started to show, her regular skirt and blouse were replaced with a black maternity dress. She started gaining a half-kilo or so each week and worried about getting fat, but Robert made no comment one way or the other. The only one who did was Taggert, who was happy with her weight gain.

Her gums became tender when she brushed her teeth, yet her lips always wished to be kissed. She spent time looking in her mirror, watching her mouth and her face. She began daydreaming about Robert. She imagined him gently kissing her body, asking her what felt good, whispering sweet words of love and lust into her ear. She felt herself get wet with the thoughts of him. Sometimes, she kissed her own inner elbows just to feel something, but that would make her even wetter. She spent so much time alone she knew she could concede to her desires, at least with her hand.

CHAPTER 15

August 7, 3163 K.E.

"IT IS AUGUST 7TH TODAY?" Abby asked Vivian as she and the maids walked into the room with her breakfast.

"So it is."

"It's my birthday."

Abby hoped that someone would tell her how old she was, but "many happy returns" was all Vivian said. The younger maids just smirked. They didn't care.

As it always was, the best part of her day was when Robert came to her door.

"It's my birthday," she told him.

"Many happy returns. How old are you?"

"With the stasis and near fast as light travel, I'm not sure," she admitted.

Robert shrugged. "Yeah, I guess I wouldn't know either. The math to figure that out is pretty complicated."

He reached out to take her hand. Even though it was not the kiss she desired, he looked even more dashing in his purple and black uniform. His sharp features softened in the warm light of the suns. As they walked in the kitros grove of the garden, she thought of what a good man he must be.

"Do you hope for a boy or a girl?" Abby asked him, rubbing her slightly protruding belly.

"It won't matter," he replied with a somewhat bored tone.

"Do you think..." she glanced up at the big house.

"Honestly, I have no idea. I take my orders from the head of security, I only see the Kyrios at the monthly duty meetings, but he has never even spoken of the child except when he asked for volunteers to guard you. I earn double time for this duty."

"Do you have a preference at all?"

"No."

Abby sniffed and wiped her eyes though they were dry. "I just want to know the baby will be loved by someone other than me. I worry about it constantly."

As she knew he would, Robert wrapped his arm around her shoulders. "I'm sure it will be. All of this will be his or hers. It is our duty is to protect it."

Abby leaned against him. Robert would never betray his household duties for her, but when the child was born, he would watch over him or her as he or she played in the garden.

That made her care for him all the more.

CHAPTER 16

September 7, 3163 K.E.

SEPTEMBER 7TH WAS LIKE ALL the other days on Kipos until Abby saw the strange green bird flit into her vision for a moment. She followed it through the garden and edged towards a fading rose bush. It ate a bud, then flew into the field of blades. Native to Kipos, the long, slender plants edged with spikes were grown in order to keep the riffraff out of Peony's and Barnett's private sanctuary. She smiled as she watched the bird flit in and out of the blades, unharmed by the sharp plant.

Abby was knocked on her back. Trying to catch her breath, she realized Robert had his full weight on top of hers. His knife sliced shallowly into her throat.

"Escaping, cunt?" His cheeks were flushed and his brown eyes looked black with rage.

"I was just following that bird," she pointed towards the field of blades.

He slapped her and pulled her to her feet. The whole right side of her face was on fire and her eyes immediately teared from the shock. He slapped her again, then gripped her shoulders with his strong hands. He dragged her back up the path towards the house. She first thought they were going back to her room, but he turned into a different part of the house where the walls were painted a deep forest green and the ceilings were a paler shade with thick, white coving boards. Potted plants hung in little nooks and family photos of happy times danced down the hallway in a staggered fashion. The windows were tastefully appointed with fabrics and the furniture was covered in rich leathers.

She had never seen such luxury, but before she could take it all in, she was in front of Barnett and Peony. The room stopped as Robert pushed her to her knees. She wobbled as she went down. Barnett and Peony had been watching a program on the Feed; behind them, Colton held a glass in the air. Watching her. He had been serving two old, well-dressed men playing chess.

The child shifted in her womb for the first time. She wondered if it was as afraid as she was.

Peony stood up. "What is the meaning of this?"

Robert sneered. "She was trying to steal the child. Escape."

Abby felt the blood drip down her neck and into her dress. She shook her head, "I was just following a bird."

One of the old men snapped, "Do you expect us to believe that when we have no birds here!"

Her fear turned into anger. She snapped back, "Whether you do or not, it is the truth. I am not a liar! There was a bird." She rose to her feet. Robert tried to hold her, but this time she pushed back. "If someone would ask about me, you would know that!"

Resentment at the unending silence of her fate and dizziness coursed through her mind. She wobbled. Suddenly, Colton and Peony's elderly guard were at her side holding her up. "Miss Boydlee, you mustn't do such things. Think of the baby."

He called her Boydlee. Closer to her real name.

"There was a bird. I'm not a liar."

She turned around looking for some encouragement, but Barnett wasn't looking at her. He was backing away. He was trying to distance himself from her.

Colton said, "I know, child. Tell the Kyria."

Abby felt the crush of Colton's gentle but firm hands as he guided her to the chair across from Peony. She felt the back of her knees brush the soft damask and the lingering warmth of Barnett on the cushion. He moved by the table to stand beside a well-dressed older man he called "Father."

Are you the one who paid for me? Abby wanted to scream at the older man.

"What type of bird, Abigail?" Peony asked. Her voice was soft and not at all angry. Though the men were glaring at her, the woman obviously did not fear her husband or anyone else in the room.

Abby answered, "Green with a bright yellow cap. It seemed to hover like a hummingbird of Earth. It ate a rose bud!" She held her hands out ten centimeters to show them the size. "It flew over to the blades. I was just watching it. I wasn't going to run away."

Peony glanced at her husband and exhaled. "Sounds like a Lunapar, most likely. Abigail, what you mistook for an avian is a reptile. A flying lizard. I'm sure the Feed has information on them. If not, Barnett will get you a nature program.

"I believe today you have had enough of an adventure."

Peony rang for Vivian, who appeared seconds later. "Please escort Abigail to her room and get her cleaned up."

THE NEXT DAY, PEONY'S ELDERLY guard came to her door.

Eli was older; he seemed to have kind blue eyes. Abby realized Eli's eyes were the first blue she had seen on Kipos. He waited until they were alone in the garden, then he gripped both of her arms with his icy cold fingers and whispered down directly into her face, "You should know you got Robert fired. Try that shit with me, I'll ruin you."

Abby said softly, "I didn't mean to get anyone fired. I just wanted..."

He cut her off. "Do you believe I can hurt you?"

She nodded.

"You may look at whatever you like, but you will stay by my side, or so help me, I will remember each of your transgressions and, once that child leaves your body, you will pay for each one."

The threat interwove with her spine. Abby did not even consider arguing. He did not seem to care if corporal punishment was prohibited. He would do whatever he felt would be most effective. It would be bad enough that she would never tell anyone out of shame and fear.

"Yes, sir. I'm sorry."

"Stop trembling. I have not hurt you yet."

Abby was careful to fall in step with him. She wanted to stop and smell the roses, but she was too frightened that this might be counted as a transgression. He got two steps ahead of her, so she took his hand. It was so cold.

His eyes grew kinder. "Continue to behave as you are and we shall get along."

After their first loop around the rose garden, Abby decided to risk talking. "What is that, sir?"

She pointed at a tailless, red-spotted rodent munching on rosehips. She had seen them before, but never asked Robert in fear of seeming stupid.

"A common garden squirrel. I thought you had squirrels on Old Earth?"

"Yes sir, but they did not have red spots and were known for their fluffy tails. May we take a closer look?"

He released her hand. "You may, but stay where I can see you."

She hoped this wasn't some sort of test as she took a few steps closer to the little animal. It glanced up and chittered up at her. She took a few steps back and went to her escort's hand.

Exactly one hour later, she was back in her room. Alone. There were no delightful feelings and self-pleasure that afternoon. Abby knew Robert must hate her now. She deserved whatever happened to her.

CHAPTER 17

September 9, 3163 K.E.

ABBY WATCHED THE RAIN AND maple leaves pelt against the window. She hoped it wouldn't rain tomorrow. The seasons changed quickly in New Alexandria. She thought of Seattle and how the coldest part of winter was only a few months but the transitional spring seemed to last forever. A few months of heat in July and August, before another lazy autumn filled with gray clouds and unending drizzle.

Abby opened her tablet. She typed in "games." The screen filled up with sites dedicated to online gaming. The parental controls would not allow her to play any adult games or bet, but there were children's word and mathematic games.

What caught her attention were the words Khlôrosan Games. She clicked on it before she realized it was exotic, hybrid pornography. The cartoon cat was scolding her again. Still, it gave her three suggestions: Khlôrosans, Hybrid races of Kipos, and Reproduction laws.

She clicked on the Hybrid races of Kipos. Her search came up with thousands of documents and articles. She looked at a history article first.

[Seeing that the human birthrate was dropping, a science team headed by Dr. Marcus Potter created the first generation of hybrids by combining human DNA with what they called the Khôlro Ray, a high speed air creature approximately seven meters across. As the rays were native to the planet and could handle high velocity, it was felt that these traits would be the best hope

in curing the ailments of humanity on their
new home.
      The first generation was born in vac-
uum tubes. The third generation had the reproductive qualities needed in order to be
mated with human volunteers, including Dr.
Potter's own son. Tall and slender, they
could take high g-force upon their frames
by the sixth generation. They were long
limbed, strong, and could run faster than
the average Kiposi. Nevertheless, their
weakness to heat and cold was obvious. By
generation twenty, the experiment had been
scrapped and all Khlôrosans living on Kipos
had been sterilized or banished.]

Abby also learned that a number of Khlôrosans still lived in a flotilla
on the outer edges of Outpost 5, clinging to the unending hope of finding
their own planet. The Kipos government wished them well in their at-
tempts; however, Khlôrosans who enter the Ilios/Kokadelfi star system are
required by law to conform to Kipos Reproduction laws and are sterilized
for the good of the gene pool.
      Abby scanned up to the first mention of <u>Khôlro Ray</u> and clicked on the
highlighted word. From the picture, Khôlro Rays looked much like a wa-
ter-born batoidea of Earth, but had a thin neck and head with fibrous teeth
within its beak. The trapezoidal body with broad flat wings and a long thin
tail for directional steering was covered with tiny hairs to protect them
from the sun. Their underbelly was sheltered by iridescent microscales
that worked as camouflaging shields. They had two pairs of eyes located
on top of the head with ear slits behind them.
      The caption read:

[The rays lived in pods composed of stable
matriarchal family groups and had sophis-

ticated hunting techniques and vocal behaviors. These behaviors were passed across generations and described as manifestations of culture. They could dive from the upper atmosphere to the surface of Kipos at speeds of over 1400 kilometers per hour. They were hunted for their DNA, hides, and meat until they became extinct.]

Abby went back to the article she was originally reading.

[The true crime is that the Kiposi did not stop with one experiment. As Kiposi birthrate plummeted again, they tried again with the garos.]

The linked picture showed a bipedal, ape-like creature with glowing bioluminescent spores for attracting mates.

[Offspring were sickly. These people's thick, wavy hair was reddish brown to black and their eyes generally brown, grey, or hazel. Their skin was always nearly dark brown. They were on average a few centimeters shorter than their colonist counterparts and their build tended to be slightly broader and heavyset. The first generations were also sterilized, though a few escaped this fate. In ten generations, most traces of the Homo garo were generally gone from the populace. The few remaining escaped to Outpost 5, where they took refuge with the

```
flotilla.
```
During the same time, a liberal Kyn branch did an experiment using the garo and created the Elykyn, who are, in the biological sense, the same species as the Homo garo.

Only on Kipos, for two viable generations, the conservative Kyn called the Elykyn the work of the devil. Refusing their sons and daughters to be sterilized, three thousand Elykyn left to find their own planet. Though it was thought that their ships had been destroyed, they have been confirmed in the Khlôrosan flotilla.]

Abby set down the tablet and rubbed the strain from her brow. Kipos was no garden.

THE RAIN DID NOT LET up the next day. Eli told her that they wouldn't be going out. At first, she tried asking politely and when that didn't work, she whined. "I'm bored!"

Eli grabbed her by the shoulders. Although the pressure of his hands was uncomfortable, he did not try to induce pain. He did not raise his voice, yet there was something in the way his words reverberated through her body that demanded obedience. "Have you come to think you're some sort of princess? You'll learn differently once you bear that child. The Kyrios won't care what we do to you then."

She cowered and whimpered. "I just get lonely."

"Maids still treat you like shit?"

She nodded.

"Stop acting like a child. Clean off that table and call for some tea." He let her go, turned around, and walked out.

Even though she knew the maids would balk, Abby did not dare disobey his edict. The maid who answered her request called her an idiot poutana.

Eli came back with a pack of cards and a cribbage board. "Where's the tea?"

"The maid…"

Eli did not wait for her to finish answering. He hit the button and told whoever was listening to get the tea service up here or Vivian would hear about it.

Tea and cookies magically appeared within minutes.

CHAPTER 18

October 14, 3163 K.E.

ABBY FELT THE BABY SHIFT in her stomach. She pushed her nightgown over her body and lay naked so she could see the child move under her skin. "If you're a boy, I shall call you Ray Lei; if you're a girl, I shall call you Lei Lei. Your grandmother's name was Lei Sun Lei and Ray Boyd Lei was your uncle."

The maid entered and dressed her as she always did. Peony entered with a new program for her tablet. It was a series of audio novels designed to help rid Abby of her Earth accent and slang.

Hoping to make Peony stay, Abby said, "The baby moves."

Peony sat down beside her. She felt Abby's stomach and laughed in delight as the child kicked. After a few moments, Peony left.

Peony and Barnett came back. Taggert rolled a small cart into the room. Upon it lay a few medicines, his tablet, and some instruments that Abby had never seen. "We need to do a test. Disrobe please," he said.

Abby undressed. Taggert had seen her naked before, but it did not stop her from feeling ashamed.

"Lie down."

Abby looked at Peony with wide eyes, but did as she was told.

Taggert applied a small amount of gel on Abby's enlarged belly. He slid a small white cylinder through this gel. There was no pain. Abby only felt the instrument against her skin.

"Take a deep breath, child."

Abby obeyed the doctor, though she could not see what he was doing or what was on the tablet Peony and Barnett were looking at. Peony laughed and began to weep happy tears. "Excuse me, Excuse me."

She left. Barnett followed his wife.

Taggert gave Abby an injection "to make it easier." It burned up her arm until her muscles relaxed. He shoved his finger into her and felt around for a few moments. With a large swab, he took a sample. That did hurt. Tears dripped out of her eyes.

"Is something wrong with my baby?"

"Seems fine." Taggert wiped off his hands on a small towel and pushed the cart out of the room.

A young maid curtsied at the doctor, entered and wiped Abby down. She dressed her in a clean dress. There was a dull ache inside her. Abby lied down in bed and clutched at her belly.

"Please be okay, little one."

AFTER THAT, TAGGERT CAME WITH his cart once a week. He told Abby to lie down on the bed and used the device to see inside her belly. If Barnett or Peony came, they got to watch the screen; but even when they weren't there, Taggert never turned it towards Abby. She longed to see the baby. He put his finger inside her, felt around for a bit, and took a sample. He always left her with the words: "Everything looks fine."

As the weather got colder, there were more days Abby was not allowed outside and she spent a few days looking at baby clothes online. Though she couldn't buy anything, it was still fun to look at the little outfits and socks. She found a store that gave free advice about parenting and going through a first pregnancy. The amount of things required to keep a newborn safe was staggering. She reviewed car seats with shuttle attachments. Babies were so small this did not surprise her, but it did surprise her that toddlers had another car seat for every year of life until around age five, they moved into another seat made of foam that contoured to a child's changing shape. They sat in this until at least age ten, when their bodies would be large enough to sit in an adult sized seat safely.

Babies and toddlers were pushed around in huge prams that often had a screen built in to entertain them. She thought about home. Mothers and fathers put their child in a carrier or sling and wore them all day in the factory. As soon as an Earth child could walk, it was expected and required to do so.

Abby did not judge one system better than the other; they were just different. After a few days of researching baby care, the parental controls popped up more often. She didn't understand what she was doing wrong. Eventually, the store was closed off to her. "Maybe it thought I was loitering," she said aloud to no one.

SHE SPENT A DAY RESEARCHING Kiposi legends but there seemed to be none. She looked up children's stories and crib tales and, though she found a few references to old stories of Earth, the articles hypothesized that the Kiposi's scientific knowledge had overcome the need for legend and fable. History and technical knowledge is more important than fiction.

The Kyn's viewpoint was the only story worth telling was that glorious God that brought them to their Garden in the Stars. He gave inspiration to <u>Jason Potolis</u> to search Vela. Abby made the leap to the Jason and the Argonauts story. She opened the word processor and tried typing out what she could remember. It wasn't much. Only he had a ship called the Argo and he was looking for a golden fleece. She remembered a woman named Medea helped him and he betrayed her when he got back to Greece.

"Alright," she said, "Jason Potolis."

A dozen articles popped up on the first page and there was at least another dozen windows to explore. Two centuries prior, the Sons of Isaac and Ishmel wrote:

```
[Jason Potolis was the commander of the
Iron Fish. Prior to leaving Earth he was a
bomber pilot for the Greecian Airforce. A
strong believer in the Heavenly Father of
Abraham, he eventually left his post for
the opportunity to scour the heavens for a
planet suitable for human life. Long range
scans first suggested 55 Canceri planet d,
but when the flotilla arrived they found
```

limited resources on a dying planet. They restocked their ships, went back into stasis, and kept going until they arrived at Gliese planet g.

In the Gliese system, Jason's beloved wife Gabriella and nearly sixty other women suffered from complications during pregnancy. With their current methods of fertility treatments, multiple births were common. During a vision, Gabriella scanned the stars and pointed to the constellation Vela, where an Earth-like planet was seen orbiting a Sol-twin with a red dwarf companion. Upon her deathbed, she begged her husband to lead the people to a land of rich soil and environmental diversity so that their son may live. She went into labor and pushed out twins—two boys—one living and one dead. She kissed the living child before she handed him to Jason. Then she held and sang to the dead child before she lay back and died.

Computer models confirmed her vision that Kipos was the garden of the Heavens. Jason Potolis wrapped the body of his dead wife and child and sent them into space. He then headed to Kipos with his newborn son.]

"What a load of shit," Abby said aloud. As she scanned the stories about Jason Potolis, she found even the most historic documents were interspersed with legend.

She spent another lazy day doing math to figure out what year it was in the Chinese zodiac. Assuming that the baby was born in the spring, he or she would be a Rabbit.

She tried to remember everything Grandma had taught her. A Rabbit looks for what is beautiful in life. Its calm nature gives it great leadership abilities. On the positive side, he or she is gracious, sensitive, soft-spoken, amiable, imaginative, lucky, and adaptable. On the negative side, he or she might be morose, detached, shallow, self-indulgent, and opportunistic. Stationed on the fourth trine just like Ray's Ram and Orchid's Pig, the baby would always be compassionate.

If she ever found them, she just knew that Ray and Orchid would love their niece or nephew no matter how he or she had been brought into the world. *Stop. Ray is dead. Ma and Da are dead. Only Orchid and Jin are left.*

Orchid will love the child. Abby would have to work on Jin. He would be angry that she was raped and the child had no father. However, he would learn to love his niece or nephew because Abby loved her unborn child.

If she ever found Rory, would he love her child? Abby assured herself. *He will. He has to. Then we can all stay together. We can be safe.*

CHAPTER 19

December 10, 3163 K.E.

ABBY COULD NOT SEE ELI through the fog. The garden kept growing, but Kipos began falling away from its edges. The hedges and rosebushes grew until Abby was in a maze with no way to get out. She had a strong pain in her belly and knew the baby would be coming soon. She tried to remain calm, but it hurt so badly. She called for help, but no one answered.

Finally she began screaming. "Eli! Vivian! Peony!" They came through the hedges staring. Abby realized that the baby had fallen out of her and now hung from the edge of Kipos. It fell. She jumped after it but, coated in wetness and blood, the babe slipped through her fingers.

SHE WOKE UP UNCOMFORTABLE WITH the strong urge to pee. After relieving herself, Abby looked nightmares up in her tablet and was glad to find that many moms reported intense dreams of giving birth to mutants or losing their babies. Of course, mutations were becoming a fairly common occurrence on this planet, but Abby was a young woman.

Abby prayed for her child to be normal. She feared what would happen if it wasn't. She knew she would be sterilized but that didn't frighten her half as much as Eli.

He was the Kyria's man. He had been in Peony's service since the death of her mother when she was five. He could be diabolically clever. If a maid was snotty about the extra tea or hot water with lemon, Eli snapped out a command and a snide remark in Greek that sent the poor woman to tears and scurrying. Even the other guardsmen feared him. Abby always gave him as much courtesy as she could, hoping it would win him over in light of the whining incident.

Every day, Eli gave Abby an hour of his time, whether it was walking in the garden or playing a game of cribbage. He made it perfectly clear that his only concern was the child growing inside her. To that end, he made Abby as comfortable as he was able. If her questions were about flowers, the garden, or nature, he would indulge her. If they were about the household or wanting more of his time, he gave her a menacing look.

She spent time on her knees begging for forgiveness for all of her faults, real or imagined. He called her an ignorant savage or a barbarian. He told her, "Instead of begging for forgiveness, learn to behave." He said her tears did not move him; she would learn penitence after the baby left her body. But he never told her what he planned to do to her.

One day, she was feeling brave and dared to ask him.

His only reply was: "You will see." The not knowing was even more terrifying.

Yet, there were days that Eli showed her consideration. Taggert had pulled out the long needle from his kit. Though she knew the futility of the action, she ran and hid in the bathroom.

Eli tore open the door. "Get out there now."

She was humiliated, her misshapen body naked in front of him. As she approached, she expected a slap, but he did not even scold her for fighting with the doctor. He pulled the chair next to her bed and took her hand. Taggert inserted the long needle through her belly. She winced against the pain. The soft back of Eli's hand touched her forehead. Too soon, he moved it away.

"Now don't worry. I'm only taking about 30 mL," Taggert said. After his collection, he sprayed a bit of stinging solution upon the puncture sight and covered it with a bit of cotton and tape. He told her to relax and drink a nice big glass of water.

Once he was gone, Abby covered her body and waited.

Eli asked, "Did he tell you what he is testing for?"

Abby shook her head.

Eli said, "Chromosome problems, maturity of the baby's lungs, development of the brain and nerves, and infection."

She sniffed. "Why would he think I might give those to my baby?"

"Just because they are doing some tests does not mean anything is wrong. Want me to stay a little longer?"

Abby nodded.

"Finish the water and I'll call for some tea and cookies." He pushed her hair off her forehead.

Abby felt safe. Eli was much too old for her to fall in love with him, but he was strong. He was smart like her Da. Perhaps he could be her second father. She would do what was required of her and he would grow to love her as he did the Kyria. If he loved her, he'd never let anything bad happen to her or her baby.

CHAPTER 20

ABBY GOT BIGGER, HER BACK ached, and she could not seem to straighten because of her belly. The maids rarely spoke to her, but they filled up her bathtub more often and allowed her long soaks. No one rushed her. Instead of socks, they gave her support hose to wear. It felt good on her expanding belly and her sore calves.

She tried to remember her mother pregnant with Orchid. Ma had done dog stretches to help her muscle cramps. Abby wasn't sure if she was doing them right, but rocking her pelvis back and forth while she knelt on all fours felt good.

Taggert came in to her room. "Keep your back a little straighter."

He helped her off the floor and told her to lie in the bed. He did his routine exam and asked her about any symptoms.

Abby said, "I have acid in my throat."

He said, "Nearly all pregnant women can be plagued by heartburn. Your uterus now takes up most of your abdominal cavity; it pushes your stomach upwards. That makes the burn more noticeable. These pills will help with that. I'll have your maid bring you more water."

She was thirsty, but having to urinate so often, she didn't see the point of drinking.

"It is important to drink for the little one. The Kyria's man will have words with you if you disobey me."

"I won't, doctor."

ABBY FELT A CONTRACTION. SHE knew it was early. She crossed her room and told the young guard who was sitting at his post in the hall. The guard called the doctor, pocketed his radio, and picked her up. He gently carried her back to her bed. His face showed his fear too.

Taggert came in. "Where is the pain, child?"

"It seems to hurt here. Right in the front."

The guard began wringing his hands. He did not want to witness the birth, yet he did not leave either. Eli came in with murder in his eyes. She felt another sharp pain in the sudden terror. If she harmed the baby or if it was stillborn, Eli would kill her. She couldn't breathe.

Taggert's hands moved over her body. "Alright, you can sit up now."

He patted her hand, stood up and squeezed the guard's shoulder. "It was actually just a 'practice' contraction. They prep the body for labor. Real ones start in the back and come around to the front, sometimes moving from top to bottom."

Eli sat beside Abby and put his arm around her. His hand was gentle on the back of her head, but he spoke to the guard. "Don't worry. You and the girl did exactly the right thing."

Taggert said, "If you are scared or unsure, you just call me. Doesn't matter what time of day. Now, I'll give you a shot to help you sleep. You just need to relax, miss. You've got a few weeks at least."

He glanced at Eli, "Daily exercise will help both the child and the surrogate and most likely make delivery easier."

Fear danced up her spine at the word "surrogate." Abby wanted to know what that meant, but Eli held her gently. She felt safe under his arm. She wouldn't spoil it.

AS THE WEATHER WARMED AGAIN, Eli walked Abby in the garden, where she began yearning for a single spot. Eli claimed not to mind, as it made his job easier. Far away from the perfect symmetry of the other gardens, flowing behind a rocky cavern into a natural pool, was a little dell. Surrounded by long blades of grass, it was always shaded and green. Stone pavers crossed the pool to a stone bench. It was only when Abby crossed the pavers did she discover small marble statues of nymphs hidden in the water.

Eli told her that Peony had made the statues when she was a teenager. She had once wanted to be an artist, though that was obviously not her fate. Barnett had built the grove for her and her nymphs when they were first married.

Abby replied, "Perhaps, that is why I love it here. Even if my child must learn to govern, I would hope that he or she might also learn to love the arts and his or her spouse."

Eli agreed that those were admirable goals.

However, what Abby truly loved was how quiet it was in the dell. It was a good place for her little Rabbit. She learned from her tablet that lunapar nesting sites were buried deep within the mud. Like her, they awaited the spring.

CHAPTER 21

February 22, 3164 K.E.

THE INTENSE PAIN WAS HARD to ignore. Abby knew she was supposed to start timing her contractions, but she could not focus. Her mind stopped working. When the pain stopped, she tried to distract herself by looking at her tablet, but she could not decide on anything to concentrate on.

The agony started again. It brought her to her knees, as did the feeling that she might be urinating on herself. Her skirt and underwear were wet, but it wasn't the gushing she expected. It was a slow, steady leak. Then bloody mucus. She did not know what that meant.

Hoping her child was alright, she crawled to the door and pushed it open. "I need help! The baby!"

She did not know the middle-aged guard who called for Eli and Taggert, but he refused to accept her hand and was repulsed at the wet gooey mess on the floor and her whimpering shaking body. Abby hated him.

As Eli came down the hall, he was not revolted or afraid. He simply picked her up and set her on her bed as if she weighed nothing at all. He asked her about timing the contractions.

She replied that she couldn't seem to focus upon anything; there was so much pain.

He did it for her.

"Ma hurt when she had Orchid. I'm okay. I'm okay," Abby whispered to herself, clutching her belly.

Taggert did a quick exam and said cheerfully, "You are definitely in labor. Eli, please assist."

She wanted to sock that cheerful look off the doctor's face. She screamed with the next contraction. Taggert gave her an injection as Eli put a mask over her face. She struggled against the mask until she smelled the sweetened air.

Darkness fell over her.

ABBY AWOKE TO: "AS WE thought, she's a girl."

Taggert cleared the baby's nasal passages with a suction bulb, measured and weighed her. The child was wailing as he quickly snipped the umbilical cord. He gave her an injection before applying some drops in her eyes.

"What are you doing?" Abby reached out, but her lower body was still hesitant and rickety.

"The injection contains vitamins. The child's responses are normal. Once I finish you may hold her." Taggert finished cleaning off the child and handed the babe to her. "She needs your antibodies. You may kiss her if you would like."

Taggert shifted a few things around for Abby's comfort as she stared into her child's face and stroked her pink, blotchy cheek. She touched the paper-thin skin surrounding her tiny fingers. She called her "Lei Lei" with a feeling of contentment. This child was hers. Lei needed her. She was her purpose.

Never before had Abby felt such joy for the life of another human being. Her child snorted and made a mewing cry that reminded Abby of a kitten. She leaned down and brushed her baby's brow with her lips.

Eli said, "You may feed her. The colostrum is incredibly beneficial to the child's digestive tract."

Abby opened her gown and exposed her breast to the child, whose mewing stopped as she latched on. She did not care how the child was created, and she swore to herself Lei would never know. All that mattered was Lei was alive, suckling greedily. Abby might have only been a mother for a short while, but she knew that an infant who cried and consumed her mother's milk would survive.

As she nursed, Abby allowed herself to dwell in the all-encompassing primal urge to encircle Lei in the safety of her arms away from the evils of Kipos. She prayed silently to her parents to watch over their granddaughter: protect her, to never allow her to be hurt. Her baby's eyes fluttered opened for a moment and then closed. Lei fell asleep as Abby stroked her fuzzy head listening to her rhythmic breathing.

"You also need to rest," Eli said as he bent down and took the child away from her. Lei began to cry again.

"Maybe she's still hungry," Abby said. She reached out towards her baby. Eli was heading towards the door.

Taggert was suddenly too close. She felt another prick and she fell back into darkness.

Da and Ma smiled upon their first grandchild. They kissed their daughter for bringing forth such a perfect little baby. There was no father's surname to add to Lei as in the case of most children, but Abby knew that her mother would like having her first granddaughter named after her. So would her father.

Grandma rocked her and told her that all her ancestors were watching her.

When Abby awoke, it took all of her strength to stand up. She felt so sore. Her breasts ran with milk and blood ran down her legs. There were smears of filth on the sheets. She was sure she was torn, but she feared looking. The baby was gone. She told herself that they just took the baby to a nursery. Barnett and Peony were wealthy. They must have hired a nurse. They must have.

Abby rang the maid's bell. She was ignored.

BARNETT CAME IN. "HOW ARE you feeling?" he asked. His eyes were no longer dull. He was happy.

She answered with a question of her own. "Where's my baby?"

"My daughter has been given to her mother," he said.

Abby shouted, "I am her mother!"

"You are a surrogate, nothing more," he said. "And you have…"

She slapped him. "I want my baby! She needs me. She's going to starve!"

It didn't even faze him. With one arm he gathered her up and with the other he hit the button embedded in his sleeve. Three men filed into the room. Eli and a younger guard grabbed her and pushed her onto the bed. Colton injected her with a sedative. She screamed, but her voice seemed to die as she fell into blackness. "She's going to starve! Please don't let my baby die."

Striking at Barnett was the wrong thing to do. Listening to the voices speak above her, Abby knew that she would be punished, but she didn't care. What worse pain could they conceive of than taking Lei away from her?

"Are you alright, Kyrios?"

"Fine, Fine."

Colton said, "Must be postpartum depression, I should think. I should have known she would be susceptible. Forgive me, Kyrios. I am at fault. I should have contacted Taggert."

Eli said, "How should we proceed with her, Kyrios?"

Abby heard the menace drip off every word. He was going to hurt her. She wasn't civilized. She had shown herself to be a savage poutana.

Colton said, "The girl obviously does not know about formula. She only thinks to protect the baby. And the engorgement of breasts can have some pain. Please, consider, Kyrios. She is very young."

Barnett answered, "Eli, I do not want her punished, but keep her sedated for a little longer. Allow her hormones to even out. She will serve me no more."

ABBY WAS NOT SURE WHERE wakefulness ended and the dreams began. She might have woken and stumbled to her bathroom. She might not have.

Monsters tried to devour her and Lei. She ran from them, but Lei got too heavy. She could not hang on to her. She had to climb. She hid the baby and tried to fight back, but heavy hands slapped her. Fingernails sliced open her back. The monsters laughed over her. Her breasts ran with milk, but her baby cried, going hungry. She choked on her swollen tongue. Blood burned her from the inside. She ached, but she couldn't defecate.

In the distance she heard a woman screaming. Orchid was screaming her name, but her brothers were calling her a whore. Abby knew the stars were lost to her. She was dead.

It was worse then death. She was alive.

CHAPTER 22

HER BEDDING WAS SOAKED IN blood and urine as if the sheets had not been changed for a few days. Abby stood up and blood ran down her legs.

She did not know the date. She did not know if she really had a baby. She hurried into the bathroom to wash off, but the blood was thick and unending. Her hands trembled. Tiny stretch marks lined her stomach. Scratches were across her back and a heavy bruise on her shoulder. Her bottom had three open sores. She climbed into the tub and made the water hot, but she could not sit in it for long.

Finally, the first sun rose over the frost-covered garden.

Vivian brought her a breakfast of toast and tea. "You may go outside without an escort now. This room needs a good scrubbing."

ABBY SKULKED AROUND THE GARDEN waiting. Her heart missed her baby. No one told her what to do or that she must go inside. The only men in the garden were pruning and picking up leaves. She walked down to the little dell and looked at the water nymphs. They seemed to be laughing at her.

She was a fool. She should have realized that they were not going to allow her to raise her child. Abby considered drowning herself, but the pool was too shallow and cold to stay in long. She thought she might jump, but feared that nowhere was high enough. She might live on, broken.

Only when the suns began to set did she go back into her room. A supper that had grown cold awaited and her nightgown was laid out on the bed.

Listening for a baby's cry, Abby tried to sleep, but neither came. It occurred to her that she might be unguarded. She stood up and went to her door. The hallway was empty. With bare feet, she padded down the hall. Breathing, music, and sounds of passion came from other rooms. She was in the servants' hallway.

No wonder everyone hated her. Barnett made them serve her as if she was part of his family when she was obviously not. Abby crawled back into bed and lay awake.

Her entire life she had been obedient and cautious, a good girl like her mother had taught her to be. Barnett and Peony knew what they were getting by her test scores. She was no longer needed, but she knew there was a chance that Barnett would start looking to have a son.

Another rape, another child she would never see. Abby closed her eyes, aware that no matter what the consequence, she had to leave.

Abby went into the bathroom and started a bath. She washed herself as well as she could through her stinging sores. She put on a bra, a fresh chemise and underwear with the thick cotton pad to catch the lochia. She did not have pants, so she put on the woolen skirt and blouse and a thin sweater. She wished there was something warmer, but it was what she had. She touched the tablet one last time. It was not hers. She was no thief. Besides, it might be a way to track her.

As the first sun rose, Abby went out into the garden. Icy dew soaked her feet. She had to leave before the rest of the house was awake, but she found herself staring at the windows, wondering which one held Lei.

As the second sun rose, Abby saw Barnett, Peony, and the old men eating breakfast on their private patio. Lei was nearby in a cradle. They were not paying attention to her. Perhaps? She could not turn her eyes away as she heard Lei cry.

Peony immediately picked the baby up and soothed her. She sang a little poem as she fed her with a bottle. Eli came beside his Kyria and looked at his new charge. He made gentle clucking noises and stroked her tiny cheek.

Though Abby ached to climb the wall and take back her baby, she knew the futility of it. Her heart scorched, she stepped to the edge of the bladed field. She glanced back. Up on the terrace, she could see Barnett's back to her. She looked forward again. The long, slender, bladed plants ended in a large head with fifty spines. Abby knew that she must walk slowly or the sharp blades would slice into her bare legs. She looked back once more. She was alone.

"Forgive me, Lei." Wiping away a tear, she took a step. No one was following her. She repeated, "Forgive me, Lei. If I can save you, I will."

Though the words gave her strength, Abby knew that she would not be saving anyone. Her daughter would be cared for and educated, even loved. Each slow step was another step away, but she could not turn back now.

Ten minutes later, Abby had made it through the sharp field. On the other side, a black asphalt road led towards the town center. The road was empty except for one man walking briskly. His black robes did not drag but swished playfully above the dusty concrete with each step. Abby felt his presence as he came closer. Contrasting with his lively flowing garment, his face was transfixed in a scowl. Without speaking a word, the man whispered, "Move, slut."

He wasn't truly calling her a slut, of course. He knew nothing about her. However Abby was sure he felt she showed too much skin; her face and hair were uncovered, as were her forearms and hands. He was Kyn. Like all Kyn, he wore all black from head to toe, trimmed with subtle gold threads to show his status, but his brown face showed his true soul. He was a sour man who wanted the planet changed according to his own viewpoints.

She hoped his kind had not adopted her sister or bought her bond, but she truly had no idea. She could not just knock on each door and ask if they knew Orchid Boyd Lei. As she glanced behind her, she wondered if Orchid was growing up to be a free woman or a slave.

Abby thought her life could have been much worse. Peony had been overwhelmingly kind to her. Barnett had been purposefully distant. They had allowed her to leave. She knew that now. If a man such as the Kyn had bought her bond, Abby would have never seen the sunlight again. It would have ended badly. It still might if she ran into the wrong type of person.

She had to get off this planet. She knew she could not go back to Earth, but perhaps there was somewhere else. Argent? Selene?

Abby glanced back once more. No one was behind her. It began to drizzle. Dry dust went into the air and mud puddles formed. Abby felt the rain soak into her clothing and turn her hair in to a heavy black mop.

She tried to remember what the speedway was called, but she could not. As she wandered towards a shopping district, she heard a siren coming. Strange. She was ninety-four light years from home and yet the sound of the white van with flashing lights sounded the same as it had on Earth. She turned down a residential street.

As she wandered further, she found another odd and disappointingly Earth-like quality to the Kiposi. Their homes were new, but built in the style of the twenty-first to the twenty-third century: two or three story dwellings spread a hectare or so apart. They were painted in various colors; most also had gnomes or cement sundials in front. They all had a few automobiles, but none as nice as Colton's.

A man called out to her, "Hey miss, need a lift?"

Abby hesitated. He might be kind or he might not. He was a Kiposi.

"No, I'm almost home," she called back, "My father would kill me if I got in with someone I don't know."

"Okay, take care!" The man drove off.

As the rain continued, puddles formed. Obscured by slick, greenish gold spiral of pollen, Abby tripped into one, soaking her socks and leaving muddy trails up her calves. She took shelter under an overpass and tried to get her bearings. She felt so dizzy. She puked into the nearest bush and looked around for a hidden spot to urinate.

There was still so much blood.

THE SKY WAS BLUE YET glazed with red clouds and a pink sliver of Selene, but Abby did not see the beauty. Dusk was falling. She was already wet and getting colder. She followed the buzz of solar streetlamps while trying to come up with some sort of logical way off the planet.

Abby found a covered train stop. The metal bench was cold, but the weight was off her feet for a moment. She slipped her shoes off and stretched her toes. Glancing up at the acrylic sign on the wall, she read it was a half credit for a ticket downtown. She had no way to pay. It was stupid for her to keep sitting there. She had to keep moving. Her eyelids ached, but she could not be caught sleeping. There were no homeless on Kipos.

Her hands were warm from walking, though her forearms were chilled. Her socks were cold and wet. Her slippers were filled with water. She puked again.

Abby tried to go into a little grocery, but she noticed the hovering bots. People paid by laying their thumbs on a screen. A man called out a "hello" and waved towards her. She hurried out.

As it grew darker, the clouds got thicker. She could not see the stars. The friendly constellations that Grandma had taught her would not be up there anyway. Exhausted, Abby did not know where she was going, only that she must walk.

Her mind wandered to prayer. *Da? Are you there? Ma? I need you.* She felt nothing. "For nine months, they never answered a single prayer," Abby whispered to herself. "The ghosts of my ancestors can't find me on Kipos."

Lost in another residential neighborhood, she saw a spaceship break through the atmosphere. *The aerospace port must be somewhere nearby!* She had been heading in the correct direction.

Abby walked for hours until she heard the beeps and clanks of machinery. A caravan of trucks, assumingly filled with bread from the painted side, exited the aerospaceport.

She shadowed a hedge and hurried towards the ships.

As she circled, Abby saw the jet planes for journeys between the cities of Kipos. She had no idea how to approach the flight crew when she had no money for a ticket. She saw the government-funded transports: sleek and white, similar to the kind that had brought her to Kipos. There was no way she could sneak aboard. If she hid somewhere not pressurized, she would die frozen and gasping. She would be burned alive if she were found; she remembered the screaming boys covered in blue flame. She tried to shake the memory from her head.

With the hope that no one would question her, she held her head high, kept walking, and pretended she did not feel like vomiting. Beyond there were privately held spaceships for both long and short-range space travel. Figuring this was her best bet, she hurried towards them.

The first ship was a large transport ship with a Kiposi crew joking about somewhere called Lathos. She did not see any women among them. The second ship also had a Kiposi crew. The third seemed to be deserted.

At the forth ship; three men were busy working a loader and quarreling about something. Abby watched them for a few minutes. Tall and long legged, they seemed to shimmer slightly opalescent olive green when the red sun hit them. She tried to remember what the tablet said about the hybrid races; these must be the Khlôrosans, explorers who could take extreme G-forces upon their bodies.

CHAPTER 23

March 24, 3164 K.E.

THE MEN COMPLAINED ABOUT BEING shorthanded. Abby tried to listen, but there seemed to be a thousand explicative's mixed in with their complaints and only half of them were in English. They wanted to take on a friend from a different ship, but it might not get there in time for the harvest. Another issue was something about needing a different environmental suit. Someone named Diane could alter an existing one.

Diane was a woman's name!

The youngest said, "Who's going to go?"

"I will."

Abby identified the female by the high melodious voice. She wondered how she had not noticed the slight femininity in her stance and the hint of breasts under her coveralls. There were no lines on her countenance, but she was not a young woman.

Abby glanced at the hull. Though there were rust spots and pieces of patched polymers, the ship was obviously well loved. Her name was *Revelation*. She watched the Khlôrosans a few more minutes; they were almost finished with loading the crates on the ship.

Seeing a chance that was quickly disappearing, Abby took a deep breath and compelled herself to ignore her nausea. She looked down at her hands and saw that they trembled. She forced them to stop. Then she stood up, smoothed her skirt, and spoke in her best Kiposi English. "Excuse me?"

The three turned to her. Not knowing what else to say, she said, "I heard you were looking for another hand?"

The elder man said, "Where did you hear that?"

She picked the first name that popped in her head. "Eli."

"Eli who?" the man asked.

Abby was not able to come up with a lie fast enough, before the woman raised her hand to stop her.

The woman's voice and golden eyes were filled with kindness and warmth. "So you want to go to Lathos. What would you do there?"

"I can work. I learn dialects pretty easily." She could see by their faces that she needed to shut up before they realized how stupid she was. She had no idea where Lathos was or if there was a colony. She went for it: "I was on Earth a year ago—not really a year. A year to me." That didn't sound much smarter.

The woman pointed at the scar on her throat. "So you're indentured."

"I was given…"

They snorted.

Abby went on, "…to a man to make a child. He took my daughter away from me at birth. He no longer has use for me."

"Will he look for you?"

"I doubt it."

"But you don't know." The elder man's golden eyes flashed as he glanced over at the other two. He did not want this problem.

The younger man said softly, "We can't just let her go. She'll be killed."

The female's eyes filled with rage, but not towards Abby. She said, "Job's labor-intensive. In four days, we leave for a relative time ten-day stint. We need someone to gather mateodeas."

"What are they?" Abby looked up at the statuesque woman.

"Large insects with a fifteen centimeter wingspan. Afraid of bugs?"

Abby shook her head. There were many more things to fear. "My name is Abigail Boyd Lei. On Earth, I was an assistant librarian. I'm not afraid of hard work."

The elder man sighed and shook his head at the woman. "Harden's going to be pissed."

Abby clinched her hands behind her back. She knew her eyes were dry, but she felt like crying. This wasn't going to work. She was an ignorant, savage poutana and the Khlôrosans knew it.

The woman said softly, "I'm Helen Tolis Alekos – executive officer." She gestured towards the elder man, "My husband Brian – ship's mechanic." Then she motioned towards the younger man, "My brother Mark –

medical doctor and biologist. Get inside before someone sees you.

"Mark, go make sure she's healthy."

ABBY SMELLED THE SAME OILINESS that she had aboard the *Vos*, yet this ship was not sterile or white. Gray metal pipes ran above her. Old blue paint was chipped off the corners though things were clean. Afraid, she glanced back at the open double doors. Helen and Brian were arguing. She wasn't sure if she could do this. She pushed down the queasiness in her stomach; she could not give them a reason to change their minds.

Mark's hands were gentle on her shoulders. "This way to the infirmary."

Just by the warmth of his hand, Abby felt strangely giddy. It had been so long since anyone had touched her with kindness. Mark probably wasn't that much older than her, just old enough to be a ship's doctor. In the cargo hold's light, his skin no longer looked shiny olive, but warm, opalescent tan. He was one of the most beautiful men she had ever seen.

Alekos. Why does that sound familiar? Abby thought.

Inside the polymer walls of the infirmary, she noticed a large wall covered in three-decimeter square drawers with lights registering which were filled and which were not. Abby could not guess what they held, but she absentmindedly touched one that gleamed "occupied."

She said nothing as Mark pressed his fingertips to the back of her wrist and counted. In less then a second, he said, "Your skin feels a bit clammy, but pulse seems strong. When did you give birth?"

"Don't know. I was sedated most of the time."

He frowned. "Disrobe please."

Abby took a step back from him and shook her head. It took all her will to push down the vomit rising in her throat.

He leaned over a console and pressed a touch pad. "Helen or Diane, come in here please?" He then bent down, unlatched a door, pulled out a sheet and set in on the table. "We'll wait. It's okay, Abby. Hippocrates haunts bad doctors."

Helen and another Khlôrosan man entered the room. His eyes were full of simmering rage as he looked directly at her. Abby pressed herself against the wall.

Mark said, "I need to examine her completely. I have a feeling she hasn't seen real medical care for awhile."

Abby whimpered, "But there was a doctor..."

The man opened his mouth, but it was Helen who spoke first. "For you or the baby? Do as Mark tells you." Her tone was kind, but it was an order with the unspoken connotation: obey or get out.

The angry man said to Helen, "She better not be a fucking junkie with a sob story," and left.

Tears leaked from her eyes as Abby pulled off her clothing and tried to cover her body with her hair and her hands. Now that the pad was removed, she felt the blood flow again. Helen patted the examination table and helped her on to it as she asked, "Alright, hon. How old are you?"

As Helen placed the sheet over her, Abby realized she had no idea. "I was almost eighteen when I left Earth... Other than having the baby, I don't know how much time has passed. I guess I'm at least nineteen. Maybe even twenty?"

"My understanding is that they used a space elevator to the ship and put you in immediate stasis, correct?" Helen asked.

"Yes."

"Birthdate?"

Abby told her and the computer began to work out the calculation. Helen said, "We'll see what the computer says, but my guess is you're probably still eighteen."

Mark quickly ran his fingers across her body, looking for injuries. "Those are some pretty nasty blisters. How far did you walk?"

"I don't know distance, but since yesterday morning."

"Look at this, Helly." Mark frowned and pointed at the obvious track marks on her arms. He turned on his diagnostic computer and noted a few half scabbed sores on her backside, bedsores likely.

A scan moved over her hands and digits. He found a microchip under her skin. "We need to take that out. They use it to track you."

Panic crept up in Abby's throat, but neither seemed angry nor surprised by its presence.

Mark said, "Broken thumb?"

"Yeah. When I was five, my little brother slammcd it in a washroom door."

"Birth order and number of siblings?"

"I'm the first of five."

"Did they all come to Kipos?"

"No. Ray the second oldest stayed behind and Joe was third, but he passed when he was two," she said. "Jin was fourth and the fifth Orchid came. I don't know what happened to them. When we arrived on Kipos, I was separated from Orchid, but was told an eleven-year-old girl would be adopted. Never saw Jin at all. He was fifteen."

Helen and Mark glanced at each other. "There are many sterile families who would have loved a young girl. Jin is old enough to be taught a trade or sent to school if he had the mind for it."

Abby saw there was something they would not say. Peony had not told her either. There was a hidden future, a fate worse than death that she had been denied only because Barnett wanted a broodmare, not a bed-slave. She needed to rescue Jin, but she had no idea where he was. The nine months she should have spent figuring things out, she had done nothing in mind-sapping luxury. "Our neighbor, Rory, came too. He was twenty. Do you think..?"

"I'm sorry, hon, but most likely yes," Helen said softly.

"H-he worked in my commune's garden. Do you think there was a chance maybe he was sent to a farm? He'd probably like that kind of work."

"Maybe, but there's no way we really can know," Helen paused, "But if you stayed on Kipos, what would you do about it? Do you have any idea how to find him?"

Abby shook her head in disappointment.

The three were silent for a while, except for the occasional beeps of Mark's scanner. Abby pointed to the white cylinder, "What is that?"

"It uses sound waves to show me the inside of your body." He moved it over her throat and turned the screen to her.

She looked at the perfectly clear view of a reddish tube with pinkish and even a few white streaks. "Dr. Taggert used something like that on me, but I never got to look inside."

"Esophagus looks a little raw. Vomiting in the past twenty-four hours?"

"Yes."

"Profuse sweating?"

"Maybe. I was walking a lot."

"Heart, lungs, kidneys – all look normal. Lower digestive system looks fine – looks like you haven't eaten since yesterday. Tell us about the father of your child?"

"I guess Barnett was in his early-thirties. He didn't say much about himself."

"Did he ever mistreat you?" Mark asked. He was looking directly at the deep bruise on her shoulder.

Abby shrugged. "He wanted a baby…"

They asked her to elaborate and Abby told them about her day-to-day activities.

Helen asked, "How did he inseminate you?"

Abby didn't know the word, but understood the question. "He took me five times. I was given an injection to make me... compliant."

Mark said, "Get dressed, Abby. Are you sure that this Barnett only took you those five times?"

Abby nodded and saw Mark and Helen share another look. They gave her a pad of bandages to catch the lochia as she pulled on the coveralls that Helen had handed to her. The clothing fit around the body, but Abby had to roll up the cuffs on both the sleeves and the legs.

Mark's voice was professional, yet held a note of falsehood. "There's some tearing. Perhaps, you had a difficult delivery and are still healing."

He opened a drawer, pulled out a bottle, and removed the cap. He measured out a foul smelling liquid. "I want you to take this."

Abby asked, "What is it?"

"Nano-contraceptive, but it has a secondary use of balancing hormones and healing tearing after a pregnancy, which is why I am giving it to you. Once you eat, I'm going to give you a round of antibiotics just to be safe."

Abby knew Mark was not telling her the whole truth. Still, she had no choice in the matter. She took a sip. She wanted to vomit. She tilted her head back and forced the rest down.

Helen handed her a cup of water. "We know how bad it tastes."

Mark set up a table beside the examination bed and positioned Abby's hand. Helen loaded a pressurized syringe, handed it to Mark and sprayed a cold liquid on Abby's skin.

He gave Abby the injection, then sliced open the flesh. She could not turn away from the spilled blood, her deep wound with torn muscles split open. It took less than a minute to remove the microchip, cauterize the wound, and knit the flesh back together. It left a tiny scar, but there was no pain. Her hand worked as well as it ever had. Abby found it all fascinating.

Helen crossed the room and opened the drawer. She pulled out a small bottle and smeared some cream on the microchip. It began to dissolve. As she turned around, she said, "Port three." She touched the intercom, "I'll be up in two minutes."

ABBY FOLLOWED MARK UP THE stairs to the upper decks. He pulled her silently past the second deck and to the third and utmost deck. They moved down a tight corridor, passing a dozen billet hatchways to the galley. Just beyond, Abby could see the empty bridge. Mark warmed up some broth and made a piece of toast for her. The idea of eating anything made her stomach turn, but she ate anyway. Afterwards, she was told to drink another glass of water and take a pill. He took her temperature once more.

Her billet was the third hatch on what Abby supposed was the port side. Mark gestured her down the ladder into a black hole. She looked up at him; she did not want to climb into the darkness. Visibly irritated, he climbed down first. The light automatically turned on when he touched the first step on the ladder.

Her quarters were clean, though they had the distinct smell of not having been in use for some time. The walls were gray. Abby guessed that it might be the original paint color. A built-in bunk with drawers underneath took up most of the floor space.

Mark opened a drawer and pulled a set of white threadbare sheets and a felted wool blanket. He showed her the built-in foldout table, chair, and two padded doors that led to a small empty closet. He showed her how to use the dimmer switch and light the clock. "The head is through that door," he said. "Get some sleep."

FIGHTING EXHAUSTION AND AGITATION, ABBY walked inside the head. The mirror was glass, but everything else—toilet, sink, shower—was a shiny white polymer. The toilet seat was not cold, but the toilet paper was rough against her tender flesh. She noticed a washer/dryer embedded in the wall. As soon as she stood, the toilet sensed her use, flushed, and spiraling disks began to clean. There was still so much blood.

From the head, another door led to someone else's quarters. The floor plan was identical to her own except the walls had been painted a soft pink, with green moths, or a similar flying insect, painted around the doors, and there was a deep rose quilt on the bed. Abby saw a few personal effects scattered about, including a few photos of an elderly couple and a teen-aged boy. She did not tarry.

Walking back to her own side, she wished for something of hers so the room didn't feel so lonely. She didn't have her old clothes, or even a photo to remind her of her old life. Wrongness lingered and fear rotted inside her stomach. Suddenly she realized she did not know if she could trust these people. *What'll happen if I fall asleep?*

Sweat began to trickle down her back as she paced the two meters of floor space, trying to figure out what to do next. She could try to find another ship. She could go back to Barnett and Peony. She didn't think Barnett would take her off planet and throw her out of an airlock. He didn't seem the type. Of course, he could just pay one of his men to do it. She shivered as she remembered that Mark had seen bruising and tried not to think of stories from the ancient times when kings threw unwanted women to their men. Her stomach revolted in terror that the monsters of her nightmares might have been real. Though vomit began pulsing back up her throat, she refused to be sick.

She heard a low hum. Curious, she opened the hatch from her quarters. A giant robotic arm polished the floor. Behind it, tiny disks moved across it and picked up the leftover polish.

She lowered herself, trying to keep her balance, but Abby was falling before she realized her legs had turned into hot tar. She reached over to pull the blanket off the bunk and wrapped herself in it. Crawling, unsure if she could stand, she forced the vomit back until she was in front of the toilet.

Coated in sweat, she puked. In the distance, she heard a plaintive cry that might have been a baby or a cat.

Intermission
The Discovery
The Canceri System: March 26, 3164

COLE PICKED AT THE LEFTOVER chicken. Saul was a great executive officer and the best friend a man could have. He never let the crew slack, and whenever Cole needed an ear or someone just to finish off a chicken, Saul was beside him. He knew they'd both pay with heartburn for eating this late, but Helen's last call had kept him up.

Harden had gone planetside for a planned engine upgrade and a test flight to Lathos. Due to their current project, he and Helen ran their ship's budget tighter than Cole preferred but they planned on picking up a little extra cash during the mateodeas harvest. However, what was truly bothering him was Helen's description of how strange Kipos had gotten.

Generations of customs agents that the family knew had become distant. They were overworked and burdened by the influx of Earthlings, especially the bonded men who tried to escape working in the mines of Argent or tried to run into the wilds. Knowing that not all the Earthlings had been placed, Helen and Brian had briefly looked into adopting an Earth child, but were told by the Bond and Adoption Department fleet lifestyle did not allow for assimilation on Kipos. She did not wail or nurse a grudge, but there was agony in her golden eyes when she told Cole their last chance at a child had failed.

Even if they found a planet tomorrow, at thirty-five, Helen knew a complete reversal of her tubal ligation was unlikely. Fleet work, especially on an explorer class ship, was dangerous; it used to be that there were plenty of orphans that needed minding. Not anymore. The Flotilla held on to their children tightly.

The Kiposi's population problems had spiraled to the fleet. Young Kiposi stopped coming for the educational benefits and experience. They didn't want to risk their lives in space when it could no longer guarantee a good job planetside.

Cole saw the incoming message from the New Alexandria Areospace Port. Knowing it was too early for the flight plan, he assumed it was Helen. He smiled at Saul and went inside his office to take the call. When his elder son's face popped up on the terminal, he was pleasantly surprised, though he immediately assumed that it was a sign of an unpleasant situation. Hopefully, the problem wouldn't be too expensive to fix.

"Dad..." Harden's gold eyes looked distant and his complexion was pale.

"Is it Helly? Mark?"

Harden sighed. "They're fine. Hel solved our personnel problem with another."

A tightness wrapped around Cole's heart. Harden generally spoke as straightforward and to the point as possible, but his words were being purposely ambiguous. This was bad. "I'm in my office. Where are you?"

"In the Burgersmith. No one's around."

So Harden was using a terminal from outside the aerospace port. *Shit, what has Helen done? A terrifying thought crossed his brain, No, she couldn't have wanted a child so badly ...* Outwardly Cole tried to remain calm and asked, "And what do you need?"

"A fleet account and work permit. I'll set up my part before we leave," Harden said. "Helen said Lathos would be pretty hard to screw up, even for an intern, and I have to agree."

Shit! Shit! Shit! "You never learned to say no to your XO. You're the fucking captain. Start acting like it," Cole snapped.

"Why did I fucking call you?"

It wasn't a question. It was an old argument threatening to rise up. It irked Cole to no end that Harden was the boss only on paper, but there was no time for this now. His kids were in danger.

Cole exhaled slowly. "I guess, eventually, you would need a better puzzle than a crossword?"

"Yeah... and Mark keeps us too healthy," Harden said.

"How bad?" Cole tried to push down the thought: *Helen needs someone to mother.*

"We know only one fact: she gave birth. Everything else she doesn't remember or has decided to forget. Mark has a horrible theory that Helen agrees with."

"Which is?"

Harden glanced behind him and lowered his voice. "The girl said she was given to a man to make a child. Helen is pretty sure that part is true, but once she bore the child, he..." Harden spoke as if he feared the very words would scald him. His normally steady hands trembled. "Her wounds suggest..."

He paused to regain control. "So, maybe, this guy passed her along to someone who decided to play rough with her; maybe a few men. She's covered in scratches. One bit her hard enough that Mark was able to get an impression from the teeth marks.

"The biggest issue is she's detoxing from an unknown sedative. Mark is pretty sure she wouldn't have lived much longer without medical intervention."

Harden's hands had formed into fists. "She found her way to the ship. She had blisters on her feet and hadn't eaten for a day or two. Heard we were hiring. She tried to hide the symptoms of withdrawal. Asked Helen for a fucking job. The kid's tough. I'll give her that. They couldn't..."

Cole nodded. He knew his kids. Mark would claim his Hippocratic oath compelled him to help her. Helen couldn't have come across a wounded girl and not tried to help. Even Harden, Brian and Diane would agree that they could not send this girl to her death and still look at each other as moral men and women. The *Revelation's* crew would keep the secret. Besides, since the dissolution of his second marriage, Harden was having a hard time staffing his ship with qualified biologists, or at least someone they could train to go planetside. They did need an extra hand.

Cole scratched his chin and leaned back in his chair. Hoping his son would understand, he asked, "So *where* did you pick her up?"

Harden did not hesitate, but he never did lie very well. "The *Vos*. Remember Donna Lee?"

"Friend of Helly's. Junior Engineer, right?"

Harden nodded.

"Terribly sad that Donna died in that recent explosion. You know, your mom once told me that clever kids always want more than just a transport. I guess that holds true in every century." He added, "You have the photo and fingerprints?"

The files came encrypted.

Cole waited for the key. When the computer matched it and loaded the image, Cole gasped at the dark circles under her eyes and the hollow look in the girl's cheeks. "She's really just a kid."

Cole scanned the documentation; he immediately saw a few things missing from Mark's recorded dictation during the medical exam, specifically the given names of who she escaped from. Harden had most likely figured out who it was. There were only two logical reasons to hide those names. Either it was someone Harden did not want to incriminate or someone that was so powerful he could be a danger to the *Revelation*. His eldest was not a great captain by any means, but he would always do what was necessary to protect the ship and crew—even from Cole and the rest of the fleet. If he thought they would get caught, he wouldn't do it.

Cole said, "I'll have this done for you in two hours."

Though he knew it was a mistake, he provided Abigail Lee with a work permit and bank account.

PART 4
THE REVELATION

CHAPTER 24

Kipos: March 28, 3164 K.E.

MONSTERS BURNED INSIDE HER FLESH and cruel fingers bruised her shoulders. She had thought she had escaped, but she realized she never would. The air was wrong. When the blackness dissipated, Abby found herself with her father. Something was off. The blankets surrounding her were softer than anything she had had on Earth. She remembered lying down in coveralls, but now she was naked except for underwear.

She whispered, "Da, I did something terrible! I lost Orchid, Jin, and my baby. I named her Lei. I know Mama would be so happy. Monsters ate me. Monsters keep coming back. I-I lost her. I'm so sorry. I just left her there. I even lost my friends in the stars."

Da just looked faded somehow. Like he was in a mist. "Wake up."

"I left her. Please don't hate me. I'm so sorry."

Her father's voice changed. It grew slightly higher and the tone was wrong. "Come on, kiddo, you need to wake up." A calloused hand was rubbing her back, but the fingers were too long and thin to be Da's.

Peeling her dry eyes open, Abby didn't know how she got into the bed she was in, but was pretty sure it wasn't hers. Covering her was a blue quilt with some sort of blue bird with long legs and a long beak in the design. Surrounding the bird were three levels of lighter blue and white diamonds intertwined with chains. As she looked beyond, there was soft lighting and the metal walls had been painted blue. The overall effect was feminine, but a man sat beside the bed. She jerked back and pulled the quilt over her naked shoulders while she tried to squash down the need for her father's presence.

The Khlôrosan pressed a hand to her forehead. "You seem cooler," he said and handed her a cup of water. Not knowing what else to do, she accepted it and took a sip. Her raw throat burned and a splitting headache seared the left side of her brain as she sat up.

The man was tall and long limbed, as were all Khlôrosans. He had no gray in his black hair, but there were slight crinkles around his golden eyes and his shoulders sloped from habitually slouching. Tiny scars lined his wrists and his tan, opalescent skin was calloused and seemed raw at the knuckles. He handed her a t-shirt—most likely his by the size of it. She slipped it over her head; its sleeves went down to her elbows.

I have become a whore. No wonder my ancestors didn't answer my prayers! I've made a child outside of marriage and now I'm an old man's whore! Please, Please! I don't want to be bound to him. He's an old man! With the thought she might have been sold again, Abby burst in to tears.

The Khlôrosan clapped a hand over her mouth and pressed her against the padded door of the closet. His voice was low and dangerous. "Shut up. I'm going to tell you this once: I don't fuck teenaged girls. Nor would anyone in my crew. We've men aboard rechecking the fusion-engine. If caught with a runaway, I'd lose my ship and licenses. Maybe go to jail.

"I'm going to take my hand away. You calm?"

Abby nodded. A mixture of tears, snot, and spit stretched away from her face. He muttered something under his breath as he pulled out a hand-kerchief and wiped off his hand before handing it to her. She blew her nose.

He turned and hit the panel on the wall, "Mark? Hurry up."

Another man's voice said, "Okay, be there in a few."

A glimmer of a memory popped in Abby's head. "Mark. Mark is Helen's brother...and a doctor?"

"My brother too. If you can keep something down, then you can still have a job. If not, I'll get you a little money. Whatever they gave you, it fucked you up pretty good, kiddo."

Kiddo? The hope that she had not shamed herself flittered into her stomach. Abby asked, "What's your name?"

"Harden Alekos. I guess you don't remember the past few days, but we've been introduced, twice now," he said with marked irritation.

"Alekos? Like the Alekos engine?"

"Yeah. You know it?"

"Not that much, I just read about it once." Abby whispered, "Harden, Helen, Brian, Mark, and Diane?" She looked up at him, "Diane? Is she your wife?"

"No. She's the engineer of this ship," he said.

"Do you have a wife?"

"I've had two, but no, not presently."

"Oh, sorry," Abby mumbled.

"No need to apologize. Both were years ago." He muttered something half in Greek and half in English. Abby didn't need to comprehend it all to understand. He was a good enough man not to dump a sick woman onto the street, but she was a serious liability. She needed to get up and show her worth before he changed his mind about keeping her.

"What's my job supposed to be?" she asked.

He handed her a well-used tablet. "This has been loaded with all the pertinent information for you to read when you feel up to it."

Overhead, she heard someone walking. She shivered. A runaway slave. She had no rights. Fear wound in her chest, but she didn't dare cry.

"Hi. Remember me?" Mark climbed down into her room. Once his feet were on the deck, he reached back through the hatchway to bring down a tray holding soup and toast.

Behind him, a massive gray and white spotted cat jumped in. "That's Rockford. He's particular to Diane, but has the run of the ship. He's been interested in meeting you."

Harden unfolded the table over her bed and Mark set down the soup. Rockford jumped into Abby's lap and purred as he rolled over on his back. She scratched his belly. His paws encircled her wrist as he nuzzled her.

Mark looked up at his brother. "See she has Rock's seal of approval."

Harden did not seem impressed. Rockford settled himself in a tight ball, purring on her pillow.

"So, how are you feeling?" Mark asked as he took her pulse from her neck.

"I guess better." Abby added, "Lost. Is this my room?"

"Yep," Mark said.

"It's a billet," Harden said.

Abby knew she should try harder to keep the sass out of her voice. "My billet was gray, wasn't it?"

Mark glanced up at his brother. "And you were worried she had brain damage."

Harden shrugged. "Still worried."

Abby asked, "You did all this when I was asleep?"

"We had extra blue paint," Harden said, "Once you puked all over the deck, it wasn't any problem to have the disks do the painting after they cleaned. So we tried to make a girl's billet. Diane and Helen made the quilt a while back. They're always working on something."

"It's beautiful," Abby said, "but I thought Kipos didn't have birds."

"They don't, but we've seen thousands of avian species on other planets. Now eat your lunch, mind Mark, and keep to your billet." With that, Harden climbed out of the hatchway.

Mark opened her closet door. A stack of coveralls, her old clothes, and a small mesh bag filled with personal items were inside. "Diane altered these to fit. These should hold you over until we get back. Helen got you a brush, comb, toothbrush, toothpaste, floss, soap, and some washable menstrual pads. Don't worry. We're not really afraid of brain damage. However, I'm still afraid of toxic shock syndrome."

Abby blushed. A man was talking about her personal needs.

"Your wounds had gone septic and I had to induce a fever to kill the bacteria," he said. "The nanos… please, tell me that you did not already forget that I'm a doctor?" he said.

She blushed deeper and shook her head. Mark explained the rest of the healing regimen: nanomites to heal a fistula, antibiotics and an antacid to coat her stomach. "I have to be honest, I've never had a Homo sapien patient, nor could I discover the exact substance in your bloodstream since I had no baseline comparison of your body chemistry. I only could treat the symptoms and watch to make sure you did not aspirate in your vomit."

"Did I say anything weird when I was out of it?"

"Weird, not really. You cried to your parents and begged forgiveness a lot, which is probably common in a person who has gone through a trauma like yours. Losing your daughter as well as your siblings is so terrible…I don't really know how to offer you comfort." As Mark reached up the back of her shirt to check her breathing, she felt her heart quicken. She took a deep breath.

Grow up! You're acting like a stupid girl with a crush.

She focused on the exam. Yet she could not deny Mark was too beautiful to be called merely handsome. Unlike his brother, who seemed faded into middle age, or his sister, who was too slender to be called a true beauty, Mark's body held the strength and musculature of youth. His eyes were more green than golden and his short black hair curled ever so slightly. Each time he turned, the slight iridescence of his embedded microscales caught the light. Abby hated that she wanted to lay back and allow him to enter her gently as he kissed her face. If he would stay there for a while, she would feel complete. Or if there could not be sex, she craved to snuggle up to his chest and fall asleep safe in his arms.

Yet their conversation was as official as any doctor and patient. She asked a few questions about her injuries, and he told her what he knew as fact, which wasn't much except that she seemed to be responding to treatment. She feared telling him about the monsters she saw when she closed her eyes, so she did not.

Finally he said, "I want you to try to eat a little more. Rocks will keep you company. Doubt I could move him now anyway." He scratched the purring ball once more and left.

ABBY TRIED TO LOOK AT the documents in her tablet, but her eyes kept filling with tears. If only she knew that Orchid and Jin were safe with kind-hearted adoptive parents. She typed in Jin Boyd Lei, but received a message that her tablet was not connected to the Feed.

She hissed inwardly, "Abby, you've been acting like an idiot all day. Stop it!" She took a deep breath, pushed down her fear and focused on the information.

The dossier described Lathos, the insects, as well as the mission objectives. Lathos was a tidal locked desert planet around Kokadelfi with 83% gravity and air pressure of Kipos. With small polar ice caps as well as liquid water, Lathos was originally considered a livable planet. However, living in perpetual light or darkness was not an acceptable option for most humans. Now it was uninhabited by humans except during the harvest.

Only seven thousand distinct species had been found on the sun-facing side, mostly waterborne arthropods. Mateodeas were nearly fifteen centimeters long and had a wingspan of twenty-five centimeters. The insects were not poisonous, but possessed a lung-irritating, foul-smelling sulfur and oxygen anal spray as a defense. This spray's antibacterial qualities made it useful in medicines. They spent most of their life in the deep water of their nesting holes. Every five years, as Kokadelfi and Ilios orbits came nearer to each other, the mateodeas would fill the sky for a week or so. The goal was to catch them and freeze them prior to death.

Each ship could land for fifty-four hours. The ship got seventy credits per bug. The purpose of this trip was to make some quick cash, which had been depleted during the engine upgrade, and test a few systems on a short interplanetary run.

Afterwards, the ship would go to Kipos for payment, rendezvous with the *Discovery*, and restock before going on a longer trip—assuming the engine upgrade held together.

The next file was filled with visuals: a map, photos, and directions from the *Revelation* to the nesting sites. The final documents were about the gear: the netting device and different types of environmental suits. Hers was made specifically for a Homo Kiposi, but they did not need to alter it to fit in Homo sapiens physiology. No one made the suits the Khlôrosans needed anymore. No one saw any profit in such a limited and dying market. The *Revelation* had only two, neither of which was fully functional. She understood why someone whose body could stand a little warmth would be needed. Abby was going to be on a hot planet for a very long day.

There was a knock on the hatchway and Helen stepped down the ladder. "Ship's clear. Dinner time. Or if you're still feeling ill, I'll bring it to you?"

Rockford jumped down from Abby's bunk and climbed up the five rungs where he stretched out across expectantly for Helen to scratch his belly. He obviously had the crew trained.

"No. I can't wait to see..." Abby pulled on a set of coveralls, blushing as Helen's golden eyes focused upon her. "And I'm hungry too. I feel like I haven't eaten for days."

"You haven't."

ABBY'S MOUTH WATERED. THE TABLE held hot biscuits, a lemony smelling soup, and what looked like some sort of meat interspersed with onions and potatoes on a kabob. She paused in the doorway for a brief moment, but Helen pulled her inside. Helen took the chair next to Brian so she sat in the open space between Mark and Diane. No one seemed to mind.

She waited to see if they said grace, but no one did. She watched to see if the either gender or the captain ate first, but that seemed not to be a concern. Helen just grabbed the soup dish, put some in her bowl and passed it to the right. So far, it was like a meal back home minus the prayer. Harden grabbed the biscuits and slathered his with butter and something that smelled like honey but sparkled a deep red before passing it on. The meat was rich, salty, and slightly chewy. She had no idea what kind it was until Brian complemented Helen on the lamb.

"This is lamb?" Abby asked before wishing she had kept her mouth shut.

"You're not vegetarian, are you?" Mark asked.

"Oh, no. I've just never had lamb," she said, her cheeks bright red. "It's good."

"We understand there were still sheep on Earth. Did your parents not like it?" Helen asked.

Abby did not hear condescension in her voice. The question seemed truly one of mere curiosity. "I'm sure they woulda liked it just fine, but our commune only had room for chickens and rabbits."

"You ate rabbits?" Mark asked, not bothering to hide his awe.

After seeing Abby's confusion, Diane said, "They are considered expensive pets on Kipos. A bun can cost up to a thousand credits."

Abby smiled. "If only our commune knew that. I bet my da could probably fit at least fifty bunnies in one of those gravitypods that held me and Orchid."

Harden asked, "Commune? We heard families were generally crowded together in a building with others. That's how your family lived?"

Abby nodded. They were obviously waiting for her to continue speaking so she said, "My family lived in one room and we shared a washroom with our floor. Thirty families total in the building."

"With five kids?" Mark asked.

"Joey died before Orchid was born so there were only four kids. Plus my parents, maternal grandparents, and my dog Tara," she said. "Everyone we knew lived like that."

Harden nodded. "There were many things the Kiposi saw on Earth that they didn't understand, including universal incest."

Abby choked and dropped her fork. Mark vigorously rubbed her back. She remembered stories of the old gods doing such things—long before there were other people—but the very idea was appalling. She swallowed her half chewed food and stared at her plate, trying to come up with something that would exonerate her planet. "I-I never heard of a family like that, but if someone did something so horrible in the commune, they'd get kicked out! I mean, we hugged and stuff, but I'd never do that to my brothers!"

"But you did sleep together?" Harden asked.

"Of course! They were my brothers. Orchid and I slept in the middle and Tara by the door."

Fury and fear blocked her ability to form any more complete sentences. Diane saved her. "You need not explain. We understand."

Helen reached across the table and took Abby's hand. She felt enveloped by the sincerity and kindness in the woman's golden eyes. "I've hugged my brothers too. If people wish to see barbarisms, they will." Helen went on to explain that sleeping together is practically unheard of, except between married couples. Siblings always had separate beds; if not, separate rooms or billets. It sounded lonely and, though she did not dare say such a thing, Abby hoped Lei was cuddled enough.

The crew had so many questions: life without sterilizers and antibiotics, her job at the library, her parents' jobs at the factory. After all, she was the first Earthling they had ever met. Abby answered, but didn't dare ask any questions herself, afraid she would seem ignorant. She carefully copied all they did as she watched for social cues. If anyone noticed, they didn't say anything.

ONCE DINNER WAS OVER, HELEN told Abby she could go back to her billet or help Brian and Diane. Curiosity—and what Abby hoped was good manners—impelled her to lend a hand. Besides, if she had to spend any more time alone, she felt she might evaporate through the air vent—or the monsters would come back.

She followed them down to the second deck and through the hatchway to the primary engine room. The lion's share of the ship was devoted to a network of cables and paneling that led to the three engines. Abby guessed the second deck was six times higher than the tight living quarters above and twice as large as the cargo hold, infirmary, and laboratory below them.

Diane told her that Kipos law required a chemical engine for takeoff. Once in space, they could turn on the grav-engine so they would have 80% Kipos gravity. When they were past Argent's orbit, they would use controlled fusion for sustained travel. Once they reached the outer system, they would turn on the tachyon generator and stabilizer unit, which enabled the ship to go faster than the speed of light.

Brian instructed Abby to inventory the spare parts and tools while he and Diane finished checking some wiring behind a heavy panel that led to the fusion engine. Abby did not know the names of the parts or tools, but it was a simple enough job. All she had to do was match up the part numbers to the list and mark the amounts on the tablet. Anything that wasn't in the inventory would be sent up to the bridge once she plugged the tablet into an outlet in the wall.

When the job was complete, Abby followed Brian through a set of two heavy paneled rings to the grav-engine. Brian opened another hatch and they entered an enclosed room.

Abby gasped in delight. Three large trees grew in the center of the space. At their feet grew soft moss, fungi, and flowering plants. There were dozens of varieties of fruits in all shapes and colors. Above them were golden and blue hanging metal lights. Between the carbon rings of the hull were portholes.

"I'd have never guessed there was a whole other world aboard ship!"

Diane said, "These are all edible. It's how we stay healthy on long hauls. You know of scurvy, beriberi, and the like?"

Abby answered in the affirmative.

"Not only do the plants give us oxygen and nutritious food, but like Rocks, the garden gives the crew something solid to hang on to. Easier to deal with problems in the black when you can come here and feel soil in your hands."

Brian pointed at a hatchway in the ceiling. "That's the real way from the galley."

"But what about zero-g during take off and landing? Don't the plants fly away?"

"Doesn't quite work like that. Even so, this room is completely enclosed." Diane explained how the ground cover and magnetic stakes worked to keep things in place. Since the grav-engine surrounded the room, there was always some gravity in the garden.

Abby found herself wondering why Diane and Harden were not together; the beautiful woman seemed to glow in the light of the garden. Abby decided that it must be a defect of his, not hers. Or what if Diane liked Mark better? Certainly Mark was more handsome than Harden. And Diane was gorgeous. What if they were together? They didn't act like it, but Abby suddenly realized she had no idea and could not chance losing her job. Ten days. After that, she would have some money and she could figure out how to save Orchid and Jin.

Brian and someone named Phoebe helped build the garden, but he gave Diane, who designed it, most of the credit for keeping it green and in working order. Abby decided that she liked Brian's gentle, easygoing way. Though she barely came to his shoulder, she wasn't afraid of him. He showed her the dew collectors and timers that mimicked sunlight. He opened up a hatch and gestured for Abby to look inside. Below the garden were heavy pipes leading to ten pumps. Kitchen and paper waste was turned into compost, human solid waste was converted to methane, and the rest was burned as solid fuel. Urine was pushed to and fro through filters until it was pure enough to drink. Oxygen from the garden was pumped into the ship. Every system had at least two redundant systems. It was dizzying, but Abby recognized a few of the parts from the inventory as Brian and Diane rechecked them all, explaining how they worked.

"*Revelation* has every function we do: circulatory system, waste disposal, lungs. My travel has been so limited, I have never seen that before," Abby said, touching a pump.

Diane chose her words carefully. "She cannot reproduce nor is she sentient. Yet the *Revelation* is a complex being. We treat her right and she treats us right in return."

They climbed back up. Diane went to go check radiation scrubbers as Brian checked each tube and pipe around the garden.

"See what you like," he called over to her.

"I can?"

"Helen said you're cooking with me tomorrow, right?"

Abby nodded and reached out for a berry. It gushed tart and sweet in her mouth with a slightly bitter aftertaste.

He handed her a small crescent-shaped nut off a tiny bush. "Try this."

It was pungent, but not unpleasing. Together, the berry and nut were exquisite.

"My brother Ray would've liked this. He liked watching things grow." She reached up and picked a piece of thick rinded green fruit. She peeled it and threw the rind in the compost bin. She broke it in half. Brian accepted and took a bite of its pinkish red flesh. "On Earth, we have a citrus fruit like this called an orange, but it is the color orange, and it's a bit sweeter. Or is this closer to a grapefruit?"

"It is a kitros and we call it 'portkali,' which is the Greek for the color orange. But they never do become orange. Probably just a mutation of the original fruit," he smiled. "I can tell you have siblings. You're used to sharing. Pick a few more. We should plan on making a solid breakfast, a cold lunch, and a minimal dinner for the take-off."

Brian discussed his plans as if Abby had a say in them, but he knew the *Revelation's* schedules better than she. Besides, pancakes with berry compote and fried mutton sounded delicious. A spinach salad with berries and portkali sounded good, too. Abby picked the required fruit and vegetables as Brian finished checking each pump.

"Been to the bridge yet?"

She shook her head. He led Abby back up through the hatchway to the upper deck. Beyond the billets and galley were two stairs to the bridge. Rubber coated metal lined the floors. Wires hidden in tubes painted white ran over the ceiling to the bow and into the control panel. Two cushioned chairs with sheepskin covered upholstery faced a large clear shield. One more was in front of the navigation station. Another three seats were folded up against a wall to maximize floor space. The pale blue polymer walls were clean, yet it was not a sterile environment. Cups of coffee sat on the control panel as Helen and Harden worked over some figures on a tablet. Helen smiled, but Harden glowered back at his figures and mumbled about the rising cost of oxygen.

Outside, there were only trucks and other ships. Abby wished for stars, but there was too much light pollution. It didn't matter. Abby knew she couldn't tell them about her friends in the stars. That would sound idiotic. Not knowing what to say, she asked if anyone wanted a piece of her port-kali.

Helen declined. "The flavor's nasty with coffee, but I'm glad your appetite's back."

Harden said nothing.

Helen asked, "You seem nervous. Still want to go?"

Brian said, "If you come to this life without wanting it, you end up in the black, spewing the ice crystals that used to be your guts. The only good part is that you freeze fast."

He squeezed her shoulder. "You should sleep on it."

As Abby walked towards her quarters, she heard Harden say, "Great, Bri. Now we'll be lucky if she ever closes her eyes again."

Harden was correct, but not for the reason he had believed. Abby went into the head and brushed her teeth, but could not look in the mirror: she feared the silly girl, the poutana, would look back at her. She kept the lights on as she slipped back into Harden's t-shirt and curled under her quilt.

Diane knocked on their shared head door and popped her head inside the room. "You alright, sweetie?"

"Yeah, I just don't want to be in the dark again."

Diane sat down on the end of the bed and touched Abby's leg through the covers. "Try to get some sleep. You'll be working with me and Brian after breakfast."

"Please, don't tell anyone I'm scared." She didn't say that it was because she feared the monsters would come back. Or she would wake up back in the big house. Or worse, one of the men of the crew would be in her rack. "I think Harden hates me."

"He hates that oxygen prices are rising and we won't get very far without it. He doesn't know you. I'll stay 'til you sleep if you want."

Abby nodded.

Diane began gently rubbing her back. "You're safe here."

CHAPTER 25

ABBY SLIPPED THROUGH THE HEAD and into Diane's billet. A sweet floral perfume wafted towards her as Diane, just wearing her robe, slid lotion up her long shimmering legs.

"That smells nice," Abby said, wishing she were as beautiful as Diane.

"You can try it, but it might make you breakout. Much oilier than the stuff I bought you. Too rich for most Kiposi's skin, and my guess is Homo sapien skin is even oilier."

"Does Helen use it?"

"Same brand, but she doesn't wear scents. I like to smell like roses— or, at least, not like the engine room."

Abby picked up the bottle and read that the lotion was a profusion of plant and flower extracts which apparently "magically made life more positive." Abby didn't know about that, but Diane's legs did look even more perfect than before. She pressed the pump down and rubbed a little into her hand. It clung heavily to her skin, as if she was going to leave a film wherever she touched.

"Feel's greasy," Abby said, "but smells nice."

She went to the head and washed it off in the sink.

Diane came in behind her. "Generally, since we sweat less, our skin is also dryer. Plus, once I turned thirty, I needed a heavier moisturizer."

"I thought Kipos didn't make Khlôrosan goods anymore."

"They don't. The lotion's made on the flotilla and sold on O-5."

"How big is the flotilla?" Abby asked.

"Seventy long range transports, all spinning in tachyon fields. Plus another twenty on the transport routes."

"How big is the Alekos fleet?"

"Three Explorer class ships, four Lathos runners, fifteen transports all FtL, twenty-five flotilla rentals with FtL mods."

Abby chewed on her thumbnail. "They seem like good people."

"They are, but I'm biased. Helen's my best friend, sweetie. We've been crew on and off for most of my career."

ABBY TREMBLED AS SHE HANDED Harden his coffee. His eyes left his crossword puzzle and focused on her. "You're still here?"

Abby nodded.

"Why did your parents allow three of their four living children to come to Kipos?"

"They wanted us to have a better life," Abby replied.

"That's fucking trite."

Helen put her hand on her brother's arm.

Harden shrugged his sister off. "She claims she was not a child on Earth. Let her answer."

"Orchid wanted to be a doctor. Jin loved to draw and design things…" Abby thought about the next part of her answer, but she wasn't going to tell them about being a questioning Serpent or her friends in the stars. "I became a librarian to escape the factories, but it only paid minimum wage. It had some benefits so my parents let me work there, but if I got married and had kids, I'd need a better job so I could feed them. Mr. Tygh…"

"Bob Tygh?"

"Yeah, he came to talk to my parents after we were tested. He said we'd go back to school…but I wanted to see another planet. Once I was offered passage, nothing could have stopped me."

Harden stared at her for a few seconds. "So you're saying if you knew what would happen, you still would have come?"

"Harden, that's enough," Helen said.

He ignored his sister and kept his eyes on Abby.

"No." she said, but inside she wondered if she had wanted to see a planet so badly that she ignored any forewarning that she might have had. *What if everything that happened to Jin, Orchid and me is all my fault?*

"How do you know this is safe?"

"I don't, but you said yesterday…"

"I could have been lying," Harden said.

Abby chewed on her bottom lip for a moment. "But you weren't."

"How do you know?"

"No one's smiling. Actually, everybody looks pretty mortified. When I landed on Kipos, everyone was trying to keep us calm. Lots of fake smiles, soft voices, and perfect organization. I knew something was wrong, but there was nothing to do. I was stuck,"

Her voice wavered, so she held her tongue still for a moment. "Last night, you asked me about a bunch of things that makes me believe the Kiposi fleet did not know what they saw when they came to Earth. We were as much a mystery to them as Kipos was a mystery to us. Mr. Johnson was so scared of the Kiposi. He didn't even come to work. Maybe he was right to be, but he knew I would be accepted and I'd go. He knew I wouldn't stay on Earth when I had the chance to see a new planet."

Harden gave his sister a look. With her eyes, Helen replied. He dropped his gaze first and said to Abby, "Last evening, you spoke as if you loved Mr. Johnson, kiddo?"

"I guess, but not in any distasteful way."

"Obviously."

"When I finished school, he's the one that got me into the librarian training even though I wasn't sixteen yet."

"How long were you in school?"

"Until thirteen." Before Harden could make another comment, Abby added, "My parents struggled to keep us all in school as long as they could."

"So the answer to my original question was poverty. Be accurate next time."

Abby wanted to hide, but she refused to let anyone know how scared she was. She ate her breakfast with the hope no one saw the slight tremble in her hands.

HELEN HAD SUBMITTED HER FLIGHT plan days prior and, though they were scheduled to take off at 13:00, their delay was not unexpected.

New Alexandria was a busy aero-spaceport and the rain was coming down in a torrent. They were delayed an extra hour and then another.

Eventually they were told that they wouldn't be leaving until 21:00.

ABBY CLIMBED ON THE TREADMILL and hit the button that Mark had showed her. She wondered how long she could run; the timer was going incredibly slowly. Feeling sweat drip down her back, she took a sip of water. It had a slight metallic taste, but it was cold. How could only six minutes have gone by?

Mark told her she must run, or at least walk, for two hours. If not, the varying gravity would steal her strength. Yet, there was another reason she ran: she was embarrassed by the softness of her breasts and belly. Even if nothing ever came of it, she wanted Mark to think she was sexy. He had seen her misshapen from the pregnancy; she wanted him to see her slender. She did not know if love was stuffing her skull or if it was lust, but she could not deny that Mark was so handsome, so kind. He was everything she used to dream about. She remembered how it felt when his long fingers slid up her back as he checked her breathing and wondered how it would feel to be wrapped in his arms. If Mark loved her, he wouldn't let anyone ever hurt her again. He might even help her find Orchid and Jin. Maybe even help her get Lei back.

She wished she had legs like Helen and Diane, but even if she lost five kilos, nothing would make her legs lengthen and shimmer. She liked the opalescent microscales embedded into their follicles; she only had fine hairs covering her body. She wondered what Mark thought about that. He probably didn't, she realized. He had seen her naked, broken. He had seen her coated in vomit.

Helen typed something else in the treadmill and the belt started shifting. "This will make it feel like you are running up and down hills. Once you are used to it, we can add bumps to simulate rocks."

As Abby ran, her mind wandered past Mark and to the coming stars. Due to the ship's internal stabilizers and gravity engine, she didn't have to go into a grav-couch. She would see them the entire way.

IT WAS NEARLY 21:30 WHEN DIANE and Brian went to the engine room. The rest of the crew went to the bridge. Helen slipped into the pilot's seat and Harden sat down in the command station. Mark folded down the seats behind the flight deck. Abby slipped into her seat and buckled herself into the five-point harness. Mark re-checked it and warned her that the first twenty minutes could be choppy, then buckled himself in next to her.

Thrill danced in Abby's chest as the chemical engines began to hum. Every second, Kipos had less of a hold on the *Revelation*. Velocity pushed Abby deeper into her seat until the planet finally let go. Abby smiled at the new sensation and glanced over at Mark. His eyes were clinched shut.

Eight minutes later, they broke out of the atmosphere. Mark took a deep breath and rubbed the back of his shirtsleeve on his brow. Smiling, he held out a stylus. It floated towards her. "There'll be a few minutes of zero gravity."

Abby flicked its end and made it rotate back towards him. They passed it back a few more times.

There was a purr as the gravity engine started to spin up. Mark grabbed the stylus before it fell to the floor. Behind them, Abby heard the slight clank of dishes and cans shifting in the latched cupboards. Ahead, there was nothing but stars. Kipos was behind them. Earth was lost somewhere among the black.

Helen slid her fingers over the touch screen, making a few final adjustments to the flight plan. Mark told her it was a standing order in Dad's fleet that someone would always be on the bridge, even if they weren't at the controls. It was one of the reasons this fleet had less accidents. Though they could be sure not to hit the moons, planets or other large objects, solar winds could send them spiraling into space or be caught and used as energy. In the black, there were rogue comets and unseen gravity sources.

"I'm going to exercise and hit my rack," Mark said. He reminded her that she was still healing and told her not to stay up too late. Abby went back to the galley and made coffee as Diane had suggested to her the night before. She brought the first two cups down into the engine room and the next two to the bridge. As she scanned the stars, looking for something familiar, in the distance, twinkling against the black, was a pale blue and gold-banded planet with vivid blue rings.

"Wow! That's Ounizo, right?" She pointed towards port.

Helen nodded. "Good eye."

"That was one of the things I hated about stasis. I never saw the rings of Saturn," Abby said as she set Helen's coffee in her cup holder between the helm and the command stations.

Harden reached out for his cup. "Well, kiddo, we've never seen Saturn either."

"We'll be passing it in six hours. Get to your billet. We'll call you so you can get a better look," Helen said.

TOO EXCITED TO SLEEP, ABBY came back an hour early. Harden gave his sister a slight frown. Abby chewed her nail and looked at their empty cups. "Do you want more coffee?"

"Sure," Helen said.

Abby made another pot and refilled their cups. Harden wasn't any more content, but Ounizo's moons and rings took up most of the screen. Abby unfolded the third seat. "One, two, three, four, … sixteen rings," she counted.

"And twenty-two satellites," Harden said. "The computer or I could have just told you."

"If I remember correctly, Saturn has nine rings and over sixty satellites. Look how much it flattens near the poles. Saturn does that too. I wonder if anything lives down there."

"Maybe. There are plenty types of life. It doesn't matter. We can't live down there," Harden answered.

"At least with current technology?"

"I doubt we will see the day that we could. After all, what purpose would a gas giant serve? Can you even fathom the amount of fuel it takes to break a gas giant's gravity?"

The expression on Harden's face was clear that his questions were rhetorical and, if she wanted to remain on the bridge, she should not be antagonistic. Abby shook her head and tucked her feet underneath her.

Helen said, "Actually, honey, they've a wonderful use. We can use them as slingshots to speed us up or use the friction of their outer atmospheres to slow us down without using fuel."

A moon rose over the north polar region of Ounizo. Reflected light from the red dwarf shone pink over the arch of the planet. Another, still in shade, seemed to be a rich purple.

"It's beautiful," Abby said, "And look at the movement of the clouds!"

Helen said, "You can magnify it on Harden's monitor."

Abby glanced at Harden for a moment before edging closer to him. "Those bright flashes—are those electrical storms?"

"Yep," His voice grew soft and became patient. "See this? We're clocking the wind at over fifteen hundred kilometers per hour."

"My understanding is that they lack a crust," she said.

"Don't know offhand about Saturn, but Ounizo lacks any surface. If we were to try to land, the gases would simply become thicker the closer we moved to the core. The pressure would eventually crush the ship. Even the heavy metals are only particles suspended in gases."

"Are there colonies on the moons?"

"No, a giant planet's gravitational pull is strong enough that its moons make unstable colonies. It doesn't surprise me that Ganymede and Triton were abandoned," Harden said.

"I didn't know you knew about that. All of Sol's colonies were abandoned in the twenty-fifth century. People always said there were too many problems on Earth for the stars."

The line on Harden's brow deepened. "You believe that?"

"No. There were a lot of people on Earth. Maybe having some on Luna and Mars would've been a good thing, but when someone mentioned it, people screamed about the homeless, polluted water, or whatever. Seems to me that there will always be problems on Earth, just like Kipos and everywhere else."

"Indeed," he said.

Helen said, "We'll be going into the main belt in a few hours and should see a shade of Lathos over Kokadelfi. You might find it interesting."

THE ECLIPSE WAS MARVELOUS, BUT Abby was disappointed in the asteroid belt. She expected to see collisions and giant rocks that Helen needed to traverse with care, but instead she learned the most unfailing thing about space is that it's really, really big.

Without prompting, Helen turned on a light and pointed it directly at the large asteroid passing nearly fifty meters away. The high points glittered copper before it disappeared behind them. Most of the asteroids appeared to be nothing more than bits of dust sparkling against the black.

"I read that the belt is nearly eighty-five percent metallic based?"

Harden nodded.

"Why don't people mine the asteroid belt if it's so high in metals?"

"The cost. We need to go sublight in the system. It's much cheaper to mine the lunar colonies, especially Argent now that it is terraformed," he said.

"Oh, I've been curious about that. On Earth, ecological problems of mining affected nearby cities."

Helen asked her, "Do you remember the population when you left?"

"Just under seventeen billion."

Harden continued his sister's thought, "Check your tablet if you want the exact numbers. There is less than a million on Kipos—including the three hundred thousand brought from Earth, fifteen thousand on Argent, and only about five thousand on both Semi and Selene. You should also look at a population density map."

Abby opened her mouth, "Three hundred thousand?" She felt a dark pit in her stomach. "There wasn't more?"

Harden asked, "How many did you think there was?"

"When we got on the elevator, even with seeds and livestock, I figured there was closer to seven-hundred fifty thousand colonists. I counted the seats and multiplied them by the number of scheduled trips on ten elevators. Easy arithmetic."

Helen and Harden shared a look. "Do you know about the deep space death?"

"Only it's a histamine reaction against the nanomites in the grav/stasis pods and two girls in our room—billet—died."

Harden said, "Forty percent died in route to Kipos. Another twenty percent died in the first month of landing due to allergic reactions."

"The stew," Abby whispered to herself.

"What?" Harden asked.

Abby looked up at him. "The people who bought my bond gave me the same foods every day. My escort, Eli, sometimes let me have a cup of tea and cookies or crackers, but nothing else."

Harden looked repulsed. "And you didn't fight them?"

"When I fought, I was sedated or punished or..." she trailed off. *Threatened. Orchid's life was threatened.*

Abby wondered what they thought. Mark was a man now, but she knew his elder siblings never left him in harm's way.

Lei was safe, but Barnett might still be able to get Orchid and Jin on Kipos. Abby hugged herself, trying to keep the heavy feeling from rising in her throat. She wanted to stay on the bridge and did not doubt they would order her to her billet if she lost control of her emotions.

It wasn't as bad as she had feared.

"Harden," Helen whispered as she tapped something into the panel. "It's on auto."

As his sister rose, Harden slipped into her station. "I didn't..."

"You never do. I'll handle it." Helen's words were curt, but her voice was gentle. She wrapped her slender arms around the younger woman and led her into the galley.

"Orchid's only a little girl, and I just left her," Abby said as tears spilled from her eyes. Helen could not provide a salve or even a Band-Aid for her aching heart, but she provided warm milk, three handkerchiefs, and a gentle embrace until Abby cried herself out.

CHAPTER 26

Lathos: April 7, 3164 K.E.

ABBY SAT IN THE AIRLOCK. From the little window, she could see Lathos was a planet of rocky canyons and deep, clear rivers. There was a slightly higher percentage of carbon dioxide and oxygen and slightly less nitrogen, but the air was within the breathable range. The problem for the Khlôrosans was the arid heat.

Claustrophobic in the tight fitting environmental suit, Abby sensed her lungs expanding and contracting with each breath. She was nervous, not about the job or the alien planet, but the fact that she must wet her pants and drink the urine at some time in the next 54 hours. The suit's base layer was a weave of polymer threads and spider silk specifically designed to wick sweat and urine away from the skin and into caches. It would be run through filters until it became potable. This repulsed her, though she knew, technically, she had been drinking urine and condensation for the past four days from the ship's recycling systems.

The internal door of the airlock opened. Mark's warm hand slipped on the back of her neck. "You okay?"

She nodded.

He gave her the final injection to inoculate her from possible pathogens. She felt herself breathe a little easier, but did not like the rash that immediately developed on her stomach and her scar.

"It itches," Abby said.

Mark handed her a pill. "Take this. It's a mild antihistamine. It'll stop in a bit."

"How do you know?"

"That's what everyone has told me," he said.

"Oh, that makes sense." She tapped her head in a sign of her own ignorance and put on the hood and covered her face with a breathing mask.

She was surprised how quickly she got used to the silvery mesh in front of her face, so finely woven it seemed to disappear.

Diane had told her it was the same anti-radiation gauze that surrounded the *Revelation*. Abby was not sure how she felt about that. It seemed so flimsy. In a strange way, her ignorance and faith of the technological superiority of the Kiposi had comforted her on her trip from Earth. There was no such comfort on the *Revelation*. Diane and Brian encouraged her to ask questions and sometimes queried her back to ensure she understood twenty centimeters of ceramic tiles coated in metallic paint, stabilizing hydraulics, three levels of silver anti-radiation webbing, and reinforced carbon—or aluminum silicate glass—were all that stood between them and the vacuum of space.

The external door opened. Knowing the crew, or at least Helen and Mark, were watching her through the camera, Abby gave an "okay" signal and waved. She hurried away from the ship. Whispering, she repeated what she was looking for: nesting holes.

The river sparkled through the deep red ravine that thrust up on the east side of her. To the west, there was a belt of rocky land where she set up the nets, just as other crewmembers had done two planetside decades before. Sweating in the shade, she hoped the crew had gotten their years right and it would be a good harvest. She knew there was no animal life on Lathos that could kill her, but she felt frightened of the alien planet. She glanced back up at the hulking ship silhouetted against the pink sunrise and took some comfort in its closeness.

In the distance, she saw another ship break atmo. It landed about a hundred meters away from the *Revelation*. Two men disembarked and waved at the Alekos ship then at her before they began to set up their gear. She waved back.

"Mark?"

"I'm reading you."

"Do we know them? What's my response?"

"Yeah. It's the *Gnosi*. Dad owns a share of that ship. Waving is enough. They might come over and talk; but it looks like they still have plenty of work to do. Just tell them the truth. You got hired on as a replacement for Pat and Becky. And just so you know, Becky's passed on, so be respectful."

"I will...and I'm sorry." Abby wondered if she was a bad person for silently hoping Becky had not died on Lathos.

Helen spoke. "Calm down, hon. Your heart is beating too fast. Take a sip of water."

Abby put her lips around the straw and sucked in the lukewarm liquid. Within minutes, the two men approached her.

"I wish I was taller," Abby whispered into her radio.

She heard Mark chuckle. "Don't worry so much. You're just slightly short for a Kiposi female."

As she stood up, she was careful to step on a rock to get a slight boost. She heard Mark's chuckle turn to roaring laughter.

"I'm Steve," the first man said. "This is Rich. Nice to meet you." She couldn't see their faces through the silver mesh of their masks, but his voice sounded like he was a man in his prime. Their bodies looked fit, though it was hard to tell through the layers of their suits.

"A pleasure," Abby replied, hoping her voice sounded calmer than she felt. "Name's Abby."

Rich said, "Damn, I love that soft voice. I need to sign on with the *Revelation*. Where are you from?"

Using the *Revelation's* external speakers, Harden's voice boomed over them. "I'm not paying you to talk, Abigail."

"It was nice to meet you, but I'd better get back to work. This is sort of a probation period and I'm hoping they'll keep me on for their longer trip."

Abby heard Helen whisper in her ear. "Excellent."

Rich nodded. "That's how I got hired too. Planned on only paying for school, but been doing it for ten relative years now. Don't let Harden get to you."

Steve added, "He yells at everyone. Becky and Pat used to drive him to obscenities."

Rich said softly, "Tell Mark we're sorry about Pat. Really sucks."

Steve agreed. "Really sucks, man."

"I'll tell him," Abby said, wishing she knew what they were talking about.

After a few parting words, Rich and Steve gestured something to the *Revelation's* camera that Abby was not sure she wanted to understand.

The scenery was beautiful, but as Kokadelfi rose higher, sweat began trickling down her back and her scalp became itchy. Abby wondered how long she would have to wait, but soon the hiss of insects filled the air and the entire ravine blackened. She had never seen anything like the swarm. She hit the first button. The loader inflated, forcing the carbon webbing into the air. As the nets closed in on themselves, she hit the cooling switch. She slipped a piece of thin metal over the hole in order to not kill any insects as her nets fell into icy heaps on the ground.

She picked them up and began walking. Abby held the nets away from her body, careful not to crush the frail exoskeletons of the insects. Heavier than expected, her arms quickly ached. The insects were sluggish, but they were awake and their wings fluttered in panic.

Harden's voice boomed over her again. She was sure the entire planet could hear his swearing about her pace. Frustrated, she bit her tongue.

There was a cart of darkened plastic jars and a checklist set up outside the ship. Abby extricated the bugs from the net and each other. She sometimes had to tickle a bug's belly in order for it to let go of another bug. All were counted.

Dead ones were thrown in buckets. These would be mashed down to make bug repellent on Argent. Since the crew only got two credits per barrel, catching them alive was preferable. She carted the jars back aboard through the first airlock. She was inside and cooled before the second airlock opened.

Mark took the cart from her and handed her a thick shake of liquid vitamins. Fake strawberry. Yuck. Why did it have to be fake strawberry? She repeated Rich and Steve's message then, seeing the immediate pain that spread across his face, apologized for not knowing this would hurt him.

"It's fine. Pat's my ex…we broke up last time we landed on Kipos. If you talk to them again, say that I was glad they were thinking of me."

Abby repeated the procedure seventeen times during the next fifty-four hour period. Mark occasionally asked about the last time she urinated, which she could not answer without blushing. At least once an hour, Harden swore at her to walk faster.

Finally, Harden signaled the last load. Exhausted, she counted the bugs she had, covered the bug cart with a thermal blanket, and pulled off her environmental suit. Feeling the cold wind of the sanitizer, she waited for Mark to clear her. Abby heard the buzz before she pushed the cart through the door and grabbed the hot towel that awaited her. Mark admired her shivering, naked body, but she quickly pulled on her underwear, a chemise, and coveralls. He took her temperature, slid his fingers across her neck to check her pulse, and then he pressed gently on her glands checking for an allergic reaction.

His hands were soft and warm. She felt herself grow slick with the wish he would kiss her. Yet she didn't dare let the crew know what a savage poutana she was. It was bad enough she abandoned her own flesh on Kipos. If they knew what she really was, they would not want her around.

Besides, just because Mark liked looking didn't mean he liked touching women. Abby did not think she could take the rejection. She smiled as she turned away. It had the desired effect. She showed camaraderie and yet created distance.

The two stowed the jars underneath an ultraviolet light. The males came perfectly into view; they had tiny bioluminescent spots on their backs glowing yellowish green. The insects were segregated by gender, packed into crates, and placed into the cargo hold. Abby touched the intercom pad.

Harden's image said, "It looks like a good take."

"Five-three males, four-two females. Dead loss one-one."

Mark showed her the numbers from the other sixteen trips. It was a good harvest: she netted 2726 males, 2412 females, and only one barrel of dead bugs.

CHAPTER 27

ABBY SAT NEXT TO DIANE, watching a sketch-comedy vid about politics on Kipos with Rockford lying behind them across the top of the bench. She didn't understand any of the current events, but she understood when people were calling their leaders moronic nymphomaniacs.

Harden popped his head outside the bridge and ordered, "Abby, get in here."

Wondering what she did wrong, she climbed the steps. He shut the door behind her. Harden sat at the navigation station and gestured at the third chair.

Fear hurt her stomach; she clutched the pants of her coveralls as she sat down across from him. Though Harden seemed to inspire love from his crew, he didn't seem all that loveable to Abby. Of course, blood and marriage relations probably helped. She reminded herself that he had yelled at her on Lathos, but never so much as pushed the cat away in anger.

Seemingly unaware of her distress, Harden said, "Helen wants to offer you a job. However, I don't have a place for lost little girls. This is hazardous work and dangerous for us to keep you. If you stay, it will be because you find the work interesting and you like the ship's company."

Abby began to smile, but Harden didn't give her a chance to speak before he went on. "You could leave the ship at Kipos. If you're thrifty, you might get by for a year on the money you've made. You're decently clever, but there's little work for an uneducated woman and plenty of people who would turn you in."

He added, "Don't think you're doing your sister or daughter any favors by trying to save them. It will get you—and possibly them—killed. You understand?"

Since Harden waited for an answer this time, Abby said, "Yes."

"Your safest option is to leave the ship at Argent. They have a service-based economy and use a cash system so it'll be easy to insert you. My family knows good people. I could get you a job as a maid or a cook. The only real danger on Argent is the mines. The only women there tend to be self-proclaimed actresses. You'll shine for all of a day, probably be dead in a month."

Abby did not fully understand his allusion, but figured he was saying prostitutes often came to a bad end. "I'd like to stay."

"We'll see." Harden went on to explain the *Revelation's* short and long-term mission objectives. Like all the ships in the private fleets, the ship was based on a profit-sharing model. Their grandmother and Cole owned 5%. The crew had their fleet standard rank allotments. The rest was owned in equal parts by Harden and Helen. They referred to themselves using the traditional ranks more for the realities of paperwork than for the belief that one was inclined to be a better captain. They shared responsibilities equally and made decisions together. (Abby would later agree with the consensus that Harden was better at the official procedure and regulations while Helen was better with personal interaction.)

Their primary long-term mission was to find a planet suitable for Khlôrosan, Clones, Garo, and Elykyn life.

"In the flotilla?" Abby asked.

"Correct. These folks only left Kipos when the Reproduction laws came down. They don't have a home and long to set down roots. While Kipos does not want them polluting their gene pool, if a planet is found, there shouldn't be a problem setting up a colony."

Abby frowned. "Wait. But why don't..."

"They just live anywhere?"

"Yeah."

"Because like an outpost, the flotilla is a closed system. Colonization is a difficult endeavor. Humans will change the planet's ecosystem and be changed by it. The idea is to stay as human as possible and set up colonies which will ensure the long term survival of all humankind."

"How many planets have you been to?"

"As a scout on my father's various explorers, over a hundred Earthlike planets; another sixty-four as captain of the *Revelation*." Harden added with a grin, "As you can imagine, such a long-term mission isn't very profitable."

"I guess not. So how does the ship make its money?" Abby asked.

"Surveying planets for the Kiposi government." Harden explained that, if upon their exploration, they found anything that might be exploited for the greater good of Kipos—medicines, new food sources, and the like—the crews were well paid for it. Abby's job would be to go planetside and take samples. She could explore ecosystems with minimal gear that the Khlôrosans could not.

"I think this work sounds great," Abby said, trying not to get too excited.

"Read this." He touched the screen and it flickered on. On the console, there was a news story about those who had died on Argent during an uprising in the mines. Abby wished she had not looked at the vid of the dead boys being piled into a shared grave, yet she couldn't turn away. She tried to zoom in on the faces. She did not see her brother, but not all the corpses had heads.

Jin's name was on the list as one of those among them.

Tears burned Abby's eyes. "The Cloud had lies on it all the time. How accurate is your news? Maybe this is wrong?"

"I doubt it. Like you, he was chipped. Even if your brother escaped the slaughter, he would then be in the process of starving to death."

She looked up at Harden. "But what if I…"

"We won't arrive for months planetside." He clicked on another link.

"If I had…"

"Listen. You'd have died. There was nothing you could have done or can do now. We found this…"

Abby looked back at the screen:

```
[On February 24, Rachel Margret DePaul was
born to Kyria Peony DePaul and her husband
the Kyrio Barnett. Her genetic structure
has all…]
```

Abby said softly, "Her name is not Lei."

"Did you think it was?"

"That's what I named her. I told them her name once she was born. After my ma. My grandma always hated my name. I dreamt that she and my parents were happy."

"There's one more."

[Orchid Stone, adopted daughter of Kyrios and Kyria Stone, won the Lincoln Middle School spelling bee. She has proven the so-called barbarians are not barbarians at all…]

The editorial went on to talk about her IQ scores and her loving adoptive parents. It mentioned how she was the pick of the litter of the four children of Cameron Boyd and Lei Sun Lei. Orchid's test score was in the top ten percent of those sent from Earth.

Abby traced the smiling face of the twelve-year-old girl until the world blurred. She tried to hold in her tears but her shoulders shuddered.

Harden handed her a handkerchief. "Are you capable of continuing this conversation? I'll give you a moment to calm down." He went down the two steps to the galley. When he returned, he brought himself a cup of coffee and handed her a cup of water. She took a sip and tried to hold herself still.

Harden patted her shoulder and put a gentle hand on her back. "Okay. I want you to make your decision in the morning."

"…" She looked up at him.

"In the morning. I don't want you to make any decisions in your state. Get some sleep. We'll speak after breakfast."

Abby went to her billet. She tossed in her bunk and paced the room. Eventually, she went to the head hoping to talk to Diane, but her room was dark. Abby took a shower, got dressed, and did her laundry. With five hours remaining until the clock would announce breakfast, she climbed back up to the bridge and tried to ignore Harden's scowl. He did not say anything, but his golden eyes were severe. Abby wished she didn't have to look up at him. Diane and Helen were both tall enough to look him straight in the face.

Helen tried to get her brother's attention, but he stayed focused on Abby as she printed out the photo of Orchid and went back to the galley. Abby dug through the drawer. She found a magnet clip and showed him what she had taken.

"I'm going back to my billet now." She wished her voice hadn't wavered.

She hurried back down the corridor. As she climbed into her hatch, she glanced back. Harden was waiting for her to go down.

Once alone, she attached the photo to her wall and whispered to it, "The only reason to leave the ship is to find you, Orcs, but the captain said if I do, I'm going to get you killed. You seem happy."

"I like this work. It's much better than being a maid or a cook. If you were here, what would you want me to do?"

Abby told her sister's photo she liked the organized way of life aboard ship. They gave her a chore and she did it. Helen, Brian, and Diane encouraged her questions. If she made a mistake—or, more often, created confusion by the way she carried out an order—they would correct her. No one ever called her names, threatened, or slapped her. She never saw anyone use the ship's informal command structure as an excuse to be lazy. They were all friends.

Abby told the photo how she liked the rotating cooking schedule and the camaraderie she felt when they dined together. Every third day, she made breakfast and dinner with Brian. Generally, the crew came together for a full breakfast. Leftovers made into sandwiches or soups were left in the smaller fridge for lunch and eaten when the crew had time, but they always came back together for a full dinner.

Da and Ma had made sure their children never went hungry, but growing up with them had brought a certain degree of monotony to the food. On Kipos, Abby felt a fear of constant scarcity due to her limited diet, but on the *Revelation* a stocked kitchen was available to her. The large, cold pantry was full of meats, fish, cheeses, eggs, dairy products, fruits, and vegetables. The dry pantry had oils, spices, sugar, cereals, and pastas. Whatever she used was added to the inventory, which was updated continuously. The list would be sent ahead the day before they landed on Kipos. When the computer recorded the jump in milk and juice consumption, she was worried, but Brian said both were cheaper and better for her than coffee. Mark added, "Especially because the *Revelation* has four coffee addicts aboard."

How could she not feel safe?

CHAPTER 28

ABBY WATCHED HARDEN THE NEXT morning, but he and Diane were focused on making and distributing scrambled eggs with green onions, cheese, and ham. After they cleaned up the breakfast dishes, Harden gestured Abby into the bridge for their second meeting.

"I heard you speak to your sister's photo last night. You have an interesting way of sorting out problems." He sat beside her, "But don't stay just because we have a full pantry."

She looked up into his face. "Why are you helping me?"

"Because my sister fucking told me to. If I had my way, I'd put you off at Argent. We'd all be safer." Yet, Harden's expression didn't match his ruthless tone. A hint of mischievousness twinkled in his eyes. He seemed almost young.

Abby said, "I don't want you to go to jail."

"We won't. When our company employed you, our father opened an account for you in the New World Bank. I have an electronic copy of your work permit in the computer."

Abby paled. "Don't they know I'm here?"

"Couldn't be helped. If I paid you under the table, it'd look as if we were doing something illegal." Harden brought up her work permit. "Your age is to our advantage. This is the first job you could get. Take a look."

ID Number	002946-LF
Name	Abigail Lee
Gender	Female (Assumed fertile)
Birthplace	Vos (Sublight LRT-783)
Mother	Junior Engineer D. Lee
Father	unknown
Class	A
Rank	Intern (Intended degree: astro-biology)
Pay	Half share plus standard fleet benefits

[History: Transferred from the Vos (LRT-783) the Revelation (Alekos Explorer-29307) via the Discovery (Alekos Explorer-29314) Lathos for Mateodeas Harvest. All duties performed satisfactorily.

Other: The Vos was destroyed November 12, 3064 in an engine malfunction on route to Outpost 4. No survivors.]

"No father?" she asked.

"Sure. Plenty of women have an enjoyable bit of planet-leave and find out they're pregnant after they are in deep space. The whole ship would have been your family. Donna was a real person. I knew her before the Earth mission. Also, that it was such a long-term mission makes it a great place for you to have been, because not only are you the correct age with the occasional stasis drop, but it makes sense that no one ever saw you before now.

"Lee's a common enough name, if someone says Abby Lee, you're likely to turn around. We completely lucked out with her hair."

He brought up the linked photo. Donna had straight black hair and a soft faraway frown, but not because she was unhappy; it was as if she was curious or concerned about something besides taking a pilot's license photo.

Harden continued, "Each week, your wages are deposited into your account from the ship's operating account, so interest works in your favor. Any taxes you owe planetside are withdrawn automatically. We never discussed your pay, but a half share is standard for an intern."

"My ma …"

"Always say mom or mother," Harden warned.

"My mom would've said you've treated me straight. Better in fact." Abby said, "I want to stay."

Harden had no emotion in his face. "There's a thousand ways to die in the black. A thousand more on every planet. We can't tell you what you will find."

Abby nodded. "I understand."

"I don't think you do. I want you to see this." He unzipped his coveralls and lifted his t-shirt to show her seven crisscrossing deep purple scars that started at his right hip and climbed up his ribcage. "You'll get hurt. There has never been a scout without scars. The animal that mauled me killed three other men."

He hit the intercom. "Helen." She immediately opened the door.

"Show her your scars."

Helen unzipped her coveralls and pulled out an arm. A long purple scar went from her wrist to her elbow. Another two crossed her shoulder. "I have another on my stomach."

"I—I still want to go. It's not just the pantry. And I'm scared. I don't think it'll be easy." Abby wished she could tell them about her friends in the stars, but that would sound stupid.

Harden pulled out a bill, crumpled it up, and threw it at his sister.

"Wonderful!" Helen said as she caught it. "You'll continue to receive your half share plus board and any needed medical care. Also, an intern is expected to complete a university level education. You don't need to major in astrobiology if you don't want, but you need to pick something that you can learn aboard ship. We could use a biologist."

Abby's stomach began to flutter in excitement. She felt her lips spread into a smile.

Helen said, "You'll start right away. We still have all Mark's courses. If you wish to study a subject not available, just let me know…"

Harden broke in, "But these courses are damn expensive, so you better finish what you start."

Helen said, "Though it does most of the work for you, you'll be trained to fly a shuttle."

Abby's eyes widened with excitement. "You trust me with a shuttle?"

Harden sighed. "If we did not trust you, we would not offer you a job."

Ignoring her brother, Helen went on to explain that basic flight was eighty hours and then, after piloting a shuttle on the job for another eighty hours, Abby could test to fly a sublight. Assuming she passed, she could take watches on the *Revelation* with supervision, then after another hundred-sixty hours she could test for a full FtL license. With a university education and FtL pilot's license, she would be qualified for nearly any job in the Fleet unless it required a residency such as medicine.

Harden's voice became harsher. "Now let us run through the plan. As an intern and the lowest in the ship's so–called command structure, I expect you to keep your mouth shut and ears open."

ABBY SPENT THE NEXT FEW days in constant study. Each morning at breakfast, Diane and Brian discussed their workload and told Abby what they expected her to do. She trailed behind them and listened as they explained a system's function and purpose within the ship. The wild swirls of entangled metal and polymers began to make sense as they worked on one system after another.

After her duties aboard ship were completed, she spent two hours with her CG Instructors learning algebra and biochemistry. The instructors seemed almost to be alive, with their ability to read her facial expressions and act accordingly. They went step by step with her and never got upset when she made a mistake. Such attention allowed her to improve her skills far more rapidly than she believed was possible, especially in mathematics, which had been her worst subject in primary school. However, they were not exactly like real people. Before the lesson, they asked her how she was feeling, but if she tried to speak about anything other than the subject they were supposed to teach, they simply nodded at her and quickly moved back to the subject. As they were programmed to follow a chain of command, when Abby told them she got a harsh reprimand for forgetting to turn off the coffee pot before going to the sack, she received another for complaining to them about it.

Abby was also given read-only access to the crew reports and ship's log in order to familiarize herself with the crew and the way the ship was run. After all, she was supposed to be a fleet brat, not a complete stranger.

The Alekos family had been starfarers as long as there had been a fleet. Their operating budgets were slightly tighter monetarily than some of the other old fleet families, but this was due to their specialization in exploration and investments in new tech.

Abby learned the Fleet Captain was currently Cole Alekos. He had inherited the job from his mother after she retired to the flotilla. Due to time dilation, he was only twelve years older than Harden. Abby was to meet this man on Argent. She hoped he was nice.

Cole's profile said that he had once been married, and his work permit listed him as a widower. Abby clicked on the linked photo. Rosemary Finch was tall and lean like Helen and Harden, but she had given her best feature—spirited green eyes—to Mark. Abby noticed the overlapping rendezvous dates on Argent between the *Endurance* and Cole's old ship, the *Antria;* it explained the large age gap between Mark and his elder siblings. Rosemary's death was listed as natural causes at the age of 117.

Abby's new "mother," Donna Lee, used to be friends with Helen and Diane when they were young women. What little records that the Alekos had access to showed a woman disappointed in the mission in which she spent nearly two decades of her life. She and six other engineers died while trying to upgrade the *Vos* to an FtL ship. The engines could be stabilized. However, the hull ripped apart during the test flight.

Harden said he was married twice and his records indicated this was the case. His first wife was Lucy Brown, an engineer with numerous accommodations, until she died at age twenty-six. Abby clicked on her dossier; she was a Khlôrosan with curly black hair pulled back in a ponytail and wide eyes. She wasn't exactly pretty, but she had a fun-loving wickedness in her smile. They had only been married for a year and a half, but had known each other for eight years. Cause of death: accidental airlock malfunction.

Abby shivered.

A decade after his first wife's death, Harden married Phoebe Willows. Her photograph showed she was a peerless beauty among the Kiposi. On the *Revelation*, she had been the Senior Biologist and Attending Medical Doctor during Mark's residency. Married for only three years, their divorce was finalized prior to the end of Mark's residency. She stayed on to finish training him before transferring to the *Polaris*, owned and operated by Brian's brother and nephew.

Records showed that Helen captained the *Tycheros Asteri* to drop tachyon relay stations. Officially, she took a demotion to pilot the *Revelation*. Abby noticed something interesting: Harden and Helen's birthdates were only fourteen months apart, though now over five years separated them. Abby was glad to discover her first impressions of Helen were correct. Passionate and confident, yet gentle and kind. Every command was given in a whisper, but obeyed immediately.

Brian and Helen met up on O-3 while she was commanding the *Tycheros Asteri*. He immediately transferred to her ship and followed her to the *Revelation*. Abby found that she really liked Brian. She felt safe when he squeezed her shoulder. His easygoing nature was a salve for the tightly wound Alekos clan. His only passion was Helen. He never even looked at the beautiful Diane with a roaming eye, much less Abby. The only thing that surprised Abby in his records was on paper, he seemed to be wealthier than Helen and Harden put together.

Abby asked him about it. All Brian said was, "I can do what I'm good at here. On a Tolis ship, I'm expected to be a Tolis. Besides, Hel's closer to her family than I'm to mine. We like her brothers."

Mark had followed his brother from ship to ship, sometimes with their father, other times just under his brother's supervision. Not surprisingly, his late teens were littered with discipline issues. It seemed one day he decided to grow up.

She asked Mark, "Do all fleet siblings stay together?"

"Some like Brian marry into another family, but only a few go planetside or into the flotilla. A family has to be careful not to split up fleet finances between offspring. Lack of funding can literally kill a ship and her crew."

Abby asked, "But what if someone is really greedy?"

"Planetside folks have to buy houses and cars, but I don't need any of that. The ship's operations budget provides us nearly everything we need. My share gives me more than I could ever spend in a lifetime. When I want something for the infirmary, all I have to do is write up a requisition."

"What if you wanted more?"

"More of what?"

"I don't know, whatever. What about a laser gun?"

Mark laughed. "What the fuck is that?"

Abby shrugged and blushed. "Something I saw in a vid."

He was still laughing as he shook his head. "Your vid certainly sounds like an accurate portrayal of fleet life."

The non-related crew was just as close knit. Helen had once commanded Rebecca Anderson's father, before she came to work for them. After she passed away, Harden was her daughter's guardian. Patrick Mason had come from a friend's short-range transport.

Diane served with the Alekoses on the *Antria*. She had rigidness in her personality, which made her a good engineer. She was born in the fleet, but left at twenty-two to pursue employment on Argent during the terraforming boom. She married a local man and they produced a son. After the moon was stable, her husband was laid off and she went back to the fleet in order to provide for them. Her husband and son stayed on Argent. Eventually, her husband got lonely and became her ex-husband. He had full custody. She was allowed visitation. When the reproduction laws were passed, her son was sterilized and eventually lost to planet-time while she lived on across her own time-line. The photos of her son and his wife still graced her walls.

Though the crew reports and her class work were interesting, the best discovery so far was made when she spent time with Brian going through the systems of her shuttle, *Revelation Chi*.

As soon as they stepped inside, Abby clapped her hands together. She didn't dare touch the controls, but behind the third seat was a four-legged robot latched in and standing quietly in his station. She kneeled in front of the robot and touched his cow-shaped body. Like the *Revelation*, his outer hull was slightly dented and worn but, as she looked closely at its optics, she noted the cameras were clear.

"Rover will be your extra set of hands on the landing. He can collect samples, traverse cliffs, and whatnot, but don't you dare leave him behind. He cost Harden and Helen over a hundred-sixty thousand credits to build."

He showed Abby the basic command structure on the wrist tablet of her environmental suit. Following Brian's direction, she programmed him. His feet clattered across the deck as she had him fetch a needle off a near-by table.

"He walks like a cow!" she said, clapping her hands together.

"I'll have to trust you, sweetie. I've never seen a cow."

"Like a sheep, but bigger, and no wool. What perfect control he has," she said as she telescoped his clamp in and out of his chest.

"As a secondary, Diane can run him and pilot the shuttle remotely, but generally will stay out of your way unless she sees a need."

"I've a question."

"That's what I'm here for."

"I don't want to lose my job, but why didn't Rover just harvest the mateodeas?"

"We tried it one year when the flu was going around. Ended up with a high percentage of dead loss. Helen had to ask Cole for some money. Harden wasn't pleasant."

"But he seems so gentle." Abby fiddled with Rover's camera functions before she unlatched his hull door and looked inside.

Brian smirked. "I can only assume you mean Rover?"

"Yeah."

Brian said, "Though he has some intelligence, AI that can make human level split second decisions are incredibly expensive. We would not profit upon anything with such technology, especially once it goes sentient. Animal intelligence is different."

"Does that often happen?"

"We don't see it so much anymore, but when I was a kid, it happened quite a bit. Once it's sentient, it's cruel to keep it—no better than slavery. They normally want to be with their own people."

A memory registered in Abby's mind. She asked, "You're birthday is March 3, 2763?"

Brian nodded as Abby frowned in thought. "On Earth, the AI left during the 27th and 28th centuries. They said they wanted to find their lost brothers."

Brian's eyes brightened. "You think the Kipos and Earth AI were in contact?"

"I've no proof, but that has been my belief since I learned your AI left."

"Mine as well. Have Rover jump."

She pushed the button and he jumped higher than she expected. She giggled in delight and Brian showed her she could make him do a side step dance.

Abby nodded. "I asked my guard, Robert, about the AI on Kipos once. He said he hadn't ever seen an android. Do they still live on Kipos?"

Brian said, "Rumored to be. Egotistical of the man to think he could pick them out of a crowd. I couldn't. Maybe my mom or Cole could. They grew up with androids. Planetside Kiposi haven't been aware of them for maybe eight, nine generations, but they are still there. Generally, living with a family who may or may not even realize that their servant, accountant, or nurse is an android until the poor soul falls apart or their programing gets corrupted."

"They ever go berserk like on the vids?"

"Not that I've heard," Brian said. "They normally shut down or freeze. My mom described it as watching a stroke victim. Even then, they try to protect their human families. They have been known to bury themselves, leave wills."

"That sounds awful. On Earth, there were broken AI. They all lived huddled together. We weren't even allowed to talk to them. My da said they were deranged."

"Probably were. With the sum of human knowledge but no internal desires of their own, they tend not to know what to do with themselves.

"Now we'll take Rover apart," Brian said, "You need to know how to fix him."

Abby reached out for Rover and patted his hull before she took the offered screwdriver. "It won't hurt him?"

Brian squeezed her shoulder. "He has no nerve endings, but it's nice that you cared enough to ask."

CHAPTER 29

Argent: February 10, 3166 K.E.

ABBY FELT THE SHIP SLOW to sublight speed as they moved past Ounzio's orbit. She felt the ship slow further as they went into the inner solar system. She was curious to see Kipos and the three moons from the other side, but a long day awaited her on Argent in the morning.

She lay on her bunk thinking about her innocence and gullibility, which had brought her to this moment. She knew it was possible she was falling into the same trap by putting her faith in the *Revelation's* crew. It would be dangerous in the black and she had tasted the exhausting work, but she knew there would be wonders so sublime that she could hardly imagine them.

Later, that night she woke up to laughter and sounds of passion through the carbon wall. She did not recognize the woman's voice, but the man was Harden, which made sense, since it was coming from his billet.

Abby giggled. He was terse and unfeeling, whether he spoke about the day-to-day operations of his ship, his younger siblings, or orders from his father. It was hard to imagine him being close to someone with such ardor. Wondering if she would have a new crewmember in the morning, she turned on some music to drown out the noise.

HARDEN AND THE WOMAN WERE having coffee in the galley; neither seemed embarrassed nor uncomfortable when Abby entered. The woman's wide-set eyes had the puffy look of someone who had drunk a bit too much wine. Her nose was slightly more prominent than most, but her face was more than the sum of its parts. Her vermillion dress was of such sheer fabric that Abby wasn't exactly sure if she was wearing a gown or nightclothes.

Hot in the face and unsure if she was supposed to say something, she said, "Hi, I'm Abby."

Harden quickly introduced them as if it were a matter of course that she should expect strange women in the galley when they were in orbit above Argent. Julia Evans was the senior biologist aboard the *Discovery*.

Julia said, "I'm truly sorry about your mother. I never met Donna, but Cole and Harden speak highly of her."

Abby thanked her as she chopped up some fruit, "Are you staying for breakfast? I was going to make scrambled eggs and fruit salad. Is that alright?"

Julia answered in the affirmative and said, "What a sweetheart your new girl is."

Abby beat eggs while pretending not to listen to their conversation since it was obviously personal—something about dinner on the *Discovery*. Harden told Julia he had a few ship errands to run on Argent and wasn't sure about that night.

She peeked after them as Harden escorted Julia down the stairs. It was strange. For all their passion the night before, their farewell was cold. There were no speeches of eternal love even if they were separated by space-time. They didn't even kiss.

ABBY CREPT INTO THE ENGINE room and climbed into the docking system that Diane and Brian were repairing. "Diane, why'd Phoebe leave?"

"Irreconcilable differences. Hand me the .2 socket."

Abby handed her the tool. "But what does that mean?"

"Why do you want to know?" Brian said. Abby heard the warning in his tone, primarily because it was the closest thing to harshness she had ever heard coming from him.

"I'm supposed to understand the ship and crew, but Harden's really cold no matter what he's talking about E. DR and M. BT."

Diane laughed. "How else would you expect him to refer to us in the ship's log?"

Abby shrugged.

Brian screwed a nut then tightened a heavy cable clamp. "Phoebe found out the hard way that Harden's first love is discovering loopholes in the laws of physics. His second love is the *Revelation*. He works long hours, and when he comes back to his billet, his mind is still at work. Between the ship's needs and Helen's influence, he's able to focus on what is happening in this galaxy, but occasionally he is still inspired and spends days working in his lab. Then there was the question of children."

"But Harden was sterilized long before they met, or did I mix up the relative timelines?" Abby asked.

Diane said, "When they got married, they talked about adopting for a while. Back then, there were still plenty of fleet brats that needed someone to look after them, but it never seemed to be the right time. It's too bad they couldn't make it work as friends. She's a good biologist. Hand me the flathead, Abs."

Abby reached back into the toolbox. "What do you think of Julia?"

Diane screwed back on the panel and gave Brian an exasperated look. "We've never worked with her, but Mark says she has some interesting ideas about hybridization. If Julia transferred to the *Revelation*, I doubt they'd even keep sleeping together. Best to keep unserious relationships off-ship."

"Do you ever think of Harden that way?" Abby asked.

Diane frowned and was obviously considering how to reply when Brian answered, "Not my type, but have you seen his sister? She's smoking hot. Don't you have someplace to be?"

Hoping to get a little more information, Abby stalled. "I left you guys some coffee and egg sandwiches."

"Thanks, but you had better not keep Harden waiting," Diane said.

ABBY HAD KNOWN ARGENT WAS terraformed, but she didn't expect to see trees and fields of wild flowers lining the spaceport's tarmac.

The former colony was now an emerald city sparkling a kilometer away against a cloudless blue sky.

The agent's image and voice asked, "How many passengers will be disembarking, *Revelation Alpha*?

"Two. Myself and Abby."

Abby waved at the camera.

"Alright, say hi to Helly for me."

"Sure," Harden replied. The agent gave them their landing clearance. He parked the shuttle in a hanger. Abby found this curious, but he pressed her to hurry into the aerospaceport. They went through the lobby and down a long escalator and a maze of crowded, dimly lit corridors. Harden turned down a long stone ramp that led to a train station.

They only had to wait a few minutes. She was surprised at the train's dinginess. Floors were sticky with spilled drinks and the faded scent of someone's urine. She almost asked a question, but Harden flicked his eyes toward the camera as he spoke about the weather and a few friends she pretended to know. Abby forced herself not to squirm, but the orange polymer seats were not made for sitting and she felt the pressure on her tailbone immediately. Harden bounced his leg impatiently until they reached their stop.

They walked up the granite staircase to the street level. Above them, was a perfect blue sky surrounded by olivine glass and steel. Only metals and glass were recycled; other garbage lined the street. Feral hens and their broods roamed freely underfoot, pecking at pieces of discarded food.

Abby smiled. "The baby chicks are so cute."

"And lice factories," Harden said.

The thin atmosphere and seventy percent gravity made it difficult to keep up with Harden's long strides until he stopped at a machine and slipped in a bill. He hit a button and a pack of three cigarettes fell behind a door. He pulled out a lighter and made an electric spark.

He took a long drag and looked at her. "Don't tell Mark I've been smoking."

"I didn't know you smoked."

Harden slowed as he enjoyed his cigarette, which made it much easier to stay close to him. "I quit after the *Revelation* was put into service. It's easy not to smoke aboard, but on Argent... anyway I made this deal with

Mark. I quit and he'll be my or dad's doctor."

"He wasn't always gonna be?"

"He talked about going planetside after his GE, then again when he finished pre-med. Helen and Phoebe talked him into staying." Harden's eyes swam as he enjoyed the tobacco high. "After these, I'll give it up until the next time we're planetside. Did you want to try? It's extremely addictive, but ultimately has its pleasures."

She shook her head.

The scent of tobacco and food from street vendors and outdoor cafes lingered between buildings. Abby's mouth watered as she wished she had time to take it all in. She saw a group of four boys smoking and drinking bubble tea. She wondered if Jin picked up the habit before his death. She felt Harden suddenly grab her wrist and jerk her along. "Keep up. If I lose you again, I'll leave you here. Fucking Helen."

THE BANK AND LICENSING DEPARTMENT was an old building made from olivine glass, as was every other building, but it still had the carbon ribs that once held glass biodomes. Harden smoked his cigarette to his fingertips and flicked what was left of it into the street. "Old custom from before terraforming. Never assume you can smoke inside a building."

Not bothering to point out she didn't ever want to smoke, she said, "I won't."

People swarmed. Above them, recording bots circled. The only people not seemingly in continuous motion were the six guards. Harden scanned the crowd. He slipped into the line he wanted. Abby stayed right behind him.

He shook a man's hand. "Hey, David. Is the Captain around?"

"This little one is a biologist?" David Anderson asked in a tone that meant he obviously knew the answer was a negative as he took her hand. David looked around sixty, brown man in a dark suit, but beneath his shirt there was a row of dark glass beads and a cross. The sign of the Suffering God?

Abby set her hand on the scanner just as Harden had instructed her. "Just an intern."

Her file came up on the screen. David said, "This picture of you looks horrid. Want a new one taken?"

Cole Alekos came up behind them and said, "Actually, we hoped to get her a new ID card. Remember the *Vos*?"

He was older than he had been in his last photo, with more salt in his black curls and a pair of reading spectacles in his chest pocket. Even so, with his straight back and heavier frame, he seemed more vibrant than his eldest son. Up close, she could see Helen was no doubt her father's daughter. They both had the same vivacious kindness ingrained in their golden eyes. Cole hugged his old friend and shook his son's hand, which Abby thought was odd. He embraced her and kissed her brow before they all sat down.

As David's eyes scrolled down the screen, he said, "Upon your mother's death, you became an automatic ward of Captain Saunders who, of course, also passed on. Now you're eighteen, technically, it isn't required that you become your captain's ward..." David paused.

As instructed, Abby shrugged, simply not caring the way any other eighteen year-old would not care about finances; she cared only about her freedom. "I don't see why I need to be anybody's ward anymore."

"Abigail, you ended up with nothing from your mother. Upon her death, she only had a few hundred credits. The money was taxed heavily. If you lose your job..."

David looked uncomfortable, but so far the conversation was exactly as Harden had told her it would be.

Harden asked, "What are the legal ramifications? She was hired to do class A work. If she's a ward, won't child labor laws apply?"

David used his finger to swipe the question across the screen. The short answer was as the Captain's ward, she was not eligible for class A work until age twenty. It was a law specifically designed to protect orphans from exploitation.

"My mom gave me permission to do class A work and I already did some on Lathos. I don't see the point of all this." Abby hated the snootiness in her tone, but Harden had told her not to worry about such things, even if Cole put a firm hand on the back of her neck—which he did.

She looked up at Cole. "I've been staying out of trouble and…"

David pinched his forefingers together under his lips and exhaled. Abby thought it might be a sign, though she did not know of what. On his next inhale, he slipped his fingers around his cross. It was a strange pantomime, but the men seemed to understand, though Harden looked shocked for a moment. Abby wasn't sure what that meant.

"Well, she's a good worker, but maybe she should go to the *Discovery*? There is plenty of class C and D work with the larger crew," Harden said to his father.

That wasn't part of the script. Abby's stomach dropped. "I want to stay on the *Revelation*," she said.

Without any anger in his tone, Harden said, "You'll go where you're ordered… Dad?"

Cole leaned back in his chair. "I hate to hold the girl back when she's pressing to move forward in her career and studies. Abby's only two months away from nineteen."

David broke in, "Which is why, Captains, it's important if you are going to offer her some protection, you do it now. It will be harder to get later if the need arises."

He tapped on the glass-topped desk and then touched his cross. Another code. Abby realized David knew who she was. Harden and Cole had not told him, but somehow he knew. She guessed he was telling them that eighteen-year-old Kiposi are not left so unprotected legally; this was a blatant sign she was a newcomer. She hoped he wasn't telling them to leave her on Argent. She slowly glanced up at the bot. They were being recorded. Abby was drowning.

Cole asked, "Is it possible to emancipate Abby per the arrangement that, if she does not perform her duties on the *Revelation* to Helen's satisfaction, she will be transferred to the *Discovery* and face the loss of her adult status until the completion of her education?"

David was visibly relieved. "No doubt that would be satisfactory to everyone involved. There is a standard three-part contract."

He swiped his fingers across his screen. Another man in a brown suit appeared, holding a pile of papers. He set them on David's desk and walked away. Abby was happy when she figured out most of the pile were just copies: one for the *Discovery*, the *Revelation*, the bank, customs, and the licensing department respectively.

The first piece was a standardized list of rules for the treatment of wards. Abby thought it was a strange thing to watch her adulthood stripped away. Cole and Harden both had wards before, so David read it quickly.

As a ward at the age of eighteen, Abby was only allowed to do C and D level work aboard ship for only eight hours in any twenty-seven hour period. Her guardian was legally responsible for giving her an education and nutritionally balanced meals of a minimum of 1800 calories a day. Mistakes or misbehavior could be punished with extra chores or confinement to quarters, but she couldn't be fired until age twenty. Though it wasn't significant at her age, if she had been under thirteen, she could face corporal punishment for reoccurring mistakes at her guardian's discretion. Abby buried her sudden worry for Orchid as David went on.

If she felt mistreated, there was a number she could type into any Feed computer, which would send an encoded message to Fleet licensing, which happened to be on the fifth floor of this building. If in her grief of her mother's demise, she mistreated a member of the crew, there would be a physiological and psychological evaluation and, if necessary, deportation to Argent's Fleet subsidized hospital.

"Now sign here. And a thumb scan from both of you," David said to Abby and Cole.

They went through the contract of her release on six months past her eighteenth birthday with the added clause that it was contingent on her working satisfactorily within reason. The *Revelation's* XO was judge of what is reasonable. David also added a clause, which stipulated if Abby wished to finish her education planetside she was free to do so. She was only required to give standard notice and have her transcripts sent to the *Discovery*. There was a form for Harden to sign stating he understood the above.

Since she had technically been Cole's ward, there was the transfer form from the *Discovery* to the *Revelation*. Then David set up Harden as her secondary granting him access to withdraw cash and file paperwork on her behalf, as he did for the other crewmembers when they came to cash-based colonies and outposts. David called down a bot. It took her picture and hovered over to his desk, connecting with a small machine. David hit another button and it printed her out an ID card.

Abby glanced down at the card. The lamination was still warm in her hand and the iridescent chip sparkled. "What's my current balance?"

"873 credits and 64 cents"

"May I withdraw 75 credits please?"

"Sure. How you want it?"

"However. I'm just going to the teahouse and hang out awhile. Maybe do a little shopping."

David handed her the bills as he said to Cole, "I wouldn't want to be eighteen again, but I miss the freedoms of youth."

Abby slipped the money into her zippered coveralls pocket and her ID card into the other as Cole replied, "Who doesn't. How's Sarah?"

The proud grandfather slid his finger across his screen and a photograph of an exquisite dark haired teenager holding a blue-scaled lunapar popped up. "Can you believe she's sixteen this year?"

Cole said, "Sure, but how old does that make us?"

The photo dissolved into another. Sarah was in an oxygen garden Abby had never seen before. Abby stopped listening to the men's banter as she watched David's life unfold backwards. She saw another ship: *The Vale*. The girl grew younger sometimes with photos of David and people Abby didn't know. Abby watched the photos until she recognized the galley walls of the *Revelation*. Sarah, around age seven, was mixing a dark brown batter with a younger fluffy Rockford watching her. There was the connection. David was the father of their crewmate, Becky Anderson, who died. Sarah had been Harden's ward until he got her back to her grandfather.

The next few photos confirmed it. Sarah was on Helen's lap in the lounge. Sarah getting a piggyback ride from Mark. Then a photo of Becky Anderson holding a toddler version of Sarah on her shoulders. Becky, Helen, and Diane making a baby quilt. Becky and Phoebe. David's arm around Becky's shoulder as she held up her pilot's license to the camera. Becky became a little girl on her father's shoulders with a woman beside them wearing the same cross that David wore now.

Abby wondered why David had left the fleet. He obviously did not blame the Alekoses. Was it the pain of his daughter's death? Did he not want his granddaughter to die in the black? Or did he retire? He wasn't a young man.

Harden withdrew cash for himself and the other members of the crew. Before he slipped them inside the inner pocket of his jacket, Abby noted that each individual envelope was marked with their names.

Cole did the same. There were many more envelopes.

As soon as they were back on the street, Cole offered cigarettes. Harden took one and leaned down to his father's lighter. Abby declined. Cole lit his own and took a long drag. Gesturing to Abby, he said, "She knows not to tell Mark?"

"She knows," Abby said.

Cole gave her a smile and turned back to Harden. "I hope you'll be coming with the others for dinner. It's been awhile since the entire family was together."

Harden muttered a reply about errands.

"Julia hoped you would be finished early." Turning to Abby, Cole said, "Don't let Harden's reticence dissuade you from attending. Though you have been my ward for all of seven seconds, you're part of the family. Don't forget that."

The words were spoken kindly, but Abby did not miss that he was reminding her of the legal ramifications of what they had signed.

FROM INSIDE THE TEAHOUSE, ABBY heard the pounding of drums and a guitar. A girl's voice moaned into a microphone. She glanced at the screen; Amanda Wolfe was the main act.

Realizing how insulated from people her own age she had been since Earth, she wished she didn't have a man as old as her father escorting her. She had the sudden urge to ditch him.

Harden muttered, "You work for a living and should not look like you made your way on your back."

Abby's cheeks flushed, but Harden's eyes had flickered toward a girl in a short skirt and a low cut blouse walking past them. "It's fucking 14:00. Where is she going dressed like that?" He didn't give her a chance to answer. "I'm going to stand over there and smoke my last cig. Hurry up. People are going to think I'm a fucking pedophile."

"Do you want anything?"

"How about you take up a sensible vice like smoking?"

Inside, Abby glanced around and stood in line. She ordered a Thai iced tea and asked the girl in front of her where she got such a cute top. She bought the main act's poster and a flash drive with the day's bands' music and biographies on it. Abby wished she could stay longer, but she didn't dare.

Still smoking, Harden started walking as soon as she approached. She punctured the cellophane and took a sip. It tasted almost like home, but even sweeter. She had to hurry to catch up with him.

"Tell me there were girls your age inside," he snapped.

"I got the names of a few stores, even one with a sale. Just down the street."

The hint of youth came back into his eyes. Abby realized he didn't particularly want to go to a store that catered to students or any place that she might want to go, but he was pleased with her.

ABBY WAS GLAD HARDEN DUCKED into a nearby bakery. Young women wandered around the shop in singles and pairs. A few were walking arm in arm with young men. There was a lot of frippery and all the young women wore makeup on Argent. Helen had told Abby that cosmetics tended to clog the gray water system on the ship. No fleet brat would spend money that way. In her plain coveralls, Abby felt like a weed among flowers. She glanced at a nearby screen and scrolled through the catalogue.

"Can I help you?" another heavily made up young woman asked. Close up, Abby noticed she wore an opalescent cream on her cheeks to mimic microscales. Abby wondered if the fad was to prove one wasn't Earthborn or to disturb parents. Her blouse was cut low enough that no doubt her dad hated it. Or did the sales girl even have a dad?

Abby bought two pairs of pajama pants—one pale green with lines of little pink hearts and the other with dancing sheep on them. She also got matching tanks, t-shirts, underwear, and socks. She used her ID card and her total was under 30 credits. She chatted up the salesgirl as she had been instructed.

She exited and glanced at the bakery across the street. Through the window, she could see Harden smoking and talking to a round woman. She hurried into the neighboring store and scanned through their clearance section. A pink striped cardigan and a matching pink blouse with scrunching under the breast caught her eye. She wished she could throw out her clothes from her time with Barnett, but Helen told her it was better not to spend too much. When they got to Kipos there would already be questions, so she must not do anything that might lead to more.

She dug deeper into the clearance section and found a pair of brown sheep slippers with pink fleece inside. She wasn't quite sure why she wanted them, but they made her smile and matched her new pj's.

Abby wandered past the fashion jewelry section. She reached out and spun the display. Just by touching such things, she felt a little wicked. Her mother and grandmother both wore wedding rings, and on holydays Abby and Orchid would adorn their throats with ribbons, but otherwise there had been no jewelry in the house. She picked up an inexpensive pendant—an olivine cherry blossom encircled with silver. It was only a single credit. It felt wicked, but it was her money. She earned it. No one would go hungry or need new shoes. It couldn't possibly hurt anyone else. She still had nearly forty dollars in cash and eight hundred credits in her account.

ABBY RAN BACK TO THE bakery. Upon her arrival, Harden pushed an apple fritter and a carton of fresh sheep's milk towards her. "Get full. We won't eat again until 21:00, maybe even 22:00." He took a drag on his cigarette as brown sugar, cinnamon, and apples melted into her mouth. "I can't believe you roped me into a family dinner. Normally, I get out of these things."

"I'd of said…"

"Don't worry about it, kiddo."

"Why did David leave?"

"He's always been a bit of a gypsy. Worked under both Dad and Helen. For a time, he was a flotilla liaison, but he has become too kindhearted for politics since Becky died. He became Sarah's guardian, began working in the bank."

"Sarah never knew her dad either, did she?"

"Nope," Harden said.

"What's going to happen to her?"

"She wants to be a dancer and actress. The kid has talent too, but as you can imagine, there isn't a lot of call for the respectable side of dancing in the fleet. Haven't seen her since she was maybe seven or eight." Harden frowned for a moment as if remembering something, but did not say what he was thinking.

"Will David stay moonside?"

"Probably. He loves that kid more than anything. I doubt it would be much of a sacrifice to him."

"Is he Kyn? I saw his cross."

"Yeah."

"I thought… I read that the Kyn always wore black robes."

"You should know how people always like to shove people into little categories," he said. "People join the fleet for a variety of reasons, but we all share a love of personal freedom."

She nodded. "So David joined the fleet. He was not born into it?"

Harden gave her a look, but Abby could not decipher if he was annoyed or impressed by her continued questions. "Yes, he wanted to marry outside his faith. They joined the fleet together and were never parted until her death." He lowered his voice. "His marriage allowed him to help raise Becky and now raise Sarah. As you know, that is not always the case for fleet men."

A rotund brown woman with a kind face said, "I love when fleet kids come in. You're so much more polite than the local riffraff, and you won't believe how bratty those Earth kids can be."

Abby wondered why people felt the need to make comments there was no right answer to. "Thank you, ma'am."

The woman slipped a cookie onto her plate. "Your mother was on the *Vos*?"

Abby glanced up. "Yes, ma'am."

"Poor baby. Try that. New recipe."

Toffee surrounded by buttery dough melted into her mouth, but Abby could have laughed. Harden had told her no one would question a fleet brat who had lost her family aboard ship. Everyone's reaction was always the same. This time she got a free cookie.

Except for a little extra paperwork, Harden's plan had gone off without a hitch. Of course, this was just the beginning; convincing the *Discovery's* crew would be much more difficult.

Intermission
The Discovery, in orbit above Argent:
February 10, 3166 K.E.

COLE AVERTED HIS EYES FROM the story he was reading on the Feed and thought *My stupid kids are going to be the death of us all.* In New Alexandria three bonded women had shown up at customs trying to find a ride back to Earth, or at the very least, to be given respectable jobs. Two had wounds so severe they were taken to the New Alexandria hospital. The third–an eighteen-year-old–was sent back to her bondholder. She tried to run and was gunned down by a customs agent. She died laughing. The article's comment section referred to her as "a poor soul suffering from delusional mania."

What caught Cole's attention was the fact she was eighteen and they were calling her a woman. Not a girl, an adolescent, or even a young woman. David had been right. If she were born on Kipos, Argent, or the Fleet, she wouldn't be referred as a woman unless she was at least twenty.

That morning he met another eighteen-year-old woman, except she wasn't. That Abby was raped and had a child somewhere did not make her a woman. At their meeting, David had pantomimed the easiest way to keep the girl safe and allow her to do A level work was to claim paternity. Even if the father was nothing more than a fling on an outpost, he could make decisions for his offspring that a guardian could not. There wouldn't have been a genetic test as long as the paperwork was in order. It wasn't completely random that Donna had sent Abby to the *Revelation* for her studies if she had actually sent the girl to her father.

To David, paternity was only about paperwork concerning a girl the captain was responsible for anyway, but the idea obviously scared the hell out of Harden. He wouldn't claim that Abby was his daughter. Perhaps Harden balked because, prior to sterilization, he had only been with Lucy. Maybe he felt it would defile her memory if he suddenly had a kid.

As for himself, Cole could admit that no one would be all that surprised to discover there was another kid wandering around with some of his chromosomes, as long as the math worked out to prior to his sterilization. A few long stasis flights and mixing relative timelines, he could easily have a kid Abby's age.

However, Harden wasn't even willing to say the girl was his half-sister. Maybe he thought it might hurt Helen and Mark for them to suddenly have another sibling, however that really didn't make sense. They both had encouraged him to lie for the girl. One logical reason could be the distribution of fleet shares, but Harden had never been concerned with money before. Of course, she might be untrustworthy.

A light on the com flashed. Cole set his fingers on the warm, tempered glass.

"*Revelation Alpha* just docked, Captain."

COLE COULD NOT HELP BUT notice Abby's black eyes watching him as he kissed Helen's cheek and hugged Mark as they came through the airlock. The inky depths seemed to be soulless. She was still staring as he embraced Diane and Brian. He did not know how many rumors of the Earthlings were true and wondered if she could be trusted. Maybe that's why Harden did not claim paternity. Yet she embraced Cole as she was expected to do. He noticed she looked too skinny for a girl with a slight tummy, but she didn't look as if she had recently given birth. Of course, at her age and with Mark enforcing exercise, she was no doubt losing the weight quickly. He told himself that if anyone else noticed, they would just look at it as a final awkward stage in growth.

Cole tried to push away his nervousness. Helen had faith in the girl; it had to be enough for Harden or he wouldn't have offered her a job. Besides it did not matter now; the girl had been his ward. At least her clothing was right. Since most of both crews used these dinners as an excuse to dress up, the girl wore a well-made black skirt with a frilly pink t-shirt in the strange mix of formal and casual that only a teenager could pull off. If he did not know her background, he would not have guessed Abby was Earthborn or even Kiposborn. She was just another fleet brat at a mixed family dinner that she probably would have bailed on if she had the choice.

As they moved through the ship, Cole was happy every surface shone under the curious gaze of those inky eyes. The only space that was not set up with as much care was their oxygen garden. *Discovery's* was bigger but less tamed, with Julia's biology experiments invading the space of more established plants. Diane's artistry had created the *Revelation's*. Thus, it was more welcoming. He could admit that.

Julia stepped towards Harden. She was always lovely, but she had obviously taken extra care in her choice of dress. His idiot son didn't seem to notice or care, though he agreed to stay the night. He muttered something about going to the bank and taking care of some paperwork. He said he hated being captain since, whether she was a ward or not, Donna's waif was his responsibility just as Mark had been his responsibility back when he was eighteen.

Cole was irked.

Julia laughed at his foul mood. She said to Abby who was still staring at the oxygen garden, "There are over a thousand species in the garden, some my own hybrids."

Abby replied, "Mark said you propagated many different types of life, including a new type of apple and fruit bearing roses. I'd like to see them."

"Sure, sweetie. Perhaps we might walk in the garden after dinner." Julia glanced at Harden in order to include him. Once again, Harden seemed to acquiesce because it was the easiest of all the options.

They moved to the upper decks through the living space, the galley, and dining area with cabinetry painted yellow and white and where the table was spread with three stuffed hens, potatoes, green beans, and a few luscious looking fruit pies.

As instructed, she stayed close to Cole. She did not flinch when anyone embraced her, but she kept fiddling with the little silver flower around her neck. He wondered if Harden ordered her to act shy. Introversion mixed with youth would be plausible excuses for any social blunders. Cole handed the girl a glass of wine and introduced her to Saul Evans.

He saw her blink at her surprise at the wine's bitterness. He was about to take it when Harden slipped next to her and exchanged it with a matching glass of grape juice. Cole wondered if he didn't want her drinking wine or just didn't want her to waste it. Harden gulped it down and Cole refilled the glass. He was nervous, but not just because of Abby. Most of the older crewmembers had known him since he was an adolescent, but Harden had always been a little uncomfortable on the *Discovery*. He could never handle these dinners without a buzz. He had no idea how to make small talk.

The junior members of the biology team loved to get a rise out of him because he had taken the well-loved Phoebe. Maybe they worried he'd do the same with Julia.

Someone asked if he heard about how Phoebe and her team had discovered a possible cure for G.I.D., the number one killer of Kyn children under six months.

Yes, he heard. "Helen speaks to the Tolises all the time."

Someone else asked if he heard that Phoebe's remarried and now a mother of a little girl.

"I'm happy for her," Harden said.

Cole knew the latter statement was a bit of a lie. Harden gave Phoebe a glowing recommendation and anything she wanted except the *Revelation*. She only asked for her half of their joint account and her own personal items. She had cried; he had not. Harden rarely thought about her at all anymore.

"I don't know what she ever saw in you," someone joked.

"I don't have a fucking clue," Harden said. That was the truth. He married her because she had asked him.

He tried to change the subject to particle entanglement, but the biology team was not ready to leave him alone yet. Someone asked about Abby's fuckability.

He replied, "I certainly have no idea or say how that child spends her personal time. You should speak to her if you're interested." There was no anger in his voice and he did not look back at the girl who was talking to

Saul, but there was a subtle movement of his finger on his glass.

Helen was ready to jump in, but Julia asked, "What ship did Abby transfer from?"

Harden answered smoothly. If anyone recognized the lie, no one showed it. In unison, the crew just nodded and gave a few murmurs of sympathy and empathy. The biologists had been shamed into silence. Cole realized either Julia had known the stock answer or she knew the truth. Julia was trustworthy, but Harden had asked that no one except Cole should know Abby's true identity. Had he told her last night?

Helen brightened the party by pointing out that Abby would start basic flight as soon as they were in space. Everyone had advice, some of it contradictory.

Cole could see by his daughter's smile and excitement in her eyes, she had big plans for her new protégé. He wished he could lie to Helen. He would tell her that he did not care if she could not have a child. She did not have to put all her hopes and motherly instincts toward this Earth girl. There was still time to find someone else, preferably someone born into the Fleet.

Of course, it was a party, so he said none of this.

Cole moved on to more pleasant topics such as the success of the *Revelation's* new engine modifications, which meant the *Discovery's* engines would also be modified prior to their mission to Scorpii.

Harden's plan was madness. However, it worked, as the idiot-genius' plans always did.

PART 5

IN THE BLACK

CHAPTER 30

Kipos: February 14, 3166 K.E.

ABBY WAS SURE SHE WANTED to be aboard the *Revelation*, but as soon as they were planetside, she glanced up and down the tarmac. She only saw other spacecraft, trucks, and the large customs hanger—no faces she knew.

Of course, she only knew a dozen or so people on the entire planet and five of them were her crewmates.

Ten days had passed for her. However, everyone on Kipos had aged two years. Lei was two. If there was ever a chance to be reunited, it was now. She would be young enough to forget Abby had abandoned her.

Mucus rose in her throat. Abby knew that, even if she could find her way back, Barnett and Peony would not let her see the child. She did not really know how to find Orchid either.

Behind her, Brian said, "If you've a brain in that head of yours, start using it. Customs will be aboard in a few minutes."

FOUR ARMED MEN WEARING DARK blue and gold uniforms came through the cargo bay's airlock; two remained outside. Abby saw the blades on their boots and the two laser weapons. They were dressed identically with bright blue planet patches on their upper arms. Two of the men had another insignia of four stars above the blue planet. As the two without the stars took position on the inside of the cargo bay doors, Abby realized she was trapped in her own ship. She was a Serpent and Grandma told her Serpents were calm and clever.

Abby recognized the one who said, "Welcome home" from the crew records. He was Patrick Mason, formerly of the *Revelation*.

"Hey Pat, Alan," Helen said as she thrust a tablet into Pat's hands. He electronically stamped it and handed it back. Abby assumed Alan was the guy checking ID cards.

Pat spoke to Helen about their movements since leaving the planet. "Sorry, but we've been searching everyone coming in from Argent. Earthlings have been causing trouble."

Alan said, "Personally, I think it was a mistake to bring such backward people into our pool. It adds too much chaos."

Pat glared at Alan, but said nothing.

Harden said, "I hadn't realized it had gotten so bad."

"Mason's wife is alright, so maybe it's just the men."

Looking uncomfortable, Pat asked Abby, "Why did you leave the ship on Argent? I see a cash withdrawal and a charge here."

"Went to a concert at a tea house," Abby said as she thought: *Harden's right. Telling half-truths is easier then lying.* "I bought a poster and a drive of songs. The charge was a new sweater."

Mark touched Pat's shoulder. "We decided to give her a try with the mateodeas. Helly's pleased with her, Harden's …well…Harden."

Pat turned back to Abby. She gave a little embarrassed laugh. "I already got yelled at for joking too much with the guys from the *Gnosi*."

Pat said, "Steve was there?"

"And Rich," Abby said.

"Those guys are such characters. Don't worry about it. I used to get yelled at all the time."

"So I heard," she said.

Mark's eyes glittered; he enjoyed this game. Harden frowned. Abby stayed silent; better not piss off her boss. Mark obviously had no such qualms of pissing off his brother. "So how do you like life planetside?"

Pat said, "I miss the ship at times, but my wife's a peach. I hear the men are just as fine, Abigail. Perhaps when the next surge comes, you can find yourself a husband. A young girl should think of her future."

Biting back the urge to scream, Abby nodded. She could not believe this man had been Mark's lover. Pat flipped on a screen and a pretty blond woman with a blue-eyed infant popped up. "My daughter's name is Megan."

Helen gushed at the baby. "She's so cute." Diane and Abby agreed.

Abby caught the shock and hidden pain on Mark's face. Pat used his trump card. The game had stopped being fun.

Pat went to check for biohazards and contraband in the infirmary and cargo decks as Alan searched the engine rooms and pump house. Once cleared, Pat seemed genuinely embarrassed as they moved to the upper decks. "Harden, I know it's a hassle, but it's best if you're present during the search of a girl's quarters whether she's your ward or not."

"Figured, no problem. She's right next to me."

"I'd have thought you would have put her in my old billet."

Harden shrugged. "We can keep a closer eye on her where she is. An untrained fleet brat was not my first choice for this job. If you ever want to come back, you're welcome."

Pat did a cursory glance through the crew quarters. They obviously looked similar. His billet was still the same color, though it was now empty. Alan commented about its convenience as it attached via the head to Mark's. When they entered Abby's billet, Harden snapped at her about keeping it tidy. She rolled her eyes behind his back. It was all an act anyway.

She purposely left her quilt a little lopsided on her bed. She had grabbed more magnetic clips and put a few photos of young people on her wall, as well as the poster of the concert. When they opened the drawer underneath, they found her sheep slippers. They opened her closet and glanced though her personal items: clothing, toiletries, a tablet filled with lessons, a constellation table from Argent, fashion magazines, a romance novel borrowed from Diane, and a small, half-eaten box of oatmeal butterscotch cookies taped shut for zero-g. They asked her a few more questions about her studies, but they obviously didn't expect they'd find anything except a girl's billet.

ONCE THE CUSTOMS AGENTS LEFT, Harden told Abby she was restricted to the ship. She glanced over at Helen hoping that she would change his mind, but Helen said nothing. They left to refill the provisions and meet with the captains of Cole's ships who were in port. Mark and Brian planned on heading out to a bar. Diane went to go change for a date with one of the men on the *Cerise*. Abby felt envious of Diane's easy beauty and obvious popularity with men.

She knew she should study. Instead she sulked, angry with Harden for reprimanding her in front of the whole crew, and even angrier with herself for not telling Harden to go to hell.

Abby heard movement. Someone was coming back up the stairs. She glanced down and Diane thrust a straw and a polymer cup of brown liquid with tiny white squares at the bottom into her hands. "It's the best I could do. I hope you like it. See you in a few hours."

"Thanks." Abby pushed the straw through the cellophane and took a sip. It was milky and sweet, so much better than the tea on Argent. The white bits were flavored with something like coconut.

Since no one was there to tell her to turn it down, Abby turned on the music loudly and sat in the galley with her tablet connected to the Feed. After drinking the liquid, she peeled off the cellophane, grabbed a spoon, and ate the softened coconut chews as she looked up Orchid Stone Boyd Lei.

The same article about the spelling bee came up, as did an article on a school field trip to the Nature Museum. There was a photo of Orchid next to her adoptive mother, Sadie, and her aunt Danielle Blackwell.

Orchid and Sadie had found each other. Harden's words echoed in her head. If she left the *Revelation*, she might get someone killed. She had to stay where she was to keep them safe. She put her spoon into the dishwasher and the cup into the recycler and watched it melt the plastic.

She wandered aft and down the stairs to the infirmary and the hundred-lighted drawers. There was a code on them. She sighed and looked around. Closer to the exam table there was a bank of latched drawers and a sink. She tried one; it opened. There were bandages and basic first aid supplies.

The second one held little vials. She typed in her tablet the names written on the side. They were comfort medicines: antihistamines, antibiotics, antacids, cough drops and syrup, pain killers. The bottom drawer was locked.

She opened the attached cabinet. There was a little broom and dustpan and a bottle of some sort of cleaning gel attached to the wall.

"What are you doing?"

Abby banged her head on the cabinet as she stood up to face Mark. "Ouch!" Rubbing her head, she said, "I got bored. I was just learning what these things are."

Mark looked at her scalp. There was no bump. "For what purpose?"

"None, I…"

The easiness in his attitude was gone. "Abby, what did you take?" He opened the medicines drawer; everything was where it should be. He looked at her tablet. He typed something into the pad on the wall and a display flashed on. All her movements of that day were recorded. She should have guessed that would be the case.

"I just was exploring. I…"

"If you're going to lie, just shut up." He watched her on the monitor. "Ten times speed."

She had been acting childish, not criminal, but she realized how truly idiotic she had been. She was a runaway and had angered her only protectors, the only people on the whole planet who had been good to her. Diane had even bought her bubble tea and she repaid them by prying.

"Your tablet and the ship support your story." Mark sounded relieved.

Abby chose her words carefully. "I'm sorry. Please don't be mad. I wouldn't have stolen…"

Mark looked at her. "This is yours to use. I was afraid you ingested something without knowing the correct dosage or side-effects."

She was tired of being treated like a kid. Or a stupid Earthling. "Do you think I'm dumb?" she asked.

"No, but you don't sleep well. It's gotten worse since the news of your siblings and daughter. Harden wanted you off at Argent. Dad…"

Pretending not to care, Abby shrugged. "They're worried about my liabilities."

"If it makes you feel better, he's on my case way more than yours," Mark said.

"You didn't get restricted to the ship," she snapped. "And you don't have to be concerned about getting fired or have your adulthood rescinded."

"Maybe not, but Harden and Helen are cross with me so Brian's crabby—and actually, I could get fired if I were to be found guilty of malpractice. I only get a crew share. Adult or not, just like you, I'd be shipped off to the *Discovery* or would have to go planetside." His voice became silky. "I didn't used to care Pat took an Earthling as a wife. I'm not sure how I feel…"

Abby knew it was a sweet lie. Desire ramping up in her chest, she knew she could swim in his green eyes. As if he was aware that she had begun to swell, his fingers moved across her ear and began gently rubbing the back of her neck.

"I thought you liked men?" Abby asked.

They walked back up the stairs and down the corridor to the living quarters. His green eyes flickered. "I enjoy the company of a fine mind more than a specific gender."

Abby knew he only wanted her to fulfill his own jealousy, but his touch made her heart beat faster. She could feel the blood coursing under her skin. Her brain was telling her that she was a poutana, but her body didn't care.

When they reached the hatch to her billet, he brushed her scar with his fingertips. She did her best not to blush and shiver under his touch. He kissed her cheek. Electricity surged to her brain. Her mouth went dry. Her arms felt heavy as she slowly tried to encircle him, but she turned her head, hoping he would kiss her lips. She closed her eyes and waited.

Nothing happened.

She opened her eyes. He was looking down at her. He seemed confused.

Then he frowned. "You didn't have a lover before you came to Kipos?"

Abby shook her head. "On Earth, or at least in my neighborhood, a girl worth her salt doesn't do such things outside of marriage."

Mark's eyes dulled with sudden uninterest. He backed away from her. "I better go. I-I-I've some work to do." He stumbled as he turned and hurried away.

Abby felt like crying. Even away from Earth, a Serpent was unlovable. Grandma had told her that she was supposed to be clever, soft-spoken, sensual, creative, prudent, responsible, and constant. She was not being any of those things. She was a mother without a child, but still a mother. She should be acting like a woman, but in fact, she was just being a stupid girl.

ABBY CRAWLED INTO THE OXYGEN garden until Kipos' two suns set. Not wanting to see Mark, she slipped out past the engine room. Inside, she could hear Brian say, "Don't worry so much, Anasa mou. Mark stopped before it went too far. Forget it or send the girl to your father, but don't worry."

"I can't send her away. Abby reminds me so much of the time when we were taking care of Sarah. It's almost like we still have her around."

Brian sighed. "You can't take in every waif that comes our way."

"Do you not like her? If you don't, then I'll send her to Dad."

"She tries hard and listens in the engine room. She's way more respectful than your brother was at her age. So yes, I like her, but that does not change the fact her presence causes problems for the ship."

"You sound like Harden," she said.

"If you want her, I'll help. You know that."

Abby could not hear what Helen said into Brian's shoulder, but his arms wrapped around her and squeezed her tightly.

She watched as Brian kissed the side of Helen's neck as he rubbed her shoulders. His mouth followed his hands. He kissed her shoulder, his hands led his mouth down her torso, cupping her breasts and unzipping her coveralls.

Abby hurried away before she was found out. *How romantic.* She wondered what "anasa mou" meant and she hoped someday someone would say it to her just the way Brian said it to Helen.

As she hurried up the stairs, she ran into Harden. "What are you doing?" he asked.

"You don't want to go back there. I saw more than I wanted," she lied, knowing her natural embarrassment would cover the fib.

Irritation spilled onto his face. "Who?"

"Hel..."

"Okay." The annoyance went away. He turned around and headed back up the stairs. "I'll talk to her later. We got our flight clearance for the morning."

"Wait," Abby blushed, not quite knowing what to say. "I don't get your rules or the way the ship is run...I'm sorry about today."

"I've no stomach for your self-pity," Harden snapped, then unsuccessfully tried to soften his voice. "Better that you looked up Orchid in your tablet than went after her. No one thinks this is easy for you. Brian hasn't seen his family since he married Helen. Diane's ex and son, have long been dead and buried. When we return to Kipos, your daughter is going to be twelve and your sister is going to be a few years older than you are."

Abby nodded.

"As for the other thing, personally, I'd rather them keep to their billet, but if Helen needs her husband, then she does. Besides, she owns this ship as much as I do. If I ordered her to do anything, she'd laugh at me. As for you, I don't know who you might bring home, which is why I better not see them in any part of my ship except your billet."

The question was out before Abby could stop it, "I can bring men here?"

Harden gave Abby such a long look that she looked at her feet again. "Honestly, when we get to O-7, fooling around with a boy your age might be a good idea. You're supposed to be a fleet brat. The more people who know your story, the safer you'll be."

"Is Mark still upset?"

"Yes. If I were you, I'd not work too hard on that crush of yours. Still, what you do is your business. I just don't want to hear about it."

He changed the subject. "I've been meaning to ask you something that's actually important." He pulled out a puzzle book out of his pocket and flipped it open. "Ten letter cutting marine Earth bird?"

She slipped to the stairs above him and looked down at the puzzle. The fifth letter was a R, eighth was a T, tenth was another R.

"It's not cheating as long as I don't look at the Feed," he said.

She closed her eyes and whispered, "Can't be a cormorant, murrelet, or pelican..." She found the answer and said, "Shearwater?"

"Excellent. Thank you." He wrote down the answer in his neat script, flipped the book closed, and returned it to his pocket. "Mark and I are heading out." He did not invite her along. Nor did he tell her she could leave the ship.

She climbed the stairs and went into the galley. She turned on her tablet and read about situational awareness or SA, the all-encompassing term for keeping track of what's happening when flying any ship. There were hundreds of variables, but specifically, Abby did a few practice equations to discover the escape velocity for any given planet.

Though, most of the time, the shuttle would do the equation for her, a computer malfunction was always a possibility. Helen and Diane had both told her to study up, as SA questions filled half of the written flight test that she would be taking in three weeks. She was nervous, but refused to believe that she would fail. She wanted to fly through the stars, discover new planets. She wanted to be the first human to touch them.

CHAPTER 31

FROM THE LONG-RANGE SCANS, PLANET b and its two moons orbited right in the center of the Habitable Zone, or the HZ as the crew called it of CD 34-4160. Though it was over ten times as large as Kipos, its rocky core was not nearly as dense. Gravity was 130% Kipos standard. From the probe, it looked like it had good potential for limited terraforming. The atmosphere had close to the correct ratios of needed gasses and pressure. A single ocean covered thirty percent of the planet. Rocky dry deserts encircled the equators, covered nearly half the landmass. Both poles were covered by icy tundra so cold that nothing but tardigrades could possibly grow. Only the temperate zone would be suitable for human life, but the landmass was comparable to all three of Kipos' continents.

As soon as they were in space, Mark explained Abby must run with a weighted belt around her waist and then her wrists to build muscle mass in preparation for the higher gravity of planet b. Every day, the weight she carried would be increased until she weighed 82.9 kilos, what she and her gear would weigh planetside.

Abby understood the logic, but some days it felt like torture. Still during these hours, she had Mark's undivided attention. Or at least her vital signs had his attention.

Between her duty and studies, Abby had almost no free time. Excited about the coming planet and nervous about her written flight test, she grew impatient during the three relative weeks in the black. The *Revelation* wasn't large enough to have a physical flight simulator, but Diane programmed a holographic game to be a perfect match for the shuttle controls. The objective of the levels was to defeat an evil reptilian alien species and rendezvous with the mother ship, but the player earned more points for completing a level using flight skills rather than weaponry. Abby played the pilot while Helen, Diane, or Brian worked the guns.

She asked the others if they wanted to play, but Mark told her immersion games gave him motion sickness. Harden told her he preferred to spend his free time far away from a teenaged girl who shrieked every time the holographic aliens blew up her holographic ship.

Abby began to mumble out an apology, but Brian cut her off. "I try not to scream, but these are damn fine graphics, brother." He grabbed the shoulder of her coveralls, "Come on, I'll play with you again."

AS THEY WERE GOING OVER the topographic maps of Planet b, Abby asked Mark and Diane if they had ever encountered real aliens.

"Sure, all the time. Plenty kinds of life out there. What do you think the mateodeas are?" Mark asked.

"I meant smart ones? Like a whole different culture."

"What, like Earthlings?" he asked.

"But we're the same."

"We came from the same people, but we aren't the same. Not anymore," he said seriously.

Abby wondered what that meant. There wasn't much difference between Homo sapiens and Homo khlôrosans. He was willing to see their similarities before her mistake on Kipos.

"So the biologist is saying we are not human?" Diane said, crossing her arms in front of her. "Because Abby refers to herself that way and so do we. Last time I checked we are all sentient beings belonging to the genus Homo."

"While we are from the same genus, there are some differences between the species," Mark replied. "For example, for her size, Abby has more muscle mass. I can only assume she heals faster because her circulatory system moves almost twice as fast as ours."

Diane stared at Mark for a moment longer. "So who is not a human, Biologist MD?"

"We are all humans," Mark admitted.

"Very good. I thought you left your brain in your billet." Then Diane turned to Abby and said, "We've only found artifacts of past civilizations. It's possible you might find intelligent life on the CD-34 4160 b."

EVERY NIGHT AFTER DINNER, THE crew spent forty-five minutes watching an episode of *Echos*, a comedy vid that took place on a ship by the same name about four male Kiposi and an android who were lost in space. Abby thought this was peculiar, but tried not to think about it. Everyone else always laughed. She wondered if she didn't understand the humor because she was originally from Earth or because being a crew-member on a spaceship was still a new experience. Some of the gags were about the paradoxes in time travel and stasis, but most were related to the cast of five heterosexual males. There were plenty of discussion of bio-logical functions, penises, sex acts, and the general lack of women.

Abby often felt her cheeks redden due to the mixed company, but it felt nice to have a beer or popcorn and sit under the quilt between Diane and Helen. Rockford always squished himself between the women. They petted him absent-mindedly and he gave them tiny love bites.

TWO DAYS FROM THE SYSTEM, Harden called Abby into the galley. She had to fight to keep her hands from trembling as he handed her a tab-let, empty except for the test questions. "You have two hours."

He told her, in order to make sure she did not cheat, he would need to sit with her. At first, she thought he'd actually watch her, but instead he did a crossword puzzle.

Abby couldn't believe her luck: word problems with multiple-choice answers. Even if she wasn't sure, she could guess. The first few questions were equations to find escape velocity. She had practiced plenty of those.

The remainder of the problems covered shuttle instruments, orbits, atmospheric issues, navigation, and checklists. The exam was much easier than Abby had expected; she finished in ninety-four minutes. She wondered if that was good or bad. She hugged herself and chewed on her lower lip as Harden plugged the tablet into the main computer and submitted her answers along the Feed to the *Discovery*.

"How long?"

"At least an hour. Maybe longer. Your test score is a low priority message," he said.

Abby began chewing on her thumbnail.

Without turning around, Harden said, "Di could use an extra set of hands on the CO_2 scrubbers. She'll show you what to do."

THREE HOURS LATER, HARDEN CAME down to the engine room with the message she passed and Cole had cleared her to begin shuttle training. Then he gave orders for the engine room to be prepared for the continued use of fusion engines for sublight and FtL once the *Revelation* was in orbit over CD-34 4160 b. No one seemed surprised by any of this.

"So what was Abs' score?" Diane asked.

"She passed."

Diane and Brian shared a look. She hit the com and repeated the question to Helen, who replied excitedly, "97!"

Harden snapped, "And I rechecked your work. You made an arithmetic mistake in one of the equations. Otherwise you'd have got it right. The other one was a wild guess?"

Abby bit her lip. "On the checklist, right? I couldn't remember what happened after the fuel cell check, so I just guessed."

"Well, don't do it when you and Helen start practicing." He passed five bills towards Diane and left.

Abby watched Diane slip the money into her front zipper pocket. "How did Helen bet?"

Diane replied, "Foolishly, if you ask me, since you didn't grow up aboard a ship. She bet you'd miss none. My bet was 96. When I took it, I got an 89, but I didn't study very hard."

Brian said, "I always bet my own score—82. Unless someone is great in math, Mark always bets 85."

Abby frowned. "Harden bet I'd fail."

"Harden bet 77. High enough that you would be allowed to retake the exam and pass the second go around with an 87. It was an educated guess considering how you've been doing in algebra," Diane said.

"Escape velocity and angles are easier than what I've been doing."

"Sweetie, they are the same damn equations. One is just theory and the other is practical application," Diane said.

THE *REVELATION* SLOWED USING BACKWARDS thrust, but to save on fuel, they used the friction of two outer gas giant's atmospheres to slow to sublight. Abby was surprised at how much the ship vibrated; she was also surprised to see Mark's head in his knees, his eyes clinched shut.

Abby hoped she wasn't giving him false impressions by putting her hand on his back.

He glanced up. "I have faith in my sister, but can never watch. Easier when we are in grav-couches."

She put her arm around him. "Don't worry. Not trying to be weird."

"Thanks, and I know."

A burst of sparkling blue flame edged across the window. "Wow! Did you see that?"

Mark glared at her, but Harden glanced back at them and chuckled to himself. Mark put his head down again and Abby rubbed his back. Another hard jolt and Abby felt the pressure push her back in her seat. She giggled.

Diane's voice crackled through the radio. Helen replied, "Cut three."

There was another jerk. Abby felt them slow even more. The vibrating softened.

Mark lifted his head. In front of them was a main sequence sun. Golden and lovely, its inner planets sparkled against the blanket of stars. She squeezed him once more. "I know you hated it, but I thought that was really exciting!"

His face was pale and sweaty, but he nodded. "Yeah. Great."

The next morning, they were in orbit of Planet b. Once Abby had the eggs baking in the oven, she slipped into the bridge so she could see it. She could not believe how beautiful it was. She popped her head back into the galley. She called, "Look, Mark!"

"Yeah, it's a planet," he said dully as he pulled out tea from the pantry.

Abby didn't understand why he wasn't excited. She glanced down at the console. "We're really in geosynchronous orbit of forty-thousand kilometers?"

"Yep, velocity confirmed sublight," Helen said.

"It's so massive. I didn't understand the scale until now. It hardly seems real."

"Scale is hard to imagine, even for me, and I've spent years behind the stick." Helen finished her checks and typed the orbit plan into the computer. Her face was serene as she leaned back. "Will you be ready after breakfast?"

As Abby answered, Planet b's minor irregular moon rose across the horizon. Even from their position, Abby could see, though much of the surface area reflected sunlight, at the bottom of the craters was some sort of darker ground. She glanced down at the scanner: three hundred and fifty kilometers at the moon's equator, chaotic rotation, and no atmosphere, yet for its size it had nearly fifty percent of Kipos' gravity.

"Must have a heavy core," Abby whispered. Then remembering she was not alone, she looked at Helen. "I guess I've only been on three planets."

Helen squeezed her hand. "Good thinking. This is exactly what I expect you to do."

ABBY RAN HER NAILS OVER her scalp to stop the tingling as she fumbled out the preflight checklist with Helen and Brian. She was sure she was forgetting something as they circled the shuttle and checked its systems.

Helen eventually guided Abby to the co-pilot's seat. Her environmental suit now had another layer: G-force cutout pants. Maybe it was just her imagination, but she felt the extra layer made her legs heavy. The shuttle had a basic control structure using a stick for pitch, roll, and yaw as well as two throttles: one for forward thrust and one for backward thrust. There was a gyroscope, plus four digital indicators on the control panel: speed, altitude, course headings, and vertical speed. There was also a sonar scanner, digital camera, and buttons that controlled the shuttle's collectors in the panel between the pilot and co-pilot's seats. It was all completely familiar and yet Abby wasn't sure she could keep it straight.

She told herself she had touched all the controls in the simulations and she had answered every single control question on her test correctly, but she did not feel ready. Her stomach fluttered when she heard Brian say over the radio, "Cargo hold secured."

The bay door opened. Helen detached the shuttle and went into zero g.

"*Chi* clear, *Revelation*. In the green," Helen said after less than a minute. "Dropping from sublight. Heading into LPO 300 kilometers."

"Copy that, *Chi*," Harden replied.

"LPO 300 kilometers, Velocity 3000kph, over." Helen said to Abby, "Ready?"

"It's my turn," she whispered in amazement. She timidly reached out for the stick and throttle. The polymer formed to her sweaty hands as Helen transferred control to her station.

Abby was surprised by the power of the shuttle as she flew in her orbit. Abby's knuckles were white and her hands felt clammy, but as instructed, she practiced a few orbital turns, then descended into a new orbit twenty-five kilometers closer to the planet. Helen frequently corrected her, either verbally or with an assist on the controls.

Abby knew she must keep scanning the indicators and instrument panel, yet the planet was so beautiful she had a hard time remembering to glance down at them. More than once, it felt as if the planet was rising up to meet her and she lost her orbit. Helen eventually dropped the radiation filter. "Start with the gyroscope indicator then glance at each of the others returning to the gyro in between. Then scan the front screen."

There were more orbital turns before Helen smiled. "Rise to LPO 500 and talk Abby."

"L…PO 275, Velocity 3012kph … All systems green. New Orders: heading LPO 500, over." She wished there wasn't so much hesitation in her voice.

"Copy that, *Chi*," Harden said through the radio.

When they were at 500 kilometers, Helen reminded Abby to speak again.

"LPO 500, Velocity 3406. All systems green," she said.

"New Orders: *Revelation* orbit 40,000 kilometers, matching velocity. Accelerating to sublight."

They practiced the landing sequence with throttle control. Abby flew back over the *Revelation*, into the landing pattern, and down to the open shuttle bay with a constant stream of instruction from Helen. Abby seemed to keep the ship steady, though she was trembling badly. She knew if she made a mistake, she would be dead. Worse, she would kill Helen.

After six take offs and touch downs, Helen said, "I think that is enough for today. Good job, hon."

Abby realized they had only been outside for an hour, but she felt completely wiped out. She would have given anything to sleep, but Helen sent her to help Brian check some wiring on the *Chi*. She wanted to skip dinner, but remembered it was her day to cook.

She made it through dinner, skipped watching *Echos*, went into her billet and, not bothering getting undressed, collapsed on her rack. Helen came in. She shook her awake and pulled off her boots. "Brush your teeth."

Abby groaned.

Another shake. A light tapping on her leg. A swat—not hard enough to induce pain—to motivate her to move. "Up."

Abby's feet touched the deck and she took a step. Not realizing it was closed, she walked right into the pocket door that led to the head. "Sorry," she said to the door.

Helen handed Abby her toothbrush and toothpaste. "Your body will go through major stress over the next few weeks while you acclimate to the speed, the last thing you need is a cavity."

Abby brushed her teeth and pulled off her coveralls. She didn't remember where her closet was, so she set them on her bed. Helen threw them in her dirty laundry.

"Okay, you can sleep."

She was too tired to notice Helen turned out the lights.

THE NEXT DAY, THE LESSON was repeated six times. They went for an hour flight, ate or did chores for two hours, then went out again. Once she got used to scanning her instruments, Abby felt the biggest challenge was communicating with the *Revelation*. The dialog between the shuttle and the mother ship was highly structured with standardized phrases; Abby just couldn't remember all of them.

Helen said, "Relax, Abby, and talk to the ship."

"I'm afraid I'm going to say the wrong thing."

"It happens to every pilot." Helen asked, "What is the worst thing you believe will happen?"

"I might crash into the *Revelation* and kill everybody."

"Honestly, the *Revelation* is too big to be taken out by the shuttle and I won't let you crash. What else?"

"Harden will yell at me."

"He won't yell at you about this, honey."

Abby was not sure she believed her.

She also had trouble with her sense of sight conflicting with the instrument panel. The stars and planets played tricks on her. The shuttle dropped into the atmosphere; the flames licking the side of the shuttle dazzled her and created queasiness in Abby's nervous stomach.

Abby was so focused on holding the shuttle steady as it bounced off the atmosphere that she almost didn't hear Helen say, "Note your heading. You'll need to apply backpressure on the stick and more thrust. Get that nose up. That-a-girl."

"If you need to puke, try to do it on the floor, not on the controls. Okay, hon, hold the entry altitude plus or minus thirty meters through the turn. Watch your heading and begin your descent…and remember to talk to the *Revelation*."

BONE WEARY, ABBY SCOURED THROUGH the cupboards. She had never wanted a cookie so badly. Or a cake. If she had a cake, she knew she could eat the whole thing herself. However, Mark didn't like keeping too many sweets aboard. She found the box of brown sugar and took a tiny lump and let it melt on her tongue. Then she grabbed a box of puffed corn cereal and ate a handful.

Diane moved into the galley and pulled out a box of dried pasta. "It seems to becoming more natural."

"Are you sure?"

"We all go through it," Diane replied. "I've felt the ache in sweaty white hands, just like you do right now."

"That's what Helen said, too."

Harden snapped, "Then assume we know what we are talking about. Don't spoil your dinner."

"I'm starving," she snapped back, but put the cereal away.

Diane passed her a hunk of freshly chopped cucumber. "I know you crave sweets, but this is better for you. I gained three kilos when I was in flight training."

WHILE THE BASICS OF FLIGHT remained the same, the atmospheric lessons felt different than the orbital lessons. They flew the speed of sound for a time to see how long it took to circumnavigate the planet, and then over a wide plain of grass where Abby and Helen spent the day faking stalls and recovering from them.

Abby knew logically, in an atmospheric stall, the engines actually had no part either in the condition or the recovery. The problem was the angle of the wing was too great to produce lift and the engine would shut down.

Though her initial response was to pull on the yoke and hit the thrusters, Abby did exactly as Helen instructed. She dropped her nose and expanded the wings to their full length, by reducing the angle of the wing, she reattached airflow, produced lift, and flew out of the stall.

One moment she felt like she was going to crash, then she had control again. It was amazing. Suddenly Abby realized her stomach had stopped hurting. Her hands were relaxed on the stick. She could fly forever.

Helen and Abby moved through different ecosystems in order to feel the differences between air pressure updrafts and weather systems. Abby flew though and faked stalls. Sometimes Helen cut an engine, in order for Abby to get the feel of a lost engine. She landed and took off and found the *Revelation* through all of them.

TWO WEEKS LATER, ABBY HAD finished eighty-five hours behind the stick, forty of those at sublight speed. If she passed her flight test, she would be cleared to scout the planet. Harden climbed into the shuttle with her.

Abby's right hand was sweaty on the throttle, her left even sweatier on the stick. She was pretty sure her feet had turned into liquid in her boots as she took off with a bit too much power. She bit her tongue. Harden said nothing. He just wrote something on his tablet. She orbited the planet using the heading of Harden's choice. She did climbing turns and went into the atmosphere. She landed on the planet and ran through her checklist. While not part of the actual flight test, Harden told her to land in a temperate region and unhook Rover. He watched as she programmed him to take a soil sample. Once completed, she reconnected him to his charging station.

Abby took off again. She did some low flying over land and water, faking a stall. She climbed out of the atmosphere without aid of the flight computer. She circled *Revelation* and landed in the correct pattern.

As she went through the after-flight checklist with Brian, Abby knew Harden was going to fail her. She missed something. She had no idea what that something was. Mark and Helen might be able to overlook her weak mind, but Harden would put her in stasis until they got back to Kipos. She would go to the *Discovery*—if he didn't just send her back to Barnett. She fought the shiver that threatened to take over her body.

Harden said, "Watch how hard you punch the throttle. Accelerating like that is a waste of fuel, same with braking. You've the rest of the night off. Get some rest. Long day tomorrow."

"I passed?" she asked.

"You passed," Harden said.

"I passed!" Abby clapped her hands and jumped up and down. She stopped when she realized the men were staring at her in amusement. She backed away from them and ran up the stairs.

Abby tried to find someone to celebrate with, but Mark and Diane were still working on the morning's exploration plan. Helen was in conference with the *Discovery*. Though Helen accepted her hug and Cole congratulated her, they were too busy to talk. Abby opened Rockford's cupboard, grabbed a long strip of knotted fabric, and went fishing.

"Here kitty," she called.

In a gray flashing summersault, he had the end of the fabric clenched between his paws. Rockford wasn't much for conversation, but at least he would always play with her.

CHAPTER 32

ABBY SUITED UP AS DIANE entered the coordinates of the day's eco-systems into the shuttle's computer. She wasn't about to admit her fear, but she was afraid. She would be on her own, connected to the *Revelation* only by radio waves. Below her, a golden sun was rising against the red-dish brown planet with strips of green covered in a shell of blue and white.

In the equatorial deep desert, temperatures soared over 100° Celsius in the heat of the day. Though uninhabitable by even the heartiest of the human species, Abby still had to assess the ecosystem for anything of value or significance. Since she had to do her sampling in the early morning anyway, Abby decided she was glad to get it out of the way on the first day.

Planetside, she turned on her camera on the shuttle before she went to take samples. The pumice was ground into an orange red powder, but as Abby pushed it aside, she found dry soil with mica flakes underneath.

Rover brought his equipment from the shuttle to the coordinates Abby had given him. Using his telescoping arm, he completed five cycles of lowering the drill barrel assembly, pulling out rocky lengths, raising the assembly back to the surface, emptying the barrel of the tubes of dirt and rock, and lowering the drills again. There were six subsurface horizons in which Abby could see colors of silicate clays, flaky golden mica, white calcium carbonate, and gypsum.

"Low concentration of organic matter, a lack of vegetative production, and no water. Definitely an aridisol."

Abby heard Mark cackle. "Nothing is definite on a new planet. Though you are probably correct."

Out of the corner of her eye, she saw a large insect with a flat, elongated body and red rostrum. She turned her head slowly and let her helmet snap a photo of it. Then she pulled a Petri dish out of her hip sack and caught it before it could crawl away.

She lifted it for a closer look. Four straight antennae were inserted near the rostrum's center. The forehead between the rostrum base and the bright orange eyes had a marked outward bulge. The tibiae of the middle and hind legs had spurs at their tips.

She set the sample in Rover's hull and began pushing the upper layer of pumice around. "I don't see any others or larvae."

Through her headset, Mark suggested, "Check around for some place cool, perhaps under a large stone or maybe some rotten vegetation. Or who knows, it might be migratory."

"Do you think it might be a baby?" Abby asked.

"Who knows," he replied, "but if it is, I wouldn't want to run into the mom."

Abby started hiking down a wide swath of sand dotted with rocky cairns covered with prickly succulents and an array of tiny wildflowers. As she leaned down to pick samples, she saw the signs of birds and small mammals bounding around the rocks. Massive exposed layers of basalt surrounded sparkling waterholes. Abby guessed aloud into her recorder these were a product of erosion by floodwaters.

She took samples of all she saw, but the air was thin and hot. She was glad to get back aboard her shuttle.

HER NEXT STOP WAS A volcanic chain running north to south. She landed her shuttle fifty meters away from the location of a high lava tube. Through her heavy boots she felt a carpet of sharp, loose pieces of rock of varying size. She checked for a breathable atmosphere. The golden light said "caution." She took an air sample and decided to keep her gear on.

She heard Mark whisper in her ear, "Harden's going to be pissed with all that air you're using."

"Tell him to come down here." She whispered back with an embarrassed laugh. "I'll check it again in a little while. Very high sulfur content. Smells terrible."

She heard the slight static in Mark's voice saying something to some-one behind him.

The heavy air tank made her imbalanced and her ankles wobbled with each step as she crossed the uneven ground. Though she did not see any complex animal life, large and small trees held soil and stone in their roots. She was surprised to see the plant diversity in such a dry environment. She collected cuttings from two trees. Then she discovered another plant with a single huge stalk that ended in a head sprouting giant reniform-shaped leaves and tiny bunches of purple berries. Abby knew the fruiting plant would make the crew happy, even if she did get a reprimand for using so much oxygen.

Abby programmed Rover to take the soil and core samples as she headed to the northwest. She tested a natural stone arch across the trench. It seemed stable enough. She slowly crossed it. Climbing a high cairn, she could see another natural bridge to the east. Below she could see the inac-tive lava tube which Mark had instructed her to explore.

The floors of the cave were covered in cracks and holes. Abby glanced up at a skylight only to fall into a shallow depression. Even through her padded protective gear, blood trickled down her leg from a scraped knee. She would have to be more careful.

She paused and shone her light up back on the ceilings. "Golden bac-terial mat covers about twenty-five percent of the ceiling of the first two hundred meters of the cave. There are large areas of black stone through empty spaces in the mats."

"Abby, your heart is beating too fast," Helen said.

"I tripped, but I'm okay. It's dark."

"Are you really okay?" Diane asked.

Abby would not admit over the radio she would rather be anywhere else than in the dark. Her light seemed to disappear too quickly. Though she knew she was alone on this planet, she felt something or someone closing in on her. She glanced around as she opened her pack of collec-tion supplies, but there was no one there. Abby climbed up the wall and accidently scraped her helmet on the ceiling. She wondered if she had left a mark and promised herself she would be more careful. Pulling out her rock hammer, she chipped off a sample of black basalt. She slipped it in an acrylic tube. Abby took out a sterile swab, collected a bit of the brackish smelling slime, put it into a Petri dish, and enclosed her sample with the screw-on cover. She repeated this procedure seven times and wrapped the samples into a tight padded drawstring sack so they could not shift or accidently open in transit.

She felt the sensation she was not alone again. Abby hurried off her perch and out of the cave. Back in the fading yellow sun, she could not shake the feeling she was being watched. She crawled over the natural bridge. She could see Rover in the distance, but fear pressed in on her. Once on solid ground, she sprinted back to her shuttle as fast as she could in her protective gear. The high gravity made every step torture for her lungs. Helen asked what was wrong, but Abby was breathing too hard to answer.

She pressed the open sequence on her command unit for the shuttle doors as she approached. She ran inside and hit the emergency close button. The first airlock sealed behind her. She looked out the shuttle window. A massive, lumbering, multi-legged black organism had followed her. Sweat trickling down her body, she ran through the second set of doors to the control panel.

She hoped that turning on the engines would frighten the beast, but it only stared at the shuttle in confusion. She hoped the camera could see what she was seeing. "Mark? Helen, Diane? Are you getting this?"

"You alright?" Diane asked.

"Yeah, but I don't think it liked me being in its house. I'm going to circle a few times, so the camera can see the organism from various angles before I pick up Rover." She pulled off her helmet and took a deep breath of the shuttle's recycled air.

She flew over the beast a few times. It stood on its hind legs and sniffed with two holes, which Abby assumed were nostrils. Could it smell her blood? Was it still trying to figure out if Abby and her shuttle were food? What truly scared Abby was the large gaping mouth filled with flat incisors surrounded by two large canines on each side. Its lower teeth looked sharp too. Each of its six legs ended in a paw with three sharp-looking claws. It could have easily killed her if it had gotten ahold of her. She only hoped Rover was all right.

The beast was lumbering back to its den as she flew over to Rover. He cow-walked aboard and went to his station. Abby connected him and patted his back.

Rover looked down at her leg, still covered by the environmental suit. He seemed to focus upon it with his camera. His telescopic claw touched her wounded knee.

"It's just a scratch," she said, wondering how Diane had known about the wound.

She went to the controls, sat down heavily, broke out of atmosphere, and docked with the *Revelation*.

Seeing she was bleeding, Mark kept her in the sanitizer for five minutes, and then snapped, "Do you know if you lose blood in zero-g, you can lose consciousness?"

Abby answered, "I tripped."

He pressed a purple nanomite goo into the abrasion. It burned for a second, then faded.

"Can I touch her?" Helen said.

Mark barely had answered in the affirmative when Helen pulled Abby into a tight hug. "You did so good today."

Abby blushed. "I thought I might be in trouble. The air mixture."

"You followed your instincts."

Before they left the shuttle, Helen patted Rover's hull and Abby was almost sure that he nuzzled her hand slightly.

TOWERING GRANITE MOUNTAINS FRAMED A wildflower-filled alpine valley in the next ecosystem. Abby set up Rover to take plant samples while she was drawn to the cliff faces. As she hiked towards them, agile six-legged rock climbers scurried across and, using their nimble front paws, reached into tiny crevices in the stone. Abby adjusted her camera's zoom to take photographs. She could not see if they were pulling out insects or plants.

Abby went onward until she found herself near the base of a waterfall that tumbled into the valley. She took water samples and chipped off pieces of stone covered in pond slime. She jumped to her feet and spun around when she heard Diane say "Abby!" through her headset, alerting her to the six-legged climber in front of Rover.

The bot was between it and its water source. Her camera took pictures as she picked up a stick and backed out of the valley.

She ignored Diane and Mark's rising panic. She could see there were climbers slowly making their way down the side of the granite cliff face in order to pin them in, but she would have to deal with them when they got there. Right now she had to save Rover. She ordered him to follow her, but he remained still. She ordered him again. He did not move in her direction. Diane said, "Abby, just go. He'll follow you."

She backed towards the shuttle. Rover did not follow instead he took one step towards the climber.

The climbing beast charged Rover. Faster than Abby would have thought possible, Rover ducked under its swiping claws. The beast jumped on his back beating his hull. He bucked it off easily. Then reared up and kicked the beast. The beast fell to the meadow floor for a moment. Then shook itself off and turned towards Abby. As it galloped towards her, though she first considered that she might strike it, she rolled out of the way of its claws. In less then a second, Rover was between Abby and the climber. Stomping at it until purplish goo squirted out of its slender body.

Without being ordered to, Rover began packing up the carcass for transport. The other climbers were watching on the hillside, but stopped advancing. He nudged Abby's shoulder. She patted his head. "Scary, wasn't it?"

Rover nodded.

"Time to go?"

He started back to the shuttle. He looked back at her once. She carefully watched the hillside, but no others came down.

Once he was reconnected to the shuttle, his screen performed its standard diagnostic.

"How long have you been alive?" Abby asked.

English words flashed on the screen above him.

```
Since before Abigail Lee, but my brothers
left me. I have no way to find them.
```

"Do you want me to help you find them?"

No, I want to stay with my mother.

"Your mother?"
No words came on the screen, so Abby assumed Rover did not understand her. Abby clarified, "I mean, who is your mother?"

The Revelation.

"Do you have a father?"

Harden Alekos built the Revelation and her
children, but Helen Alekos gave us life.

"Do they know you are smart?"
Rover seemed more and more incoherent.

I stay with my sisters, Alpha, Beta, and
Chi. I stay with my mother, the Revelation.
Gamma is dead. We are a system. Like the
Alekos System. Harden Alekos' mother, his
partner is dead, but Harden Alekos stays
with his sisters.

"Helen wasn't always with him."

```
Like Kokadelfi and Ilios. Who is Abigail
Lee?
```

Abby hit the com. "I need Harden!"

Harden's image came into focus.

"Something's wrong with Rover. He was smart, but now he's struggling."

"I saw it. Calm down. He can't die. Fuck, I thought I fixed that."

"He says he's your son, but Helen gave him life."

"I suppose that is accurate enough," Harden said.

When Abby turned around, Rover was docked and ready to travel. "He said he lost his brothers! Please tell me what to do."

Helen said, "Honey, calm down. He will be all right. His mind is working faster than he can process information."

Abby put her arms around the bot's head. "Whatever you want, I'll help you find it." Rover nestled her and then was still. He seemed lesser somehow, but now the moment had passed, Abby couldn't place why or how.

Using his speakers he said,

```
Seven minutes until launch window. Harden
Alekos, who is Abigail Lee? Rover lost Pat-
rick Mason and Rebecca Anderson. Who is
Abigail Lee?
```

Harden grimaced as Abby sat down in the pilot's seat and started *Chi's* engine. All he seemed to be able to say was, "Shit. I can't believe how quickly he showed himself to you."

ABBY TRIED TO PUSH PAST Mark checking her vitals and tried to hurry Harden to help Rover, but instead Harden told her to get showered and meet them in the galley. She tried to argue, but he repeated his order. She glanced at her shuttle where Rover was housed and back up at Harden. He was immovable, so she did what she was told.

Harden said, "About three years ago, the roverbot designation Alekos Explorer-29307 D or the *Revelation Delta* began showing signs of sentience."

Abby said, "He said you're his father, and he said Rebecca Anderson and Patrick Mason left him. I think he was figuring out where I fit."

Diane said, "Hey, Harden. Look at today's commands." She pushed a tablet across the table to him.

```
Please help me lift this rock.


Let's go to 40° 26.7717, 25° 27' 38" N.


Please take a core sample at 40° 26.7717,
25° 27' 38" N.


Once finished, please collect seven samples
of every plant at same location, 10-meter
radius. I will hike east to the wall and
take water samples of the falls. It's so
pretty here.
```

Diane was frowning in thought. "And that's just planetside. When Rockford comes near you, you always pet him. How often have you patted Rover's head or hull?"

"Almost daily? Especially if I'm doing maintenance."

"Fuck me, another girl who unknowingly uses the magic." Harden's voice dripped with irritation as he flung the tablet towards Helen.

"Magic?" Abby's analytical mind rebelled against the idea, but she was young enough to want to believe. After all, the races of Kipos were technologically superior to Earth and there was still so much she didn't know. Maybe there was some magic on the *Revelation*.

Harden sighed. "This behavior is how we think Helen turned a rover-bot into Rover. Becky did it too. Once Rover was sentient, Pat learned to do it, but not as naturally."

"How'd it happen?" Abby asked.

Harden said, "We don't really know, but it has something to do with the way he interacts with people. Sarah was around and always played with him. So that might have been part of it, but he has always said that Helen has given him life. And Helen always treated him as a member of the crew."

Helen asked, "When you first saw Rover, what was your reaction?"

"I loved him, like I loved Tara or love Rocks."

Harden nodded. "Good analogy. That is about how far his intelligence goes."

"But he can take core samples," Abby said.

Helen said, "You told us that you and your brother taught Tara tricks? It's the same thing with Rover. You ask him to do something he's been trained to do. He wants to please you. He seems smart because he speaks English."

Harden completed his sister's thought. "Rockford seems dumb in comparison, because he doesn't have opposable digits and can only say 'mew,' yet when you throw his mouse for him to fetch or fish, he obliges you the same way."

Abby thought about this for a moment and asked, "What has changed since he became Rover?"

"In his actions, not very much. However, he has changed. A roverbot can do nothing, but follow commands. Rover chooses to obey the chain of command. He questions. He has likes and dislikes. Come on. Let's go talk to him."

AS THEY REENTERED THE SHUTTLE, Rover immediately asked.

```
DNA doesn't match Donna Lee. Who is Abigail
Lee?
```

Harden, Helen, and Abby sat down in a circle beside Rover.

"You can never tell anyone, not even your sisters or mother, or you will endanger Abigail Lee." Harden said to Abby, "Tell him."

"My dad was Cameron Boyd, my mom was Lei Sun Lei. In my culture, on Earth, a child takes both of her parent's surnames. I was born Abigail Boyd Lei, but everyone calls me Abby."

```
Earth, 3rd planet from Sol. Where are Cam-
eron Boyd and Lei Sun Lei?
```

"They died. Earth planetside."

Helen looked directly at her brother. "Her parents are dead, so she is now part of the Alekos system."

Harden scowled, but did not contradict his sister.

```
After Lucy Brown comes Phoebe Willows, af-
ter Phoebe Willows comes Abby?
```

Harden said, "No. Abby is much too young to be a wife. She is an intern."

```
Who is Abby? Who is Abby? Who is Abby? Hard-
en Alekos is Abby's new father?
```

Harden said, "No."

Helen stopped him and said, "Brian, Harden and I are all Abby's new fathers. She is part of the Alekos system. We are teaching her to be a good astrobiologist."

```
Like Mark Alekos was to be a good doctor?
```

"Yes."

```
Excellent. Thank you for bringing me a lit-
tle brother.
```

He nestled her shoulder so Abby wrapped her arms around his neck. Harden said, "You must still listen to Abby."

```
Obviously. Rover obeys the chain of com-
mand.
```

He had no expression on his metal head, but if robots could be offended, he was.

```
Abby must always follow the chain of com-
mand. Ask Mark Alekos. Harden Alekos and
Brian Tolis made Mark Alekos scrub the in-
ner hull. Job took seven days.
```

"Is Mark your brother too?" Abby asked, confused about how Rover made relations.

```
No, Mark Alekos is the doctor. He is Helen
Alekos and Harden Alekos' sister. He never
gave me life. He yelled at Helen Alekos. He
made her cry.
```

AS THEY WALKED AWAY, ABBY wasn't any less confused. "If I do something wrong, he's gonna tell on me?"

"Yes, because he can't forget, but it will probably be years later. I'm sure Mark didn't need you to know that unfortunate incident," Helen said as she climbed the stairs.

"I don't get how he picks relationships."

Harden said, "Rover has a pack mentality. He has a vague idea what captain, mentor, teacher, etc. means, but he does not understand completely. He mixes up gender and relationships all the time since he doesn't have one, and if you try to give him human equivalents of extended family such as cousin or uncle, it just confuses him further.

"He has a vague idea that parents educate and siblings are playmates. The *Revelation* is his mother. She is his mother ship after all. The shuttles are his sisters. He may have picked that up from us because we use the feminine pronouns with ships and the masculine for bots. Or he might say it because his name is technically *Revelation Delta*.

"The human explorers are his brothers, except Helen and I whom he calls his fathers. Brian and Phoebe also are fathers because of the marital relationship. Diane is an engineer. Mark is a doctor. Rover doesn't really have much to do with them, but I once told him that Helen is my sister, so he says Mark is my sister as well. When he speaks of his lost brothers he is talking about Becky and Pat. He misses them terribly. And because he has animal intelligence, he can't understand death or that Pat left the fleet."

"He will wait for them to come home forever," Abby said softly. She wasn't thinking of Rover, but of Tara. She didn't mention her seared heart from abandoning Tara, who was long dead, but had grown old waiting by the door of her family's apartment. "Why don't you build him a companion?"

Harden's look was suddenly ferocious. "Do you have any comprehension of what you just asked? If I ever catch you trying to make something sentient you will be scrubbing every centimeter of this ship until I can send you to my dad."

"She wasn't even on Kipos then," Helen said, "Explain, don't yell."

Harden's jaw worked slightly, trying to choose his words carefully though he obviously wanted to shout. "Abigail, it was an accident. When an AI goes sentient, it is a terrible undertaking. It doesn't know how to find the others, so it latches on to whatever it can. Someday Rover and the *Revelation* will become obsolete. Should I turn him off? Do I have the right to end his life? I'll die of old age. Who will take care of him when Helen and I are gone?"

"Mark doesn't want to?" Abby asked.

"No, he neither has the mechanical knowledge nor the inclination to care for a non-biological being."

"Well, if I'm Rover's brother then I'll take care of him," she said.

"The promise of an eighteen-year-old girl who has just begun to discover the universe. Wonderful."

Harden turned away from her and headed down to the cargo hold to his robotic son. Helen looked at her. "I know my brother tends to forget the most significant information, so do you have any more questions or would you like to process the information first?"

"I have a million questions." Abby said as they began to climb the stairs.

"Go ahead, though I might cut you off eventually—or at least pass you off to Brian."

"How do you know when Rover hurts?"

"Rover began to act fidgety, for lack of a better word. He began to explore the ship on his own. We had to order him to stay in his charging station unless an adult human allows him out. He would sound shuttle alarms to get attention. Of course, we had to tell Sarah to stay away from him unless there was an adult present. That worked some of the time. Sometimes not so much. A roverbot, even one going through the process of sentience, is much more obedient than a human child."

"Is that why she had to leave?"

Helen gave Abby a sideways glance. "Of course not. She left because she had no interest in becoming an explorer."

Abby asked, "May I be with him when off duty?"

"As long as you stay on the shuttle deck."

"Are there any other rules I need to follow with him?"

"His sentience is not discussed outside the crew," Helen paused in thought for a moment. "You should know, either by programing or by chance, Rover's personality takes after Harden. He gets shy and nervous around strangers."

"Harden's not shy."

"You only say that because you met him as an adult. Harden progressed from shy to merely introverted. Even so, he still gets irritable after dealing with people he does not know well. And he has a real problem hiding his contempt for those with less intelligence than he has, which is practically everyone."

Which is why he always shows contempt for me, Abby thought.

"What's wrong?" Helen asked.

Abby looked at her hand. "Will Rover be like that?"

"We cannot know for sure, but I doubt it."

They wandered towards the galley. Helen looked at the coffee pot, sniffed it, and then threw it out. She began brewing a fresh pot as Abby poured herself a glass of juice and sat down.

"Brian once told me that it's no better than slavery to keep AI once they go sentient," she said.

"Any AI with an IQ higher than a human tends not to want to stay with people. They find us limiting. However, unless there is someway to move from animal intelligence into that level, Rover will always need some sort of companion."

"I know Harden doesn't believe me, but I meant what I said. I'll take care of him," Abby promised.

"I know. I meant what I said too," Helen said, watching the coffee brew. "Though I probably should have added Diane to your list of fathers, since she spends more time with you than anyone."

CHAPTER 33

CD-34 4160, Planet b:
May 14, 3170 K.E.

THE NEXT RELATIVE MORNING, ABBY walked upriver. Being careful not to damage the large round plants that lived there, she took water samples. At first glance, the water was slightly more acidic than on Kipos and Earth, but otherwise it seemed pretty normal.

She climbed over some rocks and then dropped into a cobble flat bank. She heard the rush of water and around the next bend, a seventeen-meter-high waterfall poured into the river.

Thin trunks twisted around rocks and curved in strange angles, as if trying to capture the sun and mist in their branches. Wide orange and green leaves gripped to their stems for dear life. Worried she might crush the tree's fragile root structure, Abby crept closer watching each footfall. Littering the ground between the rocks were spiny yellow fruit.

Abby took samples from the litter and from the living tree. The flesh under the bark was a strange hue of bluish gray. As Abby dug deeper, it began to shudder and bleed a pink sap. She took a sample and left the tree alone. She noticed an army of insects covering the sap, sucking on it. As she scraped some of the insects into a Petri dish, they kept sucking on the bits of sap and when the sap was gone, they began feeding on each other. The insects made her think of the old vampire stories she used to tell her siblings and the kids at the library in order to frighten them.

Abby was startled by a scurrying sound across the rocks. She looked up. A furred, two-legged creature with a slender neck and sharp beak stood in front of her. It stared with the distinct look of trying to decide if Abby was a meal.

She rose and backed away slowly while making sure her camera was photographing the creature she was seeing. Another creature jumped on her shoulder and went for the silvery mesh covering her face. She punched at it as another jumped down. Her forearm took most of the impact. The creature looked confused as it gnawed on plastic from her suit. She felt a sharp pain in her right leg. Another was on her.

She stumbled. Without thinking, she jumped into the river. She heard the animals scream and jump off her. The water moved fast, but she kept her head above it and tried to get to the deep clear pool she had seen a little ways back. She heard a chitting of the little animals. Glancing back, she saw her attackers throwing fruit towards the river.

"Are they trying to lure me back?" she said and swallowed a large amount of water.

"I really must be more careful to not get my butt kicked by creatures less than a meter high." She giggled hysterically against the pain as she climbed out of the river. With her eyes, nose, and throat burning, she panted out, "Sophisticated hunting techniques. Used to big game."

She hurried back to her shuttle. Without shutting the airlock behind her, she dove for the fresh water shower button. She ignored Mark's worried voice through her headset. Her body hurt too much to listen. She pulled off her suit and underclothes. Her torso was covered in raw spots while her legs and arms were covered in blood.

Rover entered and went to the starboard panel. He unhooked a hose and sprayed her with a pink sticky foam. She tried to get away from him, but the shuttle was not big enough. He scratched her leg wound and pulled out a little squiggling worm. The foam over her open wounds began to burn. Desperate for relief, Abby dragged her nails across her bloody limbs. She wasn't aware the airlock shut and the engines had begun to rumble as Diane remotely piloted the shuttle. She had nearly passed out from the pain as Rover strapped her to the decking to stop her from further injury once they hit escape velocity.

SHE WOKE UP IN THE infirmary with Mark holding her hand. "You were pretty banged up by those rocks. Next time, please listen to my direction."

Abby noticed her skin was soft and pink.

"We had to shave your head and give you a laser peel to completely decontaminate you. Sorry, but now we know why the river is slightly acidic.

He grabbed an acrylic box and handed it to her. Inside was a thin, translucent worm. "If the crew seems a bit pissy, it's because they had to flush out your shuttle's water and air supply and decontaminate it. Fortunately, space makes the first part easy, but no one likes to scrub the inner hull."

Mark was obviously a little pissy too. She reached up and felt the short, thick hairs covering her head. "Sorry."

The infirmary door opened and Harden walked in. "How're you feeling?"

"Better than I did planetside."

He smiled. "Did Mark tell you what you discovered?"

"We got to the part where worms shouldn't be washed off in the shower."

Harden laughed. "Did he tell you why?"

"I contaminated the shuttle's water supply." She waited for Harden to yell. He didn't.

"Mark came up with the hypothesis your worm saved your life from those septic beaks."

"Huh?"

Mark said slowly, "Julia and I have been in conference. Your blood work shows excessive activation of mast cells and basophils, resulting in an inflammatory reaction. Basically, you were having a cascading response. We gave you an adrenalin injection to stabilize you and put you in stasis. The nanomites began to mutate.

"The worm membranes are not a protein. However, they chemically bound to the proteins on your exposed wounds and mucus membranes. The resulting dermatological response to the reaction between worms and membrane proteins…"

As Mark went on she realized she had no idea what he was talking about. She glanced up at Harden.

"Look at your arm and your right leg. If Mark allows you out of bed, you gotta see your suit."

Abby glanced down at the purplish gash, nearly seven centimeters long, that had ripped across her arm. She lifted the blanket and looked; it was much worse. Two more gashes crossed her right thigh. Purple nanomite goo covered her wounds. *Mark's talking about histamine responses to a nanomite mutation and Harden's happy. Put that together and we get…*

She looked up into Harden's face and said, "Sorry for being slow. Are you saying we mighta found a cure for the deep space death?"

Harden replied in the affirmative.

She clapped her hands together. "That's terrific!"

Mark shook his head. "You fucking explorers are all insane. You have two broken ribs and numerous lacerations. I want those wounds uncovered, so stay in the gown for awhile, Abs. No constricting clothing." He applied one more application of the goo and then pulled out a sheet of an antibiotic transparent second skin. She winced, but did not cry out as Mark grafted it onto her leg. Both men helped her off the examination table.

Harden smiled. "Once we have a workable solution, imagine what we are going to make from this."

Abby asked, "Can we get new cushions for the galley benches?"

Harden nodded. "And new mattresses. My back has been killing me."

Mark frowned again. "Would you two please take this seriously? Abby, you came very close to dying out there. Your entire PH began to lower. And as I was saying, you have two broken ribs. You damaged your gear. Do you have any idea how much that will cost to fix? Harden, aren't you going to say something?"

The elder brother shrugged. "Don't really see the point, since you're doing such a good job. Can I take her?"

Abby did not know how she felt. She had faced death and wasn't scared at all, at least not of exploring. Rover galloped over to her.

"Broken ribs," Harden said.

Rover stopped and gently nuzzled her arm; she patted his head. He impatiently circled them as Abby followed Harden to her shredded suit.

"So, Mark's pretty upset."

"It's a dangerous job and everybody gets hurt. I'm just glad you're okay."

She said, "This job can really only be done by a human, I think. Rover did not save me, but Mark did by telling Rover what to do and Diane by remotely commanding the shuttle. We anthropomorphize him so much. I think I understand the limits to his intelligence. I know you told me, but I didn't really get it until now."

"Does that make you love him less?"

"Of course not. That would be like loving Rocks less because he's a cat."

"Good. Unmanned space travel only works in the beginning of the scouting stage. Humans add something to the mix that has never been duplicated by anything else. AI even admitted that before they left."

Abby asked, "Am I going out again? Do we still have more environments to check out?"

"Yeah, we've been taking some samples in the temperate zones with Rover and the short range probes, but it isn't the same. You may go as soon as Mark says you are healthy enough to do so."

ABBY HELPED AROUND THE SHIP as much as her injuries– and Mark–would allow. Diane and Brian showed her the polymer patches that would hold her suit together. A new cache had to be sewn in on the leg and the right arm had to be completely rebuilt. The needle and aluminum threads were thick, but it was no different than Diane's quilting.

She waited to see if they would scream at her for giving them more work to do, but no one did. Brian and Diane just fixed what needed fixing while Mark fixed her.

While she was in the infirmary, Abby watched Mark run tests on the worm to find a workable and commercially viable medical product. He told her, "Since I figured out I wanted to be a doctor, it has been my dream to cure the deep space death."

"That's so noble," she replied.

Mark looked surprised. "Uh, thanks. I know people who have died from the affliction–we all do. I'm really just trying not to lose anymore friends."

Mark did test after test, dictating into the ship's computer. He had his own doctor's vocabulary, and while she did not always understand what he was saying, she did not like being referred as patient AL. It sounded so cold and detached. Abby observed his steady hands while he sliced open a tiny worm and watched its innards spill on a microscope slide. He asked for a blood sample and took some of his own in order to see if there were any differences between the two races.

Other than being a test subject, Abby could not help Mark with his research. Still she liked to be close to him. She began bringing her tablet into the lab in order to do her studies. He was perfect. She felt alive every time his green eyes turned her way.

She wondered if Mark still thought about her in the romantic sense. Her tummy had become flat by the daily exercise. Though her appendages would always bear the deep scars, most of her stretch marks had faded thanks to the laser peel. Her once long black hair had been shaved off, but she thought it made her facial features more prominent, especially her obsidian eyes. She knew she should not care about such things, but she did.

By the second night of her recovery, Abby was already sick of resting in her billet. She wanted to explore more of the planet's ecosystems, not hang around the ship watching everyone else work.

She slipped into the galley. Abby could see Helen and Harden watching streaming images from the latest deep space probe on the bridge. Curious to see what they were looking at, she set her tablet on the table and took a few steps closer to the bridge. Harden's head sank to his hands. She could hear them speaking in quick, soft voices. Abby figured it was better not to interrupt them. She went back to the table and found it was hard to think about the differences between photosynthesis and chemosynthesis when it sounded like Helen and Harden were watching the stars.

Harden walked through the hatchway. He glanced over at her and sighed before he took out a beer from the fridge.

She started fiddling with her tablet. "I was just sitting here. I don't want to bother you."

"Your presence doesn't bother me, but I hate it when you act like a kicked kitten."

"Sorry."

More out of habit then actual thought, he pulled out a second beer and put it in front of her. As he sat down, he turned on the large vid screen.

She thanked him and asked, "Where's that?"

"Just images sent back from the probe. No viable planets so far, but…"

"It's a pulsar!"

"Which means it's unlikely we are going to get anything livable in this sector."

"How long ago did it go super nova?"

"Well, we are guessing only, but it looks like it might be only a few decades ago."

She scooted closer to him. "That is so cool. Mr. Johnson had a recording of a pulsar's tone in the library. How close are we?"

"We'll pass within seven light years."

"Seriously? So I could see it live?"

"That is a contradiction."

Abby smiled. "Come on, Harden, you know what I mean."

"The fuel wastage is too high," he said. "And don't try going over my head, Hel will tell you the same."

Abby considered arguing, but Harden actually seemed to enjoy this conversation with her and she didn't want to ruin it. He focused in on a desolate planet streaked with caverns. "This planet currently has no atmosphere, however…" He followed a canyon until they came to a gray concrete structure that spanned the width of the chasm.

Abby was silent for a moment. Then clapped her hands together and looked up at him in excitement. "It looks like ruins of a dam on a dried out river bed?"

"I think so, but whatever it is, there can be no question. That had to be made by intelligent life," Harden said. "And look at this."

He zoomed in further behind the "dam" where there was an empty, striated, bowl-shaped formation. Beyond that there were old pylons and rubble surrounded by a petrified forest of leafless gray snags.

"Wow, we missed intelligent life by decades, didn't we?"

"It looks like that."

"It's sad they're all gone. A whole civilization," she said softly. "If they were alive, we'd go?"

"Assuming they had a viable atmosphere," Harden leaned back and took a sip of his beer, "Ready for the next bit, kiddo?" and hit the button to the remote.

"Yeah. This is so neat."

"Yes, it is."

THE NEXT DAY, ABBY SAT in the lab with Mark twenty paces away doing experiments upon the worms. Completely distracted by his presence, she could not focus on her studies or anything else. She wanted closeness and intimacy, but she feared it would hurt and might dishonor those she loved on Earth. Part of her wanted to ask him to her billet; a few times she almost did. She felt relieved and depressed every time she chickened out. She needed advice. *I wish Ma was here.*

Tears burned in her eyes with the realization that her mother was long dead. Abby set down her tablet and slid off her chair. She climbed up to the corridor and glanced towards the galley. Harden and Brian were playing cards. Even if Brian would let her play, Abby knew Harden didn't want her around during his freetime. Remembering the quilting circle, she knocked on Starboard 1.

Connected to Helen and Brian's billet via the head the original purpose of the space was the XO's office, but other than the needed filing cabinet for fleet paperwork, Helen had turned Starboard 1 into a sitting room where Diane and Helen quilted or otherwise hung out when they wanted to be away from masculine company. They had never officially invited her before, but she guessed they would not turn her away either. Helen answered and let her in.

Abby wanted to beg for help from her insane, conflicting feelings. Instead, she asked, "So what are you making?"

Helen showed her the basic design they had come up with for Diane's new pink and green pillowcases. "Want to help?"

They showed her the list of shapes that were needed. It amazed Abby how pieces of crescents, rectangles, and triangles could be placed together to make an intricate floral design. She cut out the shapes in the padding and fabrics while they sewed.

Finally she said, "I think…"

"You're attracted to my brother." Helen said, "We all know."

"What should I do?"

Helen replied, "Depends on how much you like him, I guess."

Diane met her eyes. "Seems to me if you have to ask, you're just not ready. Give yourself time or you'll regret it in the morning."

"I do like him, but I'm scared..."

Helen put her arm around Abby, "Don't rush it. I think what you need to ask yourself—and I've told Mark this too: how much is your crush based on the proximity of an intelligent handsome guy who looks nothing like the rapist?"

Diane nodded in agreement. "And he's just young enough that you consider him a peer, but old enough that you feel safe around him."

"The only reason I hesitate is I guess I'm afraid that Mark won't be with me. I'll be nothing but a substitute for Pat." Abby blinked away her tears and tried to forget that Barnett's eyes had been clinched shut. She had once been a substitute. A surrogate. She wouldn't ever allow that to happen again. Not ever. "Sorry. I'm saying this about your brother and your friend."

Hating her childish and uncontrollable emotions, Abby waited to see their reactions, but the other women were not angry. Helen hugged her tightly and stroked her hair. "We don't blame you. Neither does Mark. That you are attracted to him means nothing. It's only how you behave that matters. Since that night on Kipos, you've done nothing wrong."

"But he never plays simulations with me. Or anything else."

"Don't worry about that, sweetie," Diane said, "As for the sims, he really does get terrible motion sickness. It's amazing he didn't puke on the approach. Seriously, he vomits all the time."

"Mark told Harden and me how much he appreciated that you stayed beside him. Normally, he's on his own," Helen said.

The two women gave Abby their opinions on suitable men long into the night; she learned two important points. First, during a one-night stand or the first few times, fleet men generally don't take the lead in matters of heterosexual lovemaking. Diane assured her it didn't mean that they were timid; they just tended to make sure the woman got what she wanted. Planetside men tended to be not so accommodating.

Secondly, Mark may or may not be suitable for her. He was still hurting over his failed relationship with Pat and, like most fleet brats, Mark started fooling around at sixteen. He was much more experienced and his perception of lovemaking would not be the same as Abby's.

Abby was disappointed. "So, I'm going to be inexperienced no matter what?"

Diane shook her head. "The boys on deep space transports have fewer opportunities to fool around. So, while you're inexperienced, you're not too far behind other eighteen-year-olds to catch up. Or go play with some girls, if you fancy it."

"I just like boys."

Diane said, "That's too bad, most fleet brats don't limit their options until after twenty, and as you've seen, some, like Mark, never do."

Helen said, "Regardless, you should have a few flings and finish your education before you even think about settling down."

THE SHUTTLE SKIMMED THE SURFACE of the water. Below seemed to be great kelp beds, but Abby could not see what lay underneath. However the sonar system picked up dozens of tiny fish and a few invertebrates. She sent down the shuttle's tubal collectors and cameras.

She landed her shuttle on sand dunes punctuated by bare rocks and conifer-like trees with an average of sixty meters in height. Abby remembered the photos of ancient sequoia on Earth. Two natural freshwater lakes wrapped around the dunes. In the smaller of the two, there was visible life. She did not understand why the larger seemed devoid of it. Still, she had seen enough to understand that, just because she could not see life, it did not mean there wasn't any.

She collected water samples from each lake and then focused her camera on the smaller of the two, where insects skimmed the surface and vertebrates swam below. She set down sticky papers and traps, hoping one or both would collect something. She set Rover to fishing.

Between the rocks, she found a single large bush, its roots cracking through the stone. She noted that all around her the bushes were approximately two meters high. Upon closer inspection, she noted the branches were laden with round berries of the brightest pink she had ever seen, approximately ten millimeters in diameter. She took her samples and a quick soil analysis that indicated it was slightly acidic and damp below the rocks.

She pried up a stone. Clear worms began roasting in the sun. She didn't hear them cry, but she felt sad about their jagged flopping. She took another sample and set the stone back into place.

Abby whistled for Rover, who came trotting towards her. She arranged her samples inside his hull. He had captured a few little fish and something that looked like a blue spiny lobster. She quickly prepared them for transport.

Mark sent her coordinates and a photo to her wrist screen.

"Copy that." Abby sent Rover to take more soil samples as she hiked across the dunes. She followed Mark's direction until the dune dropped eight hundred meters in elevation to a small gully with a wildflower carpet.

The plants had yellowish-green falcate leaves and large bundles of four petal blossoms. Abby noticed the blossoms were white on the north side of the bush, and had a reddish blush on the other three sides, almost as if it had been in the sun too long. She picked a dozen from each side as Mark had asked her to in order to test this hypothesis.

Abby collected a dozen samples of seedpods. She dug down into the red dirt and cut out a large piece of root. She found a colony of fat whitish grubs, three centimeters long and ten in diameter. She put a few into a jar. A large, eight-legged, opalescent, beetle-like creature scurried past her. She slammed a jar over it and pushed it inside. She heard a chattering above her. A rodent scurried through a nearby tree.

She jerked back, but it climbed even higher. Knowing it was as afraid of her as she was of it, she remained still in order to try to examine it. She whispered her observations into the recorder as she clicked the camera function, hoping to catch a picture. "Red eyes, body covered in grey fur, four legs, three rat-like tails, looks to have some prehensile capabilities, wait…"

Abby observed the rodent's tail swing towards a nearby limb and grasp it. Then the second and third tails followed, attaching themselves to branches and pulling the little creature higher into the tree.

"Definitely prehensile tails," Abby said.

She saw another one, this one closer. She pushed the button six times, hoping to get a good image, but the sun was setting. The light was too dim to see what she had. She wasn't even sure if there was enough light for the camera without using the flash, which might scare it away. Yet the rodent's yips and howls echoed off the dunes and she knew the recorder was picking that up. She smoothed the dirt back over the ground, quickly packed up her samples, and hurried back up to the shuttle.

HER FINAL STOP WAS ON the northern ice sheet. The sun was low on the horizon and the sunlight reflected off the snow, giving the sky an orange cast. Rover began drilling for core samples as Abby scraped the surface of a glacier. She could feel the breeze pick up, even through her environmental suit.

The sonar readings suggested the ice was thin, but even though Rover drilled six meters into the ice, he could not hit the land underneath.

Rover went back to the shuttle in order to attach his extension so he could take another sample as Abby laid guide ropes. She climbed into a crevasse in the glacier. Sheltered by the wind, but surrounded by deep blue, she felt the ice shift and groan. As quickly as she could, she scraped the wall for samples and scrambled back out.

On the surface, long, spiraling icy barbs seemed to thrust out of the sheet into the high winds. She could feel the ice shift again. In order to keep her weight distributed, she stayed low and pulled herself back along the ropes towards her shuttle and called Rover. Once inside, her skin tingled with the warmth of the air.

Simply feeling glad to be alive and thankful for the chance to explore another planet, she helped Rover place the core samples into the storage pipes below and hugged him before he attached himself to his docking area. He nuzzled her and on his screen flashed.

11 minutes 35 seconds to launch window.

WHILE CD-34 4160 PLANET B WAS marked for further study due to the acidic worms, Mark concluded the planet was not habitable for humans without terraforming. As such an endeavor would destroy the worms, it was not suitable for colonization.

Abby, Mark, Diane, and Helen went into a radio conference with the *Discovery*. Julia was excited to try a few experiments based on Mark's worm and happily reported that their survey of the Scorpii 18A planet d had identified a new yeast and tardigrade, both holding antibiotic qualities. Her team also discovered seven nutritious and delicious fruiting trees.

Abby would learn, while nutrition was somewhat easy to find, what humans would consider delicious is not.

Julia switched the com up to Cole. "I have some good news," Cole began. He went on to tell Helen that their personnel problems had ended. Pat would rendezvous with them at Outpost 7. "He's coming home?" Mark asked.

"Yep," Cole's eyes looked even happier than Mark did at that moment, then started talking paperwork with Helen.

Diane gave a sideways glance at Abby, but didn't say anything.

Abby smiled at Mark and squeezed his hand. "I'm really glad for you, I hope it works out." Though her heart throbbed a bit in disappointment, she meant it.

CHAPTER 34

AS THE *REVELATION* APPROACHED, THE large pulsating ring set against the black appeared to grow into a station orbiting a dim yellow M spectra star with three planets. Abby watched as Harden typed in the number to the bank and another long series of numbers. He glanced at her and said, "Outpost ducats are worth more than Kiposi credits. We generally don't need more than a hundred. O-7 is not more than a rest stop."

Abby nodded, but noted that Diane was actually withdrawing two hundred ducats. Curious.

"She has two dates that she knows about," Helen said. "And something always comes up."

Abby could make out the vapor trails of ships taking off and landing using their chemical engines. She had thought they couldn't use their tachyon generation units with the chemical, but obviously that was false. As she watched Helen move into the landing pattern, she realized the *Revelation's* momentum within frictionless space carried the ship to the station. The chemical engines were just used as stabilizers and secondary backwards thrust. Though it seemed to be stationary, the station orbited faster than the speed of light. She found herself giddy with the idea that in a year or so, she would be learning to pilot the *Revelation*.

"*Revelation* to O-7," Helen said, "Permission to dock for twenty-seven hours R-N-R and intel exchange. Six to disembark."

"Permission granted. Landing sequence 3. Dock 42," a male's voice said through the com.

"Confirmed. Landing sequence 3. Dock 42," Helen replied.

"In the green." The male's voice became friendly and informal. "Hey, Helly, is Di still aboard?"

"Affirmative."

"Tell her I get off at 15:00 hours, if she is interested."

"I'll let her know."

"If she's not…are you still with that Tolis?"

"Yes."

"Need a break?"

Helen rolled her eyes, but her voice still sounded friendly as she said, "Even if I did, I wouldn't take a step down."

The man laughed. "Number six a female?"

Helen smiled at Abby. "Yes. Donna Lee's girl. Brian and I love that kid like she is our own."

The man laughed again. "Point taken."

Helen pulled into the landing sequence and ordered their fusion engine to be cut. The ship began to rumble and Abby felt the ship slow to the same velocity as the station. She glanced back at Mark, whose face was fairly green. Seconds later, there was a jolt as the magnetic docking clamp took control of the ship.

"Cut engines."

The rumbling stopped.

ABBY WANTED TO SEE EVERYTHING, and knowing they would be on the space station for only twenty-seven hours, she tagged along with Harden to the bank. On Earth, Abby had seen movies with hundreds of types of sentient life, but O-7 was filled with the genetic experiments of Kipos. The Khlôrosans were a little leaner and tall. The Garo and Elmkyn were a bit stockier. The few Kiposi were somewhere in between. Abby was disappointed to realize that everyone was human.

They slipped into the bank queue and Abby glanced around. Above them, there were bots recording the scene below. There were three stations with three friendly looking tellers, but there was so many people making withdrawals, she understood now why captains called ahead and acted as secondary's at cash-based outposts. What a waste of time it would be to have a whole crew in the bank, every time a ship docked.

Beyond the long line, leaning on steel columns were three bank guards in fitted green uniforms. The first two were old men, both so wrinkled, Abby wondered how they could protect anything, but under the third column stood a trim man around forty with the manner of a kept wolfhound. Tiny crinkles lined his brown eyes and a deep crease never left his brow, though he was not frowning. He was a man with the look of someone who intimately knew violence, but he did not expect danger from anyone in the queue. In fact, he looked bored as people filed around him.

Robert?

Abby's hand jerked up to the faded scar on her throat as she put her back to him. *Shit! I'm in the black! How can he be way the hell out here?*

Maybe he was not really there. Maybe it was just her mind playing perverse tricks on her. Abby began counting, she promised herself at one hundred she would turn around. She made it to twenty-three. She glanced back. Robert was looking towards someone else. She tried to take a deep breath to calm herself, but the air in her lungs produced no relief. She wanted to run, but too afraid of making a scene. *I must act normal!*

She slid on the opposite side of Harden in order to put him between her and Robert. If it came to it, Harden would protect the ship before protecting her. She didn't blame him: she didn't want the crew to lose their licenses and go to jail.

Every second stretched into an epoch as they waited in line. The rapid shuffling of the cash dispenser mimicked her pounding heart. The constant beep of thumb scans ripped into her eardrums and tellers' friendly voices became high and tinny. She began fiddling with the snap on the cuff of her sleeve. *I will act normal!*

Harden started talking to an acquaintance. Abby accepted the woman's embrace and condolences on her mother's death, but wasn't paying enough attention to remember her name; just that she was another captain. She smiled and nodded like she was supposed to, but she felt the people close in on her as they shuffled along the queue. Suffocated by the crowd, Abby wished she could stand closer to Harden. She wished he would hold her hand, just so she might garner bravery from his proximity, but was pretty sure if she took his hand in hers, he'd jerk away. That might cause Robert to look over. *I explored a whole planet on my own; I can stand in a bank line like a normal person!*

Abby made sure her back was to Robert as they moved closer to the counter. Harden did a thumb scan and picked up the six envelopes of local currency. He chatted with the teller and introduced Abby. The teller gave her condolences on Donna's death and then asked Harden about Helen. Sweat trickled down Abby's spine as they spoke for what seemed like hours. Finally, they turned to leave. Abby's heart stopped when Robert's gaze passed over her briefly. Harden handed Abby her envelope as they walked out of the bank.

A lump caught in her throat.

"I've something to tell you, but..." She slipped the money in her zippered pocket. She glanced back at Robert. He had hardly aged since she had last seen him; the planes of his chiseled face were still handsome. Her crush seemed almost as if it had happened to someone else. The walks in the garden, the electricity of her hand on his arm, the afternoons filled with self-pleasure at the very thought of him were the distant memories of another girl, not the thoughts of a crewmember of a planetary survey team. How was she going to explain this to Harden? He would hate her if he knew. "Please, don't yell at me."

"Good looking enough, I guess, but he's too old for you, kiddo," Harden said.

"No, it's not that. Robert used to work for *them*. I got him fired." She pointed to the scar on her throat.

Harden glanced back over his shoulder. No one followed them. "You sure?"

"He thought I was trying to escape and steal Lei Lei."

Harden's scowl deepened. "He cut you?"

Abby nodded. "And hit me."

"When you were pregnant?"

Abby nodded again.

A torrent of whispered obscenities slipped through his lips before the scowl left his face. "He's lucky he didn't lose more than just his job." Harden glanced back once more. "Well, Abs, if it is the same man, he didn't recognize you."

"What should we do?"

"There's nothing to do except go have a good time and not draw attention to yourself." He glanced down at her. "Unless you want to spend the next twenty-seven hours in your billet. Hel and I have a ton of work and the rest of the crew needs to decompress. I'll see you later."

Harden turned towards the *Revelation*. Abby followed. She couldn't chance hurting the crew. Furious, another leave would be wasted; tears blurred her eyes for a moment.

Harden sighed. She heard his disappointment in her. After all, Abby was a scout on an explorer! She had a mission to learn to be what it really was to be a fleet brat. This mission was just as important to the ship's safety as exploring planets. She couldn't do that alone hiding in her quarters. Fiddling with her cherry blossom pendant, she asked, "It's really okay, if I bring a boy home? As long as we stay in my billet?" She glanced up at him, blushed, and looked down at her feet.

"I have no say how you spend your personal time, but the more people who know you, the safer you'll be," he said softly.

"Helen said they'd be nice," she whispered.

He sighed again and said, "Then I'm sure they will be."

She straightened her back and took a deep breath. "You're right. I just got scared and it's making me dumb. See you later."

Glancing over her shoulder every few seconds, she drifted down the circular corridor until she came to a busy bar with a card room and private bathing rooms. Abby scanned her hand on the door. The bouncer informed her, as a Class A crewmember and licensed pilot, they could serve her food and alcohol, but she'd better not try to buy drugs or cigarettes, which they only served to people over twenty. She could take a bath if she wanted, but she could not hire a bather.

Abby took a slow step inside and looked around. The line of four lighted fans twirling on the ceiling did not light the room well which was probably a good thing considering how sticky the floor felt under her boots. The bluish-gray metal walls were covered in peeling burgundy wallpaper and posters of people dancing that may or may not supposed to be construed as sexual. On one wall, beaded curtains led to the bathing rooms. Across was a long bar with ten taps and what seemed like hundreds of types of alcohol displayed behind it. Some people were eating some greasy looking food, but most people were looking to hook up as Diane had told her they would be. She sat down at the bar and ordered a pint of pilsner.

Out of the corner of her eye, Abby saw a dark haired Kiposi man move across the shadows. Her heart started pounding again, when he lifted his arm to wave. Her eyes opened wide and she almost spilled her pint. Then a woman went towards him and pulled him into a tight embrace.

Abby looked back down at her beer. *I'm being an idiot! If that was Robert, he is stuck at work. My hair has been shorn off; I am no longer fat and pregnant. He'd never ever expect to see me here. It probably wasn't even him! Harden knew I was being stupid—and he's one of the smartest people ever!* She took another swig, then another. She finished off her pint and tried another tap at random. Something darker to match her mood. On the first sip, she decided she did not like stout, but decided to nurse it anyway in order to study fleet interaction just as Helen had instructed.

Diane entered wearing a rose-colored dress that hugged her body perfectly. Her bob had been softened into waves and around her neck hung a strand of pearls that set off the shimmer in her skin. She smiled at Abby, but walked over to a lighted pool table, put down a fifty in front of a man and guzzled a shot of something, then downed her first beer. Knowing that even if Diane ever loaned her the rose-colored dress, she could not fill it out, Abby sighed. Curious how Diane knew how to talk to men, Abby wondered if this was Diane's first date or just someone to pass the time. The man bought the next round. Diane whispered something into his ear. He was definitely interested. The man didn't seem to care that Diane had taken his money in three rounds, especially since she used it to purchase time in a bathing room.

A man sidled up to Abby at the bar, but he was at least thirty-five, if not forty, and the smell of alcohol on his breath disgusted her. There was no one even close to her age at all. She paid her tab and left.

She wandered to the next set of open doors, which led to an arcade filled with young people playing hologram games. She saw girls walking around in pairs or trios. She tried to say hi, but was summarily ignored. Abby listened to a group of girls playing a game about killing intelligent aliens. Their giggly conversations were about boys and cg lessons. Not one was a licensed pilot or seen the things she has seen.

The boys were worse. As soon as she tried to speak to one, he told her he ached.

At first, she didn't know what he was talking about, until she remembered Rory saying something similar. She looked away.

"Why are you playing that game?"

"I didn't mean to play a game. Sorry." She backed away and went to the counter where they sold drives of music, vids, and games.

She scrolled down the list of available music until she saw the band Wish I Knew Birds.

Abby read that the band was so named because the guitarist's adopted cousin came from Earth. When heard in full, the entire album was a mix of hard vocal operatics and ballads that told the story of a girl and her pet dragon fighting a tyrannical government.

Glancing up at a cute looking boy looking through the catalogue of vids, she asked him if he knew any of the songs on the album.

He replied, "I've what you need." He flicked his tongue at her. She had no idea what that meant. Maybe she wasn't ready for this.

Abby bought the album, left the arcade, and roamed down the corridor until she came to three shops. The largest sold spare engine parts and tools. The second was filled with overpriced sundry items. Cheap cotton underwear and itchy wool socks. Nylon shorts. Skin creams and lotions. Near the back of the store was an old style soda fountain with a large selection of candy and packaged cakes. This is what she wanted so badly during her flight training. Using a small bit of cash, she bought a package of vanilla wafers and a bag of fruit candies. She bit into the crisp cookies. It had been so long since she had anything so sweet.

The third was a small relay station where one could use the com and send electric post as well as old-fashioned paper letters and postcards featuring the nearby nebula and solar system. Harden was speaking to an old man behind the counter while Mark printed a label on the worm sample canisters which would be held for two weeks in stasis for the *Discovery*. There were also two personal packages: one for Cole and one for Julia. Abby recognized the handwriting on both of them to be Helen's.

Abby offered them a piece of her cookie. Mark declined and said she shouldn't eat that crap. Harden said sure. Abby broke off a large piece and handed it to him. He ignored his brother's frown as he took a bite and shoved the rest in his mouth.

After a quick introduction, Frank, the old man behind the counter, brought out a stack of letters, postcards, and one little package. Most of the letters and postcards were for Diane from various masculine names. One letter was for Brian from his brother on the *Polaris* and the little package was from Sarah Anderson to Helen. Mark placed them in his hip bag.

She thought about Lei and Orchid on Kipos. Her daughter might not know she existed, but she wished she could write to her sister and let her know that she was alive. She wished she could write to anyone. Harden slipped a hand on the back of Abby's neck and whispered into her ear. "Want to call your sister?"

Abby nodded.

Once Mark left, Harden looked at Frank. "A pack of cigarettes, a beer for me, and whatever the girl wants…and a private call to Kipos."

"How private?"

Harden slipped a hundred ducat bill out of his pocket and slid it across the counter. Abby knew that was a lot of money since the sign said a fifteen-minute video relay to Kipos was only twelve ducats.

Frank led them to his office, through another door, and into a small dark room that smelled of stale beer and cigarettes. In front of them was a touchscreen. "Relay points?"

"As many as you can do."

"Who are we calling—the PM?"

"Close. State Secretary in New Alexandria."

Frank raised an eyebrow. He glanced at a touchscreen. "It's not even 04:00 in NAX."

"He'll be expecting this call, I gather. It's actually for his daughter, Orchid. Sender is Abby."

"Family name?"

Harden's voice left no room for argument. "Just say Abby."

Frank left the room and Abby turned to Harden. "The money for the call…"

"Don't worry about it."

Abby chewed her nail, wondering what she would say. She wanted to tell her sister she had a niece somewhere, but thought better of it. Harden told her no speaking of the *Revelation* until they saw Stone's reaction.

Frank came back in again with a pack of cigarettes, a beer for Harden, and a portkali cream soda for Abby. "It'll be thirty minutes, folks. It's 03:57 in NAX, but you're correct. The Secretary seems very interested in speaking to the girl."

Turning on a monitor so he could see his counter, Frank looked at Abby closely. "You're the first one I've met."

Abby put her hands on her hips and said smoothly, "The first intern?"

Frank chuckled. "And I heard Earthlings were too stupid for much else than warming a bunk, but you don't seem Harden's type. Too undeveloped."

Abby forced her legs not to retreat.

Harden's eyes flashed dangerously. "I don't appreciate people spreading rumors about my crew. The girl is nineteen, her mother is dead, and I'm her captain. That's all you need to fucking know."

Frank put his hands up, the universal gesture for "I meant no harm."

Harden scooted his chair back and unzipped his coveralls so only his plain t-shirt was visible from the monitor. He gestured Abby to do the same. She tied the sleeves around her waist. He turned on the monitor and made sure Abby was in the forefront. He was only slightly visible. Then they waited.

A middle-aged man's visage was first to appear on the screen. Frank zoomed out to show three people. On his left was a middle-aged woman, on his right a girl the same age as Abby.

"ABBY!" The girl said and clapped her hands together. The elder people beside her looked uncomfortable but obviously used to being on camera.

Words were caught in Abby's throat.

Harden gestured for Frank to leave. He did.

"Orchid?" Abby knew, logically, Orchid was eighteen, but the young woman on the monitor had thick black hair and expensive clothing. There was not a hint of the little girl she constantly worried about.

"This is my father, State Secretary William Stone and my mother, the Kyria Margret. Daddy, Mom, this is my sister! And Abby, look who else I found!"

Rory moved closer to the camera. The days in the sun made the skin around his eyes look a bit weathered for twenty-seven, but he was still strong. His nose looked more crooked then she remembered and one of his front teeth had a visible crack in it. "Abby? How is it that you're so young?"

"I'm in space," she said.

"Are you his whore?" Rory asked, pointing towards Harden.

"No. His crew saved me."

Rory did not look like he believed her. He started shaking. He asked to be dismissed and he was. Orchid watched him go and turned back to the screen. Though there was girlishness in her movements, Orchid was in complete control. She called the Secretary "Daddy" and the Kyria "Mom." Abby could only wonder, as a lump grew in her throat, *does Orchid even remember Da and Ma? Does she think about them?*

Stone said softly, "Miss Boyd Lei, it is a pleasure. You may not realize the trouble you have caused. We have been searching for you since my wife and I adopted our little Orchid. We thought you had shared your brother's fate."

There was no doubt in his meaning: Orchid was his daughter and he meant to keep her.

Harden spoke. "We're about to embark on a mission that involves another twelve years of your lifetime. When we return, Orchid will be over thirty, but due to the speed and stasis, Abby will still be nineteen…"

Harden summed up for the Stones everything that had happened since Abby arrived on his ship and concluded, "Abby didn't contact Orchid earlier for fear of bringing her harm, but when I learned of your promotion to Secretary of State, I knew you'd be well equipped to deal with any threat."

"What is the threat?"

Harden said, "Someone with more political power than a ship's captain had purchased her bond. She was ill used when she found her way to my ship. My doctor took her in without my knowledge. His Oath bound him to her care. As her penalty for running away would be death, he refused to allow us to turn her in."

"You could lose your license for this."

"I am aware of that, but don't see why my name needs to be brought into it."

Stone answered with just as much care. "As long as it stays quiet, if the girl comes to me, I'll buy the bond."

Harden sighed. "I want more than that."

"You will be paid handsomely for your inconvenience."

Harden frowned. "I don't want or need your money. I require your word that you'll pay for her education. I want her future transcripts to be sent to the New World Bank on Argent. The Fleet Liaison will forward them to my ship."

"You're certainly passionate for her wellbeing, mystery captain."

"As no doubt you and your wife are for Orchid," Harden said.

Someone off camera handed a tablet to Stone. "She's our daughter. You have to be an Alekos, Brody, or a Tolis. How is Outpost 7?"

Harden's frown grew deeper. Abby cringed at the ice that crept into his voice. "This girl has been a member of my crew for the past four relative months. She has a shuttle license and is studying astrobiology."

Stone smirked. "A shuttle license in four months. Astrobiology? Those who are meant to fly through the stars don't often fit into Kiposi society."

The veneer of Orchid's poise cracked. "Daddy!"

Abby felt as if Stone had punched her directly in the heart. He didn't want her, but if his daughter wanted an expensive pet, he would provide one.

Orchid rung her hands. "I remember those men grabbing you and how you tried to hang on to me. Then nothing until my parents woke me up.

"I was so frightened, but Mom promised I could look for you, Jin, and Rory. She said we'd find all of you if we could, but it was harder than she expected. The Bond Agency did not want Earth families together and much of the information was classified."

Kyria Stone said, "I would rather Orchid did not hear of such things, but we found poor Rory only on accident, when a friend was speaking about the young man who impregnated her cousin. He had apparently made her husband jealous. He was misused terribly by the man." The Kyria's eyes misted with tears as she asked Abby, "Are you... well, dear?"

"I don't think of the men anymore," Abby lied, then added truthfully, "but I worry about Orchid every day. The whole crew is good to me. They really did save me. I don't want anything bad to happen to them."

"Nothing bad will happen to them," Orchid said. Kyria Stone concurred.

Harden exhaled. Just by the sound of his breath, Abby heard his skepticism.

Abby said, "I saw you on the Feed with Sadie, Danielle, and the good Kyria. I knew you were safe and hoped you were happy before I left Kipos. I have the photo from the article on my billet wall."

Orchid grabbed a photo of herself with two kittens. "Daddy, send this to her." Stone began scanning the photo. Orchid turned back to the monitor. "You're really a pilot?"

"Yep, I love to fly. I even explored a whole other planet. I…"

Harden gently tapped her shoulder. "Be vague."

Abby finished lamely, "I—well, the whole ship—has a cat too."

Orchid frowned at Harden, but asked Abby, "With all this travel, do you still love the stars? Can you find your friends?"

Abby nodded. "It's harder than Earth, but I found them."

Frank signaled five minutes and handed Abby the photo.

Panic of ending their connection rose in Abby's throat. "Orchid, are you still going to be a doctor?"

She looked a little embarrassed. "That's my plan, sometimes I think about being a veterinarian. I really like animals. I've been getting good marks." Orchid told her about her boyfriend whose name was Jonathan. She had learned to play the violin. Sadie Blackwell was one of her best friends. Then she said, "Tell me a story about your travels. I'm sure you've seen something vague as your captain puts it."

Abby told her about the sixteen rings of Ounzio, lightening on the planet's surface and how the moons changed colors in the horizon.

Frank signaled one minute before he would need to reshift the call due to the station's orbit.

Stone said, "It seems your sister was meant for the stars, Orchid."

Abby said, "I'll still come."

Orchid shook her head. "We're sisters and I love you, but I don't need you to take care of me anymore. When you come to Kipos, you must come see me. Maybe I will have given you nieces and nephews."

"Don't worry. I'll keep Rory safe. Don't think ill of him."

"I don't."

Abby and Orchid said their goodbyes. The monitor went off. Abby turned to Harden, who was sitting back in his chair smoking. She wished it were Helen, Diane, or even Brian sitting there—anyone who would wrap their arms around her.

Harden just took a drag on his cigarette. "I knew that bastard wouldn't take you. Fucking politicians."

"Did you want him to?" she sniffed as she slid the picture of Orchid in her zipper pocket.

"Don't be stupid. I was just thinking we should have called collect."
Then he said, "Let's take a walk."

THE OXYGEN GARDEN, WHICH ENCIRCLED the outer rings of the station, was one of the most beautiful places Abby had ever seen. The nearby vents and sprinkler system created soft, moist breezes. When Abby closed her eyes, she could almost feel she was outside except for the hint of chlorine in the air.

For a time, they walked quietly in their own thoughts. Four burgundy-copper maples and four lime-green dwarf conifers lined the walkways in a pattern of a compass's star. Between the eight points, there were smaller fruiting trees every five hundred paces. There were edible ferns, grasses and smaller flowering bushes. The ceiling was lit up and painted to look like a partly cloudy yet blue sky.

Harden broke the silence, "Hey, look, a smoking station." He sat down on the bench and pulled out his last cigarette. "You still! love that guy?"

Abby shrugged as she sat upwind from the smoke.

"I saw your face and he barely made it out of the room without crying. I want you to do what's best for you. If you do not, you'll die. It'll be painful, messy, and a waste of talent and resources. I'd rather have you planetside, anywhere, than bloody ice crystals shattering against my hull."

Abby hugged herself, but failed to hold back the shudder.

"It took Helen and me a long time to recover from sterilization and I was only forced to undergo a ten minute surgery."

"You lost Lucy and the baby."

He looked her in the eyes. "You think my loss is greater than yours?"

"I dunno," Abby said, mostly because she didn't know the answer he wanted to hear.

"Lucy's death drove me to break the light barrier. I didn't know what would happen, only that there was a chance I could go backwards in time." He sighed and added, "Of course, now we know that isn't what happens when you use tachyon fields. There still might be another way."

"Would you go back if you could?" she asked.

"No." He turned his head and blew the smoke away from her.

"But why? Don't you still love her?"

He put his empty hand on the back of Abby's neck and looked her in the eyes. "Two reasons. First, it sets up a paradox that is simply fucking annoying to think about. Second, and more important, Lucy was twenty-six when she died. I'm not the same man I was at twenty-two. If I saw her today, I'd see a girl, not my wife."

Abby pushed onwards. "What happened between you and Phoebe?"

"A wife who was a medical doctor and biologist was highly convenient, but as valuable as she was to the ship, I lost sight of her needs. Or perhaps it is more accurate to say, I never took the time to concern myself with her needs at all."

"If she came back, would you?"

"No."

"Why not?"

"Fuck, kid. I don't know. I'm trying to tell you to do what you want. The Stones can protect you now. Everyone will understand if you go to Kipos."

"Even Helen?"

He gave her a crooked smile. "Brian and I will take care of Helen. You don't need to worry about her. I do hope you'll stay in touch with her and Diane."

Abby nodded. "If Orchid needed me, I'd go, but she doesn't. Rory isn't twenty anymore. He must be twenty-seven? That's too old for me. It just sucks I can't have both my family and space. It hurt to leave my parents and Ray, and it hurts now."

"That's the way life is." He took a final drag and the cigarette burnt to his fingertips. He slipped the butt into the tiny garbage slot. "What did Orchid mean about your friends in the stars? You once told me you had lost them."

Abby searched for the right words. Her answer sounded so childish. "I used to look up at the constellations when I took Tara out. I tried to show Orchid and our brothers, but they weren't interested in astronomy. And Grandma only read the stars to tell the future and talk to our honored dead ancestors."

Harden tried to suppress the mocking grin, but laughter poured out. "Someday, you can tell me about that, but for now, I've work to do. You've six hours to change your mind."

ALONE AGAIN, ABBY WANDERED AROUND the rest of the garden. Her heart felt as if it had been run over by a cheese grater. She wanted to stay on the *Revelation* more than anything, but doing so would be to abandon her parents' hopes and expectations. If she were the woman her conscious told her to be, she would get on a transport to Kipos, go to the university, get a respectable job, find a gentle husband, create a few babies, and have a loving adult relationship with her sister.

"Hello Abigail."

Abby spun around. Robert grabbed her by the neck. His mouth twisted somewhere between a sneer and a wicked smile as his fingers drilled into her flesh. With a shake he asked, "Where's the baby?"

"I left her with the DePauls." Guilt and fear left a lump in her throat. Tears sparkled on her eyelashes and his appearance blurred. She unsuccessfully forced herself calm.

"That Khlôrosan is your new holder?"

"He's a good man," Abby whimpered.

Robert laughed. "You saying, you didn't pay for your ride with your tits?"

Abby didn't know what to say. She couldn't betray the Alekoses; she said nothing while trying to focus on her escape. Robert's eyes swam. She realized he enjoyed the feeling of power that was rushing through his veins, just like Harden enjoyed cigarettes.

He slapped her cheek and squeezed harder. "I could send your ass back to the DePauls. I wonder if there is a reward. I liked my job there." Another slap. Abby wept from the pain, but focused on the fact that, though his blow might redden her cheek, he wasn't going to leave real bruises where someone might see—at least not until he got her somewhere more private. She could not—no, would not— let that happen.

Abby whispered, "I'll give you all the money I have. It's almost a hundred ducats. I was going to start a new life."

His fingers were drilling their way in between her vertebrae. "You must be pretty fucking good if he gave you a ride and extra cash. Or does he like young girls sucking his cock?"

Fear sliced away any hope of speech. Robert's face grew more terrible as she struggled against him ineffectually. He wanted her to struggle. He wanted an excuse to beat her. He whispered a few sexual positions she had never heard of into her ear. "Tell me this: did you fuck everyone, or just him?"

She tried to kick him, but he pushed her against the trunk of a tree. He whispered something else she didn't quite understand. Another slap. "Answer me!"

"I didn't know you recognized me!" she whispered hoping the subject change would buy her time before he slapped her again. She prayed for a moment to regain her battered mind and figure a way out.

He didn't give her a moment. The next blow landed on her ear. "You fucking think I am stupid enough to let you and that Khlôrosan know I was on to you?" He pulled her closer to him and strengthened his grip on her shoulders. "Maybe you think I am stupid enough to let you get me fired from another job?"

She knew she couldn't scream, that might bring the authorities and get her arrested, but remembering her time on Kipos with him, she tried wailing to see if it would garner sympathy. She accepted another slap and wept a little louder. He led her deeper in the brush, away from the trail. *No, no, no!*

She tried to lean into him, but he landed a blow on the back of her head and squeezed tighter. She let her knees crumple to the ground. He yanked her up and pushed her into a bush. The moment he loosened his grip, she tried to run. She only got a meter before he had her. She tried kicking him, and when that didn't work, she tried to fall to the ground again, but he spun her around to face him and pressed her against the nearest tree, he snarled, "I doubt DePaul will care how I return you to him…"

One moment, he had her pinned, and then suddenly, he released her. Abby did not realize why until a man and a little girl with a stuffed chicken riding on her shoulders walked down the path towards them, oblivious to her suffering. Still they could see her!

She must move. Robert was like any other beast; if she cowered, she would be his prey. She forced herself to walk, but her mind decided walking wasn't enough. With a burst of speed, she darted down the path to the main promenade. Once out of the garden, she glanced back. Robert was following her. He did not run. He did not need to. He knew the station better than she did. The employees of the bar, bank, and arcade were probably all friends of his. The only place she had friends was aboard the *Revelation*, but she didn't want to lead Robert to her ship.

Abby hurried back into the bar. She didn't know when she would be safe to leave. She glanced around. No one from the ship was there. She ordered a shot of whiskey and a beer chaser, as Diane had. She scanned the room, hoping to find a group of women, but the few women around were on laps of men or leading them into a bath. She watched Robert talk to the bouncer, but he didn't dare approach her in such a public place.

He sat down at the bar and ordered a drink, never taking his eyes off Abby. She downed the shot and chugged half the beer as she scanned the room. She thought the alcohol would make her feel braver, but instead it intensified the fear. The floor shifting under her feet reminded her of how she felt when she had been raped.

Abby saw a man on the far side of eighty. He would probably help her. His eyes seemed kind enough. She finished her beer before she approached him. "Sir, I'm sorry to bother you and I'm not trying to start anything, but I'm a little drunk. I'd ask a woman, but there doesn't seem to be any around who aren't busy. Could I just sit with you or could you help me back to my ship?"

"What ship?"

"The *Revelation*." Her stomach turned again, but she refused to let the bile rise into her throat.

"Alekos' kids still run it?"

"Yes sir."

"Don't worry, honey, Alekos' girl and her man went into a bath. They should be coming out soon." He patted her hand and gestured to the chair next to him. "First time in a bar?"

She blushed. "Actually, it's my second time. We docked this morning."

He looked her up and down. "Playing in the oxygen garden is generally frowned upon, but I'll stay with you till we find someone you know."

Abby realized the knees of her coveralls were stained. Her hands were filthy. Of course, he mistook the redness of her cheeks as a flush brought on by alcohol—or maybe sex. "It's not what you think. I just … fell down."

She felt dizzy and a little sad, but as she sat down, she positioned herself so she could see Robert. He was still watching her. She glanced at the old man. "But then I came back to the bar and I shouldn't have finished the last beer."

The old man pushed a bowl of pretzels towards her and hailed a waiter. "Happens to the best of us. Switch to a soda and eat a little—you'll feel better."

"It's weird. Aboard ship, we're all friends. Now everyone's too busy for me. Diane and Helen said I would meet boys, but there aren't any in here. I tried the arcade, but everyone seems so young. Nobody even has a pilot's license."

"Happens on both sides, girl. Most of my friends are dead or retired. I see only a sea of kids too busy to waste their time on an old man."

Robert had finished his beer and paid his tab. He spoke to the bouncer before walking through the door and out of her line of sight. Abby focused her attention to her new friend and asked, "Where do you work, sir?"

"I'm the cook on the *Dorcas*, long range transport between O-5 through O-9. You can call me Quinn."

"I'm Abby Lee." She held out her hand and he clasped it.

"Know nearly a dozen Lees. Who's your mother?"

"Donna, she was an engineer on the *Vos*."

"Poor baby. Such a fucking waste." He kissed his thumb and pressed it into her forehead.

His gesture calmed her, but she felt guilty that she told a lie to get a kiss. Abby thought, *it wasn't a lie, just a half-truth.* She was scared and she did miss Ma. She didn't have to fake that. "I thought getting drunk was supposed to be fun, but it's scary."

"You work on an explorer class ship. Your whole life is scary."

"A new planet's easy, my brain's all there."

Quinn laughed. "Suppose that's true. You'll get used to it. Look, there's your captain. Looks a little ticked off. Hi, Harden."

The men shook hands. Quinn explained Abby was afraid she couldn't make it back to the ship alone, but she had been good company. Harden thanked him and added that a bit of extra chores would sober his wayward intern. Quinn asked a few more questions about Donna. Abby knew she should be paying attention, but what she really wanted to do was throw up. The three beers, whiskey shot, soda, vanilla wafers and now pretzels were churning in her stomach. Being tipsy was bad enough, but Harden was not even hiding that he was royally pissed at her.

She heard Harden say, "She was pushing to do A level work and was emancipated conditionally. After today, I might send her back to my father."

Abby shakily paid her tab. Even though it held the threat of discipline, Abby was glad his hand was on her shoulder as he led her out.

She glanced around, but didn't see Robert anywhere.

"Harden…" she tried to say.

"Shut the fuck up," Harden said as he marched her to the *Revelation*. He helped her up the steps past Pat and Mark who were carrying two large bags of Pat's possessions towards his old billet.

"What's wrong?" Mark called to his brother.

"Drunk."

"How much?" Mark asked. Abby could see he was genuinely concerned.

"Don't worry. Quinn said she had a few beers and maybe a shot or two, but she got herself in a bit of trouble, which she and I are going to have a talk about. I'll make sure she drinks some water, then she's going to lie down."

Even though she felt humiliated, Abby did not argue. They were walking up the stairs, down the upper corridor and to her billet. He opened the hatchway. His golden eyes sparkled with fury.

"Please…" She reached out to touch his arm; he spun around and slapped her hand away.

His face contorted with rage. "Get inside your billet before I send you back to Kipos myself."

Paralyzed with fear, she didn't move. Slick, black terror coated her throat as Harden made an unintelligible sound of anger as he climbed down first. She didn't dare make him wait. As she stepped down the five rungs, Harden had his arm around her to make sure she didn't fall.

His voice was not above a hiss, but she heard every word. "Don't leave this billet. It was the biggest fucking mistake to ever let you aboard, but now what can I do with you?"

Abby bit her lip; she knew not to answer.

"If I leave you here, I endanger my dad and the whole fucking fleet. You owe me 2000 ducats. If you ever say I touched you again…" he said.

Abby paled. "I'd never say something like that. Robert asked how I paid, but he didn't give me time to answer. He told me what he thought happened."

"Exact words!"

Abby did her best to remember the entire conversation, but with her mind spinning with booze and Harden's terrible golden eyes, she knew she missed a few lines. She tried to backtrack.

"What the fuck are you rambling about?" Harden asked.

"I don't know. That's just what he said. Something about a cat." She was so ashamed and terrified she could not see that Harden had stopped frowning. "Robert asked if I-I serviced the whole crew or just you. Except he said 'fuck.'"

She couldn't stop the sobs that racked her chest. "I'll pay you back. Tell me what to do to make it right. I'll do it."

Harden sighed. "Calm down. It will be noted on your record you've been restricted to your billet for twenty-seven hours due to drunkenness. That's hardly the end of the world."

Then he turned around and climbed out.

CHAPTER 35

In the Black: June 24, 3170 K.E.

EVEN THOUGH THE CLOCK SHOWED it was dinner time, Abby was too scared to go up to the galley. She expected Harden would tell her they were going to rendezvous with another ship and he had set up transport to Kipos and her account had been emptied to pay back her debt to him. Her balance was 1602 Kipos credits. The conversion calculator told her that was less than half of what she needed to repay.

Maybe if she were quiet, Harden would forgive her mistakes. Maybe he would get distracted on one of his science projects and forget that she was even there.

Later on, she heard Diane and a male in her billet for an hour and take a shower. Then they were laughing in the galley with Helen and Brian. Harden came and went on his normal schedule. There were no sounds of passion, so she assumed he was alone. When he wasn't in there, she played music very quietly.

Even once the ship pulled away from O-7 and her twenty-seven hours were up, she stayed in her billet as much as possible. She wished she could ask someone for advice, but her neck hurt where Robert's fingers had drilled eight deep bruises.

ON HER MORNING TO COOK, Abby padded up to the kitchen to start the coffee. She saw Diane up in the bridge. She thought about talking to her, but was too embarrassed. Instead, she began slicing up apples.

Pat came in and poured himself a cup of coffee. He leaned back on the counter and took a sip, then glanced at the teapot that was nearly ready to boil. He pulled out a teabag and put it in a cup for Mark. Pat never allowed the higher gravity of Kipos to be an excuse not to exercise. He took care that his muscles were strong and there was no flab around his middle. While he was actually a few centimeters shorter, since he didn't slouch, he easily stood taller than Harden. However, while Mark's skin was still smooth, tiny lines had developed around Pat's eyes from sun exposure. Evidence he had lost nearly seven years due to his time on Kipos.

Abby loved that Mark and Pat's life had played out like a romance novel. Rory had never really loved Abby the way Pat obviously cared for Mark. He had made a mistake and searched the stars for his lost love. She was surprised to find she was not crushed about Mark, the way she had been when she saw Rory with Mary back on Earth.

Mark was handsome, but once he was someone else's, she was happy for him. More than anything, she was curious about what two men did together. She had a general idea, but found herself wondering about the specifics. The thought of two handsome men in each other's arms excited her. It was best not to dwell on such thoughts. She focused on the fact that Pat's friends had taken him back, so he must be a good man.

She reached for the brown sugar. Behind her, she heard Pat say, "What in the hell?"

"Apple pancakes."

He grabbed Abby's wrist. "Don't play dumb with me, girl. What's this?" He pointed at the scar on her hand.

"I hurt myself when I was five."

"It looks like you removed a microchip." He took a step closer.

"Don't be stupid."

"I knew something was funny with you. Do you know what you've done! You could get them killed."

She hit the intercom as his fingers dug into her shoulder. She screamed and swung up at him. He was too fast and she banged her elbow into the counter as he pinned her back against it.

"Get off of her!" Diane screamed.

Pat did not listen. "You could get them killed, you stupid cunt!"

Suddenly, Helen, Brian, and Harden were behind them. Brian held a wrench and Harden held a laser driver.

"She's an indentured!" Pat said triumphantly.

With his empty hand, Harden lightly smacked the back of Pat's head. "No shit. You think?"

Pat looked confused for a moment, but he removed his weight. Abby tried to edge towards Brian, or at least away from Pat. Brian wrapped his arm around her shoulder, which made her feel secure but also halted her retreat.

Mark said softly, "I'm the one who removed the chip. She never lied to us."

Pat's eyes landed on Mark. He opened his mouth.

Helen said, "If you've a problem with that, I'll turn this ship around and you can get the fuck off. We can still rendezvous with the *Discovery*."

Pat's shoulders slumped forward so much he seemed to wither under his guilt. "I should have realized. There is no excuse for my actions. I'm so sorry."

Abby felt Brian's hand shift on her shoulder. He pulled back on her collar. "What's that?" Brian's voice slipped dangerously low. "This why your wife left? You ever do this to her?"

Pat was now looking at the injury. "I never laid a hand on my wife. I only grabbed the girl to incapacitate her after she tried to hit me. I wouldn't have hurt her."

Now Abby felt Harden move closer. "Lay another hand on our kid and you better pray Helen gets to you before I do. She's liable just to throw you out of an airlock."

Abby felt the rest of the crew turn towards Harden. She wasn't quite sure why he was so angry, but he was livid, even more than he had been on the outpost. It took her a moment to find her voice.

"On O-7," she whispered.

Harden asked, "Did I do that?"

She shook her head. "Robert did, when he grabbed me."

"Who's Robert?" Mark said as he moved closer and glanced down the back of her shirt. He gently touched the bruises: placing his own hand, the exact way Robert had, without putting pressure. Talking over her head at his brother and brother-in-law, he said, "No permanent damage, at least not physically... what did he want?"

A sob choked out of Abby's throat before she could stop it. Now everyone would know what a problem she had become. *They will send me away.*

Looking at her elder brother, Helen said, "The crew needs to know what happened. Take Abby in the corridor until the both of you calm down. I'll finish breakfast."

Harden grabbed her wrist and started walking. Abby followed him. She wished Da were still alive. Da would know how to handle this. She could weep into his shoulder and he'd wrap his arms around her. Da would tell her what she needed to do to fix the problem with Pat and keep her job. Without realizing it, Abby wished she could jump ahead a decade or two. If she were thirty-nine, then Harden might love her. She looked up at him in the face and her crush deflated. He was just Harden, still slouching over her with crinkles around his eyes and lines on his brow. She saw herself how he saw her. Sadness flittered into anger, back into sadness, and soaked her core with shame. She was still just a stupid girl. *What's wrong with me?*

"Why are you still crying?" he asked.

"I've messed everything up for you," she said.

Harden just stood looking at her and waited for more information.

"I just didn't know what to do. I still don't. If you and Brian hadn't come to save me... I feel so stupid." That was close enough to the truth.

"You've got some super strength I don't know about?" Harden asked.

Abby shook her head.

"Explain to me how a chit like you could take a seventy-five kilo man in peak physical condition who has studied police tactics and martial arts."

"What?"

"You heard me. Explain how you could have done anything, except hit the com and scream."

Since there was no answer forthcoming, he added, "Truthfully, if Pat came after me, there's not a damn thing I could do except scream and hope that Brian showed up. So stop beating yourself up over every fucking thing that happens.

"Go wash your face and get back up here."

BREAKFAST WAS ON THE TABLE by the time Harden and Abby returned to the galley. Harden quickly ran over how he and Abby had seen Robert in the bank, had called the Stones, and their talk in the gardens. He told Abby to repeat what had happened next.

Abby's voice wavered slightly when admitting Robert had found her in the oxygen garden. She told them at first he seemed to be interested in a reward until he discovered she no longer had the baby. With her eyes on the table, she whispered a few of the terrible things to her and confessed she was terrified when he had slapped her.

"Why didn't you scream?" Brian asked.

"I thought if he told everyone I was an Earthling, you all might be in danger. He let me go when a family went by and I ran into the bar. I figured, as long as there were people around, he couldn't hurt me. I was too scared to try to make it home."

Brian shook his head and rubbed his temple.

Harden jumped in, "After you lost him, Robert found me. He said if I didn't pay him five thousand ducats, he would tell the authorities that I transported a stolen Earth girl in exchange for sex. I told him I didn't have it due to the last engine upgrade. He really just wanted the cash, so I got him down to two thousand. I was glad no one else was around or he would have asked for more."

"Will he want more?" Mark asked.

"Probably," Harden replied. "I told him I knew he cut up Abby and slapped her around when he worked for the DePauls—"

Pat interrupted with a whisper, "The DePauls? Fuck."

"Robert was smart enough not to admit it. I told him she still has the scar on her throat. That seemed to scare him." He glanced at Abby, and admitted, "Since he had struck her before, I should have guessed he hit her this time too."

"But now she has other scars. He might say…" Mark said.

"Before he approached me, he checked who we were. He knew we were explorers, but he never considered she was more than plumbing," Harden said.

Helen and Diane glared at him, but Abby just pulled at her fingers.

Brian sighed and put up his hand towards his wife. Carefully changing the subject, he said, "I don't want to be a dick, but two thousand ducats will force an inquest."

Harden nodded. "Abby, your expenses are minimal, so Helen and I decided it would be best if you pay me back over the next three outposts. You will need to go to the bank, withdraw the money yourself, and deposit it into my account.

"Remember, we have to make sure it doesn't look shady. If ever asked, I think the best excuse is a high stakes card game when you were drunk since the drunkenness is on your record. Half the station saw me drag you home."

Abby tugged at her fingers. "And we'll be okay?"

Harden looked at her with a slightly puzzled expression. Helen pulled Abby into an embrace. "Of course."

Pat sat up straighter. "Look guys, you know I love you, but I got my own kid to think about. I can't be an accomplice to a criminal offense."

"We'll transfer you," Helen said.

Pat looked at Helen. Then at Harden. "Do you even understand what they are doing to people who help these Earth kids? That's one of the reasons why I had to get out of there."

Harden nodded. "I appreciate the danger. However, Helen is attached." As if to prove his point he gestured over to his sister whose arms were still around Abby. "And the kid plans to take care of Rover after I am gone. Though I can't say I approve of every game she has taught him, they do play quite often in the shuttle hanger."

Pat opened his mouth wide. "You're shitting me?"

"Since the second day on her first trip planetside," Diane said.

"Fuck." Pat punched the table. "Harden, you should have told someone she had recognized this Robert. This wouldn't have fucking happened if someone had stayed with her."

Harden glanced at Abby and admitted, "The chances were so incredible. I thought she had just gotten scared. I didn't believe she had seen someone she actually knew."

"If she is truly one of us, then you should have," Pat snapped back.

"You're correct, but would you have wanted her hanging around with you and Mark? Because everyone else had plans."

"You could have been with her." Then Pat's brown eyes fell on Abby; she did her best not to retreat into Helen's arms. "And Abby, don't you ever hide an injury again. Fuck." He stood up and walked down the corridor. "FUCK!"

Brian watched Pat go. "That went better than expected."

Mark exhaled slowly as he stood up. "Actually, Abs, having a disciplinary action on your record is probably to our advantage. Aside from Harden, everyone we know got in trouble sometime during their internship." He followed Pat down the corridor to his billet.

Intermission
The Discovery Outpost 7:
July 11, 3170 K.E.

BEFORE THE *REVELATION* DEPARTED O-7, Cole received an updated crew manifest. Pat was back aboard, yet Harden and Helen had kept the girl. The discipline report was an out and out lie. If the girl had really gotten drunk and lost 2000 ducats on a card game, she would have received more than a day's confinement and a repayment plan; minimally she would have been shipped off to the *Discovery*.

Cole wished he could see his kids this stop instead of waiting six weeks or so until O-5, but they had a long trip and couldn't waste the time. Still, their detection of the antihistamine worms looked promising and awaited him in stasis, as did a care package from Helen.

Watching Saul pilot the ship into the correct landing pattern, Cole wished he could speak to his friend. However, entangled in the lie of the girl's birth, he felt the only way to keep his kids safe was not to tell anyone who she actually was. On Kipos, the longest indenture periods should have been over, yet people had grown used to keeping slaves. Earthlings made good workers—miners, farmers, servants, and the like. On the secondary bond market, a night with a young blond or red haired teenaged girl might bring in thousands of credits. In one Feed story, an exotic looking girl with red hair and green eyes proudly announced she brought in ten thousand in a single night, but there was something dead in her ringing tone. These girls had known nothing but poverty on Earth, but how was this life any better?

Of course, not all Earthlings were willing to be subjugated. Over the past planetside decade, a few thousand young Earthlings had escaped their bondholders or rioted. Their reputation of being wanton had proven to be false, yet plenty of Kiposi still believed they were savages. Without jobs, they formed gangs with other young people sleeping on the streets or squatting in an empty building. The Kiposi grumbled about how the Earthlings tainted their paradise, but there were not enough government agents to police the entire planet. If they were caught, they were brought back to their bondholders or simply executed.

The *Revelation* was carrying a runaway with powerful bondholders— so powerful that Harden refused to say who they were.

Still, Cole had a reason to be happy: Pat came home. The boys got into quite a bit of trouble during their internships. Nothing serious, just a few drunken escapades and a football through a storefront window. Once they had settled down, Pat was good for Mark, until his drive to procreate took over common sense. Fathers in the fleet didn't always get to raise their kids and he understood Pat's desire to be a dad, but the way he went about it was idiotic. Unlike Mark, who was bi-sexual, Pat was almost completely homosexual. Cole wondered how Pat believed he could remain married to a woman who expected monogamy and to be happy for the rest of his life.

His thoughts were disturbed by Saul who asked, "Hey, we going? Or are you going to sit in your bad mood all day?"

Cole shook his head and disembarked with his friend. As they always did, they headed to the bar. Out of the corner of his eye, he saw Julia— lovely as ever—speaking to a man. She would be hooking up with him, no doubt. She was a fine woman and a great biologist. She might even be his daughter-in-law if Harden were a normal man. However, Cole didn't particularly want to lose another biologist to his enigmatic son and Julia didn't seem inclined to leave her family aboard the *Discovery* any more than Harden wanted to leave the *Revelation*.

"What's wrong, brother?" Saul asked, then ordered two stouts.

Cole gave his friend a sad smile. "Harden's an idiot."

Saul glanced over at his niece. "Julia can take care of herself. Worried

Pat's coming back?"

Cole nodded and took a sip of the offered beer.

"Pat will understand if they trust him."

Cole opened his mouth. "Who knows?"

Saul just frowned. "Don't be an idiot. It hasn't leaked, but people like gossip. My denials have been used as confirmations that the girl isn't all she appears. Fuck, at this point half the fleet knows she exists, but I am too close to you to know the current rumor." He glanced over at Julia. She caught his look and came over to where they were sitting.

Her eyes danced with liveliness. Well, Harden always liked spirited women to counteract his intrinsic dullness. She slipped an arm under her uncle's and pulled him closer to her. "I can guess what you two are whispering about! Stop worrying. Anyone who only misses two questions on a flight exam is one of us. Right now the rumor is that she's Harden's kid. They like him better for it."

Saul laughed, but Cole was dumbstruck.

"The best story I heard so far is that Harden refuses to claim paternity, because she might be sterilized. Abby getting in to trouble could not have happened at a better time." Julia smiled. "Knowing Harden, he probably doesn't realize he acted the part perfectly."

Cole asked, "What do you mean?"

Julia looked at her uncle for support.

Saul said, "Look, all we know is Abby got in some sort of trouble. The whole fucking outpost knows Harden withdrew 2000 ducats to pay a debt then publically dragged her out of the bar. Everyone assumes she was punished when they returned to the *Revelation*. Doesn't this all sound familiar?" With a glance at Julia, he said, "Remember the shit this one used to pull?"

Getting kids through the last few years of adolescence—without killing them—was always a challenge. Cole chuckled as he remembered that, on a dare from Helen, Julia had reprogrammed seven hologram immersion games to make them more "realistic," meaning gruesome. Some of the imagery of alien species eating each other was so disturbing her mother threatened to send Julia to the Fleet hospital on Argent. Saul had quietly helped his sister take care of the damages, but asked her to allow Julia to work in the lab to pay off the debt and take accelerated classes in order to stave off any of her more creative solutions for boredom. He had gently suggested to Cole to allow Helen to do the same.

Cole nodded. "Forget the kids. Remember the shit we used to pull? My mother always said I was a terrible influence on you."

Saul laughed. "What? I thought I was the terrible influence."

His friends were correct. Everything would be fine on the *Revelation*. Helen and Harden ran their ship differently than he would like, but it was their ship. He just wished it didn't have problems keeping biologists for the planetside team. If Harden were a better captain, they would have never needed to take in the girl in the first place. Cole took another sip of his stout. It plummeted down his throat harder than it should.

Julia glanced up at the clock and said, "I've a bath scheduled at 11:00 so I have to go. Stop worrying." She reached over and squeezed his hand before she left.

Cole noticed she went into the private bath rooms alone. She loved his son, but was already protecting herself for the times when his scientific curiosity would overshadow her. He did not like thinking of his son growing old alone, but due to the indifferent way Harden treated people, he did not see any other possibility.

"I don't feel like drinking. I'm going to pick up our packages."

A GRAY-HAIRED ANDROID WAS BEHIND the counter in Frank's shop. His human disguise was nearly impenetrable, if not for his nearly unblinking eyes. "You've a message from your daughter and sons, Captain Alekos."

Where is Frank? "I know," Cole said, "That's why we're here."

"We need to go into the back."

Trying to stall, Cole said, "I like women."

"Good for you, but irrelevant," the android said. "I've someone who needs to speak with you."

"Let my friend go," Cole whispered to the android.

"He is free to leave. I hurt none who are innocent."

"Don't be an idiot," Saul said.

They followed the android into the back room. Frank was sitting there with wide eyes, speaking to a thirty-ish Kiposi in a dark expensive suit who gave off an air of strength. It took Cole only a second to recognize him: Barnett DePaul. Another man sat in the corner wearing a bank uniform, clutching his dislocated shoulder.

The android handed a drive to Barnett. "As I suspected, the girl who lives with the Stones is the little sister."

Barnett nodded and said with the utmost patience to Frank, "Thank you. Eli will compensate you for your inconvenience. We were never here." He gestured for Frank to leave and for Cole to sit. The android, apparently named Eli, brought over another chair for Saul.

Bile rose in Cole's throat as he wondered how old Barnett had been when he raped the girl. If Abby had been born in the Fleet, the *Revelation's* crew would have shoved him out of an airlock. If Barnett had gone directly to them, they still might have. "So you're the rapist? From the child's story, I expected more of a monster."

"I could suspend your license."

"You could, but it doesn't serve Kipos to have my fleet stranded, nor would it do your wife's political career any good if the populous knew you had raped a girl—Earthborn or not."

Cole did not like the way Barnett's eyes lost their sparkle as he smiled. "Your daughter's anger toward Kipos Law is well known, since she can no longer bear a child and they would not give her even one of the worst of the Earthlings.

"Helen has never said a word…"

"Perhaps she wrote a letter to a certain parliament member? Thumb scans and signatures are very easy to reproduce." His smile grew nastier as he lied. He leaned in towards Cole. "And tell me, Captain Alekos, how would your son staff his ship if it were known that he transported a bonded Earthling in exchange for sex and paid her with ship funds? Mr. Robert Jones informed us of this detail. Perhaps your son beat on him in order to hide his crime?"

No one would believe his featherweight of a son could beat up anyone, but the fleet ran on trust. Harden's alleged misappropriation of crew funds would come down on all of his ships, even though he was innocent. Cole laughed to hide his unease.

Barnett continued, "We understand each other. All I want Eli to do is deliver a message."

"I won't see my kids for a month, maybe two. That might very well be another decade planetside." Cole rapped his fingers nervously on the table.

Barnett said, "The years planetside do not concern me, but we must have an understanding with Miss Boyd Lei before she ages. The girl doesn't worry me, but the woman could become problematic for my daughter, just as some of the other bonded women have become awkward for their families to explain."

"I'll not have a rapist on my ship."

Barnett's malevolent smile disappeared. "I created a child, but I was not part of the gang rape. Still, I lost my wife's trust. She never left me alone with our daughter after that."

Saul snapped, "Step out of an airlock."

Cole set his hand on his friend's arm before Eli came closer.

Eli said, "I've terminated those who harmed the girl." Glancing towards the injured man, he added, "Robert Jones is quite fortunate. I only renewed an old wound to inspire him to give me information. My understanding is, according to fleet law, he should have been thrown out of an airlock. This was the second time he laid hands upon her. There should not be a third."

"So that's where the two thousand ducats went?" Cole looked at Barnett, then at the android. There was no answer.

"What do you mean he laid hands upon her?" There was still no answer.

Saul tried something else. "How did you get here so fast? You couldn't have flown straight from Kipos."

"We had already been looking," Eli said.

The curtness of his tone worried Cole, but he had little choice in the matter. "What can you do? My ship isn't a fucking cruise and I don't generally need people killed or beaten."

Eli blinked too slowly as he shrugged. "I have the sum of human knowledge. I can do whatever you need."

"I suppose engineering can always use another mechanic," Saul said, nervously scratching his arm.

Eli looked amused. "As you wish, Dr.—or should I refer to you as XO

Evans?"

"Aboard the ship, everyone just calls me Saul, but you'll do well to remember Mr. Alekos is referred to as 'Captain'."

"Very well. Barnett will leave out of an airlock, but as my Kyria wills, there will be a shuttle attached to it. As I will be traveling with them, you are dismissed, Barnett."

Cole could see it grated Barnett's nerves to be dismissed by a servant, but he still stood up and hurried out without a word. His strength had been an illusion. All that mattered to him was that he was finally going home.

Saul's eyes narrowed. "What was your relationship to Abby?"

Eli said, "Her escort. In fair weather, she was allowed one hour in the garden. When it was inclement, we played cribbage."

"Did she have reason to fear you?" Cole asked.

"While I did not harm her physically, I do not deny I used behavioral techniques in order to insure my future Kyria's safety. Dr. Evans, please get a hold of yourself."

Cole glanced over at his friend. Saul's face turned nearly purple, but he held in his rage. After all, Eli was an android—even together they could not take him. There was no choice but to allow him to deliver the message to the Earth girl.

PART 6

SOMEWHERE

CHAPTER 36

THINGS WERE CALM ABOARD THE *Revelation* en route to the next system. Pat hardly spoke in the lab, laying out equipment as he wanted. Every day, he listened to loud music that Abby recognized, including Bonefish and Wildins. She wondered if the music was a way to stay out of making conversation with her. It didn't really matter; most of her chores were in the engine room and, when she came down to the lab to study with her CG instructors or do an experiment or simulation, he would always leave.

He and Mark orbited each other, like dogs refiguring their territories. Yet, there was love there. Not just for each other, but for the crew. She noticed how happy everyone else was to have him back. From her perspective, it was like he had never left—or at least, they were all just picking up where they had left off. She admitted to herself that she felt a twinge of jealousy when Rover danced over to Pat and nuzzled him.

Pat was a Homo kiposi: the species link between Homo sapiens and Homo khlôrosans. Like Abby, he had a greater tolerance to heat than their crew. He was a trained biologist, while she was still a student. He was taller and stronger than she was. He had even studied police tactics. Now that he was back, did they even need her?

The silence gave Abby a chronic stomachache. It was bad enough that Mark never played with her and Harden rarely talked to her unless giving her a reprimand. Now Pat was snubbing her too. Each day, the pain grew deeper until she wished she could cut open her belly and plunge her stomach into a bucket of ice water. The feeling did not leave while on the approach to the next planet. She wanted to scream. She wanted to shake his shoulders, force him to talk to her.

Abby entered his side of the lab. "Pat, Dr. Mason, Sir, may I fly the shuttle so I can keep logging hours?"

Pat clicked off the music and chuckled. "Sure. And please just choose one name to call me. My preference is Pat."

"I didn't know if you were still mad at me."

"For what? Being smart enough to escape a bad situation?" He gestured her closer. "I've been working on the exploration proposal. Mark told me you were pretty adventurous. Since I weigh quite a bit more than you, I was thinking that maybe I should take the soil and water samples while you do the climbing."

He glided two fingers across his tablet's touch screen and brought up the long range scans then opened topography maps. He slid the tablet into the connection point, which projected the maps on the light table.

Abby scanned the surface and zoomed in on one of the three mountain ranges slated for survey. "Actually, just between you and me, I'm afraid of pretty much everything, but we'll go ahead with your plan. This cirque looks interesting. Can I climb that? Look at all the plants between the boulders."

Pat nodded. Whatever his reaction was, it was internal. He said softly, "We got to trust each other 'cause we're partners planetside, right?"

"Yeah," Abby said with caution.

"Silva could do or say whatever she wanted. She was my wife, not my slave. I never ordered her to do anything. She wanted a child as much as I did. I want you to know that."

"What happened to her and Megan?"

Pat slid down the polymer wall to the deck as he slipped a picture out of his pocket: Megan, age three. "I left her the house so I assume she is still there. Want the gory details? Mark knows, so it's only time 'til it gets around the ship."

Abby sat next to him. The deck was cold through her coveralls, but she was curious and he seemed to be in the mood to talk.

"I liked Silva, but she didn't hold my attention. She got pregnant right away. After Megan was born. Silva wanted her to sleep in our bed. By then I figured I had given her a nice house, a family, and we even had a housekeeper to help her out, so I should get a little recreation."

Pat paused before he went on. "My understanding is homosexuality is legal on Earth? Or at least it was in Paris?"

Abby nodded. "Yes, but monogamy was the rule. We didn't have working antibiotics or antivirals."

"So I heard." He went on to explain that Silva had become jealous and clingy as he spent more and more time away from home. One night, she followed him to a fleet establishment that catered to unconventional tastes. Humiliated, she locked him out. He served her with divorce papers thinking it might scare her into letting him back in. He had never loved her, but he didn't want to hurt her.

"You want to know what's fucked up? Everyone blamed her, but Silva was just a woman looking for a better life. I could have thrown her out on the street and taken my daughter away. No one would have cared. I saw some serious shit at customs.

"Left my job, called Cole. He let me sign on with the *Stark* to get to O-7. I worked there for a month while I waited for you guys. Meg has a spot in Cole's fleet or a trust in her name if she decides to go to the university, so at least she'll know of me."

He pinched his brow. "What happened to you?"

"I do not...always remember."

Pat averted his eyes and nodded, then quickly focused upon her in concern. "What do you remember?"

She tried to shove the lump in her throat down to her stomach, but the shame-filled words vomited out. "I remembered holding Lei Lei. Her hands were all wrinkly like an old woman's. They told me to feed her before they took her away. I remember how it felt. I thought I was going to raise her, but..."

Abby didn't want to relive the horrible experiences she had encountered at the DePaul's, but there was something about Pat that made him easy to talk to. He encouraged her to speak by occasionally inserted a "fuck," "shit," and once asked, "May I put my arm around you?" Otherwise he just listened.

Once he held her and she didn't have to look him in the face, it was easy to expel the words. Without knowing it, she told him everything. Things she hadn't told the others: fears her baby wasn't being cuddled enough, that she was a terrible mother for leaving, her unending nightmares, how bad the monsters had hurt her, and her fears they had made her crazy, though she couldn't be sure they were really there.

"The maids called me a savage poutana. I think that means 'whore'. They were right. They saw what I was."

He confirmed "poutana" meant whore and assured her she was not one. Simply, she never traded in sex. She was ravaged.

Clenching her knees to her aching chest, Abby told him how she fell in love with Robert, then had a love/fear relationship with Eli. She hated herself for it.

"You were stranded and DePaul's men used physical, mental, and chemical coercion to get what they wanted."

"But it was illogical to fall in love with Robert. He wasn't even nice to me. Helen loves me, but Harden hates me now. He thinks I'm stupid. Probably Mark and Diane do too…"

Someone cleared his throat in the hatchway. Abby and Pat looked up. Neither had known Harden and Mark had been standing there. Abby wondered how much they had heard.

Mark slid down the wall and sat beside them. "No one blames you for what happened or thinks you're stupid. As Pat said, you were raped, drugged, and brain fucked." Then he passed her a piece of paper. "Well, this came for you. I printed it so you could put in on your wall. The kids looked like they had fun at the party."

The top half of paper was filled with a photo showing Orchid's nineteenth birthday. The bottom half had a letter in her sister's flowing script telling her all about the party, her boyfriend, and her coming graduation.

Abby wished that she had a photo of her own nineteenth birthday to send back to Orchid, but it had just been another workday. Then she realized Mark had said the *kids* looked like they had fun. *Kids.* She suddenly understood that she was a girl to Mark, not a woman. She wasn't exactly sure when that had happened, but figured he had been looking at her that way for some time. She found she didn't mind so much. Even though Diane and Helen said messing around was expected in someone her age, Abby wasn't sure she should have a lover yet. Between work and her studies, she had enough to do. Besides, when she needed it, her hand was always available.

Pat squeezed her. "Abby's record makes no mention of rehabilitation."

Mark looked down at his hands. "I'm trained to deal with PTSD, but I've never performed therapy on anyone. After our miscommunication, I felt allowing you to open up to Diane and Helen would be best."

Pat said, "I have met a few women that needed help. At customs."

Harden looked down at the three of them on the floor. "Great, figure out what treatment she needs, if any.

Crossing his arms, he glanced over at the table. "Exploration plans done?"

CHAPTER 37

Epsilon Reticuli c:
April 17, 3172 K.E.

EPSILON RETICULI WAS AN ORANGE-RED star with an abundance of iron. The system had a gas giant planet a single AU away from its sun. The b planet and heavy star made it difficult to detect other planets in the system, though they had known of the wide asteroid belt outside the habitat zone. Then Planet c was identified by a long-range probe.

Based on orbital sonar observations, Epsilon Reticuli c was approximately sixty percent the radius of Kipos, but it had a larger, denser core. This resulted in the planet having 98% of the gravitational pull of Kipos and a breathable atmosphere with similar air pressure.

Looking at the hologram model of the planet, Mark noticed deep streaks of soil over a rocky crust composed primarily of basalt. The streaks were darkest near the three mountain ranges that soared over the world. Volcanic activity suggested an active silicate mantle maintained the planet's tectonic system.

Looking over Pat's exploration strategy, Harden said, "Abby, be careful when you climb up this ridge. This area looks to be unstable."

After the briefing, Abby followed Mark and Pat into the oxygen garden for her first of many PTSD treatments. They allowed her to pick the place. She chose the oxygen garden because it was the first place that came to mind. She wasn't exactly sure what she was supposed to do. They told her to be open and write down her goals. She didn't have any. She was only doing this because they were making her.

Mark and Pat sat on the bench across from her. She glanced up at Pat, hoping that he would say they could end this. She didn't want to talk to them and vomit up the black shame again. She said, "I promise I won't ever let my irrational fears affect my work."

"We don't think it will. That's not why you are here," Mark said.

"Why am I here?" Abby asked, hoping there was still a way out of this.

"To help you move past the trauma festering inside of you," Mark said, "Since O-7, you've been eating less and sleeping more fitfully. You've been downing antacids lately. And you've been weeping when you think no one is watching."

Abby shrugged. Denying it was pointless.

"Do you regret coming?"

"No." Abby replied. Mark was waiting for her to elaborate. She did not.

He said, "I'm installing a journal program on your tablet. You will write your dreams down. I also would like you to think about your emotional state before you go to bed. I want to see if there is any correlation between how you are feeling and if you sleep with the light on or off."

"I always sleep with my light on."

"Regardless, every seven days or so, we will have a talk," Mark said.

"Pat too?"

"If it makes you more comfortable," Mark said.

Abby did not want to tell them what actually made her more comfortable was when someone wrapped his or her arms around her. She had been a grown woman on Earth and nearly an adult on the *Revelation*; she should be able to face the whole universe on her own without being held. She huffed, "Maybe I'd be more comfortable if you'd sometimes play games with me."

Mark sighed and glanced at Pat. "I have told you before: I do not like holo-games because I get motion sickness, but if you wish to play cards, you just have to ask."

"Eli taught me to play cribbage," she offered. "I got pretty good, but I really want to learn poker? And play when you guys play?"

"Only if you promise you won't ever really get involved in a high stakes game. Helen would kill us," Mark said.

Abby agreed. She figured writing down her dreams and going to therapy in the garden would be a fair trade.

WEARING LIGHT ENVIRONMENTAL SUITS WITHOUT oxygen tanks, they landed in an open glen surrounded by forests. Giant cocoons of squirming worms hung from the trees. Pat climbed up to cut a sample while Rover took root and bark samples in the glade.

As instructed, Abby headed east to the summit of the ridge. It was a longer walk than she expected, but it was not difficult in the oxygen rich atmosphere. After about two kilometers of gentle climbing, Abby could see a panorama of seven snowcapped peaks and high rolling ridges baking in the orange glow of the sun. To the east, there was a rocky cirque where basalt boulders made sanctuaries for alpine lichen and ribbons of water streamed into a small green lake. She headed into the valley. A test showed the water to be heavily salted. She collected her samples to analyze for pathogens later.

Under the shade of a large boulder, she found a vine covered in long, feathery wisps that surrounded globular clusters of green berries. As she cut into the vine, it slithered and a white puss dripped onto the ground. More than lichen, it was part animal/part plant. She felt terrible for causing the organism pain, but she collected both the puss and a piece of the vine. She observed it for some time while taking photographs.

A long wisp fanned out and caught an insect. It stopped fluttering within seconds. She realized the insect was disintegrating from the inside; the vine was eating it.

Abby set her camera on a four second interval as she scrambled around the cirque, more for fun than research. She slid as she stepped down on a loose rock. Dusting off her scraped hands, she waited for someone to shout at her through her radio, but they must have missed it. She dropped herself to a lower ridge and moved on.

Protected by the wind, the west side's rocks were blanketed in purple, star-shaped flowers. She collected the plants and took another set of soil samples. Realizing she hadn't heard Pat in a while, she climbed back to the upper ridge.

Pat's voice was full of panic and static. She heard, "Jump down, Abs. Over. Harden, can you see her?"

"No. Come on, kiddo. Jump down to eleven."

Abby switched to a lower channel. "Copy?"

The signal was clearer. "Okay, we got her. Pat, jump down."

Pat's voice sounded more than a little worried. "I lost you for the last ten minutes."

Hoping to diffuse the situation, she said, "I found some good stuff."

"How good?"

"Lichen, an unidentified vine-type organism, and purple flowering plants in the cirque."

"I'm sending Rover to get a stone sample. Stay on this channel."

"Copy."

Rover padded his way over and began drilling out core samples. Long, striated tubes of stone were pulled out of a large boulder. A perfume of rotten eggs with an overtone of citrus lingered in the air.

"Just by sight, I'd say there are large deposits of iron and I smell sulfur and something else," Abby said.

"Take another set of gravel samples," Pat replied.

"Copy that."

ON THE SHORELINE, PAT WALKED north and Abby walked south towards tide pools. She wanted to feel her lungs fill with oxygen, then swim under the water holding her breath as long as she could. She knew she wasn't allowed to touch the water until it was deemed safe, which wouldn't happen until the water samples were aboard and evaluated. However, with the sun sparkling over it, she wanted to dive in. Abby thought of how luxurious it would feel to swim in deep water and be cleaned of the constant sweat.

Abby dipped her seven Petri dishes into the water, and then collected some of the sand between the rocks. Rover took a stone sample beside her. She packed her samples carefully and placed them in his hull.

The strange thing about the shoreline was, unlike other planets, Epsilon Reticuli c did not seem to have billions of life forms in her oceans. According to sonar scanners, they found only seven hundred different species, the majority of which were bacteria and plankton. Abby realized there were only a few gastropods and she saw no evidence of vertebrates at all, not in the sea or on the mountain range.

Abby headed down the beach with Rover trotting behind her. "You know what, Pat? No organisms here would understand the name 'Bonefish.'"

Pat chuckled through the radio, "I haven't seen any either. Let's fly over the deeper ocean and see if anything is out there."

Once Abby and Pat hauled in their samples and secured the shuttle, Abby sat down in the pilot's seat. "If everything is safe, you think we can all go planetside for a picnic? The temperature and pressure is right for everyone. The water looks great."

Pat sighed. "Harden and Mark might have a problem with that."

Abby said, "Talk to Helen. She'll win them over to our side."

"You're assuming I'm on your side."

The flight over the oceans was quiet. In the deep, scans found only a few large cnidarian-type animals. Their translucent bodies were only a few layers of epithelium sandwiching mesoglea, with large orifices surrounded by long, purple tendrils. They floated along the current until they sensed schools of tiny bioluminescent organisms. Using surprising bursts of speed, they attacked.

The smaller organisms had an advantage of their own. Their shiny exoskeletons glittered as they burst from the sea. Their three thick tentacles acted as propellers of sorts.

Pat dipped the collector into the deep water. The tube pulled out a few small organisms, along with salt water. In the dull light of the shuttle, their exoskeletons changed colors in glimmering pastels: pink, peach, yellow, minty green, pale blue, and violet.

"They're so pretty," Abby said as she took a closer look. "I'm almost sad they'll die."

"They would have been eaten anyway." Pat hit the switch and the water drained into the sample cups. He pushed a button. The organisms fast-froze. Abby figured being frozen was better than being slowly digested.

EXCITED ABOUT THE FINAL ENVIRONMENT, Abby made a perfect landing within the large volcanic crater on the only a sliver of land, surrounded by ash and magma.

Rover reached with a lengthened arm and a cup and took magma samples as Abby and Pat collected ash and mud. For the first time, they worked within five meters of each other at all times.

A sonar scan revealed a hole in the ground. Pat and Abby began digging. Within a rocky core they found a deep purple amethyst geode. As they dug deeper, they found what looked like fossilized fungi. A bright flash of light filled the sky moments before the mountain burped and spewed more ash into the air.

Pat said, "Let's get out of here."

Hearing the mountain rumble, Abby agreed.

CHI WAS IN THE AIR WHEN glowing, red-orange lava spewed upward and cascaded down into fiery rivers as a fissure cracked open the planet's crust. Propelled by intense pressure, the lava reached upwards of fifty meters.

A plume of ash rose and swallowed the *Chi* whole. Abby felt the jolt of pressure but did her best to hold the stick steady. She glanced over at Pat. His face looked white. Abby was too busy controlling the jostling shuttle to completely understand the readings, but she heard Pat tell the *Revelation* the oxygen rich atmosphere was no longer outside the shuttle as columns of sulfur dioxide clouds encircled the mountain.

Pat told Helen, "The crater just collapsed. The heat from the ash is setting small trees aflame."

Rocks and lava ejected from the ground and the shuttle was struck on its port side; Abby almost lost her seat. Pat was on the deck. Abby scanned her control panel. The outer hull had not been breached. She climbed higher, but the ash was unending.

"Fighting the current is not working, I'm going into the slipstream."

Harden said, "You don't have…."

The radio was gone. "Pat! I-I…have a plan, but it might get us killed."

Pat was suddenly above her. He slipped her helmet on her head and latched it down. He tapped it twice and she gave him an okay sign as she breathed in the pressurized air mixture. She felt his hand slide across her body as he buckled her in. "Stop asking for permission. You're the fucking pilot!"

Another rock slammed into the shuttle. This time he stayed on his feet. Even though he was right next to her, the static was louder than his voice. Finally, his helmet was on. She saw his okay sign.

"This planet hates us," he joked.

Knowing the dangers but holding back the rising panic in her throat, she punched the throttle. She turned the shuttle back downward to get out of the never-ending gray. She knew how much fuel they had. She knew there was a slim chance for rescue if it didn't work.

Seconds later, in the lower atmosphere, Pat and Abby could see the fires below and the gray above. Even though they were breaking the sound barrier, the clouds of rock and ash seemed to be moving faster. However, what Abby found much more discomforting was the constant rumbling of tectonic plates.

A few seconds went by. They traveled four kilometers from the eruption where the ground was green, though the plumes of ash still ruled the skies. After five more seconds, there was finally blue sky above them. Abby glanced at her fuel gage.

They had enough to break atmo, probably enough to get in a low orbit and get towed back to the *Revelation*. She quickly called in her plan. There was still no answer. She recorded the message and then replayed it on a twenty second repeat. There was still no answer. She pulled back on the stick and felt the jolt as she climbed.

"You still mad?"

"Never was."

"Think they are?"

Pat shrugged. "Probably not. I'm dying to replay this so we can see what is going on behind us. That was insane."

"I've never seen such a powerful explosion—even on Earth. The old vids of Mount Rainier were nothing compared to that."

"Me neither."

"Me neither, Abby and Patrick Mason." Rover flashed on his screen.

"I love that he calls you 'Abby.' Maybe we can teach him to call everybody by their first names."

Ten minutes later, they were in the black. Abby didn't want to look at the fuel gauge. She tried the radio again. No answer. "The *Revelation's* sensors will know where we are," she said, trying to pretend she wasn't scared that their orbit would begin to degrade sooner than she had anticipated.

Pat answered her with a squeeze on her shoulder.

It took the *Revelation* only two minutes to rendezvous and Abby was able to land under *Chi's* own power. As they disembarked, there were three conversations going on at once.

"What did you do to my ship? You two should be fucking dead," Harden said.

Mark frowned beside his brother. His scanner showed their heartbeats were still rapid and Abby's muscles were tight. They had suffered some bumps and bruises, but otherwise they were both fine. The crew had seen Abby half dressed before, so she wasn't really embarrassed by their presence when she changed out of her environmental gear and went through the sterilizers. However, she wished everyone would go away. If they noticed her discomfort, they ignored it. They were not even looking at her, but talking to Pat. Being surrounded by so many noisy men made Abby nauseous.

"We have the sensors watching for tsunamis and we'll see if any more tectonic activities occur," Harden said.

Once she was dressed, Brian grabbed the shoulder of Abby's coveralls and half dragged her behind the shuttle. It was completely crushed. "It's a fucking miracle you broke atmo."

The outer hull was dented from the impacts and blackened. Silver netting and wires poked through the smashed metal. Full panels of paint seemed to be sheered off. Abby briefly considered if there was a god on that planet, or if maybe her Ma and Da were watching over her.

Behind them, Pat laughed. "We'll get some samples from that."

Harden said something in reply, but Abby didn't listen to the men's banter until Brian turned to her. "You okay?"

She blushed. "Just sore. Especially my hands and neck."

In a nearly automatic gesture, Brian reached out and slipped her hand in his right and pressed his left to her forehead. "You're going to make yourself sick. You've got to relax."

His warm fingers quickly moved between her right digits, pressing the muscles until she finally unclenched. He did the same to the left. Just as smoothly, he pushed on the spaces between the vertebrae of her neck as he said, "That was awesome flying, by the way. Helen and I are proud of how you handled the shuttle. Even Harden was impressed. If Hel wasn't up on the bridge, I bet she'd tell you that herself. Feel better?"

"Yeah. Thanks." A warm happy feeling began in her stomach and expanded outward until she found herself smiling and relaxed.

Brian said, "Unhook Rover and we'll rebuild the second engine. Or do you want to go lie down?"

"I'd rather help you."

Harden asked, "How long do you need for repairs?"

"We have the parts, so maybe two days, as long as nothing breaks on the *Revelation*," Brian said.

"You have them," Harden said, then turned and headed upstairs. He hadn't said a word to her. Not really. He hadn't been impressed with her flying, no matter what Brian had said, but he hadn't yelled at her either. Abby counted that as a win. She wondered if she could have some freedom planetside. Nothing sounded more wonderful than dipping into that sparkling water, but she knew better than to say so when tsunamis were racing across the ocean.

WHILE DIANE, BRIAN AND ABBY repaired *Revelation Chi*, Mark and Pat concluded that the planet's soil seemed to be slightly alkaline and contained elements such as magnesium, sodium, potassium and chloride. The b planet disturbed the habitat zone too much for intelligent life to develop on planet c. The planet simply did not have enough potable water. Moreover, Abby and Pat had witnessed the instability of the planet's tectonic system.

It was not a good candidate for immediate colonization, but the planet could be a decent dew, mineral, and methane collection site for a nearby orbiting outpost between the c planet and the asteroid belt—if Kipos wished to build one, that is.

The water wasn't drinkable but it was clean. It had no dangerous species and it was unpolluted by natural sources.

Abby checked the system for obvious dangers and then searched for a likely safe spot on the planet. The scans found a sandy beach in the northern latitudes four days ahead of any inclement weather. A slight wind blew, but 20°C was comfortable for everyone.

At dinner, she mentioned the beach and showed Helen and Harden where it was located on her map. Rockford had no interest or intention of ever leaving his ship, but of the human crew, Mark was the only one who felt nervous about it. "What about our travel time to Sagattari?" he asked.

"We need to do a flight test to check *Chi's* repairs anyway," Harden said.

There was only a bit of discussion, and for Mark's sake, Harden made everyone promise not to wander off alone.

AS THE OTHERS BEGAN TO prepare for the picnic, Abby flew *Alpha* as Harden controlled *Chi* by remote beside her. While they went through the pre-flight checklist of both shuttles, Abby found the idea of flying beside Harden slightly disconcerting; she hoped she wouldn't make any mistakes. She told herself she was being stupid. If Harden didn't trust her flying, he would have Helen in the shuttle with him.

As instructed, Abby raced across mountains and down into valleys at the speed of sound with the *Chi* on her stern. It took ninety minutes to circumnavigate the planet.

Then Abby boarded the *Chi* and then flew in the same pattern. She did a few maneuvers and faked some stalls. Harden and Abby flew in a high planetary orbit, tested the sublight velocity fuel cells which only took seconds. Abby knew Brian and Diane were good at their jobs, but she was actually amazed that only two days prior the shuttle had been in pieces and it was just as responsive as before.

They returned to the beach where Brian had dug a hole and filled it with sea water to keep the beer cool, then lit a fire to roast three racks of sheep ribs and potatoes. Knowing that if there was something dangerous nearby it would be attracted by the smell of cooking meat, Rover kept watch. Diane and Helen strolled barefoot down the sandy beach.

Abby stripped to her base layers and waded out where Mark and Pat were running yet another PH test of the water. The water was cooler than Abby's flesh and goose pimples rose up on her skin as it got up to her knees. "Still testing? We've been gone for three hours."

Mark gave her an irritated look, so Abby walked passed them. The water was up to her waist when Pat picked her up and threw her in deeper. They glanced back Mark still testing the PH. They splashed around him until finally he splashed back. Mark never completely relaxed, but he swam with them until their teeth clattered.

Abby, Mark, and Pat came out of the sea, and the beer hole had become a winding castle around the fire. Mark and Pat wandered off somewhere, so Abby knelt down to help Harden and Brian build.

Her knees and hands were quickly covered with sand as she carved out tiny rivers with her finger and created a waterfall with rocks. Rover occasionally passed her scoops of colored rocks as he guarded.

Once the city spiraled outward nearly ten meters, Abby asked, "Rover, would you like to run with me? They will let us, as long as we have to stay together."

"Harden Alekos, I run with Abby?"

"Keep Abby safe. Stay where I can see you both and don't go bothering anyone else."

Rover tilted his head as he processed the command sequence. Abby looked at Harden in the eye.

"I know you won't, but he will," Harden said.

"Come on." Her bare feet sunk in the sand. Rover ran beside her, always at her heels. She climbed a sand dune. Feeling the sand sink back with every step she took, she finally crested it and ran down the other side. Suddenly he stopped. "Abby!"

She skidded to a stop and looked around. She didn't see any danger.

"Abby, must turn around now. Harden Alekos cannot see us in this dune." Rover began explaining the limits of the human eye and geometry.

Knowing if she continued to run, Rover would tell on her, she said,

"I'll race you back," and darted ahead.

"Cannot race. Harden Alekos would not like it if Abby got hurt."

Once again, Abby was reminded of the limitations of his intelligence.

"You didn't go very far." Harden said, turning the ribs.

"He said you couldn't see us if we went further in the dune. We're gonna keep running this way now."

Behind her, Rover skidded to a stop, but was careful not to step on any of the winding city. "Abby must stop."

Abby hopped over a wall before she turned around. Harden had covered his eyes. With her hands on her hips, she said. "You're playing with us, aren't you?"

He smiled. "Just testing a hypothesis. Give me a second to rethink his orders."

Brian said, "Once Harden told him to watch a rack of lamb until it reached seventy-four degrees, then take it out. At exactly seventy-four degrees, he pulled it from the oven and carried it to Harden, who was in the engine room. He did not bring the pan or shut off the oven."

"What was worse was he had checked the temperature so often he dried it out," Helen said as she and Diane came around the bend. "New orders are to keep Abby safe, but let Abby run as far and as fast as she wants. Don't go bother anyone else. You may race as long as you stay within ten meters of her."

There was nothing like an afternoon on the beach and the smell of ribs cooking on the fire to stimulate her appetite. After dinner, they watched the b planet rise over the sea and eclipse Epsilon Reticuli. Shivering in the temporary darkness, the humans smoothed over the beach. Careful to leave no garbage behind, they repacked the shuttles.

Mark insisted the crew go through the sterilizers upon their return to the *Revelation*, but everyone seemed happy and ready for the long trip to the Sagittarian space.

CHAPTER 38

Abby lay back on the thin mattress and smiled up at Diane as she passed Rockford to her. Pat was already in the cell beside her. She understood the idea of gravity couches was to protect the human body during high velocity and stasis would preserve food and other resources, but she still wished she could stay up.

"Don't be scared, Abs. We've never lost anyone on this ship."

"Can't help it."

Diane closed the cell door and set soft music to play while the chamber began to fill with foam. Though Abby knew she did not have to close her eyes or shut her mouth, she pinched her face shut. The foam did not feel wet as the black liquid/gelatin had, but she still hated it. She couldn't believe Mark preferred this way of travel.

Her muscles relaxed in the silence. She felt Rockford squish deeper into her armpit. Her stomach fluttered in excitement. She would awaken to explore something completely new—a planet on which Mark and the others could tolerate only for moments. She and Pat would explore it.

CHAPTER 39

The Sagittari System:
September 28, 3177 K.E.

ABBY FELT GROGGY AS THE foam dissipated. Rockford stretched. She felt the pinpricks of his sharp claws in her arm. She realized she was standing up and an arm was around her body, pulling her away from the grav-couch.

She heard Harden snap and Helen's worried voice. Mark said, "Pulse strong. Eyes a little red. Skin blotchy. The research has been limited, but this confirms that Homo sapiens just don't come out of stasis as quickly as we do. We can just put her to bed."

As she became aware of her chattering teeth, a blanket was wrapped around her. She was no longer on her feet. Abby leaned against a man's chest with one muscular arm behind her back and a calloused hand under her knees. She could hear plaintive meowing, the pitter-patter of four paws following them and hoping for a treat. A cup of water was pressed to Abby's lips.

"How did you know I was thirsty?" she croaked.

"We've gone in and out of hypersleep long before you were born," Helen said.

"Open your mouth," Mark said.

A chalky pill was placed on her tongue.

"Swallow," Mark said.

Abby swallowed it, and then drank the rest of the water.

They were moving upwards. Abby realized she was being carried upstairs and passed downward. She wanted to thank whoever was helping her, but Brian told her to lie down and tucked her under another quilt. Sleep took her quickly.

ABBY AWOKE FROM A BUZZ in the next room and a strong urge to pee. She pressed her ear next to the metal wall and heard Helen's voice through the intercom. "…been lost."

"How?" Harden asked.

"Don't know. The feed simply stopped. I'm reversing it to see if we can figure out what happened. Coming up?"

"Yeah."

Abby glanced down at the printed out letters from Orchid. She did want to catch up with her sister, but she was more curious about what was going on up on the bridge. She hurried into the head and as she sat on the toilet, pulled on a set of coveralls. She climbed up the ladder to the upper deck. She ran barefoot up to the bridge ahead of Harden.

"You shouldn't eavesdrop," he snapped at her.

"You shouldn't talk so loud."

Helen smiled in her direction. Harden looked pissed.

They replayed the feed. The probe was orbiting past a two-moon, Kipos-type planet, as they knew it would be. They saw the wide oceans, lovely green islands filled with glass buildings reaching for the sky. Suddenly, there was a golden flash, then the image blurred as it fell before it burned up in the atmosphere.

"You think it was destroyed?"

"Obviously," Harden snapped.

Abby winced. "I mean, do you think it was destroyed by the indigenous, intelligent race on purpose?"

"Could be a malfunction. There are plenty of natural reasons—solar flares and the like."

"Is that why we were woken up?"

Helen replied. "No. We found a planet in the HZ of Lambda Sagittarii."

"We're going to a planet orbiting a red giant?" Abby could hardly contain her excitement.

Harden frowned. "Haven't decided. Might be a waste of fuel."

"How…"

"Abby." Harden's voice was edged with derision.

Helen met his eyes. They had one of their unspoken discussions. Abby had the distinct feeling Helen had cautioned her brother about taking his bad mood out on others.

Harden controlled his voice. "We'll be going past the tenth planet in the system in a few hours. I realize it's Helen's day, but I need her here and Mark is still asleep. Since you're up, make some breakfast?"

ABBY BROUGHT HELEN AND HARDEN scrambled eggs and fruit salad with yogurt on top. She hoped she would hear something good, but did not tarry since they were obviously still in conference. She went back to the galley and hit the com button. She got three grumpy answers. The crew wanted sleep more than breakfast.

She hated waiting.

Helen called her back to the bridge. "So what do you know?"

"From Earth, Lambda Saggitarri marks the top of the Archer's bow in American astronomy. In Chinese astronomy, it is the two of six in the South Dipper mansion of the Black Tortoise of the North. Its spectral class is K. You already said it has sixteen planets and moons have been discovered on most of those. I also know the *Revelation* and the *Discovery* have been largely ignoring these systems."

Harden frowned, but Helen smiled again. "We're coming to the tenth of sixteen planets, an ice giant. Want to run the scan?"

Abby slipped into the third seat and focused the scanners on the planet. Scans indicated m's atmosphere was primarily composed of hydrogen and helium, solid water, ammonia and methane. The average equator temperature was 49° Kelvin, polar temp 59° Kelvin. The interior was composed of rock with an iron core…

Then she saw something really interesting. "Hey, did you guys see that m's rotational axis is tilted on its side? The planet's rings and moons move with the cloud bands. Did you know that's just like Uranus?"

Harden scowled at his sister. "Fuck me." He pulled out a bill and tossed it at her.

Helen laughed and slipped it into her zipper pocket. "Good job. We thought we found something new until we looked it up. What else?"

"Complex cloud structure. Wind speeds about nineteen hundred km/h," Abby said. "Umm, I really want to go."

"We figured as much, hon," Helen said. "Finish the system scan. You've fifteen more planets. I'm coming up with a flight plan that uses minimal fuel."

CHAPTER 40

Lambda Sagittari k:
September 30, 3177 K.E.

THE RED GIANT LOOMED IN the sky above her. She had never seen a sun so large. She remembered the autumn moons of Earth and low sunrises, but those were only an optical illusion due to light refraction, but this was not an illusion. It was darker than she had expected it to be, like twilight, though it should have been early morning. A haze of atmosphere turned the horizon the color of a deep bruise. The soil was brown and felt rich as Abby crumbled it between her fingers, but there was very little obvious life. Mosses and lichens covered the ground in shades of gold, and even one seemed to be a vivid orange. There was no greenery, no leaves. Indeed, Abby considered, for nothing could be green without chlorophyll.

Pat said, "The plant life must use some sort of phycobilisomes or something similar."

Abby walked down to the beach and looked at the vast reddish liquid. It smelled brackish and she could hear small waves crashing upon the ground. She fought the urge to run. There was something so frightening about the place, so alien. Pat had been salivating to go, but now she wondered if he was scared too.

There were large kelp or possibly algae beds under the water, but Abby could not see any vertebrates beyond that. She dipped her sample cup into the sea and lifted it out. It was clear.

Pat came up behind her. She passed him the cup. He tested the liquid. "Water. Three percent saline."

Abby programmed Rover to telescope his arm in order to move the algae aside to see if she saw any higher-level creatures, but there were still none.

Abby followed Rover back to the sandy beach and dug deeper into the ground. Cold dampness slid through her gloves, but she saw no worms. As she requested, he lifted a heavy rock. Tiny white crabs tried to escape the red light. Abby hoped her camera was recording their scurrying. She tried to catch one in a dish, but it moved too fast.

Using Rover and a piece of lichen, Pat set up a basic trap with a specimen jar as Abby climbed a large steep ridge. She scrambled upwards, feeling herself sweat. She loved the feeling of the pull in her legs, but as she reached the top, it became nearly vertical and she had to climb a crumbling embankment. She wouldn't have made it if her environmental suit hadn't been working to keep her cool.

Below, deep in the shade, was another pool. This one seemed to sparkle like a crystal. She hurried down to it.

Diane said, "Watch yourself. Those look pretty sharp."

Abby slowed down as she made her descent. She quickly took samples of the pool and broke off what seemed to be a twig from a crystal tree. She took another picture, hoping she would get clear images in the low light.

She tried using a flash, but it didn't seem to work. The light reflected off the tree. She looked back at the ground where strands of crystal glided through the sands. Wondering if they were roots, Abby took a sample of those as well.

She climbed up one more hill and saw it. "Are you guys seeing this?"

Diane answered her, "Copy that, Abs."

Below her were crumbling buildings on rusted pylons the exact same color as the ground. She had found evidence of intelligent life.

"Abby, Diane told you to be careful!" She heard Harden say as she hurried down the hillside.

Abby rolled her eyes and said, "Copy that."

"Don't roll your eyes at me!"

"Copy that." Knowing Harden couldn't see her facial expression, she stuck her tongue out towards the sky, imagining the ship overhead. No one said anything that time. It must be the tone of her voice that set him off. She would work harder to hide it in the future.

She let the camera record. Abby sidestepped down the gravel hill to the city. The crumbling pockmarked walls showed signs of long-term decay. Crystal trees slipped in and out of the ruins. She wondered if these were using some part of the buildings' materials as a food source. She dropped to her knees and dug into the ground, "Look, there is water in the soil!" She set her camera to start cycling between regular photography, illumination magnification, full spectrum, and infrared while she took samples of the water, the algae, and loose dirt.

She began to walk around the old city. She picked up some discarded pieces of building materials, shards of metal pilings and a few small bricks that looked liked they were a mixture of dirt and crushed stone. Most of the ceilings looked caved in or were completely missing. As she approached what looked like a fairly stable doorway, Harden shouted through her radio, "Don't you dare step inside!"

She peered in at the rubble, but did not cross the threshold.

She walked through the old streets before she traversed an old crumbling bridge.

"Look, an old sewer! I'm going to check it out for surface level artifacts."

"Copy that," Harden said. "Try not to touch the walls."

Abby lowered herself into the canal and looked inside. There were more white crabs, nearly a meter across in leg span. She netted one and hauled it back over the bridge. It squirmed and thrashed, but it could not break through the metal netting. She pulled a small bottle of methane dichloride out of her sample pack. She depressed the plunger and sprayed it at an orifice, hoping it was its mouth. Abby felt guilt in her chest as the crab's limbs slowed down and stopped moving.

She lowered herself back into the water and looked around. The crabs skittered away from her as she waded deeper. There was a lot of debris in the water, some of which sparkled gold. She lifted a ten-centimeter, rectangular-length, hollow, rusty piece of metal. When she turned the artifact on its end, she saw gold glittering inside. Of course, it might be iron pyrite or another shiny mineral. It was too dark to tell. She wondered what it was. Some sort of tool? It might be some sort of socket for turning bolts or piping. Maybe if she knew what the composition was, she might understand its purpose. She slid it into her pack.

She picked up what looked to be a piece of glazed pottery—part of a plate or a dish? She found a few other similar pieces and picked them up.

Abby followed the canal until she found another broken tool. She had no idea what it was. It was heavier than she had expected it to be. The long crystal shaft ended in four dulled and chipped prongs, which formed the corners of a square. If it was sharpened, it could be an eating utensil or a weapon. Maybe it was a key. Or perhaps the prongs were used for turning square headed nuts or screws. Or was it part of something bigger? She honestly did not know.

She heard Harden snap, "You've one hour. Start heading back."

"Wait, I've found this tool..."

"Now."

"I…"

"Now!"

She scooped up the last piece of the broken tool, snapped the lid on the sample pans, and went back the way she came. Once she was over the bridge, she grabbed her crab and ran back up the hill. Pat was above her on the summit. He too came down to see the city.

"Slow down! I told you to be careful," Harden snapped. "You have unstable buildings all around you!"

"Abs, your heart is racing. Make sure you are drinking enough," Diane said

"Copy that." Abby grumbled as she took a sip, angry with Harden for yelling at her in front of everyone. Again. He never yelled at Pat. Or anyone else.

WHILE PAT AND MARK WORKED on categorizing samples and dissected crabs, Abby looked over all the photographs she had taken. She was disappointed but not surprised by the photos of the crystal tree. Just as she assumed it would be, all she could see were auras of light sparkling off the branches. However, the infrared photos of the same specimen showed, without a doubt, it was a living entity. The trunk was striated with brilliant blue corpuscles.

The animal life was not diverse enough to sustain humans and there was nearly no fresh water on the planet. Water near the crystal trees had a high saline content, whereas the pools with the red algae bloom were less briny but still too salty to sustain human life.

All the information was sent back to Kipos and the *Discovery*. Mark and Pat concluded there was nothing so valuable to Kipos and certainly Lambda Sagittari k was not a place where the flotilla could colonize.

Abby went to her billet with her blood thumping. She wished she could go down to the planet again, but knew it was out of the question. She closed her eyes and tried to dream of the next solar system. Her mind moved so quickly that sleep would not come. She reread the letters from Orchid. Though they were filled with the happy occasions of her sister's life, the letters made Abby feel sad. She wanted to write back to her sister, but their lives were so different. Trying to forget her melancholy, she pulled on her cardigan over her pajamas and went up to the galley.

Outside, the window was full of the red, dim sun and a million stars but, even with star charts, she had trouble making out her old friends. Tonight, she didn't feel like doing the math to find the constellations. Diane and Harden were discussing the next engine mod for the creation and stabilization of an Einstein-Rosen Bridge.

Abby wished Harden hadn't sighed as she approached him. Still, he reached out and took the offered cup of coffee. "You want to go back?" It wasn't so much a question but an accusation.

"I know the math doesn't work," she said as she set Diane's coffee in the holder next to the com system.

"Why are you up, sweetie?" Diane asked.

"Can't sleep."

Glancing at her cup of chai, Harden said, "Maybe you shouldn't drink so much sugar this late."

"Maybe you shouldn't drink so much caffeine."

"Part of being captain, kiddo." He gestured for her to sit down. "How far have you gotten in astrophysics?"

Abby sat down beside him and sipped her tea. "I'm only on the first chapter."

He looked rather disappointed.

Diane said, "She's working full time and doing school work for four hours a day. At her age, you were still in school full time and only working four hours."

"You didn't even know me then."

"I can read a ship's log," she replied, then asked Abby. "So what's on your mind?"

Figuring that jumping straight into the discovery of the alien city would put Harden off, she told a half-truth: "Orchid's a doctor and had a little boy."

"And you regret coming?" Harden asked.

"No, not at all. That's just it. Shouldn't I? If Helen had a baby, wouldn't you want to be there?"

"She can't have children and she's sleeping less than thirty meters away."

"Harden, shut up," Diane said.

"I keep thinking Pat and I are the only humans to set foot here, maybe ever. I want to tell Orchid all about it, but I'm still nineteen. She's a mom. If she knew about Lei Lei, I don't know if she'd even want to talk to me now."

"That's completely unreasonable," Harden said,

Diane gave Harden a look. "You should write to your sister before it's too late. I still treasure every word from my son. Orchid is an intelligent woman, even if she is not privy to all the details, she knows what happened to you."

"She sends me pictures from birthdays and Landing Days and even her own wedding, but I don't have anything for her."

"Are you fucking serious? We have thousands of photos and vids of you. Just pick some," Harden said.

"Can I tell her about the constant red and gold haze and the city?"

"Not a city—ruins," Harden reminded her. "You can tell her whatever you want."

"I've been trying to think about what they must have been like. How they lived. It's hard to imagine. I wish I knew if they lived on the planet prior to the sun becoming a red giant or afterwards. That might help us guess at their physiology. It is in the HZ now, but when the star was in its main sequence, it would have been cold. Or maybe the planet was pushed into a wider orbit. Or maybe they were on a different planet and colonized this one."

She sighed. "I wish I knew more about archeology."

"If they were truly alien, it wouldn't matter. You could spend a lifetime studying them and never know. Still, I'm curious what the experts will say. If they find it interesting, people will come." Harden made a movement as if he was going to touch her shoulder, but then stopped and instead looked down at his cup.

Diane asked, "How's your PTSD treatment going?"

Abby shrugged. "I guess okay."

Diane said, "Mark mentioned you do not seem to have a viable goal of what you wish to accomplish—except learning poker, which I suppose will make you more well-rounded, but hardly makes you healthier."

Abby glanced down at her sheep slippers and began to fiddle with the plastic button eye. "I guess I don't. I'm writing down my nightmares because Mark and Pat say I have to."

"Back in the day, Spiro made me do the same thing. I still don't have a fucking clue what the mechanics of writing down dreams is supposed to do, but I did it and so will you," Harden said.

"Did you have to do therapy because you lost Lucy?" Abby asked.

"Yes and no. The first loss was a friend—her name was Miry—in a shuttle crash." Harden glanced down at his almost empty cup. "This story is pretty long and I am almost out of coffee."

Abby grabbed his and Diane's cups and ran to the galley. She heard them bicker a bit on the bridge, but she knew even if Harden didn't want to tell the story, he still would. Especially once Diane said, "It will help Abby to know she's not the only one who has gone through it."

That was a nice sentiment, but Abby simply wanted to absorb the information. She couldn't help it, whether it was a new planet or personal gossip, knowledge was knowledge. When she returned with their coffee and another cup of chai for herself, Harden began to speak: "I was only a little older than you when the shuttle crashed.

"We hit some serious turbulence and stormy weather over an ice sheet. While I am a decent pilot, I will never be as good as Hel. I was less than a foot away from Miry, but the ship was smashed in such a way that we had to cut her out. A piece of metal was stuck in her leg. By the time we got her free, she had bled out.

"For a long time, whenever it got quiet, I would try to figure out what I could have done differently, but when I ran scenarios through my head, it always ended the same or with a higher death count.

"So anyway, since I couldn't sleep, I started watching Mark sleep. He seemed so fragile. I wanted to protect him because I used to believe him to be a living last ditch effort to save a failing marriage that no one wanted – 'cept maybe Helen. She always loved our little brother. Anyway, one night, Miry's screaming got too loud, so I woke him up."

Harden hesitated as he glanced towards Diane for a moment. She gestured for him to continue. He sighed and looked back at Abby. "Even if he was sleepy, he loved my attention. So I read to him or let him read to me, or if he had trouble with a lesson, I showed him how to come up with the solution. I finally understood that he was not stupid. He was five. The only reason he could not do algebra was because he was still learning arithmetic. I detested my own little brother for nothing more than being sixteen years younger then myself. Pretty fucking idiotic, right?"

He paused again and seemed to want an answer, so Diane and Abby nodded.

"Mark would eventually pass out again, but the poor kid didn't get a decent night's sleep until Dad heard us over the course of a few weeks and forced me into therapy."

"And you could sleep after therapy?" Abby asked.

"No, I started sleeping once Lucy was sleeping beside me. She told me my pacing was keeping her awake. I was okay—or functioning at any rate—until her death."

"It all started again, but Dad and Spiro were ready for me to start my late night rambles. Dad said I could tuck Mark in and even check on him over the com if I needed to, but I was not allowed in his billet between the hours of 20:00 and 06:30. Spiro told me I could reflect on scenarios about both tragedies with him as long as I wanted, any time, day or night, but I had to accept that I'd have a sleepy doctor if I woke him at 02:00."

"Without Mark to care for, Miry and Lucy haunted me. Believing my incompetence had murdered them, I considered stepping out of an airlock more than once."

"The single reason I did not was the nightmarish vision that I would accidently decompress the whole ship. The last thing I saw were Mark's eyes crystalizing and Helen shattering against the hull."

"So I started working on the FtL engine. Helen gave me her entire savings to help fund the project. Spiro kept saying that I was the sum of my experiences. And then it came to me, the revelation that would change my direction in my research and methodology."

Abby leaned forward and asked, "Which is?"

"I can never go back. As I said before, it sets up a fucking annoying temporal paradox. It couldn't be for Lucy. I had to do this because Hel and me wanted to fly faster than the speed of light. Once I made peace with that, I knew it wasn't about the mathematics behind the speed—that had already been proven on paper back in 2688. To make it work, we needed stabilization and systems working in harmony with each other."

CHAPTER 41

ONE WAY OR ANOTHER, THE original probe had been destroyed when it orbited the fourth planet from 15 Sagittae, a main sequence star with a brown dwarf companion. Though the probe should have faithfully orbited the planet for over fifty years, something had knocked it out. They would not know exactly what happened until they reached the planet.

When they entered the solar system, they slowed down to half light speed and sent another probe towards the planet. This probe was more than just a scanning system. It sent out messages in basic mathematics and simple images of friendship. The probe entered a high planetary orbit where it remained for a week before a beam of golden light hit the camera and caused it to go crashing into the atmosphere.

The probe confirmed what the initial scans had told them. The planet was tilted on its axis at a 26°angle and orbited the main star once every 376 days. There were seasonal variations on the planet's surface within its year. The two natural satellites, both seeming to be rich in minerals, had little to no atmosphere or impact craters. The larger of the two seemed to have thick ice sheets, but initial scanning could not confirm this.

Like Kipos and Earth, it had a thick layer of mantel, a liquid outer core that generated its magnetic field, and a solid iron inner core. The planet's outer crust was divided into several tectonic plates. Volcanic activity along its coastlines and in the oceanic trenches revealed that the planet's interior was active. Saltwater oceans covered 65% of the surface, with the remainder of the surface consisting of ten landmasses filled with temperate forests, mountains, deserts, and fertile valleys. The crew could see the planet was already supporting intelligent life and discussed the possibility it could also support human life if the planet's apex species were willing to share.

"So what should we do?" Harden asked. "We've lost two probes so far, even one playing the message of friendship. I don't know the best way to contact the population and let them know we don't mean to hurt them or take over their planet."

Don't we? The thought popped in Abby's mind before she could stop it. She said softly, "When the Kiposi landed on Earth, they landed where they were welcomed. In areas where people rioted, they flew away."

"We should try the message of friendship again, but not bog it down with the math," Pat said. "And maybe we should have something ready to trade, just in case. Maybe we should start with a few crates of apples. We can work our way up to technology."

"I'm willing to try that," Harden said, "But no chances. If they fire, get the fuck out of there."

Helen said softly, "Abby, with his greater range of experience, Pat should fly."

Abby did not argue.

THEY ENTERED THE ATMOSPHERE ON the dark side of the planet first. Two large full moons filled the night's sky. As he dropped the ship into the lower atmosphere, Pat was careful to stay in the plumes of steam that rose from lighted glass buildings.

Pat headed east, toward the rising main sequence sun's glare, figuring it would offer them a bit more protection. Scanning the oceans, Abby could see there were millions, maybe even billions, of species on the planet: insects, mammals, fish. Large metal boats skimmed across the surface of the ocean. Abby felt worried as they crossed into daylight. Maybe it was a mistake to try to colonize planets that held intelligent life. She didn't know why her head hurt when she thought about such things, but she could not shake the feeling her parents would not approve of what she was doing at that moment.

Abby observed a large mammalian species that were most likely the apex that they should contact. Quick scans put them at an average height of 1.5 meters, smaller than humans. They had a total of six limbs. The back four legs were used for walking and the smaller two growing out of what Abby referred to as shoulders appeared to function as arms. Above the shoulders, an elongated neck swept upwards another decimeter to a small head with three eyes. Abby noted, "Their skin tone seems to have shades of blue. Perhaps, it's a melatonin reaction from their sun, as Earthlings have had."

Glass buildings rose towards the sky. She began magnifying down to street level. In the city, the apex species drove in vehicles and strolled on moving walkways. She said, "Look, Pat. Some are carrying small mammals! They might keep pets just as we do!"

Pat said, "Or they might be the pets."

A golden light flashed towards them.

Pat pulled back on the stick and the shuttle climbed upwards. Abby felt her stomach in her mouth. She looked at her scan; there were two flying ships behind them. Pat banked downward and skimmed along the ocean until he rolled upwards and got behind them.

"They aren't the friendliest bunch of folks," he joked. "Try hailing them."

"*Revelation Chi* to unidentified craft," Abby said. "We mean you no harm. We are explorers from the planet Kipos trying to make peaceful contact with your species."

Her hailing was answered by golden lights.

They were climbing again. Abby closed her eyes to fight the dark fear growing in her stomach which she was sure might literally vomit out. She heard the hissing of the outer hull, and smelled something burning where a bullet penetrated before she heard the emergency alarm.

"Damn. Quick fix."

Abby unbuckled herself. She fell to her knees, knowing she could not keep her footing with the bouncing. She glanced up at the sensors and unscrewed the decking panel next to the collection drawers. A small crack. She grabbed an epoxy gun. She inserted the nozzle, then hit the plunger. Foamy goo filled the crevice. She covered the goo with a patch of silver netting, snapped the panel back on to the internal hull, and bolted it into place.

The alarm stopped.

"Get your helmet on," Pat snapped.

Abby grabbed her helmet and felt the oxygen flow into her lungs. Then she grabbed Pat's and moved forward to the pilot's seat. Since both of his hands were on the stick, she placed it on his head and latched it to his suit. She waited until she got an "okay" through the radio.

Abby slid Pat's belt across his body, then slid into the co-pilot's seat and buckled herself in.

Golden streams moved past them. Pat tried to fly into some clouds, hoping to lose the other crafts, but Abby watched the planes grow larger and larger on her screen. Once they got close, she noticed they seemed to have wings as retractable as the shuttle's, but not nearly the maneuverability. However, they did have weapons.

Pat banked over to the port and then the starboard as he tried to get out of their line of fire. Then he pulled back on the stick and began to climb. Abby felt the force of gravity on her body. She pulled the tightening cord on her cutout pants in order to keep the blood from pooling in her legs.

She glanced at Pat. Through the faceplate on his helmet, he looked pale, but he did not look like he was going to blackout.

The alarm started blaring again. The shuttle began to slow and lose altitude, another hit to the external hull. The shuttle began to lose pressure.

Golden lights lit up space.

Pat shouted, "We can't reach escape velocity!"

"I'll get it!" Abby shouted back and unbuckled herself. She glanced at the board once more. The hit had penetrated somewhere near the bow. *Shit!*

Abby opened up another hatch, inserted the epoxy goop, and locked in another panel. They still could not reach escape velocity. Movement of the fabric underneath the pilot's chair caught her eye. She reached in and felt the pressure change. She slid another plate in place. They began to gain altitude again.

"My fun meter is pegged!" Pat shouted through the radio.

Abby smacked her knee into the deck as he banked again. She pulled herself back into her seat and buckled herself in. They broke atmosphere. Everything was vibrating. Something was burning. The stabilization units were breaking down.

The *Revelation* slipped from behind. The *Chi* jerked as the clamp fastened onto the shuttle. Her winch pulled them into the docking bay as they were still climbing. Pat and Abby were pulled from the shuttle and half dragged into the ship in zero G by Harden and Brian. Abby screamed when she saw the blood pooling inside Pat's helmet and drifting out of his suit.

Harden took Pat immediately to the infirmary, where Mark awaited him as Brian asked her, "Are you injured?"

Abby heard the familiar shifting as gravity reasserted itself. She pulled off her environmental suit and threw on a pair of her coveralls as Brian continued to question her about bumps she had sustained while patching the ship.

"I'm fine!" She paced outside the infirmary and bit her nails while she waited to hear something about Pat's condition. She peered in, hoping to see something, but all she could see was Mark and Harden standing over him. Blood seemed to be all over Harden and Pat's discarded environmental suit.

Brian came up behind her.

Hugging herself, she said, "I'm sorry he got hurt."

"So am I, but we all have jobs to do. You cannot help him now. Let's get down to the engine room, just in case they need us. Then, we'll see what you collected."

She glanced back. Brian put his hand on her shoulder and pushed her up the stairs.

THE *REVELATION* WAS NOT CHASED out of the system. Beyond the golden flashes of their anti-aircraft weapons and air ships, apparently, the culture did not have sublight spaceships or superior technology. Helen piloted the ship to a high planetary orbit between the outer most gas giant and its moons. Abby wondered what it would mean now that 15 Sagittae e knew they were not alone in the universe.

Of course, as soon as the report from the *Revelation* reached them, the populations of Kipos and the flotilla would know, without a shadow of a doubt, humans were not the center of the universe. There were other civilizations alive out there.

While such thoughts were interesting, there was so much work to do; Abby didn't have time to think about it for long. The shuttle needed to have permanent anti-radiation webbing reinstalled over Abby's quick patches and the stabilizers would have to be completely rebuilt.

Rover had also been shot. Brian and Abby were thankful to discover it went through his lower leg and lodged in his main outer hull without taking out any of his operating systems. By the entrance angles, both Brian and Abby realized if he had not taken the bullet; she would've been shot while she was patching the hull. The bullets were removed. Abby squeezed Rover tight and he nudged her with his camera before she left the shuttle. Brian and Diane went over a schedule to fix the shuttles and Rover while Abby encapsulated the bullets in the sample wall for further study.

Abby glanced inside the infirmary, Pat's environmental suit had been removed and Mark had mopped up the blood. The only sign of the earlier trauma was Pat's prone figure, pallid face, and the bag hung from the wall dripping plasma into his veins. Abby felt a faint yearning to comfort Mark, but she knew the best comfort for him was to simply submit to treatment.

"I'm sorry," she whispered.

"Don't worry. Pat's stable, he's just resting, he might be awake by the time we are finished," Mark said, then told Abby to undress so he could look at her bruises, especially her knee.

She did so. Since Pat was on the examination table, Mark put a sheet on the counter, which Abby climbed upon. Even through the sheet, the metal was cold and uncomfortable. Mark ran his fingers over her limbs and gave her a pass with the scanner. She admitted her knee felt tender and achy when he pressed on it, but explained when she was working on Rover, she forgot all about it.

He pulled out a sharp smelling ointment and rubbed it into her bruised knee and then her elbows, shoulders, and back. "Brian's right, you got to relax or you are going to make yourself sick. That won't help Pat or anyone else. As for Rover, I know you care for him, but he doesn't feel pain. I need to treat you prior to you giving care to him, understand?"

She nodded.

Abby slid off the counter and pulled on her coveralls. "Can I sit with Pat?"

Mark answered in the affirmative. She dragged over the chair and reached out for Pat's hand. She stroked it with her thumb and felt his calloused palm under her fingertips. It seemed like a long time before he opened his eyes.

Mark kept himself busy by pulling out sheets and bedding since he was going to spend the night in the infirmary. His movements were efficient. Though Mark did love Pat, there was no romance here. Just a wounded man and his doctor. She might not remember it, but she knew Mark had slept on the deck of her billet when she went through withdrawals.

Once he woke up, Pat smiled weakly. "Abs, help me make up a lie for Mark? He's really worried … though the bullet completely missed my artery and I have a decent doctor. So tell him, I'll be up and around tomorrow…."

"Because it's your day to cook and you wanted to make chutney chicken sandwiches?" she finished his sentence.

"Exactly, so he can sleep in our billet."

"The real prognosis is off duty for a week, then light duty until the next system as we work to build muscle mass in the wounded leg," Mark said.

"Okay, I will make chutney chicken sandwiches for you," Abby said.

"Neither Harden or Helen would appreciate the two of you joking around," Mark warned.

"Wet blanket," Pat said.

"Reckless foolhardy idiots."

"You'll like this game, Abs. Apparently the rules are to see how many adjectives we can add to an insult without repeats or swearing," Pat said. "I did one, Mark did two, and so you'll need three."

Mark frowned, but she noticed the smile in his eyes. "We could just play cards."

An hour later, Abby climbed the stairs, quietly crept down the corridor and entered the bridge. She told Harden and Helen how Pat was doing. They were glad for the update, but they still had hours of pouring over star charts and intense flight plans. Neither of them knew where to go next, but they didn't like the options. Abby wanted to remain on the bridge so she stayed quiet, listened to them discuss each nearby star and occasionally ran to the galley to refill their coffee cups. Eventually Harden said, "I guess it's time to call the *Discovery*."

By the looks on their faces, this was not going to be a pleasant call.

Abby was not sure what to do with herself, but before she could figure it out, Cole was on the com and said, "Abby, I would like to hear your report."

Abby knew he had the recordings so she wondered why he bothered to ask, but she replied, "According to the sonar there were millions of species, but the planet's apex species doesn't want us there."

Cole sighed. "Do you think we should try a second contact?"

Abby felt ice run down her back. She did wonder if they would actually ever be able to speak to them, but she was terrified of being ordered back down to the planet. Still she had a job to do. She pushed her fear deeper into her stomach. "I am curious to see if we can make contact, but we shouldn't without long-term surveillance first. We played the message of friendship. It didn't work. Pat and I were fired upon as soon as we were spotted. I'm sorry he got hurt. Rover took a bullet too. I think he saved me."

By the way Cole looked at his son, then his daughter, then his son again. Abby realized that she sounded like an idiot. She wondered if he knew Rover was alive. The look Cole gave Harden made her think otherwise.

She said, "Sir, Brian found some interesting things about the bullets. It might tell us something about the species' level of intelligence. They had some sort of tracing tech on them. If I take another shuttle down…"

To Abby, Helen said, "You will not be going down," and then to the image of her father, "Harden and I decided we are leaving this star system." Her voice was final.

Abby was glad.

Cole nodded. "I'll recommend Kipos send a public ship with a few dignitaries if they wish. Maybe they will have better luck communicating with them, but I'm not willing to waste any of the lives in my fleet and the flotilla has no capacity for contact with the new species."

Harden and Cole said a few more words about an updated timeline before their rendezvous on O-5 then Harden transferred his father's image to the infirmary.

Abby said softly, "It's weird to think now we know humans are not the only intelligent life in the universe."

"We already knew that. We've seen the ruins," Harden said. "As interesting as all this has been, we still have a job to do. The last two planets were complete busts. Assuming you enjoy eating and breathing, we need to focus on the next one."

"Sorry." Abby looked down at her hands.

"We've told you before to stop beating yourself up," Helen said gently.

Her lower lip beginning to quiver, Abby looked up into Helen's face. "But if I had been flying...".

Harden's voice was not gentle. "We played the message of friendship both on the probe and the shuttle. They fired upon you anyway. We're not diplomats, but explorers. Helen and I took a first contact training course when taking our command prep. Now we know it's completely inadequate in a hostile situation, maybe all alien situations. Pat is alive and has another scar Mark will find attractive. If you must cry, do so in your billet."

"I won't cry. I'm still just...freaked out. It's not how I imagined first contact to be. I thought it'd be like on Echoes, the holo-games, or all the movies I watched as a kid," she looked up at them, "Are you disappointed?"

Helen squeezed her hand. "In the mission? Yes. But not in you."

Harden continued the thought. "However, I am beginning to think you spend too much of your time watching vids."

CHAPTER 42

Deep in the Black

IN THE NEXT RELATIVE TWO months, the *Revelation's* crew explored six more planets in four star systems. Each one had some form of life, but none had completely favorable conditions for human colonization.

The first two planets orbited the white dwarf ZZ Ceti G 185-32. Though Pat and Abby discovered a new delicious fruit and some interesting unnamed minerals, both planets had a worriesome wobble within their orbit, and since the sun was at the end of its lifespan, it did not bode well for the long-term success of any colony there.

In HD 176051, they found a main sequence star with a red dwarf companion and a planetary configuration similar to the Ilios and Kokadelfi system. With high hopes, Abby and Pat landed on planet d. Unfortunately, as soon as they opened their airlock; both Pat and Abby went into anaphylactic shock. Diane piloted the shuttle remotely and got them back to the *Revelation*. Mark developed hives and a pretty wretched cough from secondary exposure.

Two weeks sanitation and rehabilitation was not worth further additional expense of exploration since there could be no landing party.

Abby hated being quarantined in the infirmary, especially once Mark had enforced her therapy sessions on a daily basis and Pat began lecturing her on the amount of time she focused on her studies. She realized how used to sleeping in her own billet, she had become once their snoring started keeping her awake. They were obviously bored out of their minds when they began helping her with bio-chem. Unlike her CG instructor, they got frustrated with her when she made a mistake. As they knew all of the special cases and alien variations, they sometimes contradicted the text as well as each other. She missed playing with Rover and Rockford, working beside Brian, and talking with Helen and Diane. She found she even missed Harden.

Glad to get out of the infirmary, she was thrilled when they arrived at 72 Herculis A, a G class spectral star similar to Ilios and Sol. Though stationed well within the habitat zone, planet b was too early in its ecological development. Filled with primordial ooze and single celled organisms, it would not support intelligent life.

Abby noticed Pat and Mark's orbits grew closer while in the black. They did not kiss in front of her or anyone else but, occasionally, they touched fingers while working in the lab and, when the crew sat in the galley watching vids, they leaned closer to each other.

HR 7670 had two G class main phase stars, both with reliable habitat zones in a locked binary system. A was a yellow-orange dwarf star similar to Ilios with six planets orbiting it. Scanners showed planet c did have an atmosphere of oxygen, nitrogen, and carbon dioxide, but unfortunately it had high levels of radiation leaking towards the surface.

Its companion star, HR 7670 B, had four planets. Planet d had the correct gravity and atmosphere. However, there was a strange lack of minerals in the surface soil samples. While there was evidence that it might have once held intelligent life, presently its ecosystem had been weakened. The landmasses only held a hundred species of plant life, worms and bacterium. The oceans held only ten thousand species, mostly single-celled planktons and the sea dwelling gastropods and vertebrates that fed upon them.

Back in the black, when she wasn't supposed to be listening to Mark and Pat, she heard the word marriage more than once. She heard them wonder what their families would think, what the fleet would think. They sometimes dreamed of leaving the *Revelation*. Other times they dreamed of staying. Abby observed that, most of the time, Pat worried about introducing Mark to Megan, and in turn, Mark worried about what it meant to be a stepfather.

CHAPTER 43

THERE IT WAS. COMPARED TO Sol and Ilios', HD 189733 Star A had a faster rotation and chromospheric activity, including large and widespread starspots and flares.

Planet c had been discovered over 400 years prior, but it was largely ignored due to the fact that planet b was a tidal-locked gas giant. It had been assumed by computer models that the presence of planet b disturbed the orbit of such a small Kipos-type planet, but the long-term probe in orbit showed that planet c had a stable orbit centered on 0.6 AU. The planet's axis was tilted 24°, which meant there had to be seasonal variations on the planet's surface within an orbital period of 153 days. There was not enough time for intelligent life to have evolved, or at least the crew of the *Revelation* didn't think so.

It was their best bet.

WHEN THE *REVELATION* REACHED THE solar system, they slowed to sublight and launched short-range probes. The crew confirmed what the initial scans had told them. The planet's outer crust was divided into several tectonic plates. It had a thick layer of mantel, a liquid outer core that generated its magnetic field, and a solid iron inner core. About 95% of the surface was covered with a large saltwater ocean. Thick glaciers covered the poles. The remainder consisted of one large landmass split in half by a large mountain range. Smaller volcanic islands surrounded the continent. Except for its size, Planet c was very much like Kipos and Earth.

THEIR FIRST ECOSYSTEM WAS THE mountain range in the middle on the continent. Abby programmed Rover to take soil samples as she climbed trees to gather mosses, needles, pollen-filled cones, and bark. She fought the urge to drop a cone on Pat who stood beneath her recording his observations: "The wilderness is characterized by forested slopes and volcanic peaks covered in icy glaciers. Fresh water streams. Elevations range from 900 meters at a low river in the north to 3090 meters at the highest peak. Looks like a remnant volcanic cone in the east."

Abby said, "I want to go check it out."

Pat nodded as Harden said from above, "Copy that. You've six hours before launch window."

As she climbed up the volcanic cone, she saw hundreds of six-legged, hoofed animals roaming the basins, meadows, and even wandering over the upper alpine peaks. They seemed to be herbivores, eating grasses and chewing on their cud. They watched her briefly to see if she was a threat, then went back to ignoring her. As she hiked upwards, she took samples of their hair that was left all over the valley, probably from shedding as well as rubbing against the alpine plants.

If they bolted, they could crush her, but she was not afraid of them. She felt a more looming, unseen worry. "With this large herbivore. Might be a predator around somewhere."

"Keep your eyes open," Pat said through his radio.

As she climbed, the plants were soon taken over by fields of large pumice boulders. The wind blew across her environmental suit and she lowered her shielding mask to protect her eyes and nose from the dust. At the summit, Abby looked down into a deep crater with a dome surrounded by a crystal blue lake. The volcano might be dormant, but it was not extinct. Bright blue and pink bugs fluttered through the sky surrounding her. It was surreal. Their wings were patterned with false eyes of a deeper blue. Abby watched them drink from little puddles between the stones and lick the pollen of a bright red, flowering bush. She set up a trap nearby, hoping to catch a few, but this made her sad, for she knew that they would soon die. "There are butterflies here!"

"Abby, calm down. What was that?"

"Butterflies! Do you see them?" She focused her camera in on one so the crew could see.

Abby heard the static and mumbling of her crew. "What the hell is a butterfly?" Then "How the fuck should I know?"

She realized she was being an idiot. She was not looking at the species close enough. "Wait, they're not insects. They are arachnids: eight legs and a pair of sensory arms that end in tiny mandibles."

She hoped her crew didn't think she was stupid. "But they're like butterflies and moths. The coloration seems to be the result of light bouncing off photonic crystal scales."

Pat's voice came through the radio. "Abby, that's great, but don't forget that you are up there to take soil and water samples."

Abby kneeled and tried to think of something to snipe back through the radio besides "copy that." As the seconds wore on, she knew it was too late.

ABBY AND PAT FLEW OVER the rugged western coast. The basalt headlands were covered in towering deciduous trees with bright orange bark and red leaves. Then the headlands sloped down into placid-looking coves with tidal pools teeming with organisms.

They landed on a sandy shoreline. As they exited the shuttle, avians greeted them with high-pitched squawks and screams.

Pat set Rover to take gravel samples and listened to his scanners in the shallows. "There must be millions of species on this planet," he said to *Revelation* through the radio.

Abby headed south. Black sand and pebbles twisted through pockets of orange-barked trees on elevated silt deposits. Tiny pink wildflowers peeked out from the curved roots. She observed evidence of past flooding as she collected a few plants then continued towards a procession of weather-beaten sea stacks.

"I see evidence of zooplankton, nekton, and benthos. There are insects in the sands. Rover's taking core samples," Pat said excitedly.

Abby felt sad, as she scraped a few gastropods into petri dishes, but wasn't quite sure why. She loved to hear the surf pulling back across the pebbles and crashing into larger formations.

She crept over boulders and the occasional log, feeling the wind push the water on to the rocks. Abby found a game trail heading up to the grassy bluffs. She took samples of fallen leaves and sliced off a piece of orange bark from a tree. Scaling the hillside, she came to a few large boulders. She climbed upon one and peered towards the sea. The deep blue looked like it went on forever. Abby gathered a few more samples of grass before descending her perch. She could taste the salty air. It reminded her of her childhood in Seattle.

Perhaps she felt sad, because she felt she was giving this beautiful planet away. Too bad, Earth could not bring colonists. A new thought entered her mind. She hadn't been on Earth in over a century. What if Earth had a space program by now? Maybe Earthlings could settle upon the planet alongside the flotilla. By the time she reached the shore, she decided to ask Harden about it. After all, the idea was to stay as human as possible and the flotilla took in all types of people. They probably would share this planet with Homo sapiens.

She looked up when she heard high pitch cries. Above her, fifty reddish birds rode the currents. She made sure she got a picture of them diving into the waves.

She saw something shimmering under the water. Millions of tiny stalks with feeding tentacles winding through an open mouth covered the area underneath the rocks. Abby adjusted her camera in order to capture an image of the organism. Her camera was taking a series of photos when the mouth clamped shut over a small gastropod which had began feeding on one of the stalks. Abby could see its entire head, which was covered in large plate-like scales. It was definitely a gill-bearing, aquatic vertebrate: a fish! She kept letting the camera run as it swallowed and then opened its mouth again, waiting for the next unwary prey. Then she scaled up the image to get a detail shot before she knelt down to take her samples.

Further out, Abby saw a large mass of purple flesh coming towards the rocks. The purple flesh fell back into the next wave. Then it moved forward again. She zoomed her camera lens towards it. Layers of flesh seemed to be strung together by muscular tendrils covered in tiny purple stalks ending in feathery tips twitching back and forward. At first Abby thought it might go after the plated, opened-mouth fish, but as the purple mass floated closer, the fish clamped its mouth shut and slowly swam away.

"I see a massive, cnidarian-type organism in the water," Abby said as she took a series of photographs. "I cannot say if it is a single organism or a colony of zoons."

"Either way, keep an eye on it, Abby. Don't let it get too close to you," Harden said through the radio.

Abby was careful not to turn her back to the water as she began her collection. Each wave brought the purple flesh closer to her as she grabbed a dozen rocks and a handful of tiny shells and threw them into sample cups.

"I saw that, Abby. You get yourself higher. The next wave could bring that thing right on top of you," Mark said.

She began climbing.

Between the rocks, she found nests. She grabbed a single solid egg and a broken shell with most of the fetus intact though it smelled rotten. The avians started pecking at her masked face and hands. "Crap!"

She tossed a handful of sand at them and ran down the beach. Trying to get over rocks without touching the waves was futile. She pushed down her fear, tried not to think of the purple mass in the water, and kept climbing. In her ears, she could hear her crew. The birds dove at her face, but her suit protected her from most of their attacks.

Out of the corner of her eye, the purple, fleshy mass reached up with one of its tendrils and caught a bird.

She climbed higher as the bird shrieked painfully behind her. She glanced back when the noise stopped. The bird was gone and the purple mass of flesh rode the waves as if nothing had happened. She ran down the beach until the other birds stopped chasing her. She knew she had failed in part of her collection, but she laughed. "I'm alright."

After another hour of collecting samples, Pat called her back to the shuttle. Flying over the waves, she saw a school of small fish swimming near the surface so dense that it nearly formed a solid wall. She magnified the submerged camera and saw several fish, larger in size, swimming beneath them, hoping to get a nibble.

The camera captured everything.

AS THEY CAME THROUGH THE sanitizer, she felt stronger than she had in a long time. If this panned out—and so far the prospects looked favorable—she would be credited with discovering a planet suitable for colonization. Abigail Lee and Patrick Mason would be heroes amongst the Flotilla. She wondered if she could call Orchid and tell her.

HELEN, DIANE, AND MARK CAME along for the final collections from the deep temperate rainforest. With so many hands, the work was completed quickly. As with every viable ecosystem, evidence of small mammals and crustaceans was discovered buried into the soil. There were millions of bacteria and thousands of insects.

Mark found a herd of browsing mammals with long, prehensile snouts. Their size varied according to age; most of the adults seemed to be about two meters long, a meter high at the shoulders, and between 250 and 300 kg. All had oval, black-tipped ears, stubby tails, and splayed four toes on all six feet. Females had a single pair of mammary glands and they nursed their young openly. Ranging in color from reddish-brown to nearly black, their thick skins were covered in coarse coats of short hair, with the young having white saddle-shaped markings on their backs.

"Probably camouflage," Mark said, which everyone agreed with. He put his hand out and the largest of the beasts sniffed him with its flexible snout. "Feels to be composed almost entirely of soft tissues rather than bony internal structures."

The animals nuzzled and pushed at the newcomers. They were so friendly, Mark was able to take a quick hair sample as well as look into their mouths, which held flat incisors but no tusks or fangs. The snouts of the beasts were highly flexible structures, able to move in all directions, and they occasionally grabbed a sample cup or hook out of the collection packs. Once the animals discovered the stolen item was not edible, it was discarded and they went back to eating leaves. Mark, Pat, and Abby watched the animals grab foliage that would otherwise have been out of reach if not for their snouts.

Mark said softly, "They are so relaxed. They must not have a predator here."

Pat and Abby glanced at each other. If they were browsers, they had a predator somewhere, even if the team had not come across it yet.

Eventually, the three headed southbound a few more kilometers. They walked through the temperate forest until they discovered a mammal covered in bronze bony plates surrounded by flexible black spots on its back. Its purple flanks had dark plates arranged in bronze stripes. A group of sixteen young played on a hillside as seven adults studied the newcomers with unblinking green eyes.

Over the radio, Harden screamed at the same time as the animals slunk into the underbrush. As everyone backed away, the beasts galloped towards them with a sideways gait. Abby pulled out her flare gun and took a shot.

They momentarily slunk back as the grass caught on fire.

Mark, Pat, and Abby raced back to the shuttle with Harden screaming coordinates through their radios. Grasses whipped across their legs and occasionally their hands and faces, but they didn't dare stop.

"Would you shut up?" Abby shouted. "You're not helping!"

Harden stopped shouting directions, but then just screamed, "Run, move faster!"

Once they scaled the first grassy hill, Abby panted out with the hope they would understand and not question. "I'm gonna drop my pack!"

Pat glanced at her and shouted, "Copy."

Still running, Abby loosened the straps and let her pack fall to the ground, hoping it would distract the beasts. She glanced back over her shoulder and saw the beasts circle it and tear open the polymers. Too soon, they realized it wasn't edible and darted towards the humans again. Sometimes they skulked below the grasses; other times, they ran with short bursts of speed.

Trying to keep track of the beasts, while her heart pounded in her ears,

Abby sprinted as fast as she could. Mark could have ditched them, his long limbs easily could have carried him faster then she could run, but he was beside Abby the entire time. She was mostly grateful until Mark's camera told them that the organisms can run twelve kilometers per hour.

Abby wished she could shut the camera off as she shot off another flare at the beasts coming towards her. She did not hit any of them, but another bit of grass went up in flames and the beasts slunk back again.

"Out!" she shouted to Pat.

Pat already had his flare gun in hand as they ran back through the forest.

Helen and Diane were in the shuttle. Pat made it back first, but held the door open for the other two. Mark dove through the airlock. Abby did not see the beast behind her, but she felt the heat from Pat's flare as it hissed past her. She didn't stop running until she was inside and Mark pulled her down to the deck controlling her fall. She landed hard on his body. Abby heard a beast howl and the hiss of the internal airlock door. She glanced up through Mark's arms, Pat had made it inside the shuttle, then he backed into them and tripped. The side of his boot scraped across Abby's leg and she yelped. Trying to get his weight off her, she accidently elbowed him in the shoulder. Not the most graceful of entries, but the pain and their ragged panting breath was evidence that the three of them were still alive.

However, inside the airlock, one of the beasts howled. It scratched at the inner door, grunting. It howled again.

"Prepare for takeoff," Helen shouted.

They disentangled themselves from each other and buckled themselves in. A large thud hit the ceiling. The other two beasts were outside, rounding the ship. Through the cameras, they could see the beasts scratching, snapping, and biting at the hull. The growling and barks filled the recorder.

Helen started the chemical engines. The beasts scattered. The howl from the trapped beast became strained as they gained altitude. The change in air pressure was probably driving it mad. Helen circled and dropped back down to three meters. She opened the outer airlock doors and let it tumble out. The airlock doors closed again. Abby watched it on the screen. The beast shook itself and returned to its pack.

"They were acting as a coordinated group in order to stalk and bring down prey!" Mark said excitedly.

"You think?" Abby said.

"I can't believe you've had all this fun for this long!" Mark said.

"Well, if you didn't get shuttle sick, we'd take you out more often," Pat replied.

Helen flew low over to the grassy hill to where Abby ditched the pack. Pat and Abby reloaded their flare guns as the door opened. Nothing attacked as they hurried out and picked up the shredded pack and spilled containers. They scanned the grassland for the fires, but it looked like they had self-extinguished.

Then Helen flew to where Rover was calmly taking core samples, scooping up gravel and putting them in containers. Rover ambled up to the airlock doors and entered the shuttle as he was programmed to do. He went to his station and waited to be buckled in without a concern in the universe. And why would he? Rover had finished his job and was not responsible for almost getting the captain and XO's little brother killed.

Abby expected the worst. She waited for Harden to scream. To Abby's surprise, after they came through the sanitizer, all he said was: "Everyone okay? Dropping the pack and using the flare gun was a good idea, Abby. Next time, though, just shoot the animal. Don't try to scare it."

"I was trying to hit it."

Harden smiled. "Then you need some serious target practice."

He turned to Pat. "You got a message from your kid when you were planetside."

As the men turned away from her, she remembered that Harden told her everyone gets hurt on this job. Mark had come down to the surface on his own volition. If he had gotten hurt, it wasn't her fault.

MARK, PAT, AND DIANE CONCLUDED the planet had everything the flotilla needed: a clean atmosphere, the correct pressures and gravity, billions of native species, food sources, potable water, vast mineral banks, and it was only a dozen light years from Outpost 2.

CHAPTER 44

Somewhere in the Black:
January 7, 3186 K.E.

THE WEEKS IN THE BLACK were long. Abby couldn't believe how much Pat paced on the way to O-5. Up and down the stairs, into the galley, down to the lab. There was no doubt that he was nervous about seeing his ex-wife and daughter. She witnessed Mark touch his shoulder and embrace him from behind. Pat shrugged off the touch and walked away.

The fun-loving Pat was completely gone and was replaced by a sullen man, but Mark had bigger worries. Cole insisted he sit in on the vid conference between Silva and Pat. After all, whether he liked it or not, Pat was a package deal now. If he and Pat were to marry on 0-5, which is what they both claimed to want to do, Mark would become an instant stepfather. Cole would get what he always wanted: a readymade grandkid already at the interesting age of sixteen.

Eventually, Helen decided everyone should sit in. After all, it was a family matter. Abby was glad she and Diane were invited to go too. She was curious.

Silva was a pretty enough woman of forty-one who claimed her hurt feelings were far behind her. She just wanted her daughter to have a real future, but refused to be separated from her. Megan was the only good thing that had come out of her leaving Earth, the best thing that came from her marriage to Pat.

While it would be uncomfortable, Cole thought it best that the three adults figure out how to live with one another for Megan's sake—for a few years at least. He did not want Megan to choose between losing her mother or father to time dilation.

Pat agreed. He wanted to see his little girl.

Silva first voiced her concern about how such an arrangement would affect Megan, but Mark immediately chimed in. "After my parents split up, I never saw my mother as a young woman again. We're all adults. We can make it work."

Megan seemed interested in seeing Pat and meeting Mark. She was happy she would have a friend near her own age aboard. At first, there was a question if the girls (as Harden referred to Megan and Abby) should have billets that shared a head, but Silva would not hear of leaving her daughter unsupervised with a nineteen-year-old A-level pilot—especially one who had been caught playing in high stake card games.

Though Helen tried to assure Silva that Abby was actually a very responsible young woman who had learned from her mistake, Abby didn't bother defending herself. What was there to say? She could not blow her cover.

Silva and Megan were assigned billets Starboard 3 and 4.

TWO DAYS LATER, ABBY WANDERED up to the galley where Pat was banging around preparing breakfast. Rockford rode on her shoulder, since she was carrying her tablet and a star chart.

Sick of his constant bad mood, she dropped everything but Rockford on the counter and asked, "Want some help?"

"No. Get the cat away from the counter."

"Rocks isn't hurting anything," Abby said.

"I asked you to get the cat away from the counter." He looked down at her, visibly annoyed.

Abby knew she should back off, but Pat hadn't said a nice word to her since HD 189733 Ac. He had even stopped coming with her during those stupid therapy sessions with Mark.

She rolled her eyes. "Whatever." She grabbed her things and went over to the table. She sat down heavily and focused on her tablet.

"I would appreciate it if you don't speak like that to me when Megan gets here," he said.

"I'd appreciate it if you stop being a jerk." She activated her music player, put on one of her favorite arrangements of songs, and turned up the volume in order to surround herself in safe pandemonium.

"And don't play that around her."

"You listen to this music!" Abby rolled her eyes and shouted over the din, "I wasn't planning on corrupting her on the first day."

Pat opened his mouth, almost said something, and then changed his mind and began again. He slid his finger on the touch screen to turn down the volume and said, "Look, Megan isn't dating yet. Her mother and I decided she won't be taking basic flight until she's twenty."

"I'm not dating yet either," Abby said.

"You'll get to O-5, take your test, and find a boy to celebrate with as all Fleet brats do. I don't want you dragging Megan into that. There's a big difference between sixteen and nineteen," Pat said.

Abby shot back, "It seems to me the biggest difference is if somebody has a dad aboard or not."

Pat had murder in his eyes. When he slammed his hand on the table, Rockford hissed at him. Abby was startled silent. Pat's anger faded quickly and he looked like he aged right in front of her. She was his problem. Not Mark. Not Silva. It was her. He didn't want Megan anywhere near the indentured Earthling. She was dangerous. A savage poutana. A carrier of bedlam.

If she had been considering at the moment how she felt she would realize her once persistent shame had disintegrated and its molecules had begun to intermingle into something new. However, she wasn't thinking. "So much for being partners! You don't care about me at all!" she shouted at him.

"What the fuck's the problem?" Harden said, entering the galley.

Abby looked over at him. He was glaring at her. Everyone would be on Pat's side. It would be better for all of them if she just disappeared. Even though she helped discover a planet suitable for colonization, they didn't want her anymore. "This whole time everyone's been telling me to act like a Fleet Brat. Now Pat…"

Harden said, "Pat's…"

She interrupted him, "I know! He's family and so is his kid … and I'm nobody!"

Abby didn't understand the look on Harden's face, but she knew she had hurt him. His voice was dull. "Engine room."

"You're not being fair! He started it!"

Harden said, "But you're still yelling. I have enough shit to deal with. Don't bother coming back up. I'll have food sent down to you."

"Fine," she snarled. She was glad her back was to Harden as she felt tears come unbidden to her eyes. She was crying by the time she had made it down the stairs. Diane asked her what she was so upset about.

"I-I said …I didn't mean it. I…"

"You need to calm down and tell me what happened."

Brian came around the corner, frowning. "Apparently, she just had a bit of a tantrum. Harden hopes a bit of manual labor will put her in a better temperament."

"But I…"

Diane said, "The grav-engine's internal tubes have gotten a bit rusty. Use the wire brush, no chemicals in such an enclosed space. I'll check on you later."

Abby didn't argue. She just went to the tool room and grabbed the steel wire brush. Their former kindness did not stop her fury. She crawled up into the first tube hating every single person aboard the *Revelation*, including the two people who screwed up her life—even though she didn't know them yet. Still, it really was amazing how much gunk and rust worked its way up the giant ribs. With the wire brush, she pushed her anger into the metal. As the engine got cleaner, she began to feel a little calmer.

After a while, she heard voices echoing through the tube. She crawled in deeper to hear what the crew was saying. She climbed to the next shaft and peered down at the oxygen garden through a grate.

Mark sat calmly on the bench beside Pat. Harden and Brian were sitting across from them but, due to the angle, she could not see their faces. However she could see that Diane seemed irritated as she patted Helen's hand. Helen's cheeks were flushed. It looked like she might have actually wept. No matter how angry Abby had been, she hated that she had caused Helen any distress.

"She's my kid!" Pat said.

Harden replied, "We are well aware of that, however, the entire crew isn't going to change because of Megan's presence. Your actions of late are spreading discontent throughout the crew." Harden did not remind Pat that spreading discontent was punishable by dismissal.

"It's hardly discontentment. Abby and I had a disagreement."

"That ended her screaming about not being part of the family," Helen said.

Abby felt embarrassed. She should have known that Helen would always stick up for her.

Brian and Diane said that they were willing to put up with a bit of nervous energy and short temperedness from Pat until all the wedding nonsense was over and his family was settled in. Diane said, "However, I'm also concerned about how your words affected Abby."

"She'll be fine," Pat snapped.

Helen said, "No, she won't. I don't think you understand how much trouble she's had assimilating into fleet life."

"What are you talking about? There hasn't been any real trouble," Pat said.

Diane replied, "She does fine with the six of us, but she doesn't know how to talk to people her own age. She told Helen and me other details about what happened at the arcade." She glanced at Helen for support.

"Like it or not, Megan is not a little girl anymore. She and Abby will be friends. They need each other," Helen said.

"My daughter…"

Diane interrupted him, "Is sixteen. When was the first time you fooled around?"

Harden looked at his brother before he said, "Look, guys, we all want you here, but if you have to go elsewhere to be happy, we can trade doctors and biologists with the *Discovery* or one of the other ships."

"So you'd put that kid over your own future niece's wellbeing?" Pat hissed.

Abby smirked. Pat had just let everyone know his true feelings. Maybe she shouldn't have yelled, but at least she had been vindicated. From her vantage point, she could see Mark shift uncomfortably. Even he wasn't on Pat's side.

Harden's tone was cold. "She's a lot more fucking useful to me than a woman who is trained to do nothing and a sixteen-year-old who won't even be doing D level work for the next two relative years, if not four."

Helen's voice was kinder. "More than that. Abby was Dad's ward. She's ours."

"For all of five minutes!" Pat said.

"Do you think I give a fuck?" Harden said.

Guilt spread in Abby's chest. Vindicated or not, she felt slimy for carrying on the way she had. No wonder Harden had looked so hurt before. Sure, she worked hard, but he and Helen had taken a risk on her. They brought her into their home. They protected and educated her with very little to gain. In that one moment of anger, she had disregarded the past seven months. They still were willing to take care of her. She went back to her chore with a new devotion to the task and the promise she would apologize.

ABBY DISCOVERED HOW MUCH HARDEN really had not wanted to deal with her once she came out of the engine room. Muscles aching from being crouched in the tubes and covered in grime, she expected she could go upstairs for a shower and lunch. Instead, a cold egg sandwich and an order to clean the three shuttles inside and out awaited her.

She unlatched Rover for company. He nestled her shoulder in greeting, then followed her around, telling her stories. Abby mused how nothing makes a person feel better than knowing other people's mistakes after the fourth story of Pat and Mark being punished. They had done a lot more than she ever would consider doing: breaking a window, skipping out on their lessons, ignoring orders, and their biggest offense: borrowing a shuttle without permission. Pat and Mark were actually denied a whole seven days of shore leave and told to repaint, prune, pick up leaves, and mulch the whole oxygen garden.

"Where'd they go?" Abby asked Rover.

"They flew to get a better view of Nebulae M17 with two boys."

Abby could guess what happened there. No wonder Pat was worried about Megan's purity. As she realized it wasn't only her own past that worried him, she began to giggle.

"Do you know Pat has a daughter?" she asked Rover.

"Yes. Is she still little?"

"No, sixteen, but she and her mom are coming to live with us," Abby said.

While Abby was happy Rover was excited to have another girl to play with, she could not deny the slight, familiar twinge of jealousy.

FOR SUPPER, DIANE BROUGHT DOWN a bowl of soup and toast with another order for Abby. Abby had to crawl below the garden and mop up any debris that had made its way through the crevices in the decking and into the pump housing. It gave her plenty of time to rehearse what she was going to say. Rover came with her and told her stories of places he had seen with the crew.

When she finally came off duty, she took a shower and put on a fresh set of coveralls. She glanced up towards the bridge. Helen worked on a tablet. The way she took a sip of coffee and set the cup back down on the middle of the console alerted Abby to the fact the ship was on autopilot. Remembering how upset Helen looked in the oxygen garden, Abby's guilt rolled around her head and fell down her esophagus and pooled in a thick heap in her stomach. However, Abby went downstairs to the laboratory first. She didn't want to chicken out or get distracted.

Pat and Mark were discussing something, but stopped talking when Abby popped her head in.

"Pat, I just wanted to say sorry for losing my temper."

"Yeah, me too. I've just been having a rough time figuring out how to merge my two families. That's not your fault. I shouldn't have snapped at you," he replied. "I'm sorry you got in trouble."

Abby shrugged. There wasn't any tension, but she felt the need to explain. "It wasn't so bad. Rover kept me company and told me all kinds of stories."

The men glanced at each other then back at her. Mark asked, "What type of stories?"

Abby blushed. "He was trying to make me feel better."

"Well, I hope you will be smarter than we were at your age," Pat said.

"Are you guys going to stay? I don't want you to leave."

Mark said, "Whatever gave you that idea?"

"There's a real loud echo in the grav-engine; it sounded like there was half-a-dozen Pats and Marks." She giggled nervously with the knowledge that, even if the truth was always best, eavesdropping might get her another day of chores if they told Helen or Harden.

Pat laid a heavy eye on her. "We have always planned on staying. You really took this too hard."

Mark nodded. "Still, your tantrum had one benefit. We know you're comfortable now. A few months ago, you'd have just cried." He paused for a moment. "Did you overhear the other matter we spoke on this afternoon?"

She shook her head.

Pat said, "We've decided it is for the best that you will remain Abby Lee to them, at least until Megan is twenty, and starts making decisions for herself. Agreed?"

Abby knew she was forgiven, still part of the crew. She nodded.

Mark said, "Now, Harden might not admit it, but you really upset him today. Trust me, I used to say all kinds of stupid mean shit to him. I can tell when he is hurt."

ABBY HAD NEVER BEEN IN Port 1, the billet connected to Harden's, but her first thought was that it was the most exciting place she had ever seen. The walls were painted a bright white, but covered with drawings of ships. Schematics and star charts were everywhere. Abby had to focus before she forgot the reason she was there. "I'm sorry for what I said before… and I apologized to Pat for losing my temper."

Harden glanced back at her and looked back at his large touch screen again. He might have nodded.

"Are you still mad at me?"

"No," he said.

She fidgeted, not sure if she should go back up to the galley. She took a step towards the hatchway.

Harden turned to her. "What are you doing here?"

"Apologizing. I guess not very well."

His gold eyes were cold. "I mean on the *Revelation*. What is your purpose?"

Abby's mouth went dry.

"You're a good worker, but you're also using up air, food, and water. Some days, you've been more of a hassle than you are worth.

"Now I'll admit, the way Pat had been storming around, someone was bound to lose their temper, but Helen and I were trying to figure out a way to open up a conversation with him until you went ballistic," Harden said. "You must understand everything we say to Pat affects Mark too. Not only did you offend them, but you also hurt Helen. You won't do so again or you won't be part of this crew."

Abby dropped her eyes, careful not to openly show her hurt. Holding back her tears, Abby shook her head.

"What does that mean?"

"I won't hurt Helen again. I want to be part of this crew." She sniffed and wiped her nose with the back of her hand.

"Good. Know what this is?" He brought up engine schematics on the screen.

Abby shook her head again, knowing she would never get used to the way Harden changed subjects. He stretched over to the closet and pulled out a model made primarily of bits of bent wire. It was a simple tube but each end ended in a flange that spread out until it reconnected with itself.

"Is that an Einstein Rosen Bridge?"

"Yes. My goal is to create a stable one. I've been playing with the idea for some time."

Abby took a step closer and wrapped her arms around his neck. He tensed and sighed as he reached back and patted her calf. He sighed again. "Your response to a simple reprimand baffles me," he said, looking at his model.

"Why?"

"Mark and Pat never cried and certainly never needed to be reassured with affection. So I am trying to discover if it is standard nineteen-year-old female behavior, an Earthling idiosyncrasy, or just you."

Abby let him go and shrugged.

"Do you need more time in the engine room?" Abby heard no threat of punishment; he truly just didn't know how to deal with her emotions.

She shook her head.

"I think it'll work, but there's just as much of a chance we'll all blow up or end up in some insane dimension where everything runs backwards."

"Okay," she said. "I'm not afraid to try it."

"You should be. Neither the engine nor the structural upgrades to the ship will be ready for a few relative years. If past performance is indicative of the future and you stay out of trouble, you'll be Helen's second on the bridge."

"Pat doesn't want to be? Or Di?" Abby asked excitedly.

"Di, Brian, and I will be in the engine room. Diane is still head engineer; I'll function as a mechanic just in case shit starts breaking.

"Pat, Mark, and family will transfer to the *Discovery* for the duration. Pat's a great pilot, but doesn't want to lose his kid again. Time might do some fucking weird things, so you have to be sure. There's no shame in staying behind."

"I want to go. I love this ship and you—like I should. Nothing weird," she said.

"It's bad enough you feel the need to state the obvious, but it's even more annoying that you qualify everything you say," he said as his stylus moved over his touch screen and the image of the long-range transport he had been working on reloaded.

"Helen's always fucking right, but don't go telling her I said so. I owe her another ten fucking credits because of you."

"Then stop betting against me," she said.

"Wagering that you are far too intelligent to want to travel through the first Einstein-Rosen Bridge is not betting 'against' you," Harden replied.

CHAPTER 45

ABBY PLACED HER HAND ON the smudged acrylic scanner in the testing station at Outpost 5. Her fleet permit and logged flight hours loaded on the screen. The man behind the counter asked a few questions about her flight experience and then told her to sit at the console marked "3".

As the test loaded, she was amazed that just like on the shuttle exam, it was another multiple-choice assessment. There were mainly flight planning questions and SA equations. She couldn't believe how easy it was. This time she did not worry, even though she knew if she failed the exam, she would not be able to re-test for six months.

The test ended and, immediately, her name popped up on another screen in the queue for the practical test. She was told to wait. Sitting down on one of the teal cracked faux sheepskin chairs, she noticed she was one of the youngest pilots in the room. Most were in their early twenties.

A young Khlôrosan entered the room from the test ship corridor, looking sweaty and pale. Abby noticed his freckled cheeks immediately. She didn't know Khlôrosans could have freckles. She found herself wondering when this young man had enough time in the sun to have permanent melanin clumps.

"Abigail Lee," a male voice called out.

She pushed visions of freckles from her head as she headed towards the testing area. She placed her hand on the scanner. A door opened and she went down a dingy corridor towards an airlock. She entered the double doors and felt the familiar pressure and gravity change.

The test ship was an old transport. A middle-aged Khlôrosan told her to sit down. He had her take off, do four climbing turns, enter the atmosphere, land, and escape the gravitational pull of the nearby ice giant without the aid of the flight computer. She wondered if it was just her imagination or if the sublight test was easier than her shuttle flight test. Still, the proctor gave her no encouragement or criticism; she had no idea if she did well or not. She worried she did poorly.

Her test results were sent to the *Discovery* and *Revelation*. Generally, scores over 90% were considered a pass, but it was up to her captain and fleet captain to decide whether she had the skills and emotional maturity to fly their ship in unknown deep space. After all, the *Revelation* was not just some transport on a known run.

She tried pestering her crewmates, but they wouldn't tell her anything. Brian eventually said he failed the first time as he and Helen flipped through a parts catalogue on his tablet. Mark admitted he never even took the exam as he and Rover unpacked boxes of medical supplies.

Helen said, "Find something to do or I'll find something for you." Then in a kinder tone, she suggested, "I'm sure it'd be nice to have a real haircut."

Abby headed back to the main promenade of the space station. At Outpost 5, the bathhouse was not connected to the bar. People of all ages and genders were there.

She had nearly forgotten how exquisite it felt to dip into a pool. She poured the oat and floral scented oil into the water, leaned back, dropped until the water was at chin level, and allowed it to caress her skin. "I passed. I have to pass."

Too soon, her hour was up. She got out of the bath, toweled off, and sat in the barber's chair. She showed him a photo in a book of a girl with a short bob. He complied with very little conversation.

As she left the barber, she saw the same freckled Khlôrosan from the test. He was with an older Kiposi woman. By their bone structure, Abby guessed the woman was probably his mom or maybe a much elder sister. She glanced back. The woman said something to the barber as the young man sank into the chair with rolled eyes.

HARDEN WAITED WITH HER AS the call first was relayed to the Stone residence then forwarded to Doctor Orchid Stone in her office since it was the middle of the day in Kipos.

As the screen flickered on, Abby was amazed at Orchid's beauty and embarrassed by her own youth. She caught herself wishing she was as womanly as her younger sister. At least she had a new haircut.

Orchid's eyes filled with mist. "Abby, I'm so glad you called! It's nice to see you, Captain Alekos."

"And you, Doctor Stone. I'll leave you to speak to your sister." With that, Harden stepped outside the conference room. The women began talking at once. They stopped and giggled in mild awkwardness.

"Do you like the stars?" Orchid asked.

"I love it. So many things are similar, but some are just completely different. I'm still in school. Not that Harden or Helen would let me quit, but I mean, I'm still nineteen. I just took my sublight test. What's it like being a doctor?"

"Sometimes it's wonderful and challenging. Other times monotonous, like any job."

"How are my nephews?"

Orchid spoke on her sons for a few minutes, then ended with: "My eldest is thinking about medical school. The two younger ones have not decided."

Abby asked, "I need to know…do you regret coming to Kipos?"

"I would've regretted staying more. Growing up under your and Ray's obedient shadows, I would have married young. I wouldn't have gone to medical school, learned to play the piano and violin, or learned Greek. I found a man that truly loves me and had three sons. Other than losing you and Jin, my life has been relatively happy. Rory has had a harder time adjusting. He's still my groundskeeper. His injuries from his bondage never truly healed, but his wife is very kindhearted.

"With all that has happened, are you alright?"

Abby almost lied, and then began again, "Most of the time, I love the crew, but I-I have to do therapy because of what happened."

Orchid nodded.

"Sometimes I don't like it, but Mark really does take care of me. The whole crew makes me feel safe—even when I mess up."

"You got in trouble?"

"Yeah, I got in an argument with another crewmember. Don't worry. It wasn't serious. I just got some extra chores for losing my temper. Anyway I'm rambling, what I need to know is: are you all right? Even though you're happy... sometimes I feel I abandoned you."

Orchid nodded. "Abby, I told you to go. I'm a grown woman. I am happy. I only want you to be happy too. So where are you going next?"

"I don't know. The second wave of Earthlings is coming..."

"Jonathan and I have already looked to see if any relatives are on their way. There aren't any I could find. What is actually on your mind?" Abby heard her sister's pitch change. Orchid must be using her doctor's voice. Or maybe her mom's voice.

Abby blushed. "I saw a boy today."

"Are you in love?" Orchid looked thrilled to share in the gossip.

"I don't know. I haven't talked to him yet. I just saw him twice. At the sublight test and then again at the barber."

"What do the Alekoses say?"

Abby fiddled with the edge of her sweater and met her sister's eyes. "I'm supposed to be a fleet brat... Fleet brats don't wait, but I don't want to disgrace you either. It's easier when we're in the black. There are no boys around then. So I don't want you to think I'm a whore, but I really would like to talk to him."

Her sister said softly, "Jonathan and I didn't wait. Most of my girlfriends in college didn't either. It just isn't the same as it was on Earth. Just be safe."

ABBY LEFT THE CREW'S TABLE to order the next round and she saw the same freckled young man drinking a beer at the bar. He stared into his glass with a happy look.

I bet he passed, she thought. *I wonder if he thought the test was hard. I really like his freckles.* She realized she was still staring at the young man when the bartender repeated, "Sweetheart, I said twelve ducats."

"Oh sorry." She blushed and pulled out the bills and left them on the bar and hurried back to her crew's table with the required pints.

She set the beers down and slipped next to Diane. "See, him. He just took his sublight test. I wonder... How do I..."

Harden took a sip of his beer. "Stop being an idiot and go talk to him."

Diane gave Harden a look. "I agree you should talk to him if you want, but it's perfectly natural to be nervous. I think that's Sawyer's younger boy. What's his name?" She looked at Pat, who was sitting beside her.

"Beats me. Wait... Ben, I think." Pat said as he fiddled with his coaster.

Abby slipped off her stool and slowly headed back towards the bar. She had no idea what the correct way to approach a man was, but she would learn soon enough. That is if she didn't just turn around and run back to her crew.

"Hey. I'm Abby. Can I sit with you?" *Telling him my name? That wasn't very smooth! Aren't I supposed to have an opening line or something?* Embarrassment flushed her cheeks.

The young man glanced up and blushed as much as she did. "Sure! I'm Ben, by the way."

She liked his lightly freckled cheeks, his golden eyes, and his dark freshly cut curls. She was once again glad that she had a new haircut. She wondered briefly if she had anything stuck in her teeth, but reminded herself that she had brushed them prior to leaving the *Revelation*. She shoved her doubts into her stomach as they began to talk.

Ben was twenty-one. He was much further along in school, but hadn't done any A level work. His only B level task was flying the shuttle. Abby mentioned her age and that she had done some A level work. She joked she was having so much trouble with Biochem 2 that even her CG instructor was getting frustrated. He laughed at her joke and admitted his worse subject had been planetary science.

He finished his beer, but she still had half of hers and was suddenly afraid he would leave. She didn't know how to keep the conversation going, so she asked if she could buy him another one. He smiled and nodded.

"How long are you in port?" she asked him.

"We leave in eighteen hours. What 'bout you?"

"Three days. Big refuel and resupply."

The conversation died out again. She had run out of things to say. Ben was almost finished with his second beer and she hadn't even finished her first.

Diane had told her that the general rule for adult male Khlôrosans dictated he would wait for her to make the first move. She didn't want the night to end; she wanted a whirl of romance. "Do you have your own billet?" she heard herself asking before she realized it. Then she blushed and looked at her beer.

"Yeah. Do you work for your mom?"

She chanced looking back up at him. "No. Helen and Harden Alekos."

Ben sighed in obvious relief. "Oh, you're from the *Revelation*. Cool, I always thought working on one of the explorers would be interesting."

"Do you work for your folks?"

"Yeah, but it's fine. I only asked since you wanted to go to my billet and not yours."

"I'm right next to Harden—and my mom is gone. It'd just be weird."

"You a ward?"

"Not anymore. All the Alekoses have been really good to me. They wouldn't care, but I'd be embarrassed." The half-truth came so smoothly; she didn't have to even think of the lie.

"Yeah, I get that. My folks have—or I guess I should say *had*—a ward. He's twenty-four, but it doesn't matter, he's still my brother. Mom still buys him Landing Day presents and everything. Anyway, my mom hoped to set something up with Captain Alekos when he arrived to get the short-range haul between here and 189733 Ac. You were there?"

"Yeah." She shrugged. "Varied ecosystem. We found some predators that came close to tearing us to shreds. That's a good sign." Abby realized her answer wasn't exactly articulate, but Ben seemed impressed.

ABBY BARELY LOOKED AROUND AT the ship, though she knew she would be curious about the differences in the layout of a transport and an explorer later. Apprehension slithered up her stomach as they climbed down into his billet. Helen and Diane had said, if she just acted eager and enthusiastic, it would probably hide her inexperience.

Abby repeated what else they told her: *Don't think. Just enjoy the ex-*

perience.

She noticed his billet was covered with a large mural of a comet over a desert oasis across its long wall. He saw her looking at it and said, "I painted it. When I was born, my mom left Kipos space to protect me from the reproduction laws so I've never been to Lathos, but that is how I imagined the dark side to be."

"I've only been to Lathos once," she said. "Only on the light side for the harvest. Never been to the dark side. It's wonderful." Ben was an artist. *Artists were romantic weren't they?* Abby decided that Ben must be a romantic.

Not really sure what to do, but trying to take the lead as Diane and Helen had instructed, Abby kissed him. She felt his hands wrap around her body. He pulled her down on his lap. His lips were soft and warm; she didn't want him to stop. Her heart begun to quicken and she began to feel herself swell in excitement.

She began undressing him as he unzipped her coveralls. He kicked the blankets off the bed. Once her tan shoulders were bare, he began attacking her with kisses. She went after his chest and neck. He even kissed her scars and the faded stretch marks on her belly. Embarrassed, she pushed back, but for only a moment.

"What's wrong?" he said.

"My scars are ugly."

He told her, "I expect a few scars. I guess you've spent a lot of time in deep space."

She nodded. "Is it that obvious?"

"Yeah, but it doesn't matter as long as we are enjoying it. Should I go slower?"

"No, I liked what you were doing."

He gave her a wicked grin before he headed back down. He blew on her stomach and tickled her until she squealed. She tickled him back. They chased each other around four square meters of space until they ended up kissing on the floor. Eventually, someone banged on the deck above them and told them to shut the fuck up or he would get the Captain. Some people had real jobs.

Abby giggled.

Ben blushed. "That's my brother."

Not wanting Ben to get in trouble, Abby made sure their lovemaking became more subdued. She bit her lip and asked, "Would you kiss my neck? I'd..."

She didn't have to finish her request before she groaned with pleasure. It was everything she hoped it would be. Ben did not seem displeased either.

EARLY THE NEXT MORNING, SHE opened her eyes. Ben was sleeping beside her. She glanced up at his clock. 06:23. Her meeting was at 08:00 and she couldn't go without showering or breakfast.

"I gotta go." Abby kissed him with her eyes open. She wanted to see his warm, smooth skin's embedded microscopic scales and the freckles on his nose. She sucked in his sweet cinnamon breath and flicked her tongue against his lower lip as she looked into his deep gold eyes. Ben was her first real lover and she wanted to remember this moment forever.

"You know, I have never met anyone quite like you." Ben said, "Come with us on Mom's next run. We'll have such fun."

The offer did appeal to her. Ben was sweet and handsome and everything she ever dreamed of in a husband. Still, Abby said softly, "I'm not finished with my studies yet."

"It's just a run, not forever."

Abby smiled. "I like being on an explorer. Besides, I want to keep clocking hours. We'd be fighting for stick-time."

Ben looked surprised, but not really hurt by the rejection. "You really are like no one I have ever known."

Abby said, "I hope when I make my way back here, you'd like to see me again." Then she kissed him and picked up her clothing off the floor.

Once they were dressed, they kissed once more and he hugged her tightly. "Be careful, Abby. Don't let aliens eat you."

Delight ran right through her. "You either," she said.

While Abby knew she probably would always hold some pain from her time with the DePauls, she realized her rape had not truly defiled her. She felt a strange sensation of freedom. She could never tell Ben what he had meant to her, because he could never know.

THE *REVELATION* WAS QUIET WHEN Abby returned, but she could smell bacon frying as she walked up the stairs. Once she got up to the third deck, she could hear Julia and Harden talking softly. She hoped she hadn't done something stupid by staying out all night.

"Never could figure why you don't hire a real cook," Julia said as Abby slipped into the galley.

Harden glanced up at Abby before turning back to Julia. "And miss all this?" he said as he stirred something that looked like pancake batter. They had been waiting up for her. Abby held her breath, fearing he might yell at her.

Harden only asked, "Did you eat breakfast?"

"No."

Julia slipped something to her. It was the same foul contraceptive nanobrew she had been forced to take her first day.

Abby asked, "Are you mad?"

"You think you're the first girl to decide to have a little fling between hauls? That's how most of us came into existence. I just want you to be safe and healthy," Harden said, "and not conceive until you finish your studies."

Julia's voice was softer. "Of course, it's ultimately your choice. If you had a child, our crews would handle it, but that means in four years, you'll be taking care of a toddler on the *Discovery*, not doing the test flight through the Einstein-Rosen Bridge."

"I have to drink this every time?"

"No, Mark will start you on pills after your next cycle," Julia said. "I left a few different types to try out from *Discovery's* infirmary."

"There are types?"

"They all work the same, but different formulas work better for different people. Don't worry, I've known since we met," Julia said. "Harden didn't tell me, but he's not as smart as he thinks."

Harden glanced over at her.

Julia said, "Your story about Donna is good, but something you said didn't sit right with me. When Abby was hurt, Mark confirmed my suspicions. Of course, I didn't let anyone else see her medical records so people drew their own conclusions. They guessed correctly that I was hiding her origins, but no one guessed that she was a Homo sapien."

Harden set a stack of three small pancakes and two slices of bacon in front of her. "When Mark found out where you had gone, he was a nervous wreck. Since you were sure you weren't ready, he thought he had more time to discuss birth control with you."

Abby took a deep breath and chugged it down. It tasted as terrible as she remembered, but it didn't make her want to immediately vomit this time. She chased it down with a glass of water. Then her tea and a few bites of pancake.

"You seeing Ben again?" Julia asked.

Abby dipped her bacon in her syrup and shrugged. "He's leaving in a few hours, after his mom talks to Cole."

"Maybe you'll see him the next time you're in port," Julia said as she took a bite of pancake.

"Maybe," she mumbled as she felt the pleasure rush to her cheeks. "I'd like to. He was real sweet."

"So what did you tell the Sawyer boy?" Harden asked. That was the real reason why he and Julia were up.

Abby replied, "My name and that you're my captain. He asked me if I was a ward. I said not anymore. I said you and Helen are real good to me, but I still feel weird bringing people home. We talked about the sublight test. He knows he passed."

She felt her cheeks grow hot. "We sorta just jumped in his rack after that.

"Ben paints murals. His ship's full of them. He mentioned maybe I could do a run with him. I told him I didn't want to stop my studies or fight him for stick-time. I doubt he was really serious anyway."

"Good, and you are correct," he said.

Julia gave Harden a look. "Ben may have been serious. We don't know the boy well enough to say," she said.

Abby was not worried. Harden still seemed to love her. She wasn't ruined. She wasn't a poutana. She hadn't dishonored her crew, Orchid, Jin, or her dead ancestors. She was still the same person she had been the day before. She still had her duties, a load of studying, and her meeting with Harden and Cole.

They had to allow her to fly the *Revelation*.

CONCLUSION

The Discovery Docked at Outpost 5: March 7, 3186 K.E.

COLE SAT IN HIS OFFICE wondering why he ever bothered to read the Feed. It was always filled with bad news. Of the 300,000 minds who survived the trip to Kipos, only one percent of the youngest Earthlings who were adopted into loving families made any real life for themselves. The rest of them were always protesting.

Young people, once comfortable living on the outskirts of Kipos' cities, were now in their thirties, forties, and fifties. They wanted jobs, homes, and families. Still, there was a feeling of hope for the next generation on Kipos because the population was steadily rising. Some of the strongest first generation babies would now start producing children of their own. Abby's baby would be old enough to have a baby.

Kipos had not rescinded their Reproduction Laws and Cole's offspring would remain sterilized, but he still felt the same kind of hope. Mark and Pat would be married and he would have his first ready-made grandkid. Megan was perfect: intelligent, pretty, and considerate. Silva was strict compared to Fleet standards, but she was a good woman. They both would be welcomed additions to the family.

It disturbed Cole that he might be bringing the Earth girl to harm. Abby seemed like a sweet kid. Helen adored her, Mark said only good things, and even Harden had obviously grown used to her presence, but Cole couldn't chance losing Megan for the Earth girl.

He wondered if he and Saul could take out the android known as Eli. He doubted it, not even if his whole crew helped. For the past relative month, Eli had been working in the engine room as a mechanic. Only he and Saul knew his true purpose. Now he wondered if he should have confided in Julia. She could have warned Harden.

COLE COULD NOT BRING HIMSELF to embrace Abby, so he did not stand when she and Harden came into his office. He had betrayed her. Cole could only hope that Eli was true to his word and was only planning on bringing her a message. Harden gave him an odd look, but she looked happier and more confident since Argent, as strong and fearless as any girl who had faced death and lived to tell about it.

"May I start taking watches?" she immediately asked after "Hello."

"A 94.7% on your sublight test isn't a terrible score. However, you scraped the docking clamp on landing and you're still accelerating too fast," Cole said.

Harden touched her shoulder. "You beat me. I only got a 92.4."

Abby clapped her hands together. "So can I?"

Harden glanced at him. "It's alright with me, and Helen is dying to see how Abby handles the *Revelation*."

Cole knew he had to gain control of the conversation. He couldn't think about the girl's future with Eli awaiting her. "I'd like for her to be with Helen in deep space for the first forty hours at least. Then, it is at your convenience. I also have her university test scores, but first there is another matter to discuss."

He touched the com pad. "Eli? Come in here please."

Abby stopped breathing. Her tan skin took a distinctly gray shade. As the door opened and closed, in wide-eyed panic, she stood perfectly still. The android's eyes seemed to be bluer, more piercing.

Harden put himself between the android and the girl. Cole rebuked himself for being surprised. The Earth girl was his crew. Even though he felt that Harden might be a mediocre captain, Cole saw that he loved his crew.

Cole came around his desk and pulled Harden back by the shoulders. "Just listen. I don't think he means to hurt her."

Eli inclined his head. "Captain Alekos, how wonderful to meet you. You have been transporting my stolen property for some time, the penalty for which is no doubt well known to you. Miss Boyd Lei worked nine months and twenty-one days. On the day she ran away, she had six years, two months, and eight days left on her bond or another two children."

On Cole's desk, Eli opened his bag and unrolled a thin silver tablet. With a tap on the touchscreen, a vid of Peony DePaul and a young woman the same age as Abby began to play.

"Lei," Abby whispered.

"Rachel Margret DePaul," Eli corrected, but not unkindly. "She is happy. My Kyria has raised her well. I can't imagine the knowledge that she was the product of a legal rape is beneficial to her wellbeing. Unfortunately, due to current indenture laws, the DePaul's could not just let Miss Boyd Lei go. So I purchased the bond, which I am willing to discharge for a price."

Harden said, "I don't own slaves. I could hardly afford it."

"Even a man of your intelligence is limited," Eli said. "Now Abigail, these are my terms and they are not negotiable: You will live as long as you never contact the DePauls.

"It would sadden me to destroy the birthmother of my Kyria, but for her sake, I will. Not just Rachel, but every generation forever after. Do you understand?"

Abby's voice was small. "Yes."

"If you do not wish to be an astrobiologist or whatever trivial subject you are studying, I can give you a life of luxury in a quiet residence. I will buy you a man for your pleasure and you may have other children with him as you wish. I can give you anything you desire."

Cole saw the girl's eyes grow wide with horror, but her voice was unwavering. "No, you can't."

Eli looked slightly annoyed at Harden. "Sir, you have obviously not explained the power of compound interest, though I saw the way you set up her accounts that you have an understanding of the concept." Then he turned to Abby. "I have existed for centuries. I serve the Kyria for my own pleasure, not because I need or wish for the funds. It is only for the fact that you also served the Kyria that I am giving you any options at all."

Abby set her jaw in a manner so much like Helen that Cole had to do a double take. "I mean you can't, because I already have the life I want," she said. "I don't need your help or money or anything else. I'm staying on the *Revelation*. You can't make me leave."

Eli smiled. "You're much improved, child. It gives me hope for my Kyria. Are you sure? Because I will not leave you untethered and unsupervised."

"I'm almost twenty!"

"Irrelevant." Eli pulled out a file of papers with heavy embossed borders and imbedded watermarks and placed them on the desk. "After I saw the security recordings of O-7, I took the liberty of having this drafted..."

Harden held the pieces of paper up to the light, and then handed them to Cole. The fingerprints and signatures looked perfect.

Abigail Boyd Lei, a bonded Earth teenager, was bought by Barnett DePaul and later adopted by Eli Potter and died of complications in childbirth.

Another set of papers showed the live birth on the *Vos*. DNA testing showed, though she had a Khlôrosan father, she was born without carrying the undesirable alleles; she was allowed to remain unsterilized when she and her mother arrived on Kipos. Eli provided the missing transfer paperwork and Donna's death certificate. Cole Alekos conditionally emancipated her to further her education within fleet guidelines, with the knowledge that she carried eleven of his chromosomes.

"That is insane. A simple blood test will prove she's not Khlôrosan," Harden said.

"Sir, a simple blood test would have just as easily proved that Donna Lee was not her mother. This is only paperwork following the laws of Kipos. Unless there is a reason to contest it, it will never be challenged. To me, it means nothing."

He set the paperwork in a tight pile upon Cole's desk. "Or if you prefer, this was my original plan."

He pulled out another few sheets of paper stating that Barnett DePaul had bought Abigail Boyd Lei, a bonded Earth teenager. When he had discovered she was too wild to be good breeding material, he sold her bond to Eli Potter, who adopted her as a daughter. Unfortunately due to her savage nature, Eli could not control her and sold her to Harden. He even had a receipt for a full load of mateodeas—2726 males, 2412 females and one barrel of the dead—which were exchanged for the girl. All of this was pre-dated to fit in with Abby's fleet paperwork.

Eli said, "From what I have heard, most of your father's crew respect you as a scientist, dislike you as a captain, but few who know you would ever assume you would purchase a young girl for sexual fulfillment." He paused for just a moment. "Still, I doubt people would think less of you for it."

Harden remained silent and stared at Eli. Cole knew his son would never touch the girl, but he wondered if Harden was actually thinking of taking the bond.

"Whether you want a slave or a daughter," said Eli, "it makes no difference to me. As for my part in it, I got a very nice tax deduction when I donated all those mateodeas to the university for research. More, in fact, than I paid DePaul for the girl's bond and adoption paperwork. I'll come out ahead either way."

Harden asked, "You've known where she was all along?"

"Easy enough to deduce. Her chip stopped working near NAX. There were six ships docked that day. Only the *Revelation* had a young female intern listed on the crew manifest. However, Barnett needed time to repent. He told himself it was all for the best, until the child struck him..."

"You struck DePaul?" Cole asked, amazed. His estimation of her went up a notch, and Harden's as well by the look on his face.

"When he took Lei away," Abby whispered.

Eli looked irked at the interruption. "Afterwards, he ordered her to be sedated. He did not command any injury to the girl, but he left her unprotected. Vivian and I were with our Kyria.

"Yet, I am at fault. Knowing the human gift for savagery, I should have foreseen it. I bought the bond and planned to move her somewhere quiet once she had healed. The maids had left her to die.

"The guards thought she was nothing. Worse than an animal. They were depraved, but fortunately not very imaginative. They joked about it, but her wounds could have been much worse if they were truly sadistic."

Abby whispered, "Is my daughter safe?"

"They have been terminated. Vivian and I do not suffer rapists or sloths near her." Eli had said "terminate" so smoothly and coldly, Cole had to fight the shudder creeping up his back.

Eli said, "Carefully consider how much the Stones should know."

Abby cried out, "Orchid doesn't know anything!"

"Keep it that way. Are you sure you wish to stay on this man's ship?

He has all he needs to enslave you."

"He always has," she said.

"Our brothers left us behind, so Vivian and I live only for our Kyria. If you do not forget that, you will live long."

He turned to Harden. "Proven fertile, high IQ and test scores. Add a pilot's license to the mix, and that girl is worth much more than I paid for her."

Harden looked down at the paperwork.

"You could fund your little science projects for decades by reselling the girl's bond on a nightly basis, especially since her troublesome hymen is no longer intact."

That did it. Harden's cool was gone. He grabbed a pile and snapped, "Get the fuck out."

Just by the venom in his voice, Cole realized that, in Harden's mind, there had never been a choice. Harden had played a fucking android's intelligence. After all, who knew what might come in handy in the future?

Eli picked up the other set of paperwork and slipped it back into his case. There could be no doubt the android would keep the evidence of Abby's true identity tucked away as assurance. Cole didn't doubt that, if Abby's fleet paperwork were to be challenged, it would all lead back to Harden.

Then Eli packed his tablet. He pulled out a final piece of paper and set it upon Cole's desk.

He clasped his hands together, bowed at Abby in Earth fashion, and left. Abby stood as tall as she could until Eli left the office, then tears started dripping from her eyes.

Cole glanced down. It was a simple letter of resignation with an explanation and apology that family matters precluded his ability to give the standard notice. That's the great thing about androids: they were thorough.

Turning to Harden, Abby asked, "Did I make a mistake? How could I abandon my own baby again? How could I?"

Cole was glad Abby had such trust in Harden that she did not even ask which papers he had grabbed. Still, he was disgusted his idiot son had stepped back from the girl as if her tears would burn him. This fear of emotion is why Harden would never be a great captain.

Abby cried, "I should have died for my baby. You can never trust me now, can you?"

Harden backed away even further. Cole saw that his son was struggling to keep a calm front while hiding his sheer terror that Abby would run to the nearest airlock. He didn't know what to do, so he did nothing.

Cole wondered how he and Rosemary could have produced someone so insensitive, and guided her to sit. He took her small hand in his, feeling her calluses and tiny scars. Her irises were inky black, but the whites had become red and bloodshot, full of the pain for the life that would never be.

Cole asked, "Abby, honey, do you understand, if you defied Eli, he'd have killed us all?"

She nodded.

"Personally, I can't figure out if you are the luckiest girl I've ever met or the most unfortunate. Listen, I can't even imagine the pain you must feel for losing your daughter. I don't envy the choices you've had to make, but as Eli said, you've your freedom now. You can do anything you want."

She took a deep breath and stiffened her back, but didn't let go of his hand. "Helen told me I could take an archeology course as a science elective after I pass biochem. I still want to do that."

Another shuddering breath escaped, but Abby wasn't crying anymore. She had made her choice. The resulting pain had not weakened her or made her brittle; it tempered her. She was simply not the type to step out of an airlock. "And maybe could I call Orchid? Just to make sure she's safe?"

"I'll put the call through after we finish here," Harden said, looking slightly relieved.

Cole noticed for the first time that, in the red-rimmed, soulless black, Abby's eyes glittered with a touch of gold. She would go into deep space and, when she awoke from stasis, she would take her first watch with Helen. That is what she wanted. His heart went out to the girl; the ability to make painful decisions and live with the consequences was a quality of a good captain. Helen had been correct.

"And I still wanna be secondary pilot on the Einstein-Rosen Bridge."

Cole looked at his son in shock. He couldn't even think of how to form the question. All that came out was: "When were you fucking going to tell me?"

Harden scratched his arm and glanced away before he mumbled, "Abby became part of the Alekos system on CD-34 4160 b."

"That was her first trip out!"

"Lathos was her first trip out," Harden muttered, as if that made it any better.

Cole noticed Abby was watching them now.

"Fuck, Dad, what was I supposed to do? Rover started freaking out. Helen had to tell him something."

"What did Helen say?"

Harden looked sheepish. "We were her new fathers—Helen, Brian, and me…"

Cole pinched the bridge of his nose and shook his head. In the end, Eli's paperwork had meant nothing, but it would make things easier. "And I suppose your damn roverbot is calling her 'brother'?"

"I'm going to take care of him…" Abby started to say, but Harden cut her off.

"I tried to get her back to what's left of her own family. The Stones didn't want her. And now we have the paperwork…" He trailed off before he admitted it: She's our kid. "Anyway, Julia mentioned you picked up an extra mechanic named Eli on O-7. After what happened with Robert there, I couldn't chance that it was the same guy. Abby still has nightmares about that fucker. She…they…" he trailed off again.

Cole looked at his son. Harden was terrified. He couldn't provide the unequivocal love of a father, but whatever affection he hadn't smashed down with his intellect, he was trying to give to the girl. Of course, since his son was somewhat of an idiot in that area, Abby hadn't known the depth of Harden's attachment. Helen had a mother's heart, but Cole did not doubt Brian and Harden kept her from showing the intensity of her affection until they could be sure Abby would be staying.

Abby reached out and took Harden's hand in hers. "I'm okay."

He did not pull away or even tense up, though he did look slightly confused about what he should do in response. "You are in the process of recovering from a trauma from which you may never fully mend," he said, trying to retreat back into the comforts of logic.

Abby nodded solemnly and then looked up at him with an impish smile. "Then how about: I'm feeling pretty good during this particular moment in space-time."

"As am I," Harden admitted. Then he met Cole's eyes again. The terror had not abated. He needed guidance on how to proceed and assurance that he had done the right thing.

Cole said. "Two granddaughters without having to change a single diaper. This is the best fucking day of my life."

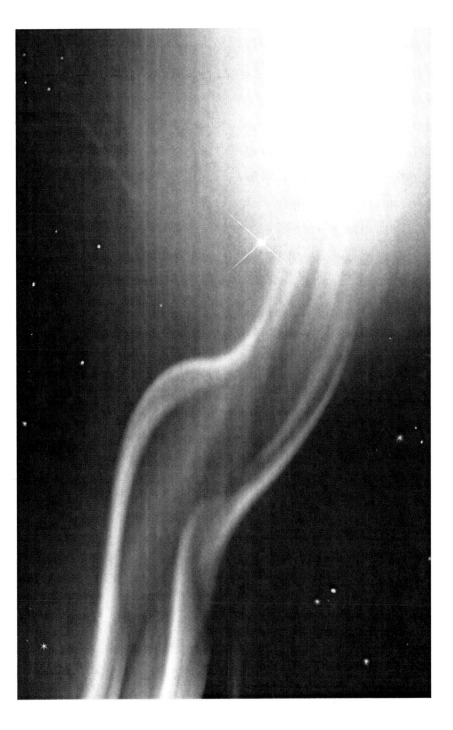

ACKNOWLEDGMENTS

I would like to give a special to thanks to Rebecca Brown, Maria Masterson, and Cassandra Vaughn for reading the book while still a draft and helping me figure out the submission process. I also would like to thank my family, who have supported my creative endeavors and listened while I rambled, especially my mother and my long-suffering husband, Dennis.

I am also grateful to Juanita Samborski and Dave Kostiuk, who meticulously edited my novel, and to everyone at 48fourteen for believing in Other Systems. Finally, a big thank you to Lon Grover who contributed his sharp eyes as a beta reader. I would also like to thank my writing group buddies, Mariann Krizsan, Linda Strout, Vivian Queija, and Steve Merlino, who helped during the daunting Round 2 Edits and anyone else who helped me get this book into the world. You know who you are.

ABOUT THE AUTHOR

Elizabeth loves to create. In her mind, she has the best job (or jobs) in the world. She gets an idea, runs with it until it leads her to generate whatever it is going to be.

Over the past decade, she has created over one hundred paintings, three graphic novels and a comic book series. Other Systems is her first published novel.

Elizabeth currently lives in Seattle with her husband and two dogs.

CPSIA information can be obtained at www.ICGtesting.com
Printed in the USA
LVOW13s1019021013

355070LV00001B/57/P